MINNESOTA MYSTERIES

Timeless Romantic Suspense in Three Historical Stories

JOANN A. GROTE

BARBOUR
PUBLISHING

An Honest Love © 1995 by JoAnn A. Grote
Sweet Surrender © 1998 by JoAnn A. Grote
A Man for Libby © 1999 by JoAnn A. Grote

ISBN 1-59310-908-3

Cover art by Getty Images

All rights reserved. No part of this publication may be reproduced or transmitted in any form or by any means without written permission of the publisher.

Scripture quotations are taken from the King James Version of the Bible.

Published by Barbour Publishing, Inc., P.O. Box 719, Uhrichsville, Ohio 44683, www.barbourbooks.com

Our mission is to publish and distribute inspirational products offering exceptional value and biblical encouragement to the masses.

 Member of the
Evangelical Christian
Publishers Association

Printed in the United States of America.
5 4 3 2 1

An Honest Love

Dedication

With love to my brother (and banker)
J. Gary Olsen and his wife Helen

Chapter 1

Constance Ward swayed against the purple plush seat, no longer noticing the rocking of the day car or the loud clacking of wheels against steel rails after eleven hours of travel.

Pinkerton's National Detective Agency hadn't given her an assignment outside Chicago since 1891, two years ago, and her gaze eagerly drank in the beauty of the countryside along the Mississippi River bordering southern Wisconsin and Minnesota.

The trip seemed more a vacation than an assignment. All that was required of her was to deliver her niece and nephew to her Aunt Libby in River's Edge, Minnesota, and become friendly with Mrs. Pierce. There was no danger involved. Mrs. Pierce's son, Rasmus, who had eluded law enforcement agencies for over five years, was reputed to be in Missouri.

A smile tugged at her lips as she watched Effie and Evan laughing with Justin Knight, the man across the aisle. The six-year-old twins looked so much like her brother, Charles, that the sight of them stung at the place in her heart that was still unhealed from his death six months earlier. Like Charles, the children had broad faces with snub noses, brown hair and huge brown eyes in contrast to her own pointed chin, green eyes and black hair, which she wore in a thick figure eight twist.

She'd been curious about the reserved Mr. Knight since he'd boarded at Chicago. When he revealed he was a banker from River's Edge, she'd found his presence even more intriguing. His acquaintance was fortuitous; she might be able to use it to advantage on her present case.

She'd thought Mr. Knight reserved until the first time he smiled at her. His chestnut brown eyes had flared with a sudden light that sent her heart tripping in a most unfamiliar manner. Then they warmed into an almost boyishly friendly glow.

Under the guise of watching the children scramble about him, she observed him as she would a suspect or so she tried to convince herself. He was about six inches taller than her five-foot-three frame, but his straight, broad shoulders and the assured manner in which he held his head made him appear taller. Brown hair parted on the side waved rebelliously just above his ears, refusing to be brought into submission.

Did his smile hint at a boyish spirit hidden inside the almost stern man that was just as difficult to tame as the waves in his hair? she wondered. Yet there was a quiet strength about him that instilled confidence. If her experiences as a

Pinkerton investigator had taught her anything about judging character, this was a man who could be depended upon in life's storms.

She couldn't recall when she'd been so aware of a man, and a stranger at that! As the day wore on, he appeared to truly enjoy the twins' attention, and she found she was beginning to like this man to whom she'd been instantly and powerfully attracted.

It was through the children they finally exchanged greetings and unsatisfyingly small slices of information about themselves. Effie and Evan practically adopted the man, climbing about his perfectly tailored suit over Constance's protests, firing questions at him about himself and the areas through which they passed.

He looked up unexpectedly, catching her gaze on him, and a thrill danced along her nerves. With an effort, she shifted her glance to the few other passengers in the day car. Besides herself, the children and Mr. Knight, there were only four: two drummers who had boarded at the last station discussing hoped-for sales, a preacher dressed in black relieved only by the white collar at his throat, and across from him a man with a Vandyke beard and long black hair that curled against the back of his linen duster, sitting with his back to her in one of the first seats, his hat low over his forehead.

The man with the long hair rose and started toward them, adjusting his gait to the swaying of the car, just before Effie darted back across the aisle to fling herself eagerly against the black skirt of Constance's mourning gown. The child's exuberant actions unintentionally knocked Constance's alligator handbag to the floor with a thud, and it slid out of her reach beneath the opposite seat.

Effie smiled up at her with shining brown eyes, her hair flowing in shiny brown waves over the large cape collar of her blue and white striped dress. "Are we almost there, Aunt Constance?"

"Only a few more miles, dear."

Constance's answer was lost in the ice-cold voice of the long-haired stranger now leaning against the seat across the aisle.

"If it ain't Justin Knight, as I live and breathe."

Constance frowned. A warning in her brain which she'd come to respect during the last three years tugged at her. Now that she saw him up close, there was something familiar about the man's face.

"Rasmus." Mr. Knight's voice was tight as he acknowledged the man's sarcastic greeting.

A chill swept down her spine like a Chinook wind. Her hand's tightened on Effie's shoulders. Rasmus! Of course, Rasmus Pierce, the head of the very outlaw gang she'd been assigned to gather information on for the Pinkerton Agency! They'd thought he was in Missouri.

He looked nothing like the photo and description of him she carried in her handbag. She must inform the Superintendent in her next report that the gang leader had let his hair grow and was now sporting a beard and a narrow, almost slinky, black mustache.

She darted a glance to her handbag, still sliding around the floor. Her stomach churned. Her derringer was in that bag. Perhaps she was borrowing trouble, and wouldn't need the small firearm. The hope was dashed when the outlaw pushed aside his long linen duster to reach for a revolver.

A grin slithered across Rasmus's face as he pointed the barrel at Mr. Knight. He spat a wad of tobacco from the side of his mouth.

"I'd planned ta git rid of ya 'fore yer weddin' this Sunday, but circumstances bein' what they are, might be I've got another plan."

Constance noticed the slight widening of Mr. Knight's eyes in a face suddenly gone pale. His hand gripped Evan's shoulder, and Constance's heart caught in her throat at the fear that sat starkly on her nephew's wide face.

"Why not be a gentleman, and let the lady and these children move out of the way before dealing with me?" Mr. Knight's voice was stiff with barely controlled fury.

The outlaw ignored him. "Where's yer pa, boy?"

Evan trembled, unable to take his eyes from the gun barrel. Even the brown locks curling just below his ear lobes quivered. His mouth moved, but no words came out.

"I said, where's yer pa?"

"His father is dead." Constance was surprised her voice was so calm. She'd been in dangerous situations before, but never with Effie and Evan near. She had to keep her wits about her, as her fellow agent, Alexander Bixby, would say. It would take all she'd learned in her years as a detective to get them out of this unbelievable situation safely.

The slimy grin moved across the man's face again as he glanced at her. "Good." His gaze dropped quickly to her gloved hands and back to her face. "You his ma?"

"No."

"You a married lady?"

Why would he ask such a thing? She returned his look unflinchingly. "No."

Effie pulled away from Constance's hands, plumped her hands on her hips and scowled at Rasmus.

"Why are you pointing that gun at my brother? You're a mean man!"

Fear spread fiery hot through her. She drew the girl back against her. "Shhh, dear. It's all right."

"He's mean! Tell him to stop being mean, Aunt Constance!"

Rasmus's eyes blazed. "Shut her up."

Dread thickened in her chest. She tried to keep her voice calm for the children's sake.

"Evan is fine. Mr. Knight is taking care of him. See?"

Mr. Knight smiled at Effie—a tight little smile, but a smile—and Constance could have hugged him. "That's right, Effie. Mr. Pierce is just playing games, as he and I used to do when we were boys."

Rasmus snorted. "Some game."

Mr. Knight jerked, and the gun lifted slightly. "Wouldn't try it, Knight. Wouldn't want a stray bullet hittin' one o' these kids, now, would we?"

His words threw a horrible picture across Constance's mind, sending terror racing through her. She pushed it away resolutely. There was nothing to be gained from imagining things.

Suddenly the train lurched, the wheels squealing along the rails, throwing the children heavily against Constance and Mr. Knight. *Somehow Rasmus's henchmen must have managed to stop the train,* Constance thought.

For the first time, she remembered the other passengers. Her gaze shot toward the men at the front of the car. Guns in hand, the "drummers" were standing on either side of the door. One was watching the next car. The other had a gun trained on the pastor.

Mr. Knight's jaw clenched. "What is it you want?"

"Why, jest a weddin' thet's all. You and Marian fergot ta invite me ta yers." He nodded toward Constance. "Figure we have a lady here with no husband, a preacher ta do the tyin', and you jest itchin' ta git hitched. Might as well do the job right now. 'Sides, might not be safe fer me ta go ta a weddin' in town. Certain people wouldn't make me welcome."

Sweat trickled down Constance's back. Surely he wasn't suggesting—!

"Trying to get me out of the way so you can wed Marian yourself, Rasmus? She'll never have you."

Rasmus dumped the smile. The fire in his black eyes shot horror through Constance. What was Mr. Knight doing? Didn't he know Rasmus Pierce's reputation? The outlaw thought no more of shooting a person than he would a jackrabbit.

"Maybe Marian won't have me, Knight. But she'll hate you, humiliatin' her by marryin' someone else right before yer weddin's scheduled. And her hatin' you is almost as good as her marryin' me."

"Even you aren't so low you'd force a lady into a marriage with a stranger, Pierce."

Never had Constance heard such cold laughter as the outlaw's. "Wouldn't bet that new house of yers on it."

"No judge would uphold a marriage two strangers were forced into at the point of a gun." Constance thought she detected a hint of uncertainty in Mr. Knight's sarcasm.

Rasmus slouched lazily against the seat facing Mr. Knight. "But yer not goin' ta tell anyone this marriage warn't jest what ya wanted. See, if'n ya do, there's a couple kids might not git a chance ta grow up." His glittering eyes swept over Evan and Effie.

Constance's arms tightened around Effie. She searched Justin Knight's face. The children's lives were in his hands. What would he do?

His gaze met hers. Fear and anger had widened his pupils until blackness shoved away the warm brown of his eyes. He seemed to probe her very soul. What was he expecting to uncover? Would he find it?

The cocking of the revolver's hammer exploded through the car like a cannon blast. "Time's a-wastin'. What'll it be? A new bride and life, or. . ." He waved the pistol from Evan to Effie and back again.

Mr. Knight's gaze still bored into hers. "Miss Ward, will you do me the honor of becoming my wife?"

The detective in her admired his calm and command, even as she wondered how he could voice the question from a face as rigid as a statue's.

She remembered her first impression of him, a man to be depended upon in a storm, and a little of the fear clutching her heart released.

Lifting her chin, she squared her shoulders beneath leghorn sleeves. She could show a good deal of "spunk" herself, as the Superintendent had said more than once. Nodding slightly, she forced a bright smile. "I should be pleased to accept your proposal."

Rasmus's evil laughter filled the rail car. He swung his pistol in a gesturing motion and hollered, "Preacher, git yerself down here! Ya got a weddin' ta perform."

The reverend walked jerkily toward them, a worn leather Bible clutched in his hands, his lips moving silently. Was he praying for safety for himself, Constance wondered, or for them? He didn't look as if he had much faith in his God getting them out of the situation. He was trembling like the proverbial leaf, and his face was whiter than his collar.

"Sir, I beg of you, leave off harassing these people. The Lord. . ."

"Yer here ta perform a weddin', not give a sermon."

The reverend drew himself up taller. His trembling increased.

"I'll not be party to such doings."

Constance stared at him in surprise. So the man had courage after all, in spite of his obvious fear. But perhaps his courage was ill-timed. Rasmus Pierce was not a man with whom to trifle.

Pierce's eyes narrowed. His lips pulled back in a sneer over yellowed teeth. "P'raps ya didn't hear what will happen if there's no marriage." He glanced pointedly toward Evan, who by now was clutching Mr. Knight's hand until his little knuckles were white.

Mr. Knight's voice was steady. "We appreciate your efforts on our behalf, Reverend. However, they are unnecessary, as Miss Ward and I are willing participants in this ceremony. We'd be grateful for your services."

The preacher looked from Mr. Knight to Constance and back again.

"Very well." He ignored Rasmus Pierce in a manner which delighted Constance. Even such a little thing gave her the pleasurable thrill of revenge.

"Miss Ward, Mr. Knight, if you would be so good as to stand beside each other in the aisle, facing me, and take each other's hands, we will begin."

Constance rose, and Effie clutched at her hand, her brown eyes huge. "Are you truly going to marry him?"

She hoped her smile was reassuring. "Yes, dear. Would you and Evan do us the pleasure of being our wedding party?" Perhaps being part of this unreal ceremony would help calm them.

Effie glanced at Evan before nodding.

Mr. Knight squeezed Evan's hand. "What do you say, old man? It would mean a lot to me to have you stand up for me."

"Okay." The boy's reply was barely a whisper.

Constance smiled her gratitude at the man who would be her husband in a matter of minutes.

Amazing what little time it takes to change the course of a person's path for a lifetime, she thought as the ceremony ended. Of course, this wasn't a real marriage. They would have it annulled as soon as Rasmus was behind bars.

Unexpected pain compressed her heart. In spite of all the roles she'd played as an agent, she'd expected to play the role of bride only once. She felt tarnished from taking the vows with no intention of keeping them.

"Ain't ya goin' ta kiss yer bride?"

Constance felt the blood drain from her face. What a reprehensible man! She stood rigid as Mr. Knight touched cold lips to her cheek.

"Ya done real good, Preacher." Rasmus straightened from his slouch against the seat, his revolver still pointed at Evan. "Now, Mr. and Mrs. Knight, don't ya be fergettin' what I said 'bout these here younguns. I don't want Marion thinkin' this marriage was anyone's idea but yers. If'n I hear any rumors ta the contrary, I'll know where ta find these babes. I've got eyes and ears ever'where. Don't ferget it."

An explosion rocked the car, throwing Constance heavily against Mr. Knight, who fell against the window. Effie's scream was the only human sound in the car filled with thuds and clangs of people and objects banging together. The reverend grabbed for the upholstered arm of a seat, missed and landed on the floor. Only the bandits remained in control of themselves. They'd been braced against the seats or doors, Constance realized, as though expecting the explosion.

Screams from the car in front of them could still be heard as Constance and the others righted themselves.

"What was that?" Evan asked through pale lips.

"Rasmus's friends blew the safe in the express car, I expect."

Rasmus raised his black eyebrows. "Good guess, Knight. In the other cars, my pals will be takin' up a collection from the passengers. But since you and the lady have been so cooperative, reckon we won't ask fer yer money and jewels."

Thank goodness! She hadn't much in the way of either, but if Rasmus discovered the card in her handbag identifying her as a Pinkerton agent, she'd be in grave danger.

Rasmus shot a glance out the window, then backed down the aisle. Grabbing his derby, he tipped it jauntily before settling it on his black hair.

"Time ta go. Be seein' ya 'round, newlyweds."

She wanted to smack the grin from his lean, slimy face, but stood quietly with her hands resting on Effie's shoulders, forcing her face to remain passive.

As soon as Rasmus and the "drummers" stepped from the car and dropped to the ground, she and Mr. Knight tore to the windows. A man with a bandanna over his face and a huge beige Stetson sat on a black horse, holding the reins of numerous other mounts. In a moment, the three outlaws were joined by others from the train, mounted and started off at a gallop.

The railroad men and passengers poured from the cars in front of them and ran toward the express car. Before Constance and Mr. Knight could follow, the reverend stopped them. She could see from his face that Mr. Knight was as impatient as she was herself at the distraction.

"I'm sorry you young people were forced into this marriage. But remember God's promise in the book of Romans: 'All things work together for good to them that love God.' "

"Thank you, Pastor," Constance murmured, and heard Mr. Knight thanking him also.

She turned to the children, admonishing them to stay where they were until she returned. Then she rushed down the aisle after Mr. Knight, one hand lifting the tailored skirt of her black traveling outfit, the other clutching her small, crepe-covered black mourning hat. Her superintendent would be expecting a report on the robbery. He would certainly not consider a wedding or a reverend adequate excuse for not discovering the details of the robbery herself.

The pastor's words swung in her mind as she ran. "All things work together for good."

What utter nonsense! This wedding would cause her endless complications. Doubtless it would eventually be annulled. But in the meantime, what would her Pinkerton superintendent say about the inconvenience caused to the investigation?

Religious people were generally tolerable, she'd found, since their Christian values kept them from involvement in too many crimes that hurt their fellow citizens. But they could be such fools, as the reverend's remark clearly showed.

Chapter 2

It was an hour before the railroad officials had examined the situation, determined the extent of the loss and damage, and were satisfied no one had been harmed. The dynamite used to blow open the safe hadn't been strong enough to blow the roof off the baggage and express car, as Constance had seen happen on other occasions. But the blast did tear apart several boxes, trunks and valises, and their contents were scattered about the car.

Constance observed everything as closely as possible in the confusion, attempting to fill her memory with facts to include in her report at the earliest opportunity. It wasn't easy with her identity as a Pinkerton operative unknown. The railroad officials tried with little success to keep passengers distanced as they considered the situation. Twice Mr. Knight suggested she return to the children. Constance pretended not to hear him.

When the train finally shivered to a grunting, clanking start, Mr. Knight won Constance's gratitude by calming Effie and Evan, praising them richly, and telling them they had acted bravely and wisely.

Before long he diverted their thoughts by encouraging them to watch for the long bridge that would soon carry the train over the Mississippi into River's Edge. They moved across the aisle, taking up residence on their knees upon the amethyst upholstered couches, noses pressed eagerly against the windows. Early-turning russet and golden leaves occasionally brightened the green pine along the high, craggy bluffs bordering the river. Steamboats and barges dotted the water. Towboats floated huge rafts of lumber from northern Minnesota and Wisconsin toward the river mill towns below St. Paul.

With the children preoccupied, Constance and Mr. Knight agreed upon a story they hoped would satisfy Constance's widowed Aunt Libby and other townspeople. Only those in their coach knew of the impromptu wedding ceremony. The reverend and the children readily agreed not to volunteer the fact that the wedding occurred on the train. The newly married couple would say they had met in Chicago—not an untruth as they met through Effie and Evan before the train left that great city.

"I hate deceit."

The vehemence of Mr. Knight's statement, coming between clenched teeth, shocked Constance. His jaw was rigid and his brown eyes glittered with suppressed rage.

It was a moment before she could rally to reply, "Surely it is necessary in this case. Anyone knowing the circumstances would understand the need for the untruths."

His gaze met hers, and his expression softened somewhat. "It distresses me that you and the children were drawn into the quarrel between Rasmus Pierce and myself. So like him to hide behind children. If it weren't for the twins' safety, I would never have agreed to the ceremony."

Of course he wouldn't, Constance reassured herself.

"I shall never be able to thank you sufficiently for disrupting your plans in order to save my nephew's and niece's lives. I have no doubt Mr. Pierce would enforce his threat against them."

"Unfortunately, Rasmus is capable of any act, no matter how reprehensible."

From the criminal's profile at the Pinkerton agency, Constance knew it was true. "Do you know him well?"

He snorted. "As well as anyone would wish to know a rattlesnake. We both grew up in River's Edge. He was always a shiftless bully. Even as a small boy he loved to see others cringe before him, would shove the weaker boys about and terrify the girls, destroying their toys and school books. Left school after the fifth grade level. Always wanted something for nothing. If he'd put half the effort into legitimate business he has into his criminal enterprises, he could be a successful, respected man by now."

"Yes, most criminals could, or so—so I've always believed." The theft and marriage ceremony must have shaken her more than she realized. She'd almost said that Mr. Pinkerton shared Mr. Knight's belief that many criminals had the power of mind to become honorable members of society if won from their evil ways.

"Miss Ward, I hope. . ."

Color rose to both their hairlines as they realized she was no longer Miss Ward. Their mutual embarrassment was relieved when Effie and Evan chorused, "The bridge! We're crossing the bridge!"

Indeed the clacking of the wheels against the steel changed subtly to a ringing clang as they moved out over the river. Relief cooled Constance's cheeks as the children's eager questions drew Justin across the narrow aisle.

The train whistle blasted through the car and moments later they arrived at the depot, a charming building with dormers in a steeply sloped roof trimmed with gingerbread. Through the window, Constance could see her graying, middle-aged Aunt Libby, reticule swinging from the hands clasped in front of her waist. Her frothy, lemon-colored gown and large hat looked frivolous on her slim-as-a-pin body with its wrinkled, almost gaunt face which ended in a jutting chin.

Constance couldn't help but smile. Trust Aunt Libby to be as up-to-date as tomorrow's newspaper. "A businesswoman in fashion must set an example if she wishes to win the women of the community," she'd said more than once while in Chicago on buying trips for her millinery.

Her grin died. What would Aunt Libby think when her niece arrived as Mrs. Justin Knight? She caught her breath at the name blazing through her thoughts.

"Aren't you coming?"

She turned at Effie's question. Mr. Knight was standing in the aisle and had opened the slotted mahogany doors above the windows to remove his duck valise and her black leather satchel with nickel plate trimmings.

Within minutes, they were descending to the platform. Aunt Libby threw out her gloved hands and rushed toward them, her high-heeled shoes clattering across the narrow wooden planks, the hem of her frothy gown moving like a cloud about her feet. She caught the children in her arms, her pale blue eyes glistening with unshed tears, her pointed chin quivering.

"You poor, poor dears! How wonderful to see you!" The crooning voice broke on the words. The children were momentarily lost in the folds of her voluminous gown.

Constance would have laughed at the sight if she weren't so concerned with explaining her new status. She felt her hand claimed by Mr. Knight and drawn securely through his arm.

Keeping her gaze on Libby, she swallowed hard and made herself ask the question burning in her mind. "Are—are you expecting the twins and me to stay in your home?"

His hand tightened over hers. "I've been fruitlessly casting about in my mind for an alternative, but in light of Rasmus's threat to the children, I don't believe we have any other options." His voice was low enough that she was certain no one else heard him. "Ma'am." The urgency in his tone drew her gaze to his. "I assure you, my actions shall in no way compromise your honor."

Was it pity lying in the depths of his eyes? She wasn't accustomed to being pitied, and found that she didn't like it.

Aunt Libby released the children, and hurried toward Constance. She was glad of the excuse to free her hand from Mr. Knight's arm to yield to Libby's embrace.

"It is so good to see you once more," she said earnestly.

"And you." Steel gray brows arched in obvious curiosity as Libby nodded to Justin. "Good evening. Returning from a business trip, I presume?"

His smile could charm a fox from its hole, Constance thought watching him remove his derby and greet Libby.

"Not completely business, Mrs. Ward. The trip afforded a great deal of pleasantry." One of his hands touched Constance's back lightly. "Your niece and I met in Chicago. I hope you will be pleased to hear that she is now my wife."

Libby struggled valiantly to remain a lady under the surprising news. "Why, I thought you. . ." Libby's shocked blue gaze met Constance's green eyes. Then her chin rose. Her smile deepened the multitude of wrinkles in her cheeks, but Constance saw the questions remaining in her eyes. "I couldn't be more pleased that marriage to Constance has brought you into the family, Mr. Knight."

He leaned down to kiss Libby's bright red cheek. "I was hoping you'd feel that way, Mrs. Ward. May I call you Aunt Libby?"

Constance caught her bottom lip between her teeth to keep from laughing at her aunt's flustered response. "Why—why, if you wish, Mr. Knight."

"Thank you. And I am Justin. If you'll excuse me, I must arrange for the horse-drawn bus to take us home."

"You are welcome to use the carriage I've rented. Of course, you will wish Effie and Evan to stay with me. You are on your honeymoon, after all."

"Oh, no!" Did her exclamation sound as desperate to her aunt as it did to her, Constance wondered. "We prefer the children to stay with us, Aunt Libby. I apologize for the inconvenience you've been put to arranging for our visit, but. . ." She looked pleadingly at Mr. Knight.

He took Libby's gloved hand solicitously and nodded toward the express car, where the local sheriff had joined the crowd of railroad personnel and curious bystanders. "Perhaps you've noticed the excitement. I wouldn't wish to upset you, but there was a robbery a few miles from town." Libby's flat, lace-covered chest rose with her sharp gasp. "The children were quite disturbed by the event. Under the circumstances, we feel it would be best to keep them with us. I'm sure you understand."

"Naturally." A tremor shook the one word reply. Libby pulled a lace-trimmed handkerchief from her reticule and mopped her skinny face. "My, it is certainly a day of surprises, isn't it?"

Constance rested a hand on Libby's forearm. "Will you be all right, dear?"

Libby waved her hand away with bony fingers. "Think I haven't had a few surprises in my lifetime? None have conquered me yet."

Mr. Knight's laugh boomed out. Constance decided she quite liked the sound of it.

When he had retreated toward the pile of trunks, boxes and valises a short way down the platform, Constance said, "Would you watch the children for me? I must send a telegram to friends in Chicago. I promised to let them know when I arrived."

Hurrying toward the station house, Constance mentally pieced together the telegram she would send. It was true it was to be sent to friends, the female Pinkerton operatives with whom she shared a home in Chicago when not living elsewhere on a case. She wouldn't dare to send it directly to the office, for fear of revealing her true identity and purpose to the wire operator. It took some doing to come up with a message that told of the robbery, the marriage, and how she could be reached without revealing her position as an operative, but she was accustomed to such challenges.

The others were ready to leave when she returned to the carriage. Libby caught her in her arms when they dropped the woman at her own home.

"I'm so happy for you, dear. See that you stop by the shop tomorrow and tell me everything." She kissed the children good-bye, and stood beside the street waving until the buggy turned a corner and was lost to sight.

Effie and Evan eagerly pointed at town sights from the back seat as they drove along. The smell of the river and the smoke from the lumber mills filled the air. Children played in the neat yards they passed, young matrons pushed parasol-topped perambulators along the sidewalks, and carriages and delivery wagons met them on the street, the townspeople often waving and calling out greetings to Justin.

"It appears to be a pleasant town," Constance murmured. Perhaps making conversation would chase away the fear clawing at her stomach. Nothing in her previous experience had prepared her to move into a stranger's home as his wife.

"I've found it so. But I expect I'm prejudiced, having lived here all my twenty-six years. The town is about forty years old. The river has made it a profitable place. It's primarily logs that keep the town finances going. You saw the barges piled with them when we crossed the river. The way the northern woods have been logged off over the years with no replanting, it won't be long before the industries relying on them will begin dying."

Was he trying to calm her by rattling on so?

Libby's two-story frame home had been pleasant looking, but built on a somewhat small lot in a common part of town. Now Constance saw that they were moving into a wealthier neighborhood. Large lots with spacious homes gently met the wide street. "Even the horses' hoofs seem quieter against the pavement here," she remarked.

"Wooden blocks have been laid beneath the pavement to lessen the noise of horses and carriages passing."

He stopped the carriage beside a horse stoop. "This is my home."

While he climbed down and secured the horse to the cast iron ring beside the stoop, Constance glanced in surprise at the new, clapboard and stone Queen Anne house. It sprawled across the huge lot, jutting and receding seemingly at random. No area of the building remained flat for more than a few feet. A three-story tower with bay windows in the first two stories stood at one front corner. An open arcade rimmed with white railings in arched openings beneath a cone-shaped roof topped the tower. A wide porch with a matching white railing ran like a wavy shoreline along the first floor, above a latticework-covered foundation. Some windows were rectangular, some arched, others round. A brick chimney stack rose from the midst of the building.

It was a grand example of the popular extreme architecture of the day, but Constance couldn't relate the house to the man she thought Mr. Knight to be. Without giving it conscious consideration, she'd assumed he would live in a home similar to the one next door, a more masculine, quietly elegant red brick Colonial Revival with stately white columns.

"Is this where we are to stay?" Effie asked when Mr. Knight lifted her from the carriage. "Is this whole house yours?"

"Effie!"

"Yes," Mr. Knight's amused voice cut into Constance's low protest. "The whole house."

The children's eyes met and they grinned. Constance stomach tightened in apprehension. She'd seen that conspiratorial grin before. She took Effie's hand firmly. "I expect you and Evan to behave like a little lady and gentleman."

"Yes, ma'am."

"Yes, ma'am."

Their joint agreement didn't reassure her for a moment. She kept Effie's hand in her own as they started up the walk. Experience had taught her that if Effie was subdued, Evan's proper behavior was assured.

Mr. Knight opened one of the double doors with etched glass windows, and invited his companions to enter. Constance tried to ignore the anxiety that tightened her stomach. When she was attracted to this man earlier, she never thought she'd be married to him by day's end!

The size and elegance of the foyer fairly took Constance's breath. Marble covered the floor, rich mahogany lined the walls, an elegant gas and electric chandelier hung from the second-story ceiling, which was covered in a fresco of clouds and cherubs against a robin's-egg blue sky. A wide stairway curved invitingly upward between gleaming mahogany posts.

"Justin, welcome home!"

A dainty blond woman dashed toward them, her pink organdy gown drifting across the marble. A wave of lily of the valley scent surrounded her. The delicate features above a pointed chin were radiant with welcome as she held out tiny hands to Mr. Knight. He took them immediately, but stared at her as though in a trance.

This is the girl he loves, Constance thought with a pang.

A sweet laugh rang through the hall.

"I see I succeeded in surprising you. I've planned a homecoming dinner. Mrs. Kelly has helped me. Please don't scold. I know this won't be my home until Sunday, but it was such fun planning the dinner."

"Of course I'll not scold, Marian. It was just unexpected, seeing you here." He was pale beneath his wavy hair, and Constance's heart went out to him. To have to face his fiancée so soon!

Marian tucked a tiny hand beneath his arm possessively and smiled at Constance. "He never can bring himself to reprimand me. A wonderful quality in a man, don't you agree?" Not waiting for a reply, she looked up at Justin. "Aren't you going to introduce me to your friends?"

"Why don't the children and I look about your yard while you and Miss Marian greet each other?" Constance suggested.

Relief and gratitude relaxed his face. "There's a stable and carriage house out back. Perhaps the children would like to see the horses."

"Oh, yes!"

"Can we, Aunt Constance?"

"Of course, dears," she replied, leading them through the door. "Good evening, Miss Marian."

"Good evening." The confusion in Marian's voice cut an unexpected mark of guilt into Constance's heart. Why should she care that the girl, she couldn't be more than nineteen, should be hurt? The marriage had been necessary to protect the children, if not to save Mr. Knight's life. In her work, subterfuge was often required in apprehending the criminal element. Never had it disturbed her before.

But as she followed the children around the rambling house to the stable, she felt uncomfortably as though her principles were decidedly smudged.

Chapter 3

Justin Knight stood in the open door and watched Marian rush down the lane. The wide-brimmed hat which matched her pink gown tilted unfashionably, teetered as though about to fall. She hadn't taken time to secure it before rushing from the house.

She had, however, taken the time to throw a choice porcelain figurine in his direction, fortunately with poor aim, and tell him exactly what she thought of a man who would wed another woman two days before he was to marry her. His face still burned from her contempt. It didn't help any that he agreed with her every sentiment.

The familiar scent of her lily of the valley fragrance lingered in the air that still reverberated with her anger. He hated like fury to hurt and humiliate her. He wished things were different; wished Rasmus hadn't effectually barred him from telling her the truth about his marriage by threatening the children.

His fist struck the mahogany door with a force that set the leaded, etched glass trembling. How he hated deceit!

Yet if excitable Marian discovered the true reason for his marriage, she would never be able to keep her knowledge of it from Rasmus. The toe of his shoe brushed at the fragments of broken figurine covering the marble floor, a tangible reminder of the whirlwind Marian created when he told her he had married someone else.

His lips stretched in a tight grimace. May as well admit the guilt he was fighting wasn't only over Rasmus's enforced deceit. A man in his position should feel he'd lost the most precious of life's gifts. He didn't.

His affection for Marian had never been the overwhelming attraction of which he'd heard so many men speak regarding the women they married. When he was the only remaining bachelor amongst his friends, he'd decided he'd over-estimated the emotions involved with love.

At twenty-six, he sometimes felt like an old man. Since taking over the bank when his parents died in a train accident three years ago, he hadn't much time for youth's lighthearted pursuits. Being with Marian, who faced life eagerly, made him feel young again. And so he'd proposed to her.

Even so, he'd never told Marian he loved her and she'd never asked for his love. Had he been unfair to her, asking her to share his life without loving her more than life?

Regardless, it was behind him now. He was married to Constance.

Even if his parents hadn't drilled into him the belief that marriage vows were inviolate, his own commitment to the Lord left him with the same conclusion. He stuffed his fists into the pockets of his gray trousers. The circumstances of the ceremony didn't change the sanctity of the vows.

At least he'd had the opportunity to tell Marian of his marriage before she heard it from someone else.

"Thank Thee for that, Lord. Help her through this time."

The broken engagement would be difficult for her pride if not her emotions. It would be socially embarrassing for her and her family. Anger burned through him. And Rasmus would bring such pain on Marian in the name of love!

A mirthless laugh jolted from his lips. He'd always been so conservative. Marrying a woman he'd known less than a day and taking responsibility for her and two children, one could hardly call that staid.

"Beggin' yer pardon, Mr. Knight."

He turned to face the short, round, middle-aged woman with deep red hair piled above her face. Tantalizing odors of oyster stew and roasting beef clung about her.

The woman must have heard Marian's temper tantrum, he realized at the sight of her flaming cheeks. Her plump hands were settled above her stomach on the thin linen apron covering her cotton house dress. Disapproval oozed from every pore of her face.

"What is it, Mrs. Kelly?"

"The meal Miss Marian was havin' me prepare for ye—will ye be wantin' it?"

He smiled into the eyes stuffed beneath thick red brows. "Is there enough for two adults and two hungry children?"

She drew her short self up straighter. "Have ye ever known there ta be a lack of food on me table?"

"Not once in all the years you've cooked for me." It felt good to chuckle. "Before dinner, would you clean up this mess in which we're standing? Also, my wife and her niece and nephew are in the backyard. Please ask them to come inside. If Terrence, the stable boy, hasn't gone home for the night, ask him to bring the bags from the carriage before returning it to the livery."

She bustled down the marble hallway toward the kitchen, the large bow of her apron dancing on her ample hips.

Justin entered the parlor, his frowning glance taking in the new, luxurious furnishings chosen by Marian. So many items for which he had yet to pay. Marian had cut no corners with their prospective home, he thought. He'd given her a spending limit, but he'd been so busy with the bank that he hadn't thought to see that she kept within it. She'd spent extravagantly. He'd thought he had enough to cover the debts she'd accumulated when he started home from Chicago. Rasmus's robbery of the express car was going to complicate his ability to meet those bills.

The thought crossed his mind again an hour later when he led Constance and the children into the room following dinner. He pushed a wall button, brightening the large, high-ceiling room with electric light from the cut-glass chandelier.

He watched Constance's gaze run swiftly over the pale gold patterned wallpaper topped by the wide, hand-painted frieze of blue and gold, to the tasseled, dark blue fabric window cornices over the soft golden draperies in the bay window. Beneath them stood a long, graceful rosewood sofa covered in blue damask. Matching chairs sat opposite the fireplace, where an elegant brass and crystal clock was chiming the hour of nine upon the silk lambrequin covering the mantle. A mass of fresh flowers filled the room with fragrance from a crystal vase upon a marble-topped, elegantly carved rosewood table beneath the chandelier. The Persian rug brought bright splashes of red into the otherwise softly-colored room.

"I like your house, Mr. Knight," Effie said decidedly. "May Evan and I explore the rest of it?"

"Effie!"

She lifted her eyebrows innocently at Constance. "But I said 'may we'."

Justin scuttled a laugh. He was sure Constance wouldn't appreciate his undermining of her disciplinary attempts. "Tomorrow you may explore to your heart's content, but just now I'd like to speak with you."

When Constance and the children were seated on the sofa, he pulled a matching gentleman's chair close. Leaning forward, elbows on his thighs, fingers linked loosely between his knees, he smiled at Effie and Evan.

"Have you ever been to Sunday school?"

They nodded in unison.

"We learn lots of Bible verses there," Effie offered. "I can say more verses than anyone else in our class. Evan can say almost as many, though."

"Do you remember learning that we must forgive our enemies, and those who hurt us?"

Effie nodded vigorously, but Justin noticed that Evan's nod wasn't nearly as eager, and his large brown eyes were wary.

"You were both very brave on the train today when Mr. Pierce stopped to talk with us."

Evan jerked up straight, his back no longer touching the sofa. "He was a mean man! He pointed a gun at me!"

Constance laid an arm over his wide sailor collar. Her eyes met Justin's, and he cringed inside at the pain he saw there for the children.

"And you did exactly the right thing when Mr. Pierce did that, Evan," he continued. "Perhaps you remember in your Bible stories that when Jesus was taken prisoner and his enemies accused him, Jesus answered them not a word. Sometimes keeping silent, as you did today, is wise. There's more wise things we can do, even though Mr. Pierce isn't present."

Evan leaned slowly back against the sofa once more. "What?" he asked tentatively.

Effie, sitting on the edge of the cushion swinging her feet, held her hands palms upward. "Yes, what?"

"We can pray for him." He was watching Evan, but he noticed the jerk of

Constance's head toward him at his comment. A sadness slipped through him. On top of everything else that had happened, was he married to a woman who didn't revere the Lord? Perhaps he misunderstood her action. Perhaps she did follow God and was surprised to find that he did, too. Well, there'll be time to explore that later.

"Rasmus Pierce is older than you children. He's bigger and he has a gun. But you are stronger and richer than Mr. Pierce."

"We are?" Effie grinned.

Evan just continued looking at him skeptically.

"You are. Because you love Jesus. When you have Jesus beside you, it doesn't matter how tough things seem, because Jesus is stronger than anything or anyone. And He's promised to never leave those who love Him."

Effie nodded. "We learned that in Sunday school."

Evan nodded slowly. Justin breathed a small sigh of relief. Was he beginning to reach the boy? Evan had been as tense as a wound up tin top ever since Rasmus drew his gun. Not that he could blame him. But he couldn't bear to think of the boy living in a world of fear because of Rasmus.

"We can pray for Rasmus. We can ask God to forgive him, and make him His child."

"Yes, let's!" Effie's curls bounced in the light.

Evan nodded slowly, pushing himself forward on the cushion. "I'll pray."

"All right, old man." Justin bowed his head, then peeked to see what the children were doing. Both had their heads lowered solemnly over folded hands, their eyes squeezed shut. Constance's troubled gaze was on Evan.

"Dear God," Evan began, and Justin shut his eyes. "Please forgive Mr. Pierce for bein' a bad man and pointin' his gun at us and robbin' the train. Make him love Jesus so he'll be a good man. Amen."

"Amen," Effie repeated.

Evan's anxious brown eyes were waiting for his own when Justin lifted his head. "Will he be a good man now, and not point guns at boys?"

Justin pressed his lips together firmly. He wasn't going to find it so easy himself to forgive Rasmus for frightening the children. But even if he had the luxury of refusing to forgive the thief, he couldn't afford to set an example of unforgiveness for Evan. If the boy held hatred and fear to himself it would only make the harm Rasmus had done worse and longlasting.

He swallowed hard. "Sometimes it takes a long time for God to finish His work in a man. It might be quite a while before Mr. Pierce learns to love Jesus. But we'll keep praying for him, won't we?"

"Yes," Evan said in a low voice. "But I wish God would work quick."

Justin grinned as he stood. "One thing we can count on, old man; God's time is always best, even when it seems slow to us. By the time on that brass clock on the mantle, it's getting mighty late for small boys and girls to be up. You'd best be getting to bed."

Constance slipped a hand on each of the children's shoulders. He liked the brave, sweet smile she gave them.

"I'll go up with you. Say goodnight to Mr. Knight."

"Miss Ward, when you're done, please meet me in the library."

He thought for a moment she would refuse, but finally she inclined her head.

It was a half hour before she came to the library that served as his study. He rose behind his desk and watched as she examined the room from the doorway.

This woman is my wife. The thought set his heart quick-stepping. She was lovely! Not in Marian's bright, bubbly manner, but in a gentle yet self-confident manner that surrounded her in an aura of serenity. The light from the gasolier glowed off her thick black hair swept to the back of her head in a delightfully simple but elegant twist.

From the beginning he'd been fascinated by her eyes. Unexpectedly, deeply green, clearer than emeralds. More unexpectedly, they met one's gaze frankly, without the proper dropping of lashes or the twinkling of a flirtatious tease. They were eyes to be trusted. *"The heart of her husband doth safely trust in her."* The verse from Proverbs 31 slipped across his mind. It fit this woman.

Since meeting her in Chicago (could it truly have been only this morning?) he'd wanted to know more of her, rejoicing in the bits and pieces that were revealed in his conversations with her and the children during the twelve hours on the train.

Each time they'd shared a smile over the children's antics, a warm joy rippled through him. It was as though his heart had tumbled to her and was no longer in his keeping. The knowledge had left a burning ache in his chest. Why did she come into his life now, when he had no right to be attracted to her? He had asked the Lord to forgive him, had tried to keep his eyes from her face, his ears from listening for her voice.

And now she was his wife.

What did she think of all that had happened today, drawing her to his home as his bride? When they'd stopped before the house, he'd thought he recognized fright staring starkly at him momentarily from her wide eyes, and fury with Rasmus had raged within him.

"What a comforting room. It appears much more like you than the rest of the house." Her warm, rich voice preceded her as she crossed the Brussels carpet of wine, gold, and brown toward his desk.

His neck and face burned. Had he been staring blatantly at her all this time? "Marian designed and furbished the house, except for this room and my bedchamber. I insisted on having my way with those."

She stopped near the inlaid desk, her fingers linked lightly together in front of her straight black skirt of moire silk. "That explains it, then. Your house is fine and beautiful, but I thought it unlike you. It is like Marian—bright and gay and especially choice."

"You are most kind."

"But I believe I prefer this room. The bookcases filled with volumes behind the leaded glass doors, the wine velvet draperies, the leather furniture, the frieze that matches the border of the carpet. They fill the room with welcome and warmth."

She stepped closer to the bookshelves beside them to examine the volumes. He liked her peaceful ways, her low, gentle, rich voice, the graceful way she moved without ever appearing to rush, her quiet hands. Marian's hands were in constant motion; she never seemed to rest.

"You have a wide array of interests, judging by your books. Longfellow, Thoreau, James Fenimore Cooper, Mark Twain, Dickens, History of France, a journal by Lt. Zebulon Pike, and several volumes by Allan Pinkerton." She glanced over her shoulder. Was there veiled amusement in her eyes? "Didn't Mr. Pinkerton found the Pinkerton National Detective Agency?"

"Yes. His works aren't particularly literary, but he does describe common methods used by bank robbers, forgers, counterfeiters and such, which I've found useful in my position with the bank."

He cleared his throat and stepped out from behind the desk, indicating the long leather sofa beneath the doublewide window on the opposite wall. "Won't you be seated, Miss—may I call you Constance? I'm afraid people will consider it odd if I continue addressing you as Miss Ward, and I'm sure you would prefer to be called Mrs. Knight only when necessary."

Color flooded her face above the high black lace collar, but she answered steadily. "Thank you. Under the circumstances, Constance will be acceptable."

She lowered herself gracefully onto the sofa, her straight back not touching the upholstery. He settled himself at the other end of the sofa, allowing a comfortable, nonthreatening distance between them.

"On the train, you and the children told me a little about yourselves and your trip. I know you are all from Chicago, the children's mother died years ago and their father almost six months ago; that you were traveling to River's Edge to visit your aunt, Mrs. Libby Ward. Beyond that, I know very little."

Her green eyes met his with complete composure. "There is little else to tell. Aunt Libby and I are the last of our family. I could hardly raise the children alone. Who would stay with them when they were not at school and I was at work? Aunt Libby offered to give the children a home. Between her and Mrs. Chandler, Aunt Libby's housemate, the children could be cared for more properly."

"There is no young man you pledged to marry who would share the responsibility of the children with you?" At her slight drawing back, he hastened on, "I assure you, I wouldn't ask such a personal question on our short acquaintance under other circumstances. This situation is untenable for you, to say the least, and I only hope that it will not also damage a friendship which is important to you."

"I am promised to no young man."

Had she hesitated before answering? Was there perhaps a man who had not asked for her hand, but who carried her heart? He hoped fervently not, for her sake as well as his own. Wasn't she enduring enough already because of him?

She leaned toward him slightly, her hands clutched in her lap. "I am most distressed that your marriage to Miss Marian has been interrupted. I do hope she will forgive you when Rasmus Pierce is behind bars and the truth is revealed. Naturally, we shall then obtain an annulment, and. . ."

"There will be no annulment."

Her eyes met his, shock glinting off their green depths. "Pardon me?"

He'd been hoping to avoid this discussion for a few days. Well, may as well get it behind them.

"There will be no annulment."

Chapter 4

C onstance shot to her feet. It took all her training to keep her voice low and even rather than shouting at the top of her lungs as she wished.

"No annulment? Surely you jest."

He stood also, meeting her gaze evenly. She wished he'd remained seated. It did nothing for her self-confidence to have him towering above her with his masculine strength well defined beneath his gray jacket.

"I assure you, I do not jest about vows taken before God. I am sorry your life has been inconvenienced, but. . ."

"Inconvenienced? You call it an inconvenience to be married to a man whom I have known less than twenty-four hours?"

"Have you so soon forgotten the vows we exchanged? 'Until death us do part.'"

Was she as pale as he? Even his lips were white. He had been engaged to Marian, she reminded herself; he can't want this marriage to be real. Her shoulders relaxed slightly beneath the black silk.

"Do you believe I shall betray the temporary nature of the marriage and endanger your life? Please rest assured I shall not. My niece and nephew's lives also stand in danger, you may recall."

"You've been stronger through this ordeal than I would have believed possible of any woman. I am certain you will not forget for a moment the danger that remains to the children. As I said, it is the vows. . . ."

"Might I remind you that we were wed at gunpoint? As you yourself told Rasmus, no minister or judge would uphold such a marriage against the participants' wishes. Nor would the strictest of society's matrons expect such a marriage to be honored."

"I expect to honor my vows."

His quiet tone frightened her; it was chillingly convincing.

"Regardless of my feelings in the matter? Regardless of the disruption to my life and the children's? I cannot believe a highly principled man would insist on binding an unwilling stranger to himself. Do you feel it is your faith which requires this?"

"Yes." He seemed surprised she would even ask.

"Isn't God supposed to be just? Yet you have asked forgiveness for a criminal, and believe God would force strangers to honor vows exchanged at gunpoint! I do not understand your God."

"My God? Aren't you a believer?"

"I—I. . .are you now challenging my faith?" She wasn't a believer. In these enlightened times, it was embracing ignorance to accept the beliefs of past centuries in a God who created and ruled the world, she thought. Yet she knew she would win no favor or respect from this man by expressing her views.

"Do you believe I am a heathen because I do not feel compelled to remain married to you for the rest of my life? I assure you, under normal circumstances, I, too, believe in the sanctity of marriage."

"If you had believed our marriage to be permanent, would you have entered into it?"

She stared at him, wanting desperately to say she would not have married him under such circumstances. Even as instantly attracted to him as she'd been, in her wildest imaginings she wouldn't have considered marrying a stranger.

Yet. . .she took a deep breath, dropped her gaze to the colorful Brussels carpet, then raised it again to his, squaring her shoulders.

"If it were the only way to save the children's lives, or yours, yes, I would have entered into the marriage even believing it to be permanent."

His eyes widened slightly at her admission that she would have entered into the marriage even to save him. Had he thought she would allow a man to be killed if it was within her power to prevent it?

The stoniness in his chestnut brown eyes softened. "It is all right then."

Whatever could he mean? she wondered, but he continued before she could ask.

"There is nothing to be gained from continuing this discussion. Are we agreed that until Rasmus Pierce is under lock and key, and solidly under, the marriage must at least appear permanent?"

"Yes," she agreed grudgingly. "Is it possible the minister is an accomplice of Rasmus Pierce?" Recalling the timid, trembling man, she doubted it, but she would grasp at any straw at this point.

"You mean, could he be an impostor? I'm afraid not." There was gentleness in his voice and pity in his eyes. "I know his face. He's been serving at a church in Red Wing, a few miles north of here, for five years or more."

"I see."

"It has been a long day. You must be exhausted."

The thought she had suppressed since the vows were exchanged pushed its way to the forefront of her mind. Her breath seemed to stop, though her heart hammered on faster and louder than ever beneath her tailored black silk bodice. He'd explained during dinner that he only employed day servants, so not even Mrs. Kelly would be in the home this evening. She had thought Mr. Knight too fine to insist that. . .she couldn't complete the thought. Had she been mistaken? If he considered the marriage permanent, would he expect. . . ?

"Your bags have been taken to your room, which is beside the children's. My room adjoins yours." He pulled his hand from his pocket and held out a key. "This is the only key to the door connecting our rooms."

Her lungs almost hurt from her breath of relief as she accepted the key.

"Thank you," she murmured. Almost immediately she knew her relief was for more than her own physical safety. She would have hated to find Justin Knight was not the honorable man she had instinctively believed.

The realization frightened her. She was trained not to trust people; trained to believe anyone capable of deceit. How, why, had she allowed this man to penetrate her usual defenses?

She explored the discomforting thought further in her room as she worked over her required daily report to the Pinkerton agency. It shook her to the core to realize that she'd let her guard down with Justin. To do so was extremely dangerous. If an operative trusted the wrong person, it could mean death to oneself and others. Never had she allowed herself the luxury of trust in the past, not beyond her family and fellow agents.

She replaced the silver pen in its ornate holder on the graceful mahogany writing desk which stood beneath the double windows draped in pale blue damask. The material matched that on the chaise lounge at the end of the lace-canopied bed and the bench before the vanity whose top was covered with delicate silver appointments. One of these was a fragile atomizer filled with lily of the valley fragrance such as Marian was wearing earlier. She herself hadn't worn scent since becoming an agent. It was too distinctive for someone who must change identities frequently and remain in the background more often than not.

It is a lovely room for a bride, Constance admitted, observing it as she rose. What joyful anticipation Marian must have known in decorating it! How awful for her to have her plans in tatters!

She fingered the delicate cream lace draping a bedpost. For that matter, wasn't her own life in tatters? She, who had always prided herself on the control she had over her life. Who had pitied friends whose lives were dictated by their fathers or husbands. Not for her a life such as that.

How she'd enjoyed being a Pinkerton operative! The excitement of knowing she was helping the cause of justice. She hadn't been tempted once to exchange it for marriage, even though she'd now reached the rather advanced age of twenty-three. The agency had a strict policy against the employment of married women.

She might have been tempted to marry Alex otherwise. He was such fun when they worked on cases together. He had a brilliant mind for counteracting criminals, and was a wonder at acting the parts necessary in their cases.

Although they had never courted because it was against agency policy for agents to see each other romantically, he had asked her to marry him when her brother Charles died. She had refused.

Occasionally, she'd allowed herself to wonder what it would be like to spend her life with Alex. There was no one she knew with whom she would prefer to be married. But she certainly wasn't ready to give up control of her life to any man yet.

She pushed away from the bedpost impatiently. "Well, it certainly appears you have done so!" she whispered, crossing to the window to peer unseeingly out at the large back lawn flanked by the stable and carriage house.

Lately her life had careened more and more out of her control, culminating in this afternoon's fiasco. Within the last six months, her brother Charles died, she'd been left with the care of his children, and now she was married to a stranger, and her career was threatened.

"All things work together for good to them that love God."

Constance gave an unfeminine snort as the quote slipped uninvited into her mind. The thought might be comforting, if she loved God.

Charles had loved God. He'd taught Effie and Evan to love Him, also. Charles had tried to convince her that she was a sinner in need of God's love and the salvation He offered through His Son, Jesus Christ.

She'd only laughed at him. A sinner? She set high ideals for herself. Her life was devoted to bringing lawbreakers to justice. Surely if there was a just God, He would have to admit she had done everything humanly possible to become a good person. What more could He expect of her?

Honesty.

The word shot through her mind and burned into her heart. Her very spirit seemed to writhe in discomfort. Loyalty to the law was her highest ideal. Honesty, unfortunately, was often forsaken in her commitment to justice.

Justin had hated to be dishonest, even to save his own life and that of the children. She could still hear the distaste in his voice as he'd spoken of his hatred for deceit.

She was unaccustomed to people who held themselves to such a high standard of integrity. As a detective, she dealt regularly with criminals to whom truth was foreign. In order to trap them, it was common for her and other operatives to pretend to be people they weren't and to make promises they had no intention of keeping.

This marriage was only another of many roles. It was unreasonable for her and Justin to consider their vows unbreakable under the circumstances. Yet she couldn't help but admire his insistence on keeping them. To do so would mean losing the woman he loved and taking responsibility for herself and the children " 'til death us do part." In the face of such self-sacrifice, she felt almost unworthy beside him.

She tried to shed the thought with her wrapper, but it remained to climb with her between the crisp new sheets slightly scented with lily of the valley. The deep lace trimming the top sheet tickled her chin as she drew it up. She wished she felt as clean inside as the bed linens felt to her. Always she'd been proud of her high ideals. It was extremely uncomfortable feeling unworthy. She didn't care for it, not one whit.

❧

Justin watched Constance leave the library. His brows puckered. Had he been unspeakably cruel, insisting there be no annulment? The day must have been murderous for her, valiant though she'd been through the improbable events.

A wry smile twisted his lips. This was his wedding night, and he and his bride had spent the evening discussing an annulment. His admiration for the woman who was now his wife had multiplied as they talked. Even though horror, then anger, had followed disbelief in her eyes at his sudden declaration, her voice hadn't risen from its rich, low tones.

He tugged a chain and plunged the room into darkness before crossing to a window to stare out at the black night. Did he have any right to expect Constance to act according to his beliefs, to spend the rest of her life with him, simply because she had been on a certain train at a certain moment in time? But always he'd believed a marriage vow unbreakable. If she chose to leave him when Rasmus was apprehended. . . . His heart contracted painfully at the thought. If she chose to leave, he'd remain true to his vow.

The thought of a future without a loving companion beside him left him feeling as alone as a man on an ice floe.

"All things work together for good to them that love God." He clutched at the hope in the promise.

Chapter 5

"Hᵒw many boats do you count, Evan? I count twelve!"

Constance and Justin exchanged smiles at Effie's exuberance. The child stood on tiptoe in the open third floor of the corner tower, her hands clutching the six-inch-wide railing topping the short wall. Even with their lithe little bodies stretched to their limits, the twins were barely tall enough to see out the arch which was open to the weather.

A good thing, Constance thought. If the wall were shorter, Effie's enthusiasm might endanger her. The way she threw herself at life, one day that child would land in a powerful lot of trouble, or Constance missed her guess.

"I count thirteen boats," Evan answered after his usual careful deliberation of the situation. He pointed a thin little finger toward where the river rounded a bend to be hidden from their view. "See that towboat comin'?"

"It wasn't there when I counted," Effie informed him with a toss of her curls.

The sound of Justin strangling a laugh brought Constance's gaze to his face, half hidden behind one of his large hands. The laugh sparkling in his eyes slipped into sadness as he looked out toward the ribbon of water.

"One day there won't be many boats left on the Mississippi. The railroads are taking over the transporting of goods and passengers which are the lifeblood of river economy, even the transporting of the logs on which River's Edge's economy relies. Already the river traffic has diminished substantially."

She could think of nothing encouraging to say about his comments, so changed the subject.

"What do you call this area? It reminds one of a widow's walk, where a sea captain's wife would watch for her husband's return."

He shook his head slightly. "There is no special name for it."

"Look! A bird is sitting right beside me!" Effie's stage whisper should have scared the sparrow away, but it didn't. The tiny brown bird sat on the pot of bright geraniums inches from Effie's hand, turning its head this way and that as it viewed the giggling girl.

A river-scented breeze caught one of Effie's long brown curls, and the sparrow darted away. She spun around. "I'm going to call this room the Bird Cage!"

Justin nodded decidedly. "The Bird Cage it is."

Constance tucked behind her ear a stray lock of hair with which the breeze insisted upon playing. "The view is spectacular, most of the town, the wide expanse of water dotted with islands, and the beautiful craggy bluffs."

"There's an eyeglass in my office. I'll leave it here for your use," Justin offered. "Lieutenant Zebulon Pike explored this region in 1805, two years after the area was acquired by the United States. In describing the area he said, 'It was altogether a prospect so variegated and romantic that a man may scarcely expect to enjoy such a one but twice or thrice in the course of his life.'"

Hands on the gleaming white railing, her gaze drifted over the landscape. "I agree with the Lieutenant. It would be lovely to spend one's life in the midst of such beauty."

She turned to question him concerning an unusual building, but the words died in her throat at the unexpected, fervent light burning in the eyes watching her. Whatever was he thinking?

His attention was diverted by Evan tugging at his sleeve. "May Effie and me sleep out here, sir?"

"Effie and I," Constance corrected, as she did twenty times a day.

He nodded solemnly. "Yes, Effie and I. May we sleep out here?"

"Oh, yes! May we, Mr. Knight?" Effie was jumping up and down, unable to contain her enthusiasm.

"It might be cold," Constance suggested. "It will be dark, and there may be mosquitoes."

Effie waved her little hands in a dismissing motion. "We don't mind. Little things like that don't bother us."

"No, we wouldn't mind," Evan seconded in his serious tone.

Effie threw her arms about one of Justin's legs, almost throwing him off balance in her ardor. "Please, Mr. Knight! It would be wonderful!"

"Your aunt and I will discuss it. Run along to your rooms and collect your hats. We're going to the business district."

Effie's whoops disappeared as the children ran through the house, the door to the Bird Cage slamming behind them.

"Those two might have your nice new home torn to bits within a few days."

His grin was pleasant. "Effie is quite a charmer. It isn't easy to resist her beseeching brown eyes."

Constance started to smile in sympathy, but the remembrance of Miss Marian's similar comment last evening stopped the smile cold. "He never can bring himself to reprimand me. A wonderful quality in a man." At the memory, a chill settled about her heart like a fog. It took her quite by surprise. *Why should I feel. . .almost jealous? How absurd!*

"There's something we forgot yesterday."

Instantly her nerve endings served warning. His voice was so smooth that she knew instantly he was about to broach a topic to which he feared she would object.

"The wonder would be if we did not forget something in the unprecedented melee."

He dug in a small vest pocket with his thumb and forefinger. A ring flashed in the fingers he held toward her, destroying the atmosphere of pleasant camaraderie.

Her hands clutched the railing the children had recently vacated, and she fought the wave of weakness that threatened. She'd faced guns in the hands of criminals with less fear.

"Surely that isn't necessary."

"You needn't stare at it in horror, as though it were a viper. It's only a wedding band."

"It—it makes everything seem so. . .permanent."

"Isn't that the image we wish to portray?"

They stared at each other, neither making a move to relent. After what seemed aeons, Justin asked gently, "Don't you believe, too, that it would be wiser to wear the ring? Truly?"

She gave in then, but couldn't gain command of her voice, so only nodded.

He took the hand she reluctantly extended and slipped the ring on her finger. It felt as heavy as the huge anchors she'd seen on steamboats.

He released her hand immediately and she let it fall back upon the railing. Sunshine danced off the gold band, drawing her gaze to it like a magnet. Delicate orange blossoms were etched about it, and the sight of them caught her heart in a little twinge. It was too sweet. She would have preferred a plain band. Was this dear little ring the one he'd chosen for Miss Marian? The thought repulsed her, but she daren't ask. He needed no reminders that he wasn't married to the woman of his choice.

"I took the liberty this morning of stopping by the newspaper office. Rasmus will be looking for an announcement. I spoke with my lawyer, also. We're to stop by his office this afternoon to sign the special marriage license. The judge is a friend of mine, so there was no difficulty obtaining it."

Did he think she would rejoice at the news? He had simply taken care of necessary details.

Simply. Among his friends, people who respected him. People who wouldn't understand his apparent ungentlemanly behavior toward Miss Marian. The least she could do was be civil.

"Thank you for looking to these details. It cannot be easy for you."

He leaned a hip against the short wall, ignoring her sympathy. "Marian had calling cards printed. You'll find them in the writing desk in your room."

She nodded. Something else of Marian's. Of course she must use them. A lady needs calling cards, and it would be silly to go to the expense of printing others which would only say the same thing, Mrs. Justin Knight, or Mr. and Mrs. Justin Knight. For a moment Constance felt as though she'd lost her identity, as though she'd been swallowed whole in Justin Knight's personality. Mrs. Justin Knight. The title left no inkling of the woman who was Constance Ward.

"Aunt Constance! Mr. Knight! Yoo-hoo!" Effie's yell from the yard below broke the uncomfortable silence.

"Coming!" Justin hollered between cupped hands.

Constance shook her head. "I despair of ever molding her into a lady."

"I confess I like her quite as she is."

So did Constance. It pleased her that he was fond of Effie, but she knew better than to believe her exuberant niece's manner would be acceptable as she matured.

The afternoon was more trying than Constance expected. Everywhere they went people stared. A number of matrons refused to respond to Justin's greetings, pursing their lips primly and shooting him disapproving looks from beneath their bonnets. Dusky color darkened his face at their actions. Constance's heart went out to him, and she lifted her chin slightly higher and made her smiles for him especially warm as they walked along the bustling streets.

He pointed out buildings of interest, shared pieces of the town's past, his hopes for its future. He kept the conversation friendly without a hint of intimacy, and Constance discovered herself relaxing and enjoying an easy camaraderie.

The smell of the river and nearby lumber mills, and sounds of boat horns and whistles, added unusual elements to the air of the business section. The normal sounds and smells of the horses, carriages, delivery wagons, trolley cars, and smokestacks couldn't hide the effect of living along the Mississippi.

When they passed the post office, Constance took the opportunity to post her report to headquarters, explaining to Justin casually that she'd written a short note to a friend the night before.

They stopped at his bank and he introduced Constance and the children to the officers and clerks. She glanced about with keen observation, noting with approval the discreetly cautious yet respectful manner with which his employees treated the bank's patrons. But she found it disconcerting to be introduced as his wife to the people with whom he worked intimately. Each hour, each introduction, added another snarl in the web of deceit begun with their marriage.

"Your aunt's millinery is only a few shops up the block," Justin said as they left the bank. He nodded toward a building on the opposite side of the street. "That general store is owned by Rasmus Pierce's parents."

Had he heard the catch of her breath at his revelation? She knew, of course, that Mr. Pierce's parents had a shop in River's Edge. It was for that reason her superintendent had been eager for her to bring the children to the town. She had been expected to work undercover, simply keeping her eyes and ears open, listening to local gossip, and managing an introduction to Mr. and Mrs. Pierce in the innocent position of Libby's niece. The children would not have been placed in danger if things had gone as planned.

Inside Libby's millinery, Justin shifted uncomfortably in the midst of the bonnets and trimmings. Constance viewed his discomfort with ill-concealed amusement. He soon announced he'd wait at the bank while she visited.

Upon Justin's departure, Libby requested her assistant, who had been busy trimming hats at a table piled high with hat forms, laces, ribbons, ostrich feathers, and silk flowers, to help Effie select a new bonnet, and Evan a new sailor hat. As soon as they were out of earshot, she demanded her niece tell all concerning the unexpected marriage.

Constance only smiled mysteriously, fingering the black silk roses bedecking the wide brim of a bonnet on a cast iron display stand.

"Surely you know the ways of love are unfathomable, Aunt Libby."

"Hmpf! If Mr. Knight hadn't been Marian's intended, I'd have thought it perfectly lovely to find you married to him. As it is, customers' heads and tongues have been wagging all morning."

"I'm sorry for any embarrassment caused you." The waves sent out by that abominable ceremony lapped everywhere.

Once the apology was received, Libby put the offense behind her.

"Never you mind, dear. I know you wouldn't intentionally act improperly. What is done is done. You are now Mrs. Justin Knight, and that is that." She bounced her palms off her skirt and looked Constance up and down. "My dear, hasn't your mourning for Charles ended yet? Surely the six months is nearly up."

Constance looked down at her black gown. "I've grown so accustomed to wearing mourning that I seldom notice it now. The six months were past last week, but I didn't even remember to bring anything but mourning wear from Chicago." If only mourning in one's heart could be put off so easily and at a socially prescribed time!

"Never you mind, dear. Mrs. Clayton, who rooms with me, has her garment shop next door. It will be great fun helping you select a new wardrobe."

"Oh, but I can't possibly afford an entire wardrobe! A few pieces, perhaps. Black silk is still considered proper and fashionable, is it not? The mourning gowns will be sufficient for most days."

"With the mourning period over and you the new bride of one of the town's wealthiest and most respected men? They certainly will not be sufficient. Mr. Knight can afford the finest wardrobe to be had for his wife, make no mistake."

"I shall certainly not allow Mr. Knight to purchase my wardrobe!" Constance swallowed her pride at the sight of Libby's shocked face. It wouldn't do to show an unnatural reluctance to spend her husband's funds. "A bride should supply her own trousseau," she finished lamely.

"At the threat of insulting you, my dear, I am quite certain you cannot afford the manner of wardrobe required by the wife of a man of Mr. Knight's stature."

Another unexpected complication! She had some funds, but she couldn't afford to spend all her money on clothing.

"You'll soon see I'm right about this. Until then, let me furnish you with some outfits." Libby held up a hand as Constance started to protest. "I hadn't the pleasure of purchasing an engagement or wedding gift. The least I can do is furnish a few pieces for your trousseau."

To that Constance agreed.

It was rather fun trying on new readymade garments, and selecting patterns for others from Mrs. Clayton's supply. She needed everything new, from undergarments out.

Libby held up a sheer yellow organdy with a wide, fluttery collar that settled lightly over huge sleeves. A yellow satin sash secured the waist. "This is just what you need, my dear. Women are either a flat or a fluff this season, according to the New York World." Her gaze ran over Constance's black gown contemptuously. "With your severely tailored outfits, you have been a flat at its most extreme. It's time you showed that new husband of yours that you are a woman."

The statement sent tingles along Constance's nerves. The last thing she needed was to remind her temporary husband of her femininity. Her fingers played with the delicate fabric of the collar. "It is lovely. But I'm afraid it's entirely inappropriate."

"Nonsense. This pale yellow, butter yellow it's called, is all the rage, and will set off your black hair to advantage."

"But. . ."

"I have not been in the business of fashion all these years without knowing what enhances a woman's best features. Now stop arguing and try this gown on. I declare, you are more difficult than little Effie."

Constance laughed softly to herself as she slipped into the frock. What would her fellow female operatives think if they saw how easily her aunt destroyed her resolve?

The gown is becoming, she admitted to herself, turning in front of the tall mirror. Libby was right. The color was perfect with her hair. She fingered the cream-colored lace edging the collar. She'd forgotten what color could do for a woman. What would Mr. Knight think of her in this gown? Dismay swept through her. What did it matter what Mr. Knight thought?

"Please help me out of this, Aunt Libby."

"I have a large, soft leghorn bonnet with all manner of flowers in my shop that will be perfect with the dress. And a parasol of crinkled crepe with a flowered handle."

"But the gown doesn't suit me."

Libby's hands stilled on the tiny buttons running up her back. "Doesn't suit you? Are you blind, girl? It suits you perfectly. You shall take it and that is that."

Well, the rest of her life was out of her control. Her wardrobe might as well be, also, Constance thought.

Before Libby was through, Constance had also acquired an outing suit of dark blue serge lined with gray silk, which extended out over the revers on the collar of the Eton jacket. Matching gray satin in flat piping was stitched in rows around the bottom of the skirt. Libby contended it was a bit too moderate a style between a flat and a fluff, but Constance claimed it a compromise. To complete the outfit, Libby selected a straw sailor hat with a broad navy ribbon about the crown.

Libby agreed to a simple gray tailored skirt and white shirt front with a French lawn tie. "Terribly popular this season." A swivelled gingham gown of rich green was Constance's favorite purchase. It looked like a soft silk poplin, and enhanced her eyes as no other gown she'd ever owned.

Outside Libby's shop, Constance paused with the children beside her. Did she dare take time to stop at Pierce's General Store? Why not? Justin had said they were to meet him at the bank, but hadn't set a time.

She'd forgotten the extent of variety in a general store. It had been years since she'd been inside one, what with all the specialty shops today. The comforting smell of leather from shoes, saddles, and harnesses mingled with the pungent odor of kerosene. Both odors dwindled as she neared the counter, replaced by the smell of vinegar in the pickle barrel she passed, and the more subtle scents of lavender and rose from colognes and soaps.

Impulsively, she selected a bottle of lavender scent and a box of matching powder. Perhaps if she eliminated Marian's lily-of-the-valley claim on her bedchamber, her guilt would lessen somewhat while in that room.

Effie and Evan passed up the small display of tin toys, dolls, and board games for the candy display in front of the counter. While they studiously considered their choices, Constance looked through the school supplies nearby and studied the woman wrapping a fold of red-flowered cotton in brown paper. Could she be Mrs. Pierce?

The woman was as slender as Aunt Libby, but was shorter and appeared to lack the milliner's strength. Her hair was skinned back unfashionably into a plain bun, with no curls to soften the bony face. Her eyes were like wells of perpetual sorrow.

Undoubtedly the man working among the barrels at the back of the store was Rasmus's father. They had the same long, lean face and pointed chin. But instead of swaggering conceit, this man's face was filled with anger. His tense, thin shoulders rode permanently up beneath his ears.

"May I help you, ma'am?" the woman behind the counter asked as her customer turned away.

Constance rested her folded, gloved hands on the counter and gave the clerk her most friendly smile. "Yes, please. The children will be entering the first grade level, and will need items for school. Perhaps you could advise me?"

It was a practical purchase, she assured herself. Whether the children remained in River's Edge or returned to Chicago, they would need school supplies.

The clerk joined her at a display, Effie and Evan close behind, eager to discover what they might need for their new experience. From the variety of pencil boxes the old woman showed them, Evan selected a simple maple box. Effie preferred one in the shape of a closed parasol, with a silk tassel. Both contained a pen, a holder, lead and slate pencils, chalk, a ruler, an eraser, and a sponge.

The clerk added a small slate and a book strap for each child. "That should hold them until their teacher advises them further. The total will be $1.20."

"I'm purchasing these, also." Constance indicated the containers of lavender scent. "Would you like to select some candy, children?" She hadn't discovered nearly enough about the Pierces to leave yet.

She didn't have to ask the twins twice.

"They are fine-looking children." The woman's gaunt features softened slightly as her sad eyes rested on the whispering, pointing children.

"Thank you. They are my brother's children. Excuse me for being so forward, but I noticed the name of the store is Pierce's General Store. Would you happen to be Mrs. Pierce?"

She nodded shortly, eyeing her warily.

"I'm pleased to meet you. I'm sure I'll frequent your establishment. You see, I'm newly married. My husband and I only arrived in town last evening." She lowered her lashes and traced a black-gloved fingertip along the raised edge of the oak counter, hoping she appeared properly nervous as a new bride. "I'm certain I'll be needing many items once we've become established."

"Have you married a local man?" Neither voice nor face indicated sincere interest; the question was merely polite.

Constance pretended not to notice the lack of interest and gushed, "Mr. Justin Knight."

The woman's gaze jerked to her. Was she surprised because Justin had been engaged to Marian, or because she hadn't expected to see the woman her son had forced to marry standing in her store?

Bony hands slid down the woman's white apron. "I hope you'll be happy."

Constance's murmured "thank you" was lost in the slam of a door at the back of the store. She followed Mrs. Pierce's gaze to her husband and a man who appeared to be a farmer, talking in low voices behind the barrels.

The farmer looked up and tipped his wide-brimmed hat to Mrs. Pierce. She nodded at him briskly. "Good day, Mr. Meeker."

The children placed their selections on the counter, Evan a striped peppermint stick and Effie a gracefully curved piece of ruby ribbon candy, and Mrs. Pierce collected Constance's money with shaking fingers. The woman's attention was no longer on Constance and the twins, but wandered constantly to the two men. What disturbed Mrs. Pierce so about the farmer?

When Constance turned at the door, she noticed Mrs. Pierce hurrying toward the two men, her new customers forgotten.

⌘

That evening for dinner, Constance wore the new green gown. The admiration in Mr. Knight's eyes when he saw her in it took her breath. Each time their gazes met across the perfectly appointed table, she was so aware of him that she'd lose her train of thought. She couldn't recall when the look in a man's eyes had caused her to feel so flustered.

To her delight, Justin had asked Libby to join them for dinner. The older woman's presence gave the meal almost a party atmosphere, and lightened the tension between the newly married couple.

The only pall on Constance's evening was the continual reminder of Marian's broken engagement, by the use of the exquisite crystal, china, and silver she had selected.

They were almost through dessert when the robbery came up in conversation.

Quite natural that it should, since it was the most popular topic in town, next to Justin and Constance's wedding. When Libby mentioned the robbery, Justin dismissed the children from the table, and Constance was glad of his concern for them.

"To think that one of River's Edge's own boys should come to this!" Libby puffed like a tugboat at the thought. "Rasmus Pierce always was a troublesome youngster, but never in my wildest dreams would I have believed he would become a thief!"

"Does he appear freely among the townspeople?"

Justin's brow furrowed at Constance's query. "What makes you ask?"

"I thought perhaps with his parents living in River's Edge and having been raised here, the townspeople might tend to look aside if he visited his family or friends."

"Hmpf!" Libby's flat chest heaved in indignation. "As though a man such as that would have friends!"

"I shouldn't be surprised if he visited his parents," Justin offered, "though I've never seen him do so or heard anyone mention seeing him. Not since his chosen vocation became known."

Libby sighed dramatically. "My heart goes out to his poor, sweet mother."

"Yes," Constance agreed. "I've always felt that parents would be shamed by their children's criminal behavior."

Libby lowered her crystal water goblet and shook her head until her tight gray curls wobbled. "I don't believe it's shame Mrs. Pierce feels over Rasmus. It's sadness, pure and deep and simple. Sadness, because her son has made choices that can't bring happiness to his life, and that bring unhappiness to others."

A knock at the front door interrupted the discussion. Mrs. Kelly hurried out of the room where she'd begun to clear the table. A moment later she was back. "There's a man to see ye, Mr. Knight. A stranger, he be, by the name of Alexander Bixby."

Alexander Bixby! Constance hoped her face didn't reveal her shock.

Had the Superintendent assigned Alexander to the train robbery case? She wasn't aware of a contract between the Pinkerton Agency and the Chicago, Milwaukee and St. Paul Railroad, but it was common for railroad and express companies to hire the Pinkerton Agency for such cases.

Her heart was beating faster than a steam engine at full throttle. *What will Alexander think, finding me married to another man?*

Chapter 6

Constance could barely keep her attention on her conversation with Aunt Libby. What are Alexander and Justin discussing? At Justin's instructions, Mrs. Kelly had taken Alex directly to the library. He and Justin had been there ten minutes already, and Alexander didn't even know she was in the house.

"Aunt Libby. . ."

Constance started as Justin spoke from beside her. He stopped in front of Libby, giving her his wonderful smile.

"The man in the library is a Pinkerton agent, here to discuss the train robbery. Since Constance and I were on the train at the time, he would like to speak with both of us. I do hope you will forgive the extreme breach of etiquette if we speak with him?"

At the word "Pinkerton" Libby had clasped both hands to her lace-covered chest and drawn a breath so deep that Constance was sure it threatened to break her stays.

"A Pinkerton agent! How thrilling! But what does he think you can possibly know about the robbery?"

"I'm sure he's speaking with everyone he can locate who was on the train. Doubtless he will find our account unenlightening. I know I needn't tell you that he doesn't wish his visit known. You're much too wise to spread confidential information."

"Why, of course I'll not divulge it! I'll just take my leave. You needn't see me to the door. I'm only family."

"I knew we could count on you to understand. I've asked Mrs. Kelly to have the stable boy harness the carriage and see you home. Come, Constance."

Alexander was examining some of Justin's library volumes when they entered. She knew from his position that the books he was looking at were the Pinkerton volumes, and she couldn't help but smile.

"Mr. Bixby."

At Justin's voice, Alexander swung to face them, his hands clasped loosely behind his back. "Allow me to introduce my wife. Constance, this is Alexander Bixby of the Pinkerton Agency."

Alexander's eyes peered at her, like glittering pieces of onyx, from deep beneath his brows. His face paled so it almost rivaled the white collar of the shirt beneath his gray suit, his black hair and mustache not enhancing his color. If the situation were not so serious, Constance would have laughed. Alexander, the star performer of their Pinkerton division, speechless, she mused.

Before either she or Alexander could respond to Justin's introduction, Effie came tearing into the room like a miniature whirlwind, with Evan close at her heels. She swung against Constance's skirt, her feet pushing the Brussels carpet into a ridge as she skidded to a stop.

"Have you and Justin decided if we can sleep in the Bird Cage tonight?"

Constance steadied her with gentle hands on the girl's shoulders. "You mustn't. . ."

"Alex!"

At Evan's exclamation, Effie spun toward the guest. "Alex!"

This time it was Effie following Evan across the room. Each of the children chose one of Alex's trousered legs to lean against while bombarding him with questions. "When did you get here?"

"Are you going to live here, too?"

"We came on a train!"

"Bad men came on the train, but we weren't scared!"

"Are you goin' to marry Aunt Constance now?"

"Silly! He can't marry her. She's married to Mr. Knight."

Justin's gaze, filled with questions, met hers.

Why did she feel so defensive, as though she should have told him about Alexander earlier? She'd had no reason to think the two men would ever meet.

"Alex, Mr. Bixby, was my brother's good friend. When Mrs. Kelly announced him, I had no idea he was the same man we knew back in Chicago."

He didn't look convinced, yet there could be no doubting that the children knew Alex well. She hurried toward them. "Alexander is here to discuss business with Mr. Knight. I think you should go to your room and dress for bed."

"But we want to see Alex!" Evan protested.

"Can we show him the Bird Cage?"

"Perhaps another time, Effie." Constance held out her hands to the children. "I'm sure after coming all this way from Chicago, Alexander wouldn't leave River's Edge without seeing you."

"Not a chance of it!" Alex squatted down. "Do I get a hug before you run upstairs?"

Effie threw her arms around his neck, but Evan stepped back and held out his hand. "Boys don't give hugs," he informed earnestly.

"Can we sleep in the Bird Cage?" Effie asked again, turning from Alex.

"May we. Yes. I've already requested Mrs. Kelly place bedding out for you."

"Thank you, Aunt Constance! C'mon, Evan!"

The children raced from the room. Their feet thudding against the marble hallway and then up the stairs kept the adults abreast of their path. Once the sounds died away, Alexander began questioning Justin and Constance concerning the robbery. Neither Alexander or Constance revealed her association with the Pinkerton Agency.

Seated at one end of the leather sofa, Constance kept her gaze on Alexander. He was as professional as always. What did he think of her marriage to Justin Knight? The color that had fled when Justin introduced her was back in his strong, lean face with its high cheekbones beneath shiny black hair.

When Mrs. Kelly came to the door to make a request of Justin, Alexander took the opportunity to whisper to Constance, "Meet me at the stable out back at midnight."

Minutes later, Alexander took his leave.

Constance started for the stairway. "I'd best check on the children."

"Mrs. Kelly is with them. I'd like to speak with you before we retire."

Reluctantly, she re-entered the library. Taking a deep breath, she turned to face him. Might as well put the discussion behind her.

He leaned back against his desk and crossed his arms. The mellow light from the lamp beside him didn't reach his face, and the shadows made his eyes seem dark and unfathomable. "Is Mr. Bixby your friend as well as your brother's?"

"Yes. We met through Charles."

"Evan asked Bixby whether he was planning to marry you. Yet when I asked last night whether you were engaged to anyone, you said no."

"I am not engaged to Mr. Bixby, or to anyone else."

"But he's in love with you?"

She felt the color rise to her cheeks at his impertinent question. "I cannot answer as to the state of another's heart."

"Has he asked you to marry him?"

"Does it matter?"

The silence after she snapped the question seemed to last an hour, though the monotonous ticking of the mahogany-encased clock on the desk counted off less than a minute before Justin answered.

"Forgive me. I have no right to pursue this."

His willingness to retreat destroyed her stubborn attitude. "It is I who should beg your forgiveness for being snappish. Your engagement is broken because of our marriage. It's only fair you know about Alexander."

She turned away from him, crossing toward the fireplace with its wide mantle at the end of the room.

"Alexander did ask me to marry him after Charles died. The children love him, as you could plainly see this evening. He would have taken them into his home if we married, and raised them gladly."

"You turned down his offer?"

She nodded. "As you know, he is a Pinkerton operative. That is a dangerous life. He would hate to leave the agency or pursue a less adventurous career. And I would hate for the children to lose a second father."

"So you refused him for the children's sake, and for his own?"

She turned to face him across the room, her hands linked lightly behind her back, but didn't reply.

"I wonder if you could have refused him so nobly if you were in love with him."

Indignation flooded her chest, and her nails bit into the flesh of her palms. She fought to keep her voice calm.

"You walked away from your own marriage plans to protect the twins. Do you think you are the only person capable of honorable actions?"

He crossed the room, stopping only inches from her. She forced herself not to retreat, though she quivered inside at his nearness. His eyes studied hers until she felt he'd taken her heart out and examined it. When he finally spoke, his voice was low.

"No, I don't think I'm the only person capable of honorable actions. But I believe if you loved a man, you would not be such a weak creature that you would refuse him out of fear that he might die on you."

She turned sharply away. How could he think he knew her so well after such a short time?

"Mr. Bixby seems like a fine man, but I think I pity him."

Pitied Alex? "Because of me?"

"Because of the profession he's chosen."

Constance whirled about in surprise. "But he loves his profession! And he's very accomplished at it."

"I'm sure he is. But I've read Allan Pinkerton's accounts of some of the cases his agency has handled." He waved a hand toward the bookcases holding the volumes Alexander had been examining when they entered the library earlier. The light danced off the gold lettering on their maroon leather bindings. "Sometimes the detectives. . ."

"Operatives."

"Pardon?"

She flushed. "Alex says Pinkerton agents are not to refer to themselves as detectives, as the title has negative connotations. Agents are called operatives."

"I see. Sometimes operatives are required to perform unsavory acts to capture criminals."

"If you've read Mr. Pinkerton's works, you are aware that he believed the ends justify the means." She flashed him a smile. "You see, I have read the volumes, also. Don't you agree with his philosophy?"

"I most decidedly do not. Without limits, it's difficult to tell where the line is that separates justice and injustice. How does your friend Mr. Bixby know when, or if, he has crossed that line?"

"I assure you Mr. Bixby is a fine, upstanding young man. His morals are unimpeachable."

"No man is so perfect that he can rely solely upon his own instincts of right or wrong. We must have a guide if mass confusion is not to reign on the earth."

"And upon what do you believe one should rely to make such judgments?"

"The Bible, the Word of God."

She should have realized that would be his solution. "You think the book infallible? Much injustice has been committed over the years in the name of God."

"Unfortunately, that is true. Still, man has trusted the book through centuries. I would rather rely on it than myself, knowing how easily a man's judgment can be swayed by his emotions."

Seated at the desk in her room later, she paused in writing her day's report for the agency to reflect on Justin's words. From the time she first began hearing of Allan Pinkerton's work and the good he'd done in the name of justice, he'd been the nearest thing to a hero in her life. She'd believed in him so strongly that she'd never questioned his belief system. "The ends justify the means" was a basic tenet in his philosophy.

He would likely have given little weight to anything Justin Knight had to say. Mr. Pinkerton was an atheist, and had no qualms in admitting it. She'd embraced his thoughts on religion as eagerly as she had on other topics.

She had told Justin that the Bible was not infallible. Neither was Mr. Allan Pinkerton, she had to admit.

Justin's face with his steady eyes drifted across her mind. He'd sacrificed much for her and the children. He was an intelligent, honorable man even though a Christian. Or perhaps because he was a Christian? She didn't like the way his faith made her feel the inadequacy of her own standards of right and wrong, and set the stirrings of doubt threatening her own system of beliefs and ideals.

With a sigh, she returned to her writing. The faint scent of lavender she'd dabbed on her wrists earlier drifted to her as she signed the personalized stationery upon which she'd penned the report. Guilt pulled another string in her heart at the sight of the delicate golden script at the top of the linen page which indicated the sender was Mrs. Justin Knight. She should have found other stationery upon which to pen the report. Hadn't she appropriated enough of the items Marian had selected to use as Justin's wife?

She folded the note and placed it in an envelope, then rose impatiently. She hadn't felt as much guilt in years as she had since that disgusting marriage ceremony less than two days earlier. What a useless emotion! She wouldn't allow herself to become so maudlin again.

The bong of the grandfather clock in the lower floor hallway solemnly and unhurriedly announced the midnight hour. She plucked a paisley shawl from the chaise lounge at the end of the bed and pulled it over the shoulders of her green gown.

It seemed providence that the children were sleeping on the third floor of the tower. Justin had thoughtfully offered to sleep in the room off the Bird Cage in order to be close by if the children needed something or became frightened during the night; so like him to do so. She wouldn't need to worry at awakening any of them as she stole out to meet Alexander.

She didn't like that word *stole*.

There she went again, allowing her Justin Knight-influenced conscience to prick at her, and when she'd determined not to let guilt muddy her heart or mind!

The moon was full, the cloudless sky studded with stars that watched as she hurried across the lawn. It was a good thing the tower was in the front of the house. No chance of Justin seeing her in this bright moonlight.

The door of the stable stood slightly ajar. Was Alexander already there, awaiting her? She slid into the darkness. Fresh hay, oats, leather, and less pleasant, more pungent odors, surrounded her. Was that the sound of mice scurrying in the hay, or was it Alex moving about?

"Alexander?"

"Here." He touched her sleeve a moment after answering her in a whisper no louder than her own. "Let's stay by the door where there's a little moonlight, and fresh air. Why did I say I'd meet you here rather than the carriage house?"

She could hear the laugh in his last statement. One of the horses snorted, and the hoofs of another thudded lightly against straw-covered floorboards. The stable may be more odorous than the carriage house, but the sounds would help cover their voices.

Her eyes were growing accustomed to the darkness, and in the faint light of moonbeams, through the door which stood slightly ajar, she made out Alexander's face, the mustache a black shadow beneath his straight nose. His eyebrows were like a small ledge above two caves that were his eyes.

His hand remained on her arm. It tightened slightly now. "Are you all right?" His voice was hoarse with anxiety.

"Yes."

"Thank God! When I heard you'd been forced into a marriage with a complete stranger. . ." His broad shoulders drooped slightly beneath the gray coat that looked black in the moonlight. "Thought I'd lose my mind for worry over you." He cleared his throat. "Came up to the house immediately upon arriving by train tonight. Couldn't wait to make certain no harm had come to you, or the children."

His concern was heartwarming. "We're all fine, as you saw for yourself."

"Knight hasn't made any, demands on you?"

"Alexander!" Even in the darkness she knew her cheeks flamed at his question, and she tugged her arm from his hold. "Justin Knight is a gentleman, in every sense of the word."

"I'm sorry if I offended you by asking, but you never know what kind of bounder. . ." He caught her about the waist and pulled her close. "I should have married you back in Chicago. Should have ignored your excuses. Then you and the children wouldn't be in this mess. But I knew how important it was for you to continue as an operative, and didn't press my attentions."

She pushed against his chest with both hands until he released her. "I shall excuse your behavior this evening due to the trying circumstances. But I have never given you permission to touch me in such an intimate manner, and I expect that you shall not do so again!"

"You know I love you, that I. . ."

"Please, Alexander!" She wanted to shout at him instead of whisper. "It is all I can do to keep fear for the children aside and act professionally in the present situation. Please do not ask me to assume the added emotional distress of another proposal at this time."

"As you wish." His voice was tight with anger. She knew if the light were brighter, she would see that his lips were tight also. "You haven't told Knight that you're an operative?"

"Of course not! Have I ever revealed my position to anyone without the Superintendent's approval?"

"Sorry. Had to be sure."

"What—what did the superintendent say about the marriage?"

"He thinks it's marvelous. Thinks your position as a prominent banker's wife may serve the agency's purposes well." Bitterness all but rattled his teeth. "Didn't seem concerned that Knight might be a rounder, that you might be endangered living in the man's home. Said that of course an annulment would be obtained when Pierce was apprehended."

Should she tell him that Justin was against an annulment? No. Even in the darkness, anger shouted from the tense manner in which he held himself. She handed him her envelope.

"Here is my daily report. I suppose you'll wish to read it, since you're on the case now. When you have, would you post it for me?"

He stuffed it into an inside coat pocket. "Sure. Might as well bring you up to date on the case. From what you and Knight said earlier, you're already aware Rasmus Pierce and his mob pulled the strike on the train."

"I almost forgot to tell you! I posted the information in my report last night but," she stepped closer in her eagerness, "Rasmus doesn't look anything like the image on his Bertillon card. He's grown his hair and wears it rather like Buffalo Bill Cody, back behind his ears, though his is limp and stringy instead of full and curly like that famous man's. And he has a Vandyke beard."

"You're certain it's Rasmus and not another member of the mob you're describing?"

"I'm certain. It was he who insisted on the marriage. He threatened to harm Effie and Evan if we didn't agree to the ceremony."

"You shudder like that again and I'll forget my resolve to be the gentleman you requested."

She stepped back hurriedly with a slight gasp.

"You needn't be afraid of me." The pain beneath the anger in his tone caused her to regret her actions immediately.

Before she could apologize, he switched the subject. "No wonder you went along with the marriage, if the children were threatened. It's going to be a real pleasure putting that bounder behind bars." His thick eyebrows met. "Think I'll check out that minister. Haven't spoken to him yet. Maybe there's a chance he's not legitimate."

"Justin says the man serves a church in Red Wing. But, of course, it would be good to verify that." Not that she believed for a moment that Justin would lie, not honorable Justin. But her experience with the agency had taught her that no one is to be completely trusted. "What else have you learned of the robbery?"

He gave her a quick report, but revealed nothing she didn't already know, with the exception of the listing of other agents who were joining him in the area. Most were going to be in disguise, working at menial positions about town where they could be available if needed, and where they might pick up information from local gossip or observation. He was to be the agent in charge.

When he'd revealed all, he poked his head cautiously through the door to glance about. "All clear. Better let you out of here before you begin smelling like a stable hand. That would prick Knight's curiosity!"

But she didn't leave.

"Alex, do you ever wonder about the morality of the deception we use as operatives?"

He scowled and shrugged. "It's necessary. You know that." Impatience tinged his voice. "Can't expect to walk up to a criminal and say 'by your leave, I'd like to arrest you. Would you be so kind as to give testimony against yourself?' "

She smiled at the scene he portrayed.

"What brought on this attack of conscience?"

"I was thinking of the danger to which I've exposed the children, and. . ." she shrugged slightly.

"Charles was my closest friend. The twins' safety is important to me, too."

"I know. I'll not allow sentimentality to sway my good sense again."

She'd just started through the door when he detained her with a hand on her shoulder.

"You know where I'm staying, Constance. I'll be keeping as close a watch as possible on you. If anything changes, if you should find the situation with Knight. . .I'm here if you need me."

She covered his hand with her own; released it after a quick squeeze. "Thank you." She was tempted to tell him that in spite of her earlier actions, she liked him very much. She'd best not. It would be cruel to encourage him unless she knew she loved him, especially as she was presently married, temporarily, to Justin.

When had she begun thinking of him as Justin instead of Mr. Knight? she wondered, hurrying across the new lawn. The spicy scent of the bright yellow and amber chrysanthemums in the plaster urns beside the back walk hung thickly in the air.

She wished the Superintendent wasn't so enthusiastic about her position as Mrs. Justin Knight. It was clear from Alexander's comments that the Superintendent expected her to keep her position with the agency a secret. She'd been hoping to be allowed to tell Justin the truth.

In the past, she'd been proud of her ability to deceive. It was that which made her such a valuable operative, after all. But it disturbed her more every passing hour to deceive Justin. She'd never met a man who held honesty in such high esteem. She'd like to have his respect. What would he think when he discovered she was an operative? If only he believed that the ends justified the means, she wouldn't worry so that he would despise her when the truth was revealed.

Chapter 7

Attending church had never been such a trying experience.

After Charles's death, Constance had attended faithfully, knowing it was important to him that his children be raised in the church. Usually, she allowed her mind to drift during the sermons, and afterward enjoyed pleasant visits with friends and neighbors. It was a friendly, comfortable place to be in spite of her lack of faith.

Today was different. The congregation's eyes were on her and Justin more than on the pastor. Certainly few people in attendance paid any attention whatever to the sermon. Constance, however, couldn't avoid listening to the sermon. Its theme was the same verse the minister had quoted on the train: "All things work together for good to them that love God." Was it a coincidence? Surely the pastor couldn't have chosen the verse because of her and Justin; he wasn't aware that they hadn't married of their own free will. Was the verse true? A longing to believe it tugged at Constance. It would be comforting to have such a promise to grasp in a world where terrible things happen to people and evil often appeared to triumph.

During the closing prayer, she spread the palm of her left hand over the skirt of her filmy yellow organdy. Her wedding band raised a small lump beneath her pale yellow glove. The ring should have been presented to Marian this afternoon. The thought made her cringe.

The benediction over, the congregation rose to leave.

"Think you can play the part of the happy bride?" Justin whispered beneath the brim of her flowered leghorn before turning to Effie and Evan.

Could she play the part? If only he knew the extent of her experience as an actress mastering all manner of roles for the agency. When he turned back again, she slipped her hand beneath his arm and smiled so rapturously up at him that he blinked in astonishment.

The fun died in her when, walking down the aisle, her gaze met Marian's. The girl's blue eyes were shooting sparks above pale cheeks.

Guilt and sympathy flooded Constance, and it was all she could do to keep smiling as they swept past Marian's pew. As if the girl hadn't been humiliated and hurt enough!

And she, Constance Ward. . .uh, Knight, was taking part in causing another human being such pain. She hated herself for it.

But I have no choice!

Once outside in the early September sunshine, a few of the men tipped their hats and greeted Justin, only to be tugged hurriedly away by frowning wives. Other than the pastor and his wife, only a handful of bachelors were brave enough to offer their felicitations.

The congregation had mostly dispersed when a middle-aged man, his slender face twisted in red fury beneath his hat, fists clenched, stepped from beside a fringed buggy.

Justin touched his wide Boston derby and nodded slightly. "Mr. Ames."

Marian's father! She should have known. Would he create a scene?

"Knight, I once considered you one of the finest men I ever had the privilege of knowing. But you're nothing but a disgusting, cheap, smelly old skunk."

Before Constance realized his intentions, the wiry man flung a fist at Justin's face. It landed with a disgusting crunch on Justin's nose, and she felt him stagger against her.

Dropping her parasol, she grabbed Justin's arm just as a second blow struck his chin, toppling him backward to the ground. Her hold on his arm carried her with him.

She was barely aware of Evan and Effie's raised voices, or the few remaining members of the congregation who stood in stunned silence. All she noticed was the blood streaming from Justin's nose as he struggled to a sitting position and helped her do the same.

"Get up and I'll give you more of the same!"

Surely the older man didn't expect Justin to actually fight him? He would be no match for Justin's youth, she had time to think before Effie flung herself against the man's leg. One little foot flashed from beneath her ivory organdy skirt in a series of wildly aimed blows, occasionally landing on Mr. Ames' shins.

"You mean old man! Don't you dare hit Justin! Don't you dare!"

"Effie! Stop this instant!" Justin fairly roared.

Effie spun and faced him. "But he. . ."

"That's enough, Effie."

The girl's eyes flashed fire. She dropped to her knees beside Evan, who was trying to stuff his handkerchief beneath Justin's nose.

Justin remained where he was, knees drawn up, one hand taking the kerchief from Evan. "I know what I did to your daughter is as close to unforgivable as a man's actions can come. I cannot justify myself to you or Marian. I can only say that I am sincerely sorry for any harm."

"Sorry!" The man turned his head and spat. "That's for your apology. You aren't worthy of a woman like Marian. Good thing she discovered in time what a rotter you are. Just see your bank try to stay afloat in these hard times now that the entire town knows how little stock they can put in your word."

He strode to the buggy, still shaking in anger. Marian was waiting for him there, a triumphant smile on her beautiful face.

What must Justin be feeling, Constance wondered with a pang, to be publicly attacked before the girl he loved?

When the buggy was clattering down the street, Justin slipped a hand beneath Constance's elbow. "Have you been hurt?"

"No. But your nose."

"I've had bloodied noses before. Of course, the last time it was over a baseball, and I was the ripe old age of ten."

Her concern fled in a grin at his words and the twinkle in his eyes. She reached to straighten his red satin tie, which had pulled from his vest and twisted beneath the pointed wings of his high linen collar.

"I could grow accustomed to your smile, Mrs. Knight." His low, ardent tone made the words as intimate as a caress. She stared at him, incredulous, lips slightly parted, her fingers frozen at his vest.

He turned to Effie and Evan a moment later, and she was glad of the opportunity to recover her composure.

"Thanks for the handkerchief, old man."

Effie propped her fists on her hips, her mouth screwed into a pout. "Why didn't you hit him back?"

He pushed a curl behind her ear. "Remember the talk we had the first night in our new house? We should always do what we think Jesus would do. I didn't think Jesus would hit Mr. Ames."

"I suppose we better pray for him, too." Evan sighed resignedly. "Like that mean old Rasmus."

Justin grinned, pushing himself from the ground. "You've got the right idea, Evan." He bent to assist Constance to her feet.

Effie crossed her arms over her lace-covered chest and snorted. "Pretty soon we're going to have so many people to pray for that we won't have time to do anything else."

"Life could hold worse possibilities," Justin replied, grinning, and handed Constance her parasol. His gaze fell to her skirt. "I'm afraid your gown has been ruined. There's both a grass stain and a tear."

"It's only a dress." She tried to keep the disappointment out of her voice. She'd felt positively frivolous in the gown at first, after months of black gowns and mourning hats, but she truly liked it.

"I'll buy you another."

"That isn't. . ."

"You look like sunshine in it."

Her heart skipped a beat. She had to lower her gaze from his to allow herself to catch her breath. What had beset the man that he was making such boldly personal comments?

"Perhaps it can be repaired. I'll speak with Aunt Libby about it Monday morning."

They began walking the five blocks to the house. The children ran on ahead, clambering over every horse stoop, and balancing along the tops of occasional stone fences, with Effie leading the way as usual.

"I—I. . .there is something I should like to say."

His smile could have chased away clouds. "Is it so serious you must pucker those lovely eyebrows into a frown?"

"This entire situation is serious!"

"But not tragic, I hope. What is the problem?"

"It's only. . .I. . .it's your wedding day. Or it was meant to be. It shall likely be especially difficult for you to have the children and me in your home today instead of Miss Marian. If you'd like, I shall take the children to Aunt Libby's for the afternoon."

His smile faded somewhat, but didn't disappear altogether.

"You are most thoughtful, but that won't be necessary. I'd much prefer your company to your absence."

Did he hope their company would help divert his thoughts? He is such a kind man. If only he could have been spared this heartbreak.

It must be awful for him, unable to explain the situation, allowing people to believe he has gone back on his word, Constance thought. The townspeople should know him better than to believe the worst. Why she'd only known him two days and she already knew he would never renege on his word unless it was impossible to keep it.

What was happening to her good sense? She knew better than to trust anyone.

Justin drew her hand through his arm solicitously. "Is anything wrong? I thought I heard you gasp."

She denied it with a quick shake of her head, disturbingly conscious of his touch.

Constance gave up trying to argue with her detective training and allowed herself to enjoy the rest of the walk home, well aware that the newlyweds made an interesting spectacle for the neighborhood: Justin with a bloodied nose and herself in a torn, stained gown.

Her brother would have liked Justin. Not only because the man shared her brother's faith, but because he lived it.

She was accustomed to men with high morals. It was required of Pinkerton agents that they not have addiction to vices such as drinking, smoking, card playing, or low dives, and that they be of "a high order of mind."

Yet, she didn't know another man, including Charles, who would have had the strength of character not to at least retaliate in words when Mr. Ames struck him. He forgave Rasmus, forgave Mr. Ames, and kept silent about the cause of their marriage to his own detriment in order to protect the children. Not only the character of every other man she'd known, but her own character as well, seemed weak by comparison.

The front door slammed behind the twins, rattling the lovely etched glass. Constance and Justin were halfway up the front walk before it opened again and Effie stuck her head out, brown curls bobbing.

"Hurry! There's a present on the dining room table."

"Oh, dear," Constance said, entering the door Justin held for her. "That reminds me. What of the wedding gifts you and Marian received?"

"They were displayed at Marian's house. I assume she will see to returning them."

The nightmare never seemed to end for Marian.

A large package wrapped in beautiful mauve paper sat in the middle of the linen cloth covering the dining room table. She reached for the card, then dropped it as though it were on fire.

"Rasmus!"

Chapter 8

Justin grabbed the card. "'Best wishes to the Bride and Groom. Fondly, Rasmus.'" In a quick, fierce gesture, he crumpled the card in one hand. "How dare he intrude in my house, threaten my family!" The balled-up card bounced against the tiny, cheerful gold print of the wallpaper on the opposite wall and fell upon the red, cream, and gold carpet.

My family. The words echoed through Constance's mind, even as she grasped the edge of the table with her yellow gloves.

"He's showing us that he meant what he said, isn't he? That he can easily reach and harm the children if he chooses."

"I'm afraid so, yes." The words were tight, furious.

She turned and darted for the door, grasping her pale yellow skirts. "The Bird Cage! If he departed within the last few minutes, perhaps we can see him from there!"

He was past her in an instant, taking the steps two at a time, coattails flying.

When she reached the open tower room, his hands were resting on the wide railing. She knew without asking that he hadn't seen Rasmus. Disappointment was in the sag of his shoulders, the dejected line of his lips. Still, she rushed to one of the openings to search for herself, snatching up Justin's eyeglass, making her gaze stop at every movement until convinced Rasmus was nowhere in sight.

"I expect he came during the church service, Constance. He'd know we have no live-in servants, that the day servants would be at their own homes on Sunday and there'd be no one to see him enter."

Suddenly lightheaded and nauseous, she leaned against the balustrade surrounding the tower room. She could taste fear on her tongue, feel it in the rage in her chest. The children—she could hear their laughter from the open window of their bedchamber below—to think anyone would be so vile as to threaten them.

The Justin was gently urging her head against his shoulder. It was so comforting in his arms. Too comforting.

She pushed herself away, instantly missing his strength.

He caught her elbows lightly, but didn't try to draw her back into his embrace. She stared at his gold scarf pin, avoiding the disturbing intensity of his eyes. "I've never known a woman with your strength. But you needn't be strong every moment. I'm going to be beside you, sharing your burden for the children until Rasmus is behind bars."

His fervent promise almost crumbled the weak defenses she'd built against her attraction to him. She didn't doubt the sincerity of his concern for the children, but she mustn't forget he loved Marian.

"Rasmus is only trying to keep us frightened, Constance. If we continue to do as he requested, he has no reason to harm Effie and Evan."

She took a deep breath and met his gaze.

"Perhaps we should contact Alex, Mr. Bixby. He may wish to speak with the neighbors, to see whether anyone saw Rasmus."

His mouth tightened slightly. "I'll try to catch him at his hotel."

While he was gone, she changed from her torn frock into her new white shirtwaist, navy silk tie, and gray skirt. She worried every moment he was away. The house was so huge. How would she know, until too late, if Rasmus returned? A dozen times she looked in on the children, assuring herself they were safe.

When she heard the front door, Constance rushed for the hallway. Relief flooded her at the sight of Justin and Alex.

Justin was hanging his pale gray Boston derby on the walnut and brass hat rack when he saw her. He squeezed her hands and smiled down at her, and the world seemed steady and safe again.

"Mr. Bixby and I decided to come directly back and talk here. Is the gift still in the dining room?"

"I've removed it to the library to prepare the table for luncheon." Had Justin suggested the men return here to speak because he realized how upset she was at being alone with the children?

"Then we'll be in the library if you need us." He dismissed her with a nod.

"May I join you?" She ignored Justin's raised eyebrows at her severe breach of etiquette, inviting herself to a business conference between men.

"Of course, you may." Trust Justin's gentlemanly nature to win out. His voice and manner didn't show a hint of disapproval or surprise, in spite of the shock she'd seen in his eyes a moment earlier. He took her elbow and ushered her into the library as though it were the most natural occurrence in the world.

She lowered herself onto the edge of the leather wing chair to which Justin led her, uncomfortably aware he remained standing beside her. Was he not so subtly reinforcing to Bixby that she was his wife? She dismissed the idea immediately as absurd.

"Guess you can tell for yourself, Bixby, that the fancy-wrapped box on the desk is the gift. Constance and I won't object at all if you do the honors and open it. You've already read the card."

She recognized the almost imperceptible tightening that deepened the lines at the corners of Alexander's dark eyes, warning of his displeasure. Did he think Justin's actions toward her too proprietary?

"Nothing unusual in this," he said, pulling out a pair of tall, exquisite silver candlesticks. "Expect they were purchased with stolen money."

"Your mistake. They belong to Marian's parents."

Constance couldn't contain a gasp at Justin's revelation. "You're certain?"

"I doubt there are two pair of candlesticks of that size and quality in this town. Hadn't heard the Ameses had been robbed. We'll have the dickens of a time trying to return the candlesticks. How do we explain why Rasmus would steal them, then give them to us as a gift?"

Alex shook his head. "That crook doesn't miss a trick. I'll return them for you. Don't worry, I won't let the Ameses know where I discovered them. I'll just say I came across them in the investigation, and that it could damage the possibility of capturing the criminals if I reveal the details."

"Thanks, Bixby."

"I'd best get some agents started on checking out the neighborhood, see if we can locate anyone who saw Rasmus this morning." He picked up one of the candlesticks and quirked an eyebrow. "Might try the Ames's neighborhood, too."

He paused beside her. "You and the children stick close to Knight this afternoon. I'll arrange for an operative to pose as a stable and yard man, so there will be someone with you and the twins when Knight's at work. The man will be on the place by dusk."

Dusk still seemed a long way off, Constance thought at six that evening, looking out across the Mississippi from the edge of the steep limestone bluff just north of town. Behind her, Effie and Evan were chasing a butterfly across an expanse of rock-strewn meadow.

How thoughtful it was of Justin to get them out of the house. Had he realized she'd been looking around corners since they'd discovered Rasmus's gift?

She smiled at him as he lowered himself to the plaid blanket covering the large gray rock.

"It's so peaceful here. The river doesn't look like the Big Muddy today, with the waters bluer than the sky. I would never have guessed the Mississippi was this wide. I can barely see the bluffs on the opposite side. They look a hazy blue, like mountains from a distance."

He leaned against the trunk of a scraggly pine, one of many scenting the breeze, resting his forearms on his updrawn knees. He'd changed from the formal suit he'd worn for church to soft brown trousers topped by a Norfolk jacket.

"This is one of my favorite places. The pines on the craggy cliffs hide numerous caves where I played with friends as a boy." He broke a twig idly between his fingers and tossed it over the edge of the bluff. "For a time, when Rasmus and I had a questionable truce, he even joined in our escapades here."

Evan appeared suddenly, throwing his arms about Justin's neck and almost knocking him over.

"Hey, old man, practicing to be a football player?"

Giggles were his only answer. The boy lay panting on the blanket beside him as he continued. "My friends and I would pretend we were Tom Sawyer and his friends. We had quite the spine-tingling adventures. There's even a cave in these bluffs we dubbed Pirate's Cave. We pretended it contained smuggled treasure."

Evan jerked up. "Pirate's Cave?"

"It was only make-believe." Justin rumpled the brown curls. "Your sister's calling."

The boy was off to join her in a flash.

When Justin turned his attention back to Constance, his eyebrows shot up. "You're laughing at me. Why?"

"It is difficult to imagine you as a child. You seem so. . .comfortably adult."

His mouth curved down temporarily. "Old and staid, that's me. That's why I thought Marian. . ."

He didn't finish the sentence. Did he think he would insult her by speaking of his fiancée? How silly. And he certainly wasn't old and staid, with his warm brown eyes and rich laugh. Every time she looked at him, she felt his arms about her as they'd been earlier.

"Marian would bring life and energy to any home." The admission hurt.

"So do the children." She followed his gaze to them, where they played leap-frog with awkward grace.

Eventually her gaze drifted from the children to discover him watching her, two lines cutting between his brows.

"I'd thought for a time, Constance, that coming here had served the purpose I wished and relaxed you, but the tension is back in your face."

"I can't put Rasmus's threats from my mind after his visit to your home. Is there anyone more vile than a person who threatens children?"

"No!" His fists tightened into white knuckled balls. "But we shall continue to do all we can to protect them."

Constance remembered his words when he saw Rasmus's card, "How dare he threaten my family!" and a sweet longing stole through her.

She played idly with one of the blossoms amidst the pile of fragrant wild-flowers, clover, and dandelions which Effie had deposited in the lap of her gray skirt for safe-keeping.

"I know you shall. Your goodness to myself and the children continually amazes me. It is myself, and Rasmus, with whom I am upset."

"Yourself?" He leaned forward earnestly, arms about his knees. "But you have done nothing for which you should be upset. On the contrary, you've acted bravely."

"If I hadn't brought the children to River's Edge, they would not have been endangered."

"But you couldn't have known that in advance."

Would he protest so vehemently if he knew she had come to gather information on Rasmus?

"Nevertheless, I feel I've failed Charles." She lifted her hands slightly and her shoulders raised the white lawncloth shirtwaist in a dainty shrug. "Six months ago I was content with my life. Then Charles died, and I acquired sole care of the children. I love them, but I've brought them into danger. Now we are trapped in the role of your family, not knowing when the charade will end. I no longer have control over any aspect of my life."

"Do any of us have control over our lives?" He asked gently. "Isn't such control merely an illusion?"

At least he didn't reiterate his refusal to consider an annulment, she thought in relief, though she'd noticed him wince when she mentioned the charade. "I suppose you mean that God is in control."

"Yes. He allows both good things and hard things to happen to us, but He makes 'all things work together for good to them that love God,' remember?"

Did she have the courage to admit what she was thinking? Not if she continued meeting his eyes, she thought. She turned her gaze out across the river, welcoming the pine and clover scented breeze that cooled her hot cheeks and fanned the tight little curls about her forehead.

"I always considered myself a morally superior person, priding myself on my high standards. Until I met you, I didn't realize the inadequacy of my own goodness. Your standards shame me, they are so much higher than my own."

Shock sat plainly on his features. "I can't imagine that your standards would be lower than mine in any manner. You are one of the finest examples of gentle womanhood I have ever known."

The sincerity in his husky voice humbled her.

"Thank you for your gallant protest. But I do not attempt to make God's standards mine, as you do."

"I fail miserably numerous times daily in attempting to live up to those standards. The Bible says only God is good. We cannot judge our actions by comparing ourselves to each other. We must compare ourselves to Christ if we wish to know whether we are good. In that comparison, we all fail."

A shaky little laugh slipped out. Strange, she didn't feel like laughing.

"That makes Him sound rather like a stern schoolmaster watching for mistakes and handing out demerits."

"Jesus wiped away all our demerits when He took our sins on Himself and paid our debt with His death on the cross."

"I saw the change believing in Christ made in Charles's life. I've seen the evidence in your life, also, so strongly that I can no longer deny His existence or power."

Something glorious leaped in his eyes.

"Charles always told me that if I believed Christ was the Son of God, and had taken my sins on Himself, all I needed do was admit to Him my need for His goodness, and He would forgive me, and be with me in a close manner. Is that what you believe?"

Was it guarded hope she saw in his eyes?

"Yes. It is what I did as a boy of fifteen. The decision to follow Christ has made all the difference in my life."

She ran the tip of her tongue quickly over her suddenly dry lips. It was such a simple little thing, just a prayer, why was it so frightening, as though she were stepping off this rock into nothing but air?

"I—I'm not experienced with praying. Would you. . .do you think God would mind if you prayed with me?"

One of his hands covered hers. Could he feel her trembling?

"I'm certain He'd not mind, and I would be honored to do so."

"Dear Lord and Father, we thank Thee for putting within us a longing for the good and true in life. Thank Thee for revealing to us the inadequacy of our own attempts at goodness, and our need for Thy goodness, which is given us through the sacrifice by Christ of His own life, though we are completely undeserving of it. Thank Thee for accepting my request for Thy salvation when I was just entering manhood. We humbly request Thy gift of salvation for Constance this day, and thank Thee that Thou hast promised that Thou wilt turn away no one who comes to Thee. In Jesus' name, Amen."

Was she supposed to say something to God now, too? Were there rules about talking to Him? Constance couldn't recall when she'd felt so ignorant. She peeked up at Justin through her lashes and caught him watching her with softly glowing eyes.

"Is that all?"

"Unless you would like to add something."

"No. I—I wouldn't know how, even if I wished to."

"God isn't as concerned with the words we use as He is with what is in our hearts. You can talk with Him whenever you wish, however you wish, and He will listen to you. Don't worry if prayer seems strange to you at first; it did to me, too. As time goes along, you'll grow more comfortable talking with Him, the same as with people with whom you develop a friendship."

Effie slipped to her knees beside her, and Constance was glad for her timely arrival. It had been unusually exhausting discussing her decision to trust in God. She was accustomed to people who ridiculed such faith, or tolerated it in polite society, only to laugh about it behind people's backs. What would Alexander say if he knew of her change of heart?

Effie flung her arms out wide. "I'm hot! I wish I could wear short pants like Evan when we play. But I made a good frog, even in my dress, didn't you think?"

Constance bounced a fingertip off Effie's snub nose. "I'm not a very good judge of frogs. I am glad you aren't green with spots, but are a pretty little girl instead."

Where would all their lives wind up after the cruel joke fate, in the form of Rasmus Pierce, had played on them? For a moment panic threatened Constance's newfound peace of spirit.

"All things work together for good to them that love God," she repeated to herself. She hoped it was true.

Chapter 9

Justin leaned against the white pillar on the back porch and stole a glance at Constance, who was watching the twins with the gift from him. She was so near he could smell the delicate lavender fragrance she wore. The scent suited her, subtle, lingering in one's senses but not clinging.

The gentle light of early evening played on her hair, and he stuffed his hands hard in his pockets to keep from caressing it. He could still feel its softness against his cheek when he held her so briefly in the Bird Cage yesterday. He longed to have her in his embrace again. But more than that, he wanted the love and respect of this sweet, courageous woman.

She looked up at him with a smile in the green eyes that so fascinated him.

"You shall spoil the children with your generosity."

"They've been through some difficult times. I hope the pony will let them forget those times for a few minutes, anyway." He nodded toward them. "They appear to have taken to Zeke, in spite of that misshapen nose above his thick black mustache." The short, slender man in the bicycle hat, a collarless tan shirt, brown corduroy knickers, and suspenders was checking the harness under Evan's watchful eyes.

"Looks like he's been on the losing end of a few bouts of fisticuffs."

"Alex made a wise choice in his selection of an operative to stay on the grounds. The children have been following him about the stable and carriage house most of the day. I must say, he's been extremely patient and agreeable with them."

Justin certainly hoped he was a wise choice. Zeke Endicott had been waiting when they returned from the bluffs last evening. It had relieved his mind a great deal while at the bank to know Zeke was watching out for the three people who had become so important in his life the last few days.

He'd feel better if he were watching out for them around the clock himself, but that wasn't possible. He couldn't ignore his responsibilities at the bank. Too many banks had floundered and closed their doors the last few years. Difficult growing conditions and low rates for wheat hadn't helped midwestern banks. The current silver situation threatened even more. With the northern forests overcut and the increasing use of railroads to carry logs, the local economy, largely reliant on lumber carried on the Mississippi, was teetering precariously.

No, it was no time to be neglecting his duties, even if it did send his heart to his throat to think of leaving Constance and the children each day.

He smiled broadly as Evan climbed into the tall wooden cart and took the reins. "No, Effie. A gen'leman never 'lows a lady to drive. You're the passenger this time."

"Looks like Evan is finally standing up for himself," he said to Constance.

"He is a reserved boy, but not so timid as one might think. He chooses his battles well. Those he chooses, he generally wins."

"I expect he takes after a certain aunt in that respect."

She turned from watching the children to regard him steadily, but did not take up the challenge in his comment. "Since you and Mr. Endicott are watching the children, I believe I shall take care of my correspondence."

He watched her enter the back door, moving gracefully as always. He wished she had stayed; he enjoyed her company.

Sitting on the top step, he leaned back against the huge round planter filled with geraniums, and let his gaze move back to the children taking the cart up the drive and down, the spotted pony bouncing faithfully before them.

Only four days had passed since the forced marriage ceremony. It seemed a lifetime. Already he thought of Constance and the children as his family. He wouldn't have thought it possible for one's heart to be captured so quickly and irrevocably.

Constance had been a real trooper about this marriage. They hadn't discussed the permanency of it since that first night, though he'd been tempted to do so yesterday when she spoke in passing of the time the "charade" would be past. But there really was no point in arguing about it until Rasmus was captured.

His lips tightened at the memory of his proposal. When Constance realized Rasmus's intent to harm the children if they didn't marry, the blood had drained from her round face beneath that awful black mourning hat, but her gallant spirit had risen to the occasion. Calm determination routed the fear and dismay from her emerald eyes in less time than it takes to blink. He'd half fallen in love with her at that moment. If the situation had to happen, God had placed the right woman there.

And now she'd accepted Christ. The knowledge left a glow around his heart.

Would the Lord be able to convince her that her place was now here, beside him? As a new Christian, she couldn't be expected to understand or embrace all the Bible's teachings overnight. And there was Alexander Bixby. Did Constance love him? He wasn't certain about the legalities of an annulment, should she still choose to try obtain one against his wishes. Could one be gained on the grounds that one was forced into the marriage contract under duress?

Constance, even her name implied loyalty and faithfulness. She was a woman in a million. Even if she obtained an annulment, his heart would belong to her forever. Yesterday she'd said she felt "trapped" as his wife. The memory left a burning wound inside him. Would he be able to win her love before Rasmus was apprehended?

"Great kids, aren't they?"

Justin jerked upright.

"Didn't see you come up, Bixby." Some guardian he was proving for the children and Constance!

Shadows had formed beneath Alex's eyes since yesterday afternoon, Justin noted.

"Thought I'd stop by to let you know the latest developments."

Justin glanced at the children. Zeke was still with them; they should be safe. "Let's talk in the library."

"Is Constance about?" Alex asked as they entered the booklined room. "I'd like her to join us."

Justin felt the muscles around his mouth tighten, that stupid jealousy again. "I hate to worry her any more than necessary."

"The children are her responsibility. I should think it would worry her more not to know how the case is progressing."

"She and the children are my responsibility now."

"I know the details of that marriage ceremony, remember?" Justin didn't like the way Alex's eyes narrowed and his voice lowered threateningly. "Constance may be forced to live with you for now to protect the children, but if you do anything to harm her," Alex poked a blunt-edged finger toward him, emphasizing his point, "I'll tear you limb from limb. She's not your wife permanently. Don't forget it."

As if he had to be reminded that he hadn't his wife's love and commitment! The knowledge added to the anger Alex's challenge had lit.

"Is threatening innocent people part of your job?"

"I expect to marry Constance myself when this case is over." He jammed his hands into the pockets of his brown-checked sack suit. "Now that you know how the land lies, do you want to discuss the case or not?"

Regardless of his anger with Bixby, the man was right, the children were Constance's responsibility. Besides, what did he expect to accomplish by keeping the two of them apart? Did he think Constance would forget the man? Confound it, he even liked Bixby, except for his attraction to Constance. He was intelligent, easy to meet, and obviously cared about Constance and the children.

"I'll ask my wife to join us."

His fury continued to seethe as he went in search of her. First Rasmus entered his home and threatened his family, and now Bixby entered his home and brazenly announced his plan to marry his wife! Whatever happened to the idea that a man's home is his castle?

When Constance and Justin returned to the library, Bixby didn't have all that much to relate. The Ameses had been glad to receive the candlesticks back. Apparently nothing else but an ornate silver frame holding a likeness of Marian had been taken from them. The items had been taken sometime last night while the family slept. No one in either neighborhood recalled seeing Rasmus in the area.

All known abandoned buildings in and around River's Edge had been searched since the robbery, with no sign that Rasmus's gang had been inhabiting any of them. Rasmus's parents' establishment, along with their home above the store, were under constant watch. Again, there was no indication Rasmus or any of his criminal friends had been there the last couple days. Storekeepers, horse dealers, and real estate merchants were being interviewed in hopes of discovering large or unusual purchases. No leads there yet, either.

Justin rested his elbows on the desk and pyramided his fingertips together. "So all that's been discovered so far is where Rasmus is not hiding?"

The slamming of the back door and Evan's high-pitched holler interrupted Alex's reply. Justin and Constance were at the library door by the time Evan reached it. His eyes were almost as large as the round straw hat he'd been wearing earlier.

Justin caught him by the shoulders. "Whoa, old man! What's the problem?"

"Effie fell out of the cart! She made the pony go fast. The wagon hit a rock, and Effie fell out. She's sleepin' and won't wake up!"

Justin was down the hall before Evan finished. He could hear Constance racing behind him. Terror flooded him as he dashed toward the still child lying on the ground with Zeke kneeling beside her.

"She's alive, sir," Zeke assured as Justin fell to his knees beside the girl. "Out cold, though. May have a concussion."

Justin set trembling fingers alongside Effie's neck to reassure himself Zeke's words were true.

Constance dropped beside him to take Effie's limp hand with a strangled sob, her eyes large with fear. Justin longed to comfort her, but couldn't afford the luxury. He squeezed her shoulder.

"Steady, dearest. Doctor Thomas lives only a few doors down. I'll bring him."

It was almost midnight before Dr. Thomas left. Effie had two black eyes, a swollen nose, and had lost her two top front teeth. But long before the doctor left, she had regained consciousness and was fast becoming her usual bossy self. The doctor assured them her injuries looked far worse than they were.

Little comfort, Justin thought, staring glumly between the wine-colored library draperies into the black night. He'd never forgive himself for leaving the children with the cart and pony. It had only taken a moment for Zeke to turn his back and the accident to happen. For the first time, he realized the extent of the responsibility he'd assumed for the children.

"Justin?"

He turned to find Constance close behind him. She looked like an angel in the mellow light from the desk lamp. If the accident had terrified him, how much more must it have frightened her?

He opened his mouth to comfort her and instead heard himself say, "Effie could have been killed."

A hurt sound broke from her throat. She swayed toward him, opening her arms. In two steps, he had her in his embrace, burying his face in her soft, fragrant hair.

"You mustn't blame yourself, Justin. You mustn't! Zeke was with them. He couldn't prevent it, and you wouldn't have been able to, either."

The words did nothing to ease his guilt, especially accompanied as they were by the tears in her voice.

"It must have shredded your heart to see her like that."

She pushed him away just far enough to grasp his shoulders and give him an ineffectual shaking.

"You must stop accusing yourself. In a few days, the only sign of this evening's misfortune will be the lack of Effie's two front teeth, and her temporary teeth at that. Can you imagine her trying to boss Evan about with a lisp?"

Her attempt to lift his spirits caught his heart in a twinge. If anything ever happened to this brave little woman. . . . Despair flooded him. How could he prevent it? He hadn't even been able to keep Effie from harm with a pony and cart. He swallowed the lump of anguish in his throat.

"I'll sell the pony tomorrow."

"We cannot protect the children from every possible harm. Wouldn't it be better to teach them how to act wisely around the pony?"

He recognized the wisdom of her words, but he couldn't stop wishing he could protect Effie and Evan always.

One of her hands slipped tentatively from his shoulder to rest along his cheek, setting his heart reeling. The eyes so near his were almost black, filled with pleading. "Please forgive yourself, Justin. You must know Effie and I lay no blame upon you."

Sincerity filled the sweet, whispered words that began to ease the weight of guilt in his chest. Wonder swept through him that she had come to comfort him.

He gathered her gently closer. His gaze locked with hers and he bent his head, allowing her plenty of time to draw away. Instead, joy flooded him when her soft hand slipped from his cheek to the back of his neck the instant before his lips touched hers.

Chapter 10

Justin's kiss was incredibly tender, and Constance ached to stay forever in his arms, her husband's arms.

In the arms of a man who was in love with another woman.

The thought brought her to her senses as effectively as a dunking in ice water. She drew away from his embrace, disappointment swamping her when he released her immediately. What was the matter with her? Hadn't she wanted him to release her? Had she lost all ability to reason, because a man kissed her?

Because the man she loved kissed her. The realization brought a small gasp. She loved him!

Justin caught her lightly by the shoulders. "Have I offended you so? Must I. . .shall I beg your pardon?"

His low words trembled slightly, adding to the turmoil in her chest. She dared not look at him for fear he'd see the love in her eyes. How could she expect him to ask her pardon when she had welcomed his kiss with all of her traitorous heart? Hadn't he realized how her lips had yielded to his?

"There is much I'd like to say to you, Constance, but this isn't the time. It's been a trying evening for both of us. I apologize if I've made it more difficult for you. But I'm grateful for your comfort."

She nodded slightly, noticing his hands clenched at his sides. Was he remembering Marian also, and regretting their embrace? "I. . .thank you for caring so deeply for the children. Good night." She wanted to race for the door and up the steps to her room, but she forced herself to keep a ladylike pace. It wouldn't do to let him know how deeply she'd been affected by the last few minutes.

She glanced in passing at the grandfather clock at the bottom of the stairs. A quarter past midnight, and she was to have met Alex at midnight. The knowledge quickened her steps. In her concern for Justin, she'd forgotten the meeting.

In her room, she pulled her paisley shawl over her white blouse to hide it from the moonlight. Opening her door an inch, she listened tensely for Justin to retire to his room so she could leave the house without risk of being seen. The minutes ticked by with slow regularity, but he did not ascend the stairs.

Her lips still throbbed from his kiss. She wished she could put it from her mind, forget the way it felt to be folded tenderly next to his heart. "I'm grateful for your comfort," he'd said. Likely he had only kissed her in gratitude for her forgiveness over Effie's accident.

Her admiration for him, which began on the train, had grown as she watched him caring for the children and dealing with the townspeople's contempt. But tonight, after experiencing his pain as though it were her own, she couldn't deny her love for him.

She had never believed love could come so swiftly. But normally one wouldn't have the opportunity to know someone so well within such a short time, her heart argued. One's true character was revealed quickly by life-threatening circumstances such as they'd encountered together.

Love was so much more than her friends had said, more than a delightful fire racing through her veins, as uncontrollable as a magnetic force. It was a sweetness and warmth that filled her at Justin's kindness to her and the children, at his devotion to them and care of them that left her aching with the knowledge it was beyond repayment. She could never be worthy of such a precious love.

Justin had explained to her that, according to the Bible, marriage is a symbol of the relationship between God and His followers. Now that she'd committed herself to God, she did wish to please Him. The thought of an annulment was unsettling in light of her new faith.

But falling in love with Justin was foolish. It only invited heartbreak. He may have kissed her, but he loved Marian. The knowledge twisted cruelly through her heart.

Well, even if she could never have his love, she could try to give back a portion of the kindness and devotion he gave her and the children, until the case was over and they parted.

"Lord, help me. Show me how to be a blessing to him," she stumbled over the unfamiliar words. "Thank You, whatever the future holds, for these days You've allowed me to spend with him."

Was her prayer sufficient? She was still uncomfortable speaking to God. But Justin had said that would change as time went on, she reminded herself.

A footfall! Finally he was coming up the stairs! She closed her door softly, leaning against it, waiting for his footsteps to pass her room. Had they paused slightly before continuing on? She held her breath until she heard the door to Justin's room open and close.

She hated sneaking out of his house to meet Alex. It was only proper that Justin should know of her position as a Pinkerton operative. She'd tell him tomorrow at the first opportunity, regardless of the Superintendent's command.

The decision lifted some of the weight from her spirit. She latched the back door softly and ran lightly across the lawn to the carriage house. It wouldn't seem so strange if voices were heard there tonight, since Zeke was staying in the second story. The moon was especially bright tonight. She glanced over her shoulder at the softly lit windows of Justin's bedchamber. No sign of him. What would he think if he looked out and saw her? The thought put wings on her feet.

Holding her breath, she carefully lifted the heavy wrought-iron door latch. She'd barely opened the door when a hand clasped her wrist and pulled her inside.

"I thought you'd never get here!"

"Alexander!" The breath she'd caught whooshed out.

"Zeke said Effie wasn't seriously harmed. Has there been a change?"

She shook her head, then realized he couldn't see her in the darkness. "No."

"Knight still acting like a gentleman?"

The memory of his kiss swept back. "Y—yes."

"Sounds like you're shivering. Cold?"

"On this warm night? Don't be silly. What news have you for me?"

"I had the minister on the train checked out. Just as Knight said, he's ordained. Nothing to indicate he's tied up with Rasmus Pierce."

This time last night the news would have only added to her frustration. Now, now her heart tied her to Justin more securely than any vows. Married or not, she loved him.

"How is Knight getting along without the money he lost in the robbery?"

Shock burst through her like a lightning bolt. She tried to speak, but her vocal chords were paralyzed.

"Did you hear me?"

Her fingers pressed against her throat. "I didn't know Justin had any money in the express car. I assume you are speaking of the train robbery?"

"Right. A good piece of the money belonged to him, almost $50,000."

Constance flattened her hands against the wall behind her. She wished she could see something to sit upon. Her knees were threatening to fail her.

"There must be some mistake."

"It's no mistake. The Superintendent believes Knight was in on the robbery."

"Surely you are jesting!"

"Not a bit of it. Superintendent is usually right about these things. If he's correct this time, your position in Knight's home, much as I hate it, is a gift. Has he said anything that might substantiate his guilt?"

She tried unsuccessfully to push aside the pain tearing through her. As Alex said, the Superintendent was seldom wrong about these matters. Experience on other cases had taught her that a woman's heart wasn't a good judge of a man's character. But this time, it was her heart!

Reluctantly, she scanned her memory, terrified of finding incriminating evidence. All of Justin's actions appeared honorable. Relief unknotted the tension in her stomach.

"I can think of nothing to condemn him."

"Start keeping a watch out with the possibility Knight is in this with Pierce. If you get a chance, go through his papers." He snorted. "Why am I telling you what to do? You're one of Pinkerton's best operatives. You know what to do."

The knot was back in her stomach, tighter than ever.

"Yes. I know what to do. I'd best get back. If Effie calls for me, Justin will discover I'm out." Besides, there was a very good chance the tears burning her eyelids were about to let loose in a shower, and she didn't want Alex around if that happened. There was nothing more foolish than falling in love with a suspect!

Moonlight streamed in the door when Alex pushed it open, silent on its new hinges.

"Be careful, Constance. Knight's life isn't worth yours."

She nodded, no longer trusting her voice.

The night air felt good against her hot cheeks as she hurried back to the house. She wished it could blow away the horrible suspicion Alex had planted.

She wouldn't be telling Justin she was an operative after all. She'd been feeling guilty for deceiving him. Was he deceiving her instead? Had he and Rasmus somehow discovered on the train that she was an operative? Did they think that by marrying her to Justin they could remove her from actively pursuing Rasmus and remove any suspicion of Justin's involvement with Rasmus at the same time?

When she finally slipped between the lavender-scented sheets in the room meant for Marian, she buried her face in her pillow to keep her sobs from passing through the wall to Justin's bedchamber. It had been difficult enough realizing she'd fallen in love with him knowing he was in love with Marian. But to think he might be so dishonorable as to be a thief! It was more than she could bear.

Chapter 11

With Justin spending his days at the bank, Constance had ample time to search his room and library. She did so with dread. Would she unearth something that would tumble Justin from the lofty position in which her heart held him?

She found no money, notes, or bonds in the house. Nor did she see any sign of a safe or other likely hiding place.

In his library desk drawer, she found a carved box filled with bills for the house and furnishings. The number of them took her breath. Had these bills driven him to a desperate act?

If it weren't for the suspicion planted by Alexander, she would have rather enjoyed life with Justin. During the days she supervised the servants, shopped, or visited Libby. In the evenings, he took time to play with the children and have a family time of Bible reading and prayers. The children had begun attending the first grade level of school and were full of tales each evening.

After the children were in bed, he would work at his desk. Constance joined him in the library, doing needlework or reading. Often she spent the time reading the Bible. Justin was never too busy to set aside his work and answer the questions that invariably arose during her readings.

Occasionally she'd glance up to find his gaze on her with an expression that sent her heart pattering wildly, though he hadn't attempted to kiss her again or broach an intimate conversation.

The role of Mrs. Justin Knight was the most difficult she'd ever attempted. Over the years she'd played a gypsy, a wealthy socialite, a nurse, a young widow, and a poor type writer, among other things. As Mrs. Justin Knight, she played herself. Except she couldn't reveal her vocation, or tell her husband she loved him. And she might be working to put the man she loved in prison. Her heart clutched at the thought. How could anything so difficult be asked of one?

If only he would mention the loss of his money in the robbery, she thought. Why didn't he tell me of it? Why?

Constance spent as much time as she could spare visiting with Libby. The woman was always full of town gossip. It helped keep Constance's mind off Justin and the constant fear that the Superintendent's suspicions might prove true. There was also the possibility that something her aunt innocently revealed in her tattles would provide a hint that would lead to apprehending Rasmus.

One day she tried to casually introduce a topic often in her mind since her last talk with Alex.

"Have you heard any rumors about Mr. Knight's bank? Being a business-woman, I thought perhaps you would hear things I would not. You know how tight-lipped husband's are about business."

Libby's busy hands stopped tugging at the black lace and silk flowers adorning a straw hat. Her steel-gray eyebrows lifted in surprise.

"Now, dearie, what would make you suspect your husband of having business troubles?"

Constance settled a broad-brimmed leghorn on her black hair and looked into the viewing mirror, trying to appear casual.

"The last few years haven't been healthy for banks. And then, Mr. Ames did threaten that people would remove their funds from Justin's bank."

"I haven't heard of any run on his bank. Marian's father was just letting out some temper."

"There's the new house, too. It must have cost Justin something dear."

"Mr. Knight deals with money every day. I doubt he'd overextend himself." Her long, thin fingers closed about the brim of the leghorn. "Here, dear, allow me to adjust this for you." Deftly she folded up the back brim and attached it to the crown with a glittering black jet butterfly. "There! Isn't that better?"

"Yes," Constance replied absently. "Then you haven't heard of workmen complaining of overdue bills for the house?"

Fists propped on her navy skirt, Libby set her narrow lips in a prim line. "Workmen wouldn't know what to do with their lips if they weren't complaining of overdue bills. Now, I expect you'll place your trust in Mr. Knight and not ask any further indelicate questions."

How was a woman to place trust in her husband when a Pinkerton superintendent was suggesting that same husband might be involved in unsavory crimes?

She longed to confide in Libby. It would be nice to have someone help her sort out her thoughts and feelings. But what could she tell her? It was unthinkable to share information regarding a case.

And concerning Justin, what could she say? "The most awful thing has happened. I've fallen in love with my husband."

She groaned. Her aunt would think her feebleminded.

～

That evening when the family gathered in the parlor for devotions, Justin stopped Effie beneath a softly-shaded lamp and propped her round chin up with his fingers.

"It's been over a week since your accident. How is your face feeling?"

"Good."

It was an awfully colorful face, Constance thought. The swelling had gone down a bit, but her nose and eyes were the colors of the room: blue, yellow, and magenta.

Justin chose the fourteenth chapter of John for the text that evening. One verse stood out especially clear in Constance's mind: Jesus saying, "I am the way, the truth and the life. No man cometh unto the Father, but by me."

The way, the truth, and the life. Her thoughts stuck on the phrase, and she didn't hear the rest of Justin's reading. She felt as though the word *deceiver* were emblazoned in large letters across her forehead.

What would Jesus, who was the truth, think of her profession? She'd always thought of her vocation as promoting justice and banishing evil. But what would Christ think of using deception for such an end? There was so much she had to learn of Him!

"Shall we pray?" Justin's question brought her back to the present in time to see Evan and Effie, seated on either side of her, folding their hands and bowing their heads. Effie's long shiny brown curls slid forward and hid her cheeks. Evan's legs stuck straight beyond the end of the cushion, the blues in his favorite sailor suit almost black against the china blue damask.

She always listened closely to Justin's prayers, trying to learn the proper manner to speak to God, in spite of his insistence that there wasn't such a thing, only a proper attitude of heart and mind.

"Dear Lord and Father," Justin began in his rich voice, "I thank Thee for the pleasure Thou hast given me by bringing each of the people in this room into my life. Please make me the man Thou wouldst have me to be for Effie and Evan. Teach me how to be a help to Constance during this trying time. Thank Thee for her infinite patience, and the peace and order she brings to our home. In Christ's name, Amen."

Tears stung behind Constance's eyelids. Did he mean those words? She daren't meet his gaze, for fear he'd see in her eyes the love for him that was growing daily.

"What'th a 'trying time'?" Effie was leaning forward, hands still clasped in her lap, brows meeting in puzzlement.

"It's when things aren't the way we wish."

"But thith ithn't a trying time," she protested. "We like being married to you."

"Yes," Evan agreed promptly. "We like the big house and the Bird Cage, and the pony and cart. And you, too, Justin."

A smile broke across Constance's face at the last comment, and destroyed her resolve to keep her gaze away from Justin.

"Glad to hear it, old man."

"Maybe Aunt Conthtanth wouldn't think it a trying time if you gave her a pony and cart."

"Effie!" Laughter tangled with disapproval in Constance's exclamation.

"I guess that's something to consider. Thank you for the advice." His amused glance met Constance's.

He could be such fun! If only they weren't caught in this untenable situation. Perhaps under normal circumstances, he would have fallen in love with her, and there would be a chance for a real future together for them.

Except that under "normal circumstances," Marian would be Justin's wife now. The thought drove the joy from her heart and brought her to her feet. She held her hands out to the twins.

"Time to dress for bed, dears."

Effie rested a pudgy hand on Justin's knee. "Will you come up to kith uth goodnight?"

"I will. I couldn't sleep without your hugs."

It would be difficult for the children when the time came to leave him, Constance thought as they went up the stairway together.

It would be difficult for her, too, but at least she knew what to expect, could try to protect herself against future pain, though the longer they stayed here, the more it seemed her attempts were like too few sandbags piled against a rapidly rising river.

Half an hour later Justin pulled the door to the Bird Cage closed.

After the way his prayer had touched her heart, Constance didn't dare spend the rest of the evening across the library from him in the usual manner.

"Good night." She hoped her bright smile would keep from him any suspicion of her tangled emotional state. At his surprised look, she added, "I must take care of some correspondence. There are so many people to keep in touch with when one is away from home."

"Please join me first. There's something I must say to you."

A tension underscored his words, sending shivers of apprehension along her nerves. As much as she wanted to give herself a chance to repair her barriers against her attraction to him, she couldn't deny his request.

In the library, he stepped behind the desk. Constance stood on the opposite side, linked her fingers together in front of her skirt, and watched him silently. His mouth was a tight line in his rigid face. What had he to tell her? She breathed slowly, trying to calm the mad thudding of her heart.

He clasped his hands behind him. "A widow, Mrs. Healy, was in the bank today. Her husband was once one of the wealthiest men in town. In the recent difficult financial times, he turned most of his investments into cash with which to keep his company afloat. In addition, he borrowed heavily. With the common belief that a gentleman doesn't burden a woman with business problems, Mr. Healy kept the facts from his wife. When he died last month, Mrs. Healy was shocked to discover she is no longer a wealthy woman, but barely a step beyond poverty."

What had this story to do with her? Constance thought. The eyes that met hers were black with repressed emotion. A deep breath lifted his jacket, and he squared his shoulders. Opening a drawer, he pulled forth the carved box which she knew to be filled with slips of debt for this house.

Opening the cover, he let it rest against its hinges and pulled out a handful of bills. He tossed them to the desktop, where they spilled out in a fanlike pattern. "My debts." His voice was tight. "For this house and furnishings. I had thought they would be paid in full by now. Rasmus's robbery of the express car changed that."

"Why are you telling me this now?"

"Mrs. Healy's situation made me aware of how selfish and proud it is for a man to keep all knowledge of a couple's affairs to himself."

"But. . ."

He held up a broad palm. "I know you do not consider us truly married." Bitterness iced his words. "I'm not going to argue the facts with you at present. If something happens to me, if I die before Rasmus is apprehended, the law will consider us married, and my debts will become yours. You have a right to know that."

If he died! A shiver rolled over her.

His face twisted violently. "I'm sorry."

She longed to tell him that it wasn't the thought of debt that had scared her, but she couldn't admit how dear he'd become to her.

"I don't wonder you stand there staring at me in horror, Constance. It seems Rasmus's attempt to keep Marian from me never ceases to complicate your life."

She lowered herself onto a nearby leather chair, her hands grasping the wide walnut arms.

"You deal with money daily. How did you arrive at such a state as this?"

He snorted and dropped into the tall leather swivel chair, resting his elbows on the desk. His hands plowed through his hair.

"I was concentrating too much on bank business and not enough on my personal finances. I'd given Marian a free hand in furbishing the house, though I stated the limitations on funds I'd planned for the project. She spent far more than I allowed. I'm not excusing myself. I should have asked for a regular accounting. But I spent the time and effort on bank business instead."

"Why did you indicate that the express car theft hampered your ability to meet your debts?"

"I'd been to Chicago to sell property that I'd inherited on Prairie Avenue."

"But that's one of the wealthiest sections of the city. Real estate prices there are very high."

"The prices I received for the sales would have almost paid off these debts. Now Rasmus will be spending the money instead."

She rose, her eyes meeting his steadily.

"Thank you for sharing your financial situation with me. I hope you will find a solution. Alexander said there's no sign of unexpectedly large purchases made in the area recently. Perhaps the thieves won't have spent the money before it's recovered."

"Rasmus has been at large for a good while. I admit to having reservations about the Pinkertons' ability to apprehend him."

"The agency has a commendable reputation."

"That they do," he admitted grudgingly. "Whatever happens, I hope you'll not become responsible for my debts."

"That hasn't happened yet." She crossed to the door and paused, her hand on the woodwork, to seek his dear face across the room. "And if it should happen, you would be forgiven."

She strode quickly from the room, not wanting him to see the truth in her eyes, that she would forgive him almost anything. But she hadn't turned quickly enough to miss the widening of his own eyes, warmly brown in the soft light from the desk lamp.

❧

Justin's gaze met hers across the dimly lit room. Her voice was like the richest velvet: "If it should happen, you would be forgiven."

Justin's heart stopped, then plunged on thunderously. Could she possibly mean the promise in her words and voice?

"Constance!"

He stepped toward her, but she whirled about and disappeared into the hallway like a frightened doe.

For a moment he was tempted to follow her, take her in his arms and not let her go until she admitted the love she'd hinted at. Common sense stopped him. It was too soon. If love for him was beginning to flicker in her heart, he didn't want to extinguish it by rushing her. He'd promised when she moved into his home not to make demands on her; he meant to keep his word.

It had been extremely difficult honoring that promise during the week that had passed since Effie's accident, the night he'd taken Constance in his arms and kissed her. His arms had felt empty ever since. Her lips had yielded to his so sweetly, and so briefly. But she hadn't demanded the apology he'd offered, and the knowledge left his heart brimming with hope.

His mouth spread in a smile. *Lord willing, I'll win her love yet.*

❧

"Constance!"

She ignored his soft, eager call and hurried up the wide, sweeping stairway. She had endured all she could of his sweet presence tonight.

She continued all the way to the Bird Cage on the third floor, where she checked on the children. They were sound asleep, Effie's arms thrown back in abandonment, Evan's tucked beneath his pillow. They were such dears! When this case was over and the marriage issue resolved, would she be able to leave them with Libby and return to her work in Chicago as originally intended? It would be like tearing out part of her heart. She hadn't realized when the plans were made how much a part of her life they had become.

The breeze through the open portals was cool against her cheeks, fragrant with the spicy scent of geraniums from the boxes attached to the railings.

Justin had finally told her of his money stolen from the express car. She had been waiting and hoping for this since Alex's revelation days ago. Why then did it give her no joy? Why was her chest taut with pain and fear? Did Justin's sharing not indicate his trust in her? Did it not indicate he wasn't party to Rasmus Pierce's crimes?

Or did it mean he knew she was a Pinkerton operative? Had he somehow discovered that Alex had told her of Justin's loss, and told her of it himself only to avert suspicion?

"No, it's not possible." She could barely hear her own whisper. "Justin is a Christian. He would never conspire with Rasmus."

Wouldn't he? How could she be certain? What did she actually know about him? Except that he held her heart.

She stared unseeingly at a row of distant street lamps in the business section near the always-active riverfront. There had been the well-known Pinkerton case involving Michael Rogers. Mr. Rogers was a wealthy man, a "pillar" of the Methodist Church in Council Bluffs, Iowa. Local authorities had laughed at Mr. Pinkerton when he told them of his suspicions. Yet it was eventually proven that Mr. Rogers was a member of the infamous Reno gang.

But there was more to being a Christian than being an upstanding church-man. Thanks to Justin, she knew now that it was Christ in one's life that made one a Christian. Justin carried his faith into every aspect of his life.

At least, into every aspect he allowed her to see. Such a disquieting thought.

The breeze was suddenly cold. She wrapped her arms over her chest, rubbing her palms briskly over her upper arms, crushing her voluminous, pleated white sleeves in the process.

Moonbeams danced over the children's round faces. She stopped to tuck the blankets about them more securely. They looked so angelic in sleep! How they loved Justin. She hated to think of the pain it was going to cause them to leave him.

She understood Libby's comment about Rasmus's mother now. If Justin was a criminal, she couldn't condemn him or be ashamed of him. She would only hurt achingly, eternally hurt, for the choices he made that kept happiness from his life.

Tears pricked at her eyelids, and her heart echoed the unspoken cry in her mind, *Lord, don't let Justin be guilty!*

Chapter 12

Constance stood outside Aunt Libby's shop, Evan and Effie on either side of her, waiting for the clanging red and gold trolley to pass. The moment it was safe, the children darted across the street, adeptly dodging pedestrians and horsedrawn vehicles.

She shook her head resignedly as she followed. The stop at Pierce's General Store following the almost daily visit to Libby's millinery was becoming an eagerly-awaited ritual.

She paused for a wagon to pass, smiling at the driver when she recognized Mr. Meeker. He lifted his broad brimmed, sweat-stained brown hat and nodded to her cheerfully. He'd been at the store a few times when she stopped, usually delivering crops or baked goods in exchange for supplies, and Mrs. Pierce had introduced them. The last time she saw him, he'd mentioned that his bride of a year had returned to Missouri for a few weeks to see her ailing mother. She wondered idly when she'd return.

Her brow wrinkled in a frown as she hurried toward the store. Libby continued to insist her wardrobe inadequate for the wife of such a grand man as Justin. Constance did not intend to add to his pile of debts, and she certainly would not share the news of his financial problems with Aunt Libby, even if she had shared it with Alexander. She'd hated the gleam of satisfaction her news brought to her fellow operative's eyes.

Her concentration was so complete, she almost collided with a tall man in a gray suit. She stepped back quickly, the man's hands steadying her.

"Justin!" Joy at the unexpected encounter danced like sunbeams on her heart.

He smiled down at her. "Where to in such a hurry?"

"Following the children to the general store. They love to stop at the candy display there."

"I should think they would prefer the wider selection at the confectionery. Under the circumstances, I'm surprised you choose to shop at Pierce's."

She ignored his guardedly curious look.

"The children must always part with their precious pennies at the confectionery, but Mrs. Pierce has been known to give them each a piece of candy on occasion."

"Not tough-as-flint Mrs. Pierce? When I was a boy, she chased me and my friends from the store with her broom more times than I could count."

"Due to your fine manners, no doubt."

His twinkling eyes sent her heart tripping. "But what else? It was during our Robin Hood period."

She stopped short. "Robin Hood? You don't mean. . ."

A melodramatic sigh accompanied his nod. "Afraid so. We thought it chivalrous to take her candy sticks and give them to the poor new immigrant kids."

"It never occurred to you to purchase the candy?"

"That was impossible. Robin never paid for the food he gave away, you see."

Dismay spread across her chest. Did he have a natural criminal tendency, or had he merely been a typical lad?

"Of course, when our parents discovered what we'd been doing, we had to pay every cent back, by the sweat of our brows."

"I would consider it a personal favor if you kept the exploits of your wayward youth from Effie and Evan."

His chuckle won her smile as they entered the store.

She spotted Evan and Effie at the candy counter, as usual, near a young blond woman speaking with Mrs. Pierce.

Her attention on the children, she barely noticed the cheap glasses and kerosene lamps she passed that lined the window shelves, sparkling in the sunlight. The prisms of a hanging gas lamp sent miniature rainbows darting about the aisle and merchandise, but her attention was on the woman beside Effie. Could it be Marian?

Mrs. Pierce smiled. "Good day, Mrs. Knight."

The blond's shoulders stiffened beneath gold braid on violet silk, but she didn't turn about.

"Hello. I hope Effie and Evan haven't been any trouble." The children paid no attention to her arrival, but continued a whispered argument over which candies to purchase.

"Those two dears? I should say not. Brightens my day to have them stop." Constance watched the pale eyes in the age-lined, skinny face move over her shoulder to where Justin stood. "We don't often have the pleasure of your company, Mr. Knight."

The blond's gloved fingers tightened on the glass countertop. Constance was certain now that it was Marian.

"Mrs. Kelly usually does my shopping for me."

Marian swung around to face them, blue eyes sparking above her perfect, tiny nose. Despair swept through Constance. How could she ever hope that Justin might fall in love with her? Marian had captured his heart, and she was as different from petite, fair-haired, fiery-spirited Marian as River's Edge from Chicago.

The young woman's pointed chin lifted. "It seems some woman is always doing your shopping for you, Mr. Knight."

The pile of bills Marian had charged flashed on Constance's mind.

Before Justin could respond to Marian's challenge, she continued. "I don't believe I've had the pleasure of being introduced to your wife."

Constance allowed him to pull her hand through his arm and keep it firmly in place with his clasp. "Mrs. Knight, this is Miss Marian Ames. Miss Ames, my wife."

Constance inclined her head slightly. "It's a pleasure to meet you, Miss Ames."

Marian's eyes were hard as sapphires. "Thank you."

Justin ignored her rude reply. "And these are Mrs. Knight's niece and nephew, Effie and Evan Ward, who live with us."

At their names, the children turned. Noticing Justin holding his derby, Evan whipped off his round straw hat. Justin gave him a solemn wink of approval.

Marian barely glanced at the children. Her attention was fully on Justin. "I shouldn't keep you. I only stopped to speak with my future mother-in-law."

"You're to be married?"

The shock in Justin's voice was reflected by the muscle which jumped in the arm beneath Constance's hand.

"Yes. To Rasmus."

Justin's face was whiter than death. Pain shot through Constance at the way his eyes grew old before her. Was he thinking he had lost Marian's love forever? That he couldn't bear it?

Marian's face glowed with satisfaction at her announcement's effect, and anger rippled through Constance. Wasn't it enough that she hurt Justin horribly? Must she gloat over it?

"Ith Rathmuth the man from the train?"

Constance nodded. "Yes, Effie."

Effie's red cotton gown swung as she whirled to face Marian. "You muthn't marry him. Rathmuth ith a mean man. He pointed a gun at Evan on the train and made Aunt Conthtanth marry Juthtin."

"Effie!"

"Effie!"

Constance's protest was effectually lost in Justin's roar, which brought dusky color back to his face.

"Is it true?"

Pity flooded Constance at Marian's husky whisper.

Evan grabbed his sister's arm and shook it. "We weren't s'posed to tell!"

Effie dug her few remaining top teeth into her bottom lip, and looked cautiously at Constance. "I forgot."

"It is true." Marian's sounded desperate. "If it weren't, the children wouldn't have been ordered not to speak of it." A sob burst from her. She pushed her way past them to tear down the narrow aisle.

"Marian!"

Constance clutched at Justin's arm as he started after her. "We must help Mrs. Pierce!"

The woman was leaning weakly against the countertop, her face as gray as her work gown.

Justin reached her before Constance did. With strong hands below her shoulders, he lowered her to the rickety chair behind the counter before she slumped.

"Fainted. See if you can find some spirits of ammonia."

She searched quickly among the crowded counters and returned with the bottle. Justin had loosened the high collar of Mrs. Pierce's gown and untied the long apron which covered it.

It was only moments before Mrs. Pierce revived, though her eyes looked so tragic that Constance wondered if it wouldn't have been a kindness to allow her to remain oblivious to the world a few minutes longer.

The woman struggled weakly to sit up by herself, but Justin kept a hand below her arm.

"Take it easy, Mrs. Pierce. You've no other customers at present. Rest a few minutes."

"Rest." The tired voice cracked on the word. Wrinkled lids covered the washed-out blue eyes. "Do you think the mother of Rasmus Pierce can ever rest? I tell myself there isn't anythin' new in crime or plain deviltry that he can do. But always he finds more ways to hurt people." The lids opened slowly. Her troubled gaze rested on Justin's face. "I'm sorry he wrecked your plans to marry Miss Ames. I didn't know."

He smiled through tight lips. "It doesn't matter. The woman I married instead is superb, don't you agree?"

Constance's heart felt as though it would burst. If only he meant it!

Wrinkled fingers plucked at his sleeve. "But Miss Ames, she's young and headstrong. No tellin' what Rasmus will do if she accuses him of ruinin' her marriage to you."

"I'll try to locate her and explain everything. But not until I know you're well."

She straightened bony shoulders beneath the thin cambric dress.

"I've lived through a lot of things in my time, boy. Expect I'll make it through this, too." Her skinny, blue-veined hand patted one of his. "I'd give my life to have had my boy turn out as fine as you."

Even Effie and Evan were still subdued when the four left the store upon the arrival of Mr. Pierce a few minutes later.

Settling beside Constance on the wide, red leather seat beneath the black fringed carriage top, Justin picked up the reins.

"I have to try locate her."

Constance nodded. Of course he meant Marian.

"If she says anything to Rasmus, and if I know Marian she'll repeat what she's heard loudly and completely, it could mean trouble. He won't like it that she's found out."

"I know." She kept her voice low, like his. It wouldn't do to frighten the children who were in the seat behind them. Was he remembering, as she was, the wedding gift? Remembering how easy it was for Rasmus to enter their home? Could they protect the children should Rasmus decide to carry out his threat?

"I'll leave you and the children at the house. Zeke will be there with you. I'll tell him what's happened before I leave."

She nodded. Zeke's presence would help, of course. But she felt safer with Justin close, in spite of the Superintendent's suspicions. She laid her hand in its soft black glove on his arm. She kept her eyes on it even when she knew he was looking down at her in surprise.

"Please, hurry back to us, Justin."

But when the twilight faded into night and the lights warmed the house against the darkness, he still hadn't returned.

Constance alternately stared out draped windows watching for him, and paced the floor until she was sure the new, thick carpet would be in tatters by morning.

Zeke had gone up to bed with the children. His plan was to sleep on the floor inside their door. They'd led the children to believe his presence was a special treat for them. The twins had been allowed to bring cookies and milk to their room, and Zeke had promised to tell them stories.

"Keep them safe, Lord, please." She repeated her plea for the fiftieth time since Justin left. She'd felt so sure of the Pinkertons' ability to protect people in the past, but this time it was Effie and Evan being guarded, and the famous company's reputation didn't reassure her one whit.

A lantern glowed outside the carriage house, then went out.

That would be Alexander's signal. She hurried through the kitchen and out the back door. Wind snatched it from her hands to slam it against the wall. She struggled to shut it.

The wind pulled at her hair and green skirt as she bent against it. The derringer she'd slipped into the embroidered muslin pocket hanging beneath her skirt was heavy against her hip. She didn't intend to be caught without it again should Rasmus appear.

A hand on her arm sent her heart hurtling to the ground and back. The grip kept her from reaching her derringer. Rasmus?

"Constance, it's Alex."

Relief almost took the stiffening from her knees. "Thank the Lord it is you!"

His voice was at her ear. "Can't hear you with this wind. Guess you couldn't hear me, either. I called to you twice." He pulled open the door, and they slipped inside.

The friendly smell of leather from new harnesses hanging on the wall greeted them. At the sound of a small scratch, sulfur filled the air and a long match flickered.

"Did you hear what happened at Pierce's Store?" Constance asked breathlessly.

His dark eyes peered at her through the small blue and yellow flame. "No."

Quickly she poured out the story, reminding him of Rasmus's threat to harm the children if Marian discovered the truth about Justin's and Constance's marriage. Long before she'd finished, Alex had shaken out the match.

"Zeke went looking for you as soon as Justin left this afternoon, Alex. He couldn't stay away long. We were both concerned for the children."

"Of course. Their protection must come first, at all costs."

She breathed a sigh of relief. She hadn't been certain he would feel that way.

"We'll need to have an agent watch Marian. Obviously she's been in contact with Rasmus. We should have thought of that angle earlier."

Yes, they should have. What would Rasmus do when Marian spoke to him? Would he harm her? The thought sent shivers up Constance's arms.

"I'd best get started. Sooner we begin watching the Ameses' home the better."

A minute later he was closing the carriage house door behind them, and they were back in the wind.

He started to say something and she leaned nearer to hear him, bending her head until it almost touched his shoulder. His hand was at her waist, steadying her against the buffeting winds.

"Be careful, Constance. Keep your derringer at hand. We're up against a bad one this time."

She lifted her head to reply, but she never had the chance. He was torn from beside her and thrown against the door.

She grasped for the pocket with the derringer.

"Keep your hands off my wife, Bixby!"

Even the wind couldn't hide Justin's yell. It stilled her reach for the gun and sent her heart plummeting. When had he come? They hadn't heard his horse's hooves.

Alex pushed himself to a standing position, straightened his coat, stepped closer to make himself heard, though he, too, had to yell to accomplish it.

"You've got it wrong, Knight. We're talking about the case."

"Why not meet at the house if that's true? Get out of here, and quick."

Constance clutched at Justin's lapels. "Don't be foolish. We need him. We can't protect the children or apprehend Rasmus without him."

Bixby flexed the shoulder that had hit the side of the house with force at Justin's earlier shove. "We're all in this together, Knight. We may not like each other, but we can at least be civil."

"Just keep your hands off my wife, understand? Now get off my property."

Alex leaned down and picked up the hat that had flown to the ground at Justin's attack, crushed it on his wind-blown hair, nodded at Constance, and shouted, "Remember what I said!"

Justin's grip remained on Constance's arm until they entered the kitchen, where he released her abruptly.

She shoved back the wisps of hair the wind had pulled from their pins and tossed across her face. "What enticed you to act so abominably? Alexander is helping us."

"Helping himself to my wife." The words snapped with anger. "He told me he's in love with you, expects to marry you when Rasmus is behind bars."

"But I. . ."

"You may as well get him out of your mind and heart. You're married to me, and you'll stay so."

Chapter 13

"You're married to me and you'll stay so!"

Those angry words had been going around in Constance's mind like a steamboat wheel. Would they ever stop?

Constance slipped the purple bolero vest trimmed with black braid over her white shirtwaist. Tugging slightly at the bottom of the vest to straighten it, she looked in the floor-length swinging mirror. The vest went perfectly with her new purple and ivory striped skirt.

Round amethysts surrounded by tiny seed pearls dangled daintily in gold from her ears. It was nice to wear something other than silver and onyx mourning jewelry.

"Hoping to cheer yourself with the earrings and your new outfit, aren't you?" she asked her reflection. "Neither has removed the bags from beneath your eyes."

No wonder. She hadn't slept a wink all night. Justin's accusing eyes and voice had kept her company no matter how hard she'd tried to push them away. It hurt unbearably to think he believed she'd meet Alexander clandestinely. If she could tell him she was an agent. . .

That still wasn't an option.

She'd best be starting downstairs. Mrs. Kelly would likely have breakfast prepared soon.

The enticing odors of coffee and sausage greeted her when she entered the hallway. She poked her head into the children's room and urged them to hurry their dressing. She'd learned months ago that they no longer appreciated her offers to help.

She hesitated halfway down the stairs. Justin was leaning against the library door reading a newspaper. Her heart lurched when he looked up and saw her. She continued her descent, resisting the desire to turn and bolt back up the stairs.

He folded the newspaper briskly and tucked it beneath one arm. Stepping forward, he waited for her at the bottom of the stairway. The eyes that had always been so warm and friendly were shuttered. The determined line of his mouth set her trembling inside. The man obviously had something to say and intended to say it.

Didn't he say enough last night? At the memory, heat filled her face. She stopped on the last step, hand resting on the smooth balustrade.

"Good morning."

"Good morning. I wanted to speak with you first thing."

That was obvious. "Have you more indiscretions of which to accuse me?"

He winced at her comment, and she hated herself immediately for having made it. She might hear what he had to say before attacking him. If the gray shadows beneath his eyes were any indication, he hadn't slept well last night, either.

"I thought you should know that I wasn't able to locate Marian yesterday."

His formal, reserved tone assured her she wasn't yet forgiven for last night and sparked her anger.

"When you didn't return until so late, I was sure you'd found her and the two of you were having a heart-to-heart conversation." Or that Rasmus had found them together and harmed him, but she wasn't about to let him know she'd feared for his safety. Her heart was too raw from last night's vocal beating.

Even his lips grew white at her taunt. "I haven't spoken to Marian out of your presence since we married."

How easily that phrase slipped off his tongue—"since we married." The words always had to struggle through her throat.

"Constance, we need to put aside our differences and think of the children. If Marian has reached Rasmus, we cannot guard Effie and Evan too closely."

He was right, of course. She shifted her eyes from his tense face. She couldn't indulge her pain at the expense of the children.

"Zeke slept in their room last night."

"No he didn't. I did."

"You. . . !"

"I stopped to check on them before retiring. Zeke almost knocked me out before we recognized each other. I sent him back to the carriage house, and I took his place. I thought it would look pretty strange if anyone discovered he'd spent the night in our house instead of his room."

"Of course." How would they have explained such a thing to Mrs. Kelly? She hadn't even thought of it when she and Zeke concocted the plan. But then, the children's safety had been uppermost in their minds.

"Now that we've come to a cease fire. . ."

Her hands clutched the banister and she took a shaky breath. "Before the subject is entirely put to rest, there's something I'd like to say."

His gaze locked with hers. "I'm waiting."

"In spite of the fact that I entered into this marriage with the expectation it would be temporary, I would not be unfaithful to our vows while the marriage exists. I did not meet Alexander for indiscreet or unsavory purposes. I met him to tell him of Marian's engagement to Rasmus."

"Why should he care what Marian does?"

She struggled to beat down the anger flamed by his contempt. "If she's meeting Rasmus, the Pinkerton agents can follow her to locate him. At least, that's what Alexander said they would do when I spoke with him."

His gaze bored into her eyes, searching their depths as if to discover the truth. She met his scrutiny unflinchingly.

He wasn't the only one with doubts. Her heart still tried to override her reason and say Justin was innocent of connection with Rasmus. But was he? What if her heart was wrong? What if she told him she was a Pinkerton agent, only to discover he was a partner with Rasmus? In such a case, he might decide to get rid of her, and then what would happen to the children?

A pounding at the double doors a few feet away broke the strained silence. A glance through the etched glass revealed a round, middle-aged man with a red handlebar mustache and a derby that appeared two sizes too small.

"Sheriff Tucker! What in the world can he want?" Justin had the door open almost before the words were out of his mouth. "Come in, Tucker. What's the news?"

Constance's breath caught in her throat. The sheriff! Could he have news of Rasmus? Had the local authorities captured him?

The rotund man took time to tip his derby to Constance. His face was florid. "Excuse me for intruding."

"Please give it no thought. We know you wouldn't do so without cause."

"Cause! I'll say I have cause!" he managed between puffs. "It's your bank, Mr. Knight. It's been robbed!"

❧

There was no doubt in anyone's mind that Rasmus and his gang had performed the heist.

Dynamite had been used to explode the door to the vault. In the noise of the storm, the explosion went undetected until the chief clerk opened the bank for the workday. Debris was scattered throughout the building from the force of the explosion. Numerous repairs were required.

Three evenings later, Constance sat in the wing chair across the room from Justin's desk, the Bible open in her lap.

Justin worked in his shirtsleeves, striped in wine and white tonight. He rested his forehead on his fist and studied the financial statements before him. His hair was in disarray from running his fingers through it. Her heart twisted at the sight of his face, gray with exhaustion, carved with lines that hadn't been there when they met on the train.

Depositors had barely given him a moment's peace for worrying over their lost savings. She sympathized with them, but Justin felt personally responsible for each loss, and she feared the burden was too great for him.

To make matters worse, Marian Ames had disappeared. No one had seen her since the robbery was discovered. Her parents were frantic. Was Justin's heart just as frantic over her safety?

Justin was certain Marian had contacted Rasmus and Constance expected he was correct. One more matter for which he felt responsible. When he'd heard of her disappearance, barely repressed fury had burned in his eyes.

"Deception! It never breeds anything but trouble."

She bit back the sigh that threatened and moved to his desk. "Won't you retire? It's nearly midnight."

He rubbed his hands over his face. "Not yet."

Rising, he straightened his shoulders and moved out from behind the desk, holding out his hand to her. "Will you sit with me?"

She hesitated only a moment before placing her hand in his. It was the first time he had touched her since finding her with Alexander, and she quivered inside. Her heart ached for the camaraderie they'd so briefly shared.

They sat side by side on the sofa. His gaze was locked on their hands, where he played idly with her fingers.

"Did I tell you that the night the bank was robbed, we were holding $70,000 in payroll for one of the local lumber mills?"

"It was in the newspaper."

"Seventy thousand dollars. All those workers without wages. I've arranged with some of the local merchants to give credit to the employees until they receive their next pay, but that will be weeks away."

That was so like him. Admiration surged through her.

"Insurance will only cover a portion of the loss. If Rasmus isn't apprehended, I don't know how I shall make restitution to the lumber mill, to say nothing of the other depositors. I may need to sell this house. It won't be a great help, since the sale would barely cover the unpaid cost of building and furnishing the home. The law doesn't require me to make restitution, but I can't live in a fine home like this while the lumber mill employees go without money they've worked hard to obtain."

"Of course not." Tears glistened on her lashes, blurring his profile.

"The owner of the mill is worried about the forest fires raging in Wisconsin and northern Minnesota, too. They've been burning for two weeks, and destroyed not only thousands of acres of trees, but a few small towns. The mill owner may have to let some of his men go if his lumber supply is affected. Which means the men need that payroll more than ever."

The strain in his dear face was like an enemy. If only she had a solution to offer, some comfort to give, Constance thought. But she could only think of platitudes that would appear patronizing and be of no true benefit.

"I've no major investments left to liquidate since selling the Prairie Avenue property in Chicago. Of course, Rasmus has his dirty paws on that money, also."

He swallowed hard. "I've decided to make Rasmus an offer. He can keep the portion of the train and bank money that belongs to me if he will return the rest. In exchange, neither the railroad, express company, nor bank will press charges."

Such compromises were common, she knew. Usually they were arranged through secret negotiations by a lawyer retained by the thieves. Pinkerton had always detested such compromises. He felt it imperative that robbers not be allowed to negotiate as though they were law-abiding businessmen. She had always agreed.

"Are you certain this is the only way?"

"Yes." The word was sharp and harsh.

"How do you propose to contact Rasmus?"

"Through an ad in the local newspaper."

In spite of Justin's pain, a ray of joy touched her heart. She was finally convinced beyond a doubt that he was in no manner a partner with Rasmus. He couldn't be, he was threatened with the loss of all his material possessions, and had already lost the respect of many townspeople.

Perhaps she could win back a little of the respect and trust that she'd lost when he'd found her with Alex at the carriage house. She hadn't yet obtained leave from the Superintendent to reveal her employment, but. . .

His hands tightened on hers. "I'm sorry you and the children have been caught in the midst of this mess. I can bear it for myself. Giving up the house is no great sacrifice for me. I wouldn't mind living as cheaply as possible for years while paying back the payroll loss. But you and Effie and Evan, you don't deserve this."

She gave him a trembling smile. "Have you forgotten? Even though everything looks hopeless from our viewpoint, God is in control. 'All things work together for good to them that love God.'" She could hear the hesitation in her tear-clogged voice. Why did it make one feel so vulnerable to speak of God? "Isn't that the way the verse reads?"

A small smile tugged at one side of his mouth. "Yes, that's the way it reads."

"When the pastor quoted that verse on the train, I wanted to bounce my pocketbook off his head. I thought it the most ridiculous statement I'd ever heard. But something good did come of our forced marriage. You shared your faith with me. Because of you, I believe in God now. Is there anything greater you could possibly offer me and the children? Surely you don't believe that money or a grand house is of more advantage than faith."

One hand cupped her cheek. The chestnut brown eyes she loved so well glowed as he smiled tenderly down at her.

"You are a wonder, Constance Knight. An absolute wonder."

His touch chased away her breath. It was all she could do to speak.

"Has—has the financial situation changed your mind about the annulment?"

The tenderness in his eyes was instantly eliminated by anger. She longed to grab back the hand that dropped from her cheek.

"Still hoping to go back to Alex Bixby? Sorry, but my belief in the sanctity of marriage vows hasn't changed, even if I am sorry to bring my financial problems down on your shoulders."

Resentment charged through her. How could he be so abominable? She opened her lips to retort. Clamped them shut. Wounded pride was urging her to build another wall of lies between them. She wouldn't. There had been enough deceit. There would be no more on her part.

The resolution straightened her shoulders. Boldly, she reached for the hands which had only moments before touched her so tenderly. The unexpected move brought Justin's puzzled, still angry eyes to hers.

"I was not thinking of Alexander. I inquired only that I might know whether I dared tell you that—that in spite of the 'mess,' as you refer to it—together we can get by, you and I and the Lord." Her words trailed off.

His fingers crushed hers. The hope in his eyes drove her lashes down in astonishment and wonder. "Do you mean that?"

She nodded, unable to trust her voice to answer his hoarse question.

His hands framed her face, lifting it until she could not help but look into his joy-filled eyes.

Now was the time to tell him she was a Pinkerton agent. Before she lost her courage. She laid her fingers gently on his lips to prevent them from claiming her own. "There's something I must tell you. About. . ."

"Aunt Conthtanthe, I can't find Regina."

They drew apart instantly at Effie's unexpected question.

The little girl stood in her linen nightgown, rubbing her eyes at the lights in the room, her face screwed into a tired pout.

"I thought you were asleep hours ago, dear."

"I woke up and couldn't find my doll."

Constance smoothed the girl's sleep-rumpled hair. "You probably left Regina in my room. Remember you were playing with her on my bed after dinner?"

"I'll go look for Regina with you, Effie." Justin picked the little girl up. He smiled broadly at Constance, the thinly-veiled ardor in his eyes sending her heart tumbling. "I don't want you to get sidetracked, Mrs. Knight. There's one or two things I mean to say to you before you retire. Wait for me here."

Constance waited. The memory of the light in his eyes kept her company. It seemed only moments before she heard him re-enter the library. "Did you find Regina?"

"Yes."

The curtness of his reply stunned her. His face could have been set in granite. What had happened in the few short minutes he'd been gone?

"The doll was lying on your writing desk. Beside this."

He dropped a crumpled piece of her personalized stationery into her lap as though he couldn't stand bear to touch it.

"Sorry it's not in the pristine condition in which I found it."

"Oh!" She didn't have to unwad it to know what it was, the unfinished daily report on the Rasmus Pierce case she was writing for the Superintendent.

Contempt twisted his lips. "I thought you so fine, so pure and trustworthy. And all along you were living in my home under false pretenses. A Pinkerton agent!"

Chapter 14

A Pinkerton agent!"

The words echoed off the booklined walls. The scorn in his voice and eyes burned her very soul. "I was going to tell you. . ."

"When the case was over and you were ready for that annulment, I suppose."

"No, it was what I started to tell you when Effie interrupted us."

"Convenient story."

"You must believe me!"

"I shall never believe you again."

"Justin, please, let me explain." The words were a tangled sob.

"Explain? How can you possibly explain choosing such a degrading profession? You must have seen many unsavory situations in your work, been involved with people with whom no decent woman would associate. No wonder you hadn't a problem meeting another man clandestinely while married to me!"

"I told you why I met Alex."

"And the children, how could you expose those sweet kids to the danger inherent in your profession?"

"I never intended them to be exposed to danger. I was simply bringing them to Aunt Libby's. My assignment was to become friendly with Mrs. Pierce and try to obtain information from her regarding Rasmus. The agency didn't even know Rasmus was in the area. We thought he was still in Missouri. It wasn't my fault he robbed the train we boarded. Nor that he insisted we marry."

The muscles in his neck stood out like cords of rope. "Excuses! How could you help but realize you would be putting the children in danger bringing them along while you worked on a case in any capacity?"

He paced four long, sharp paces toward the marble-trimmed fireplace. Four paces back. Glared at her.

" 'Everything that deceives may be said to enchant.' Plato said that, in case you've forgotten. He was certainly correct about you. You were completely enchanting. You're very good at deceit. I never suspected you were a detective."

Indignation brought her to her feet, her hands clenched into fists at her sides. "Of course I'm good at my profession! Why shouldn't I be?" Was that her voice, high and shrill? "Why shouldn't I honor the pledge I made to my employer to keep my purpose here secret? Why give criminals advantages they don't give law-abiding citizens? Did Rasmus warn you that he was going to rob the train or the bank?"

"Why did you become a detective?"

"Because I love justice."

"Justice?" His lips twisted in an ugly sneer. "Don't make me laugh."

"Yes, justice. And yes, love for it has put me in many unsavory situations among people with whom you would likely never associate. Do you believe, truly believe, that women should close their eyes and ears to the evils perpetrated in this world? That women should have no part in combating them? Aren't they as often victims as men? Have they no responsibility for sustaining justice?"

"There are other ways women can fight injustice, ways that don't involve deceit. Such as by raising children to love the Lord and goodness."

He grabbed his jacket from the back of a chair and she watched, fuming, as he left the room. A moment later the front door slammed. Was he so angry he'd left the house?

She rushed to the hall, almost tripping over her long skirt. His favorite hat was missing from the hall rack. Desolation swept over her. He had left, furious at her, despising her.

"Good riddance," she muttered, walking back into the library. She dropped down on the sofa, crossed one leg over the other, swung it back and forth furiously. Stood up. Started pacing.

No use trying to relax. Never had she been so angry. Never had she allowed her temper to break from her control. Never had she yelled at anyone.

She stopped abruptly at the fireplace, ran a finger along the edge of the mantle. "Never have I been so in love, or so afraid," she whispered.

Would he ever let himself trust her again? Living with his contempt would be unbearable. If only she had told him earlier that she was an operative!

She threw herself down on the cool leather of the sofa, cushioning her face in her arms, and sobbed herself to sleep.

It was hours later Constance awoke. She stirred uncomfortably and looked about. The lights were still burning. What had awakened her? She sat up stiffly. Lowered her head into her hands with a groan. Had her crying spell brought on this crushing headache?

The clock in the hallway began chiming the hour. One—two—three—four—five. Five in the morning! It couldn't be.

The back door slammed. Justin! Her heart began beating louder than the grandfather clock. If only he would forgive her! She raced down the hall, through the swinging door to the kitchen. A man's figure was silhouetted against the screen door by the light from a battered tin lantern on the rectangular oak table.

He swung around.

Her blood turned to ice. "Rasmus!"

❧

From the end of the dock, Justin stared into the black waters of the Mississippi lapping at the wooden posts. The smell of the river and the sound of its gentle waves were usually soothing when he was battered from life's battles. He found no peace here tonight.

Pain more intense than he'd ever known gripped his heart relentlessly. With a deep groan, he squatted down on the damp wood, plowing his fingers through his hair. His hat fell unheeded to the planks beside him.

Boats steamed past, their lights reflecting in waving paths. The voices of dockmen rose and fell. He was oblivious to it all.

Constance's face filled his mind, with the timid pledge in her eyes as she whispered, "Together we can get by, you and I and the Lord." He'd thought in that moment the Lord had handed him heaven on earth, only to have his heart torn out by the roots minutes later when he found her note.

"Enchantress!" The bitter indictment rent the gentle night breeze.

He hadn't suspected the snags and quicksand and currents that lay beneath the image of the peaceful, strong, compassionate woman. She was only playing a role, one of numerous roles she must have played as a detective. Would he ever know who she really was? Would he ever dare allow himself to trust her again?

He hadn't known betrayal could spiral through a person, burning and piercing all at once, wrapping one in despair and fury. And making the future look as black as that water flowing past.

Is this what Marian experienced when he told her of his marriage to Constance? "Forgive me, Lord, for hurting Marian. Heal her, regardless of the reason. Heal her, and bring to her the good that Thou hast promised to those who love Thee."

Healing. His heart was so raw that healing seemed impossible.

He buried his face in trembling hands. "Lord, I thought if we honored the vows, this marriage would have Thy blessing. I don't understand why Thou hast allowed our lives to be joined, or why Thou hast allowed me to love Constance beyond reason, when Thou must have known it would bring this pain. I beg that Thou wouldst heal me."

He didn't know how long he sat there, reliving the joy of Constance's presence in his life, the thrill of believing earlier tonight that he'd finally begun to win her love, the fire of knowing he'd been deceived.

The walk home was like walking to his own hanging. Constance would be there. He'd have to see her and speak to her and be constantly reminded of her betrayal. It was more than any man should be expected to endure.

Forgive her.

The words stopped his steps on a street corner near his home. "I can't. It's too soon!"

Constance had been amazed that he would forgive Rasmus. That had been easy compared to forgiving her. He'd never given Rasmus his heart.

But there would be no peace for him without forgiving her. His throat tried to close against the words.

"Lord, help me to forgive her. And please, make our marriage the union Thou dost desire. In Thy Son's name. Amen."

Could they have a real marriage without trust?

Had a light flashed from his parlor window? It must have been his imagination, there was no light there now. Certainly Constance wouldn't be waiting up for him. He shrank from the thought of facing her.

But what if something had happened to the children? How could he have allowed himself to become so wrapped up in self-pity that he had forgotten the need to watch over them?

Fear swamped him as he hurried up the steps, and his heart reached for the Lord with a prayer he didn't know how to put into words.

Chapter 15

Lantern light flickered grotesquely on the kitchen walls.

"Right the first time, Mrs. Knight. Rasmus Pierce, at yer service." His chuckle raised the hair on the back of her neck. "Or more precisely, yer at my service."

In the light from the battered lantern, his face was gray between his black derby and the thin beard that covered the bottom half of his face. His hair no longer curled over his collar, and the Vandyke beard had been sacrificed to an over-all beard. No doubt to better disguise himself from the Pinkerton agents whom he must know were searching for him, Constance thought.

A dark farmer's jacket reached just below his hips, covering a checked flannel shirt tucked into brown corduroy trousers. Her training had recorded her observations of his looks and dress in a moment. What caught her attention were his eyes, and the triumphant look that glittered there. It chilled her to the marrow.

Is he here to harm the children? Stop that! Get your emotions under control, she chided herself. *Don't let him know you're frightened. Remember your training.* She took a deep breath, disguising it somewhat by lifting her chin. *Let the breath out slowly. That's better.*

"What may I do for you, Mr. Pierce?"

"For starters, ya kin git inta the parlor, where we'll be more comfortable waitin' fer yer husband."

"My husband hasn't risen yet. Since you are so eager to speak with him, I'll waken him for you."

"Stop right there, Mrs. Knight."

She froze with her hand on the swinging door. Had that brushing sound been a gun being withdrawn from its holster? Why, why had she removed the pocket with her derringer earlier in the evening? She forced herself to turn about and swallowed her heart which had settled in her throat. Rasmus had a pistol leveled at her.

Zeke is in the carriage house, she encouraged herself. *Surely he'll rise soon, and realize something is amiss.*

"I thought you wanted to speak with my husband?"

"It'll be easier ta do when he gits home. Ya see, I know he went out last night and hasn't come back."

"But. . ."

"I told ya on the train thet I have eyes and ears ever'where. If yer expectin' thet man out back ta help ya, ya kin quit yer waitin'. He's tied up pretty as a present."

Obviously no help would be forthcoming from that quarter. At least Zeke was still alive, or Rasmus wouldn't have bothered to tie him up. But there was still Justin, somewhere out in the night.

He moved past her to push open the swinging door with his back. "Lead the way ta the parlor."

She walked slowly down the hall, her heels clipping softly on the marble floor, trying to portray a calmness entirely lacking inside her. If only the children would remain sleeping until—until what? *Please, God, protect them!*

She touched a wall button when she entered the parlor, filling the room with brilliant light from the chandelier. Perhaps when Justin returned, he would see Rasmus through the window.

"Douse thet light, pronto!"

"But, Mr. Pierce. . ."

He pushed her away from the wall and punched the switch. The lantern light seemed impossibly dim after the chandelier.

Would the semidarkness hide her movements long enough for her to subdue Rasmus? Only if she managed it before his eyes readjusted to the lantern light. Her knowledge of the room was to her advantage. Her mind cast about for a weapon. The fireplace tools? She started in that direction.

"Hold it. Set down in this here chair."

Disappointment threatened to overwhelm her as she lowered herself into the blue damask-covered rosewood ladies chair. It was nowhere near the fireplace. *Don't think as though you are already defeated,* she shook herself mentally. *Something else must be available. Remember, Pinkerton operatives must be ever ready to take advantage of the most trifling circumstances.*

Rasmus pulled the heavy drapes over the windows. "Don't want the mister seein' the light 'fore he gets inside."

Darkness enveloped her heart. He mustn't harm Justin!

He perched on the edge of the grandfather chair opposite her, setting the lantern on the marble-topped table beside him. "Ya try ta git away, and I'll hev ta hurt ya."

Her hand clutched at the neck of her white shirtwaist. "Get away? From one of the country's most dangerous criminals? You credit me with a great deal more courage than I have."

Had her high, squeaky voice fooled him? One of the things she'd learned from watching women on her cases was that their voices invariably rose with fear.

Even in the dim light she could see the grin splitting his beard. "One of the country's most dang'rous crim'nals, huh? I like thet."

He would, with his demented values, she thought.

Rasmus pulled a can of chewing tobacco from his coat pocket, pushed the top off with a dirty thumb. She could barely control a grimace as he stuffed a pinch in his cheek and grinned with stained teeth.

It seemed a decade before Justin's step sounded on the front verandah, though Constance knew from the brass and crystal clock on the mantle that only fifteen minutes had passed. The footfall sent fear and hope spiraling through her together.

Rasmus's derby dropped over the lantern. "Not a sound, Mrs."

The front door opened. A prayer for Justin's safety flew from her heart. Her fingernails cut into the palms of her hands. She forced them open, spreading her fingers along her purple and cream striped skirt. Took a deep breath. She must stay as relaxed as possible.

The sound of the door closing. Footsteps in the hallway. They stopped. Came nearer the parlor.

She opened her mouth to yell then suddenly shut her teeth hard in her lips. With Rasmus armed and expecting him, would her warning further endanger Justin?

"Constance?"

Should she answer his hesitant query?

"And company, Justin." Rasmus lifted the derby, accidentally brushing the box of snuff from the table to the carpet. Light flashed off the barrel of his pistol, which was aimed directly at the door.

"Come in and join us."

He looks awful, she thought when Justin entered. Pity fought with fear in her chest. A day's growth covered his chin. His eyes were black hollows from sleeplessness, his hair rumpled.

She could see his face turning as he searched the room, stopping when he recognized her.

"Have they harmed you, Constance?"

"No." She blinked back sudden tears at the repressed anger in his voice. She wished they could see each other better in the lantern light, so he would be more apt to believe her. "Mr. Pierce, now that my husband has returned, may we turn on the lights?"

He rose and hit the button.

The sudden light set spots dancing before her eyes.

"Set yerself down, Justin. No, a little further from the Mrs. Thet's the way," he approved as Justin lowered himself to the edge of the sofa.

Justin's gaze was searching her face as though to prove to himself she had truly not been harmed. Did he care so much? Did it mean he had forgiven her? She smiled slightly to reassure him.

His attention shifted to Rasmus. "What's this all about?"

"Heard ya have a proposition ta make me," Rasmus said around the tobacco forming a ball in his cheek.

Constance stifled a gasp. Where had Rasmus heard that? The announcement hadn't appeared in the newspaper yet.

Justin didn't show any surprise at Rasmus's knowledge. "That's right. A compromise."

Rasmus leaned back until the grandfather chair creaked and stood protesting on its back legs. "Let's hear it."

"A good deal of the money you stole from the express car was mine. Seventy thousand of the money you took from the bank was payroll for one of the local log mills."

"Read 'bout the payroll in the paper. Glad ta hear I did ya out of a might on the train, too." His shoulders shook in a chuckle.

Justin waited for his mirth to cease. "This is the proposition. You keep the money that belonged to me, and return the rest. In exchange, the bank, express company, and railroad will drop all charges against you and your men."

Rasmus's bark of a laugh cut off abruptly. The front legs of his chair dropped to the thick carpet with a soft thud. "Ya think yer the only ones lookin' fer us? Why, even the Mrs. here knows I'm one of the most dangerous men in the country. What do I care if'n charges are dropped fer a couple of measly strikes? Won't stop ever'one chasin' me."

"People in this area would stop, and they'd have a softer spot in their hearts for you. After all, until now, you've never been known to steal from your former neighbors and your parents' customers and friends."

"Friends! As if anyone gives my folks the time of day 'cept fer people curious 'bout me."

"That's not true!" Constance interrupted eagerly. "Your parents are well liked and respected. At least they were until you blew the express car."

"Oh yeah? An' what would a little lady like yerself know 'bout it?" With an oath, he jerked to his feet. "No more 'bout my folks from either of ya. I've listened to yer offer, Knight. Now ya listen ta mine. Those two little kids been livin' here, some of my pals took 'em out of here 'bout two hours ago."

"No!" The word exploded from Constance's lips, terror whipping through her. Justin bolted from the sofa.

"Stop right there, Knight!"

Justin stopped at the sight of the pistol leveled at him, the muscles in his cheeks working, hands clenched menacingly at his sides. "If you've harmed those youngsters. . ."

Was her face as pale as his beneath his stubble? It felt like it. She was hot and cold and lightheaded all at once. *"All things work together for good to them that love God,"* she reminded herself silently. Surely that promise is for children like Effie and Evan, also. It had to be!

Yellowed teeth showed in Rasmus's beard. "Didn't think we'd get 'em out of here without wakin' the Mrs. from her nap in the lib'ary. My men had jest started down the street with 'em when she found me in the kitchen."

This couldn't be happening. Was he bluffing? Perhaps the children were still in their beds.

"You mentioned an offer. What is it?" Fury filled Justin's words. His face was so rigid it was a wonder he could speak at all.

"Ya give me five thousand dollars, and I give ya back the kids."

Constance gasped.

Justin glanced at her and back to Rasmus. "I haven't the money. You've taken everything. My investments have been liquidated to pay for this house, or a portion of it."

The grin slithered across Rasmus's face again, broader than ever. His eyes glittered. "No kiddin'! I've made the great Justin Knight a poor man?"

"A tough man like you doesn't need to hide behind a couple of children, Rasmus."

"Nope. But I'm not ag'inst raisin' money on anythin' I can, kids included."

"I told you, I haven't any money."

Rasmus waved his free hand. "But there's all this. A fine house, horses, and carriages. Should be able to raise 'nough cash fer the kids. If not," his shoulders lifted the dark canvas jacket in a shrug, "I'll keep 'em for comp'ny fer Marian, leastwise 'til they git on my nerves."

"Think Marian would still agree to become your wife if she finds you stoop to stealing children?"

At Justin's sneering comment, all semblance of patience dropped from Rasmus's face. His voice sent white fear slithering along Constance's veins. "We wouldn't of taken the kids at all if'n ya'd kept yer word. Marian said ya told her 'bout yer weddin', an' she was breakin' our engagement. But she promised ta marry me, and she's goin' ta marry me."

"Planning to kidnap her, like you did the children?"

"No need ta, banker. She's already at my place."

"Not by her choice, I'm sure."

"It will be her choice, 'ventually."

"You're wrong, Rasmus. You can't force people to love you."

Didn't Justin know better than to goad him? Anger was turning the man's face purple.

"Don't need no sermons from you, Knight." He pointed the gun at Constance, setting her skin crawling. "You, git over here with me. Goin' ta be daylight soon, I got ta git ridin'. The Mrs. will be goin' long fer pertection. Spot anyone on our trail, she's dead." He frowned at Constance. "What ya waitin' fer? I said git over here."

She rose shakily to her feet. Slowly she began walking. She sunk her top teeth hard into her bottom lip. *Think, Constance! There has to be a way out. There always is, one only has to recognize it.*

Rasmus spat his tobacco wad out the side of his mouth unto the carpet. "Move it, woman!"

The tobacco!

With a swift, graceful move, she knelt to pick up the can of chewing tobacco that had been knocked to the floor. Thank the Lord not much had fallen from the can. Could Rasmus hear the exultant beating of her heart?

She held the can in her palm as she rose. "You dropped this." Her breath stopped. She'd only have one chance.

He snorted a laugh. "Quite a lady you married, Knight. Even polite when she's bein'. . ."

She tossed the tobacco directly into Rasmus's face.

Chapter 16

Rasmus clutched at his eyes with his free hand, swearing liberally.

"Git it off! It burns! Git it off!"

Justin lurched for the outlaw, knocking the pistol from his hand. It fired upon landing at her feet. Her courage nearly failed her as she felt the wind of the bullet whiz past her ear. A moment later she grabbed the gun and trained it on the struggling men.

"Sit down, Pierce!" She was amazed that her voice wasn't shaking like laundry in a windstorm.

Still swearing, Pierce dropped to the floor with tears streaming in rivulets through tobacco on his cheeks.

"There's some rope in the pantry." Justin disappeared and was back in a minute that seemed like a year.

She'd been taught to shoot a variety of firearms, but she wasn't accustomed to handling them for any period of time. Her wrists were protesting severely by the time Justin had Rasmus secured hand and foot.

"Where's Zeke?"

"Rasmus said he was tied up in the carriage house." She lowered the gun, but didn't put it down. One thing she had learned well through the years was not to trust any criminal, even those who appeared harmless.

She glanced quickly at Justin and back to Rasmus. "Do you think he was bluffing about the children? Could they still be in bed?"

He was out of the room before she finished speaking. His feet pounded up the stairs and down the upper hallway. They didn't pound on his way back down.

"Not there," was his terse statement when he re-entered the room.

Rasmus stubbornly refused to tell them where Marian and the children were being held. Constance was thankful for the years of experience as an agent that helped her keep her emotions from spinning out of control at worry for the children. She could only be a help to them if she kept calm.

Finally they gave up questioning Rasmus, and Justin rang up the sheriff.

While he used the telephone, Constance released Zeke, whose black and blue eye distinguished the effort he'd made against capture.

When they arrived back in the house, Justin was just hanging up the telephone, and she asked whether Sheriff Tucker would be coming for Rasmus.

"No. Zeke and I will be taking him to the jail house." He turned his attention to Zeke. "Bixby was with the sheriff when I rang up. The plan is for you to gather the agents in town. Some will stay with you and the deputies to guard the jail in case Rasmus's pals hear of his arrest and try to spring him. Bixby and I and the rest of the agents will form a posse and join Sheriff Tucker in searching outlying farmhouses and abandoned buildings once more. I'll be ready to go as soon as I change."

While Justin changed clothes, Constance changed, too, exchanging her purple and cream striped skirt and purple bolero vest for a blue serge divided skirt and matching Eton jacket, the better for horseback riding. The flap that disguised the trouserlike aspect of the skirt would also serve to hide the pocket carrying her derringer. She would not be caught without the weapon again.

She was waiting in the hallway when Justin came out of his bedchamber. He'd changed to a flannel shirt, corduroys, and boots, but hadn't taken time to shave.

"I'm going with you."

"Like fun, you are." He brushed past her.

She grabbed his flannel sleeve. "Effie and Evan are my niece and nephew, not yours. I'm the Pinkerton operative, not you. You have no right to keep me from joining you."

"I have the right of a husband, or perhaps you've forgotten." His eyes scorched her.

Her cheeks burned. "I've forgotten nothing. But I'll not sit here and knit while you look for the children."

His hands clasped her shoulders, crushing the pert pleated sleeves. "When I came home and found Rasmus here. . ." His voice cracked and he pressed his lips fervently to her temple. "Don't you know how thankful I am you weren't harmed or killed?"

The gravelly words whispered into her hair sent waves of hope through her.

He cleared his throat and pulled away far enough to look into her face. "It will be difficult enough keeping my mind clear of my fear for the children. I won't have the added distraction of your safety. Either you agree to stay here, or I shall lock you in your room."

"You wouldn't dare!"

"Wouldn't I?"

The challenge in his eyes and voice answered that question.

"Will you stay?" he demanded.

"What choice have you given me?"

Couldn't he understand that she didn't want to worry about his safety any more than he wanted to worry about hers? Why did men think the more valiant part of courage lay in fighting, and not in waiting and praying while your heart burned itself out in worry and fear and love? But how could she admit her fear for him when such an abyss of problems lay between them?

His grip loosened and his voice gentled. "Will you include me in your prayers while you wait? I've no doubt your heart has been sending forth prayers for the children since the moment we heard of their abduction, as has mine."

She blinked back the tears that suddenly threatened. "Of course."

He turned to go.

She clutched his sleeve. Her recent hope washed away when she saw his eyes. How could they be so cold and remote, after those words, after that kiss? They almost frightened her from asking, but she had to know. "Is—is there anything I can offer God that will make Him more likely to answer my prayers for Effie and Evan?"

"You mean, to make a bargain with Him?"

She nodded, her lips clamped hard in her teeth.

"No. We cannot bargain with God."

"Do you think God would allow something awful to happen to the twins because—because I wasn't forthcoming with you about my position with the Pinkerton agency?"

"No!" She cringed at the thundered word, and his face twisted. With a shuddering sigh, he cupped her cheek with one hand. "You mustn't torture yourself with such a thought. The Bible tells us God is love. Would love harm two little children for the purpose of punishing you?"

"I suppose not."

"Of course not. I don't know why He allows some of the hard things. I can't guarantee Effie's and Evan's safety. But their abduction is not God's way of punishing you."

"Thank you."

At her muffled whisper, he dropped his hand.

There was one more request she must make before he left. If anything happened to either of them. . .

"Please." She allowed all the yearning in her heart to fill the word.

He hesitated at the top of the stairs, his wary gaze locked with hers.

"Please forgive me for deceiving you."

His gaze didn't falter. He didn't blink. A muscle tightened in his cheek. "I already have. But forgiveness doesn't restore trust."

And then he was gone.

She stood transfixed, listening to his footsteps recede, not wanting to believe his words. Would her chest continue burning for the rest of her life?

Dashing tears from her lashes, she hurried downstairs. She must be about her plan. It was the children's safety that mattered, not her justly battered heart.

From the back door, she watched Justin mount his favorite riding horse, a huge black, and ride off to meet the posse. As soon as he was out of sight, she dashed to the barn and saddled a small roan.

She rode quickly down to Pierce's Store, securing the roan at the back of the building. She didn't want to chance identification of either herself or the horse if Justin came by with the posse.

As usual, Mrs. Pierce was alone in the store when Constance entered. There was no welcoming smile on her face, only the spine-chilling reservation of hope-lessness. Constance was certain she'd already heard of her son's arrest.

Mrs. Pierce stood silently, waiting for Constance to speak, the palms of her hands sliding idly up and down the blue cotton apron covering her hips. Constance resisted the impulse to take those hands in hers and quiet them. Strange, she almost felt guilty for having a part in the arrest of her son.

"I'm sorry, Mrs. Pierce."

The narrow, gray-topped head nodded once, slowly. The woman's eyes never left Constance's, but there was no accusation in them.

"They say he was arrested at your home. That you and your husband over-powered him."

"Yes."

"Well, it had to happen sometime. Seems I've been waitin' for it since he was a kid." Her chin trembled. "They're sayin' he stole your kids, Evan and that pretty little girl."

"Yes." Relief sighed in the admission. She'd been wondering how she was going to interrupt the woman's grief to introduce her own. Mrs. Pierce was the only one who could and would help them find the children, she was certain. There was little chance the posse would locate the hideout that had so long eluded local law enforcement and the Pinkertons.

"I'm that mortified over his takin' them that I can hardly think to work. What you must be goin' through, worryin' about them!"

"As a woman and mother, of course you must understand my concern."

The door to the back room closed with a soft thud, and they turned toward it. Mr. Meeker, wide-brimmed hat in his hands, was racing up the rickety stairs to the second floor.

Constance turned back. "I came for your assistance."

Iron-gray eyebrows peaked in surprise. "Help from me?"

"Yes." She lifted a quick prayer for guidance. "You have probably heard that a posse has been organized to find the children, and Marian Ames, whom your son is also having held against her will."

"Miss Marian?"

She couldn't let herself be sidetracked by the woman's apparent shock.

"If the posse locates your son's hideout, people on both sides of the law are apt to be hurt, possibly killed. That would only make things worse for Rasmus."

Why did the woman keep glancing at the back of the store? Constance wanted to shake her bony shoulders and make her pay attention. "Mrs. Pierce, I'm sure you don't wish the children's and Marian's lives endangered any more than I. Should they be harmed, Rasmus is certain to receive the harshest punish-ment. But if the men with whom he was associated can be taken peaceably, and the stolen money retrieved, perhaps the law will be more lenient."

Mrs. Pierce lowered herself slowly to the top of a barrel beside the counter, glanced again at the back of the store. Bony fingers fidgeted with the tiny black bow at the neck of her plain gray dress.

"Why come to me?"

"I think you know where your son has been staying."

The washed-out blue eyes swung back to observe her, but she didn't reply.

"I can understand that as his mother you couldn't betray his hiding place earlier. But he's behind bars now and there's nothing further to be gained for him by keeping his secret." Her voice had broken on that last sentence. My word, she wasn't going to break down and cry, was she? She couldn't afford to give in to such emotionalism now, of all times, when Effie and Evan's safety depended upon her!

Footsteps pounded down the stairs. Mr. Pierce was settling an old gray hat on his head. "I'm goin' with Meeker, Ma."

Mrs. Pierce started up from the barrel, her hands out pleadingly. "Pa, no. . . !"

"Don't know when I'll get back," was his only response before the two men left through the back entry.

Constance wouldn't have thought it possible that the woman's face could have grown grayer. What had happened that she hadn't seen? Two men leaving. . .could it be, was it possible that Mr. Meeker was connected with Rasmus's gang? But he'd only moved to the area recently! Still, stranger things had happened.

She grasped Mrs. Pierce's arm. "Where are they going?"

"I–I'm not certain."

"Please! You are the only one who can help Marian and the children!"

The woman stared at the door where she'd last seen her husband. After a few tense moments, she squared her thin shoulders beneath the gray dress. A strange peace softened the lines in her face.

"Rasmus's men are stayin' at Meeker's place."

"Thank you!" She darted for the door.

"Mrs. Knight!"

She looked over her shoulder, impatient at the interruption.

"I'll go with you. I know where his farm is. Besides, you'd have difficulty gettin' the men to listen to you. They know me."

Constance hurried back to take the woman's shoulders in her hands and smile into her old face. "If a mother's love can do anything to undo the sins of her children, your love is doing so today. Thank you."

"I'll have to get a horse at the livery."

"I'll ring Zeke at the jail house and tell him where we are going. I will meet you at the livery."

Zeke didn't care for her plans, but she didn't tell him where she was calling from. She knew she and Mrs. Pierce would be on their way before he could stop them.

Constance had difficulty keeping her fears at bay as she followed Mrs. Pierce. She tried to ignore the aching in her chest, tried to clear her mind of all the frightening possibilities. She had to keep her wits about her, as Alexander would say.

They didn't take the main road. Mrs. Pierce insisted the back road would be quicker with the horses.

"Likely we'll get there before Pa and Mr. Meeker. Meeker's wagon will slow them up a might. 'Sides, they won't want to arouse suspicions by travelin' fast."

Mrs. Pierce would make a good operative herself, Constance thought.

Along the way Mrs. Pierce told how Meeker had carried messages between Rasmus and his parents. Meeker and his bride had moved to the area a year ago, no one here had any reason to suspect he had ridden with Rasmus in Missouri. Meeker didn't want his bride to know of his criminal association, so when he married and purchased the farm, Rasmus and the others kept their distance. But when Meeker's wife returned to Missouri to care for her ailing mother at the same time Rasmus and his men needed a good local hideout, Meeker offered his farm.

The farmyard was quiet when they reached it. They rode straight into the yard with no attempt to hide and tied their horses to the porch rail.

One of Rasmus's men met them at the door. He was tall with a lean face, a shaggy mustache, and stubble at least two days old. The suspenders holding up his baggy corduroys slipped over the shoulders of his dirty, collarless shirt. He carried a rifle, but greeted Mrs. Pierce with a smile.

"Never 'spected to see you here, ma'am." The smile faded. "Guess you heard 'bout your boy."

"Yes, Tom."

"Don't you worry none. The boys are on their way to get him out a there."

"Why would they do a fool thing like that?"

"Ma'am?"

"Least in prison, I don't need to worry about his gettin' shot up."

"Now, ma'am, Rasmus ain't goin' to get shot. That one has the luck of the gods, he has."

"Hmph! Can see this discussion is goin' nowhere. And you can quit looking at this lady like she's an ice cream soda. She's married to Justin Knight."

Tom's mouth dropped open and snapped shut. "Mrs. Knight! Not the woman who married him on the train? The woman that. . ."

Constance nodded. "Yes, that woman."

"Well, Tom, where are Miss Ames and the two youngsters Rasmus had brought here?"

Tom glanced warily from Mrs. Pierce to Constance and back again. "Uh, I'm not sure Rasmus would like me sayin'."

"Don't be a fool. How would I know they were here if my son didn't tell me?" She stepped past him and started for a shut door. "Are they in the parlor here?"

"Well, yes'm, but. . ."

"Come along, Mrs. Knight."

They had barely stepped through the door when Effie threw herself against

Constance's skirt. "Aunt Conthtanthe! I knew you'd come!"

Evan was close behind. His fingers clutched her skirt and didn't let go, though his eyes met hers fearlessly. "We've been here a long time," he said accusingly.

Constance knelt to hug them both, trying hard to keep back the tears that threatened to form in her eyes and throat. "I know, dears. Say hello to Mrs. Pierce."

They didn't let go of her while they greeted the older woman. Constance used the time to glance about the room. It was furnished simply, with a braided wool rug in the midst of an astonishing variety of cheap furniture. Chromos of flowers and dogs and kittens hung against the cabbage-rose patterned wallpaper. Marian sat on the round stool in front of an ornate parlor organ, her eyes wide.

In one corner, a man sat in a chair upholstered in wine plush. A rifle stood against the wall beside him. A pistol pointed directly at Constance was propped casually on his corduroy covered knees. The sight of it set fright slithering like an eel down her throat and into her stomach. After all these years, she'd never grown accustomed to looking into the "business end of a pistol," as Alexander often stated it. And with the children in the room. . .

The man himself was the opposite of Tom. The dim light from the simple, two-shaded gas ceiling fixture gleamed softly off his bald head. His neat mustache seemed too small for his fat face. His red collarless shirt strained past the stomach falling over the top of his trousers.

Constance didn't like his eyes. They were beady and small and she hadn't seen them blink once since she entered the room. He was going to be far more difficult to reason with than Tom.

She felt Tom stop inches behind her. "Guess you know Mrs. Pierce, Gent. This here's Justin Knight's wife."

Gent! Gentleman Jake. She should have recognized him. Although his Bertillon card back in Chicago showed him dressed as a dandy. Her heart sank a little. He'd be even more difficult to convince than she'd originally thought.

He removed a fat cigar from his mouth. Keeping his eyes on Constance, he addressed Mrs. Pierce. "You know Rasmus wouldn't want you out here. 'Tisn't safe for a lady like yourself."

"Don't talk patronizin' to me, Gent. Guess I can be here if I want. When Rasmus takes to holdin' women and children against their will, it's time somebody steps in."

"Now, ma'am, don't get riled."

"I've come to take Miss Ames and the youngsters home."

"You know we can't let you do that, ma'am."

"I'm doin' it just the same."

With one quick move of his fat thumb, Gent cocked the pistol. Constance felt her eyes grow wide and the eel slipped down her throat again. She hugged the children closer.

Gent's words were terrifyingly unhurried. "No, ma'am, I'm afraid you're not."

Chapter 17

She would be reliving this scene in her mind's eye for the rest of her days, Constance thought. The pistol in Gent's flabby hand could wreck the lives of each person in that room.

"Hmpf!" Mrs. Pierce threw back her scrawny shoulders. "There isn't a man in this gang that would have the spunk to shoot me and face Rasmus."

Constance stared at her. She was magnificent! And very probably correct. The thought restored her hope and reason.

Behind her, Tom shifted from one foot to the other.

"What do you think, Gent? Should we let 'em go?"

"Now what do you think Rasmus would say when he gets back here if he found Miss Ames and the children gone? Use your head, Tom."

Mrs. Pierce propped her fists on her skinny hips. "Now you listen to me, Gent. It's my son in prison, and I'm not so sure as you are that he's goin' to get out anytime soon. I don't intend on his facin' the law for abductin' females and youngsters."

"Seems like that should be his choice, ma'am."

"Hogwash. I said I'm takin' these people with me, and I'm takin' them and that's that."

"Mrs. Pierce, I reckon you're right about me not shooting you," Gent drawled. "But I don't think Rasmus would mind if I played target practice with one of these kids, or Mrs. Knight."

Mrs. Pierce whirled around. "No way to sic the law on a person faster than hurtin' women and children."

Gent rolled his cigar around with his tongue. Shoved it to one corner of his mouth.

"I'm getting mighty tired of this discussion. Suppose you sit down somewhere and make yourself comfortable. Because I promise you, none of you are going anywhere."

His voice was too smooth, too devoid of emotion. It was now he'd be at his most dangerous, Constance thought, if her knowledge of people gained from similar situations was any barometer. She touched Mrs. Pierce's arm.

"Let's sit down on that sofa. Mr. Gent's patience seems to be wearing thin."

The older woman pressed her lips together until they almost disappeared, but she followed Constance to the sofa. The children tagged along, still clutching Constance's skirt.

Evan climbed up on Constance's lap, and Effie leaned against the blue serge divided skirt covering her knee. Why, the twins were still in their nightclothes, she realized with a start.

"The men are mean, Aunt Conthtanthe. I dropped Regina, and they wouldn't pick her up. And they pointed gunth at uth."

"But we remembered what Justin told us," Evan said, his brown eyes serious.

Constance smiled at him. "What was that, dear?"

"He told us we're stronger than mean men, because Jesus lives in our hearts, and He's stronger than mean men. Don't you remember?"

"Yes, dear, I remember now."

"We prayed for them, like Justin told us."

"But when we prayed and athked God to make him good, that fat man jutht got madder."

Constance gaze darted to Gent. Had the children prayed aloud for him and Tom and the others? No wonder he'd been angry. What is more infuriating than to hear a child point out your sins?

The wooden clock on the paisley, gold-fringed cloth covering the top of the organ showed an hour had passed before Marian crossed the room and sank to the floor beside Constance. Her sapphire and gold striped skirt spread around her in a sunburst of color, though its wrinkles bore evidence of days of wear.

"Have you been treated well?" Constance asked in a low voice.

Marian nodded. "No one laid a hand on me or the children. They just refuse to let us leave."

"Marian wath kind to uth."

Marian smiled slightly and laid a hand on Effie's head. "And Effie and Evan have been kind to me. They've reminded me of some important things today."

Effie leaned harder against Constance's knee and whispered loudly, "Don't you think Marian ith pretty?"

Lovely color tinged Marian's cheeks and jealousy stabbed through Constance. "Very pretty." Justin couldn't help but think so, also. Could a man who had been attracted to Marian's delicate, golden beauty ever find her own dark looks attractive? What did her looks matter? He didn't trust her. Could love exist without trust?

Constance shoved at the desolation threatening to overwhelm her. If she allowed herself to dwell in that emotional quicksand, she and the children might never leave here alive.

She urged Effie and Evan to sit with Mrs. Pierce for a few minutes.

"I think she could use some hugs." Besides, the closer they were to Mrs. Pierce, the safer they were. As the woman had said, Gent and Tom wouldn't want to chance hitting Rasmus's mother.

When the children had transferred their attention to the older woman, Constance turned back to Marian.

"Thank you for trying to comfort them today."

Marian shook her head. "They were braver than I." She took a deep breath.

"This is the third day I've been here. I've had a lot of time to think. I don't know how or when we might leave here, or even if we will, but there's some things I must say to you."

"To me?"

She nodded, lifting her delicate features a trifle higher. "I should never have become engaged to Justin. I've always liked him, and was flattered he asked me to marry him, but I wasn't in love with him."

"Please, you owe me no apology."

The blond woman shook her head vigorously. "I must tell you. Until Justin told me of his marriage to you, I thought my life was almost perfect. I was betrothed to the town's wealthiest bachelor, all my friends envied me, God seemed to be giving me everything I wanted, and demanding little in return. And then you and Justin married, and life became unbearable."

"I'm sorry."

Marian ignored her interruption. "I tried to hurt Justin by agreeing to marry Rasmus, but I only hurt myself. . .and them." She nodded at Effie and Evan, who were carrying on quite a conversation with Mrs. Pierce. "When I discovered the true reason for your marriage, I foolishly flung my knowledge in Rasmus's face. How could I have been so silly as to think a nineteen-year-old girl would be any match for a hardened criminal like Rasmus?"

Constance didn't know what to say. She laid a hand on Marian's shoulder, and the girl continued.

"Listening to the children ask God to forgive these men, I realized how much I've taken God for granted over the years. When I was Effie's and Evan's age, I trusted Him as they do. Anyway, shortly before you arrived, I asked God to forgive me for becoming so self-centered, and recommitted my life to Him."

Constance's heart gave a little leap. Another good thing that had come from her strange marriage to Justin!

"I'm so glad."

Marian clasped one of Constance's hands tight in her own. Blue eyes met green ones. "I don't know how you feel about Justin. I can't imagine being forced to marry as you were. But Justin is a good man. If you decide to stay with him, I hope you will be very happy, and never waste a moment feeling guilty about me."

Constance pressed the girl's fingers. "Thank you."

Marian flushed and pulled her hand away self-consciously. "Oh!" She reached back to touch Constance's wedding ring. "What a lovely band."

Embarrassment heated Constance's cheeks. "I've felt a hypocrite each time I looked at it. It should have been yours."

Marian's curls bounced as she shook her head. "That isn't the ring Justin bought for me. I know, because he asked me to accompany him to select my ring." She turned around and rested her head against the sofa.

Constance glanced at the simple band with the delicate orange blossom design. Had he truly selected it just for her? She touched her lips to it softly.

Thank You, Lord, her heart rejoiced.

Poor Marian. She might not love Justin, but she had endured a great deal because of Rasmus's love for her. The guilt that had hounded Constance since she first met Marian swept over her. In spite of Justin's love for truth and her own questions regarding the ethics of using deceit to obtain a "noble" end, she could forgive herself for deceiving criminals. But had her deceit hurt others, like Marian? She'd gone merrily on her way after each case was completed, not once looking back to see if her actions had brought harm or sorrow to the innocent.

Marian shifted her position and groaned. "We may never get out of this room."

Constance darted a glance at Tom, still leaning against the door to the hall, and then at Gent in the plush velvet chair. "You mustn't think in such a manner," she urged in a low voice. "Pray, and keep your eyes and ears open. Who knows what opportunities God may give us?"

Marian nodded, but Constance didn't see any hope in her tired, drawn face.

In spite of the few hours sleep she'd had the night before, Constance wasn't tired. She was too nervous and frightened to be tired.

Justin hadn't slept at all. Was he tired now, or was he as wide-eyed as she was? Where was he? Had the posse come across the men attempting to free Rasmus? Had Justin been caught in a gunfight? Her heart twisted at the thought of him, of his beautiful chestnut brown eyes, the rich low laugh she loved, his steady commitment to the Lord, the loving way he'd taken responsibility for the children, his loyalty to the townspeople in spite of the way they'd treated him after he married her.

Would she ever have a chance to tell him that she loved him? Would he care to have her love? Would she ever again feel the touch of his hand on her cheek, or his lips against hers?

Constance sat up a little straighter and folded her hands in her lap. She was going to do everything in her power to see him again!

"Excuse me, Tom."

He jerked his surprised gaze to her and stood straighter.

"What will happen if your friends are unable to free Rasmus, and are themselves apprehended?"

Gent snorted. "Sheriff Tucker couldn't catch a rat in a trap."

Constance gave him her sweetest smile. "I'm sure you know the man's abilities better than I. I've only been in River's Edge for a fortnight or so."

She turned her attention back to Tom, easily the most gullible of the two. Dividing the enemy would give her more advantage. She opened her eyes wider to give Tom her most innocent look. "But suppose, for the sake of argument, that your friends were apprehended. What if they told where you are staying? If the Sheriff found you and Gent here with the children and we three ladies, wouldn't you two be accused of abducting us, rather than Rasmus? Surely no one would believe that Rasmus had his own mother forcibly detained."

From the corner of her eye, she could see Gent hitch forward.

"Shut your mouth, woman!"

Tom shuffled his feet again. His lean face crumpled into a mass of furrows. "She makes sense to me, Gent. Mebbe we should let 'em leave."

"I'll do the thinking around here. Can't you tell she's goading us?"

"I don't know. Mebbe. . ."

"You in the house!"

The holler from outside brought instant stillness to the room.

"Justin!"

Constance didn't need Marian's whisper to know it had been Justin's voice. Lord, help us. Keep Justin and the children safe. Show us what to do.

Grunting, Gent pushed himself from the chair and crashed against the wall beside a window, trying to make his round body flat.

Tom slipped to another window.

Effie and Evan hurried back to Constance.

"That's Justin," Evan announced.

Constance nodded and put a finger to her lips.

"We know you're in there."

Justin again. Constance's heart started tripping at another level. God had at least kept him safe until now.

"There's a posse of twelve armed men out here, mostly Pinkerton agents. We don't want trouble. We just want the women and children released."

Tom's face was deathly pale against the cabbage roses on the wallpaper.

"Pinks, Gent!"

"Shut up." Gent swung the barrel of his pistol against the glass. Constance heard the tinkle of it falling.

"You want them?" Gent hollered, his fat chin wobbling. "You come get them!"

Chapter 18

Gent's holler reverberated through the room.

Constance slipped her hand into the pocket beneath the panel of her split skirt, grasped the pearl handle of her derringer. Her gaze was glued on Gent. She opened her mouth to tell the children to get down.

Gent poked his pistol barrel out the broken window and fired before she could speak.

She was vaguely aware of Marian dragging Evan to the floor. She reached for Effie, but was hindered by her pocket.

Horror held her motionless, her mouth went desert dry, watching Effie tear across the braided rug toward Gent in her linen nightshirt and bare feet, her curls flying.

A moment later Constance was on her feet, the derringer pulled from her pocket. But by then, Effie's fists were pummeling Gent's stomach, her high little voice screeching furiously. "Don't you dare shoot Juthtin! Don't you dare!"

Constance felt as though she was moving through molasses. Terror tumbled through her. Would she be able to stop Gent in time?

He turned with a bellow, pulled back his arm as though to strike the child with his pistol. He mustn't harm her!

A sound rang out. A vibration ran up her arm. The pistol dropped from Gent's hand and his bellow increased.

Had she fired the shot?

A loud thud came from behind her, but she didn't dare turn around. Gent was diving for his pistol, grasping for it with his good hand. If he reached it. . . Her derringer was no good, it only held one shot.

"Move away, Effie!" Her voice finally worked.

Effie ignored her and stomped her heel into Gent's injured hand. Howling, he forgot the weapon and huddled over his hand.

Constance shoved Effie out of the way, kicked Gent's pistol from his reach, and hurried to retrieve it. She swung around, pointing it at the groaning, swearing man. He glared at her with pain-glazed eyes.

She glanced around. Mrs. Pierce had Tom's rifle in her arms, pointed at Tom, who was lying on the floor. Had that been the thud she'd heard?

Evan was still with Marian on the floor beside the sofa. Effie was leaning against a chair, panting from her efforts.

Suddenly she recalled the men outside, that shouts and a smattering of shots had filled the background during the storm they'd been through in this room.

Had anyone outside been hurt by the one shot Gent had gotten off?

Careful to stay out of Gent's reach, she leaned close to the window and called, "Come into the parlor, gentlemen. We have some gifts for you."

❧

Constance watched the last of the posse leave, taking Tom and Gent with them. Mrs. Pierce accompanied them. Would she lean on God during this difficult time? Constance hoped so.

Resting her hand on the side of the organ, she surveyed the small room. What would Mrs. Meeker think when she returned from her mother's to find her husband in jail and her home the sight of a gunfight? She wished she could spare the woman the pain of her husband's betrayal.

Had Justin felt as betrayed when he found she was a Pinkerton operative? She'd almost hoped he was learning to love her, until he made that discovery. Would he ever let himself love her now?

He hadn't spoken to her since entering the room, but his eyes had slashed at her more sharply than knives ever could. Even now his back was turned to her, his anger dividing them more effectively than the space between them. The children were demanding all his attention, and he was squatting before them, listening to their eager tale. Even with Justin's resentment tearing her heart to ribbons, she was overwhelmingly grateful to the Lord for keeping him safe.

Alexander moved away from Marian and Mrs. Pierce toward Justin and the twins. "Aren't you two going to let old Uncle Alex in on your stories?"

They turned their attention to him eagerly. After a minute, Justin turned to face her. Anger still stood plain on his face, so hot she was certain it would melt her.

He came toward her slowly. She tried to tear her gaze from his, but it was as though they were cemented together. Her chest ached with her held breath. She would have retreated if she weren't already against the wall.

"I told you to stay at home." Fury cracked like a whip in his low voice. "When Zeke caught up with us after the attempt to free Rasmus was squelched and told us you were headed here with Mrs. Pierce. . ." Both hands plowed through his hair. "How could you have done such a foolish thing?"

Marian's beaming face was suddenly beside him. "What the man is trying to say, with a gentleman's usual finesse, is that he was terrified you would be harmed, and he doesn't know how to express his joy at your safety."

Justin's face flushed. "I said exactly what I meant."

Marian jerked at his arm with her dainty hands until he scowled at her.

"Justin Knight, you're a fool. You have no call to be so angry with Constance. You should be thanking God for such a courageous wife. Why, she married you, a stranger, and went to live with you in order to save your life and the children's. How did she know you were a gentleman? You could as easily have been a reprobate. Don't bother protesting, you could have been, for all she knew. And today she risked her life to save not only the children, but her husband's former fiancée and the mother of the man who forced her to marry a stranger. If you cannot appreciate what an extraordinary woman you've married, well, you don't deserve her."

"That's telling him," Alex called laughingly from across the room.

Justin glared at him. "I'd appreciate it if you two allowed my wife and I to work out our own affairs."

Constance's heart gave a little leap at his words. Did that mean that he wanted to work things out between them?

"Yes, sir," Marian said with exaggerated meekness. Her brow furrowed. "How did you know where to find us?"

Justin dug his hands into the pockets of his corduroys. "We found Effie's doll a couple miles down the road, just about the time Meeker and Mr. Pierce came by in Meeker's wagon. Didn't take a Pinkerton agent to figure out this was a likely place to look."

Effie swung about, eyes wide. "You found Regina?"

Justin nodded, his face softening. "She's in my saddlebag."

"Ooooh! Thank you!"

Evan's serious eyes looked up at him from beside Alex.

"Will you take us to Pirate's Cave, Justin?"

"Pirate's Cave?"

"You said you played there when you were little like us. Gent said Rasmus put loot there." The round face puckered into furrows of curiosity. "What's loot?"

"They must have stored the stolen money in the cave!"

Excitement snapped in Alex's eyes. "You know where this cave is located?"

"I could find it in my sleep. It's in the bluffs above the river between here and River's Edge."

Alex was on his feet instantly. "Then we can recover it on the way back to town."

It was all Constance and Marian could do to keep the children from joining the men in their search when they reached the bluffs where they'd picnicked their first Sunday in River's Edge. Constance's heart lodged in her throat while she watched the men descend the gray cliffs. But it wasn't long before they were back with bags and gunnysacks filled with money and bonds, which they piled in the bed of a wagon borrowed from Meeker's farm.

When they returned to town, they all went first to Justin's home. The group was barely off their horses and out of the wagon before Aunt Libby and Mrs. Kelly rushed across the lawn, followed by a short, stocky man in a brown checked suit, with round wire-rimmed glasses perched on his short nose, holding a pencil in one hand and a notebook in the other.

Justin's jaw dropped. "Benson! What are you doing here?"

The short man adjusted his glasses. "Sheriff Tucker said this was the best place to come for the complete story on Rasmus Pierce and his mob. Since I'm our paper's top reporter, here I am."

Justin rubbed a hand along his unshaven jaw. "Couldn't we do this another time? We'd all like to clean up."

"But the town's jumping to hear the facts. The editor's holding the presses for me."

Justin glanced at Constance. "Can you bear up a while longer?"

She nodded. Did he think speaking to a reporter was trying? It wouldn't weary her nearly so much as one more minute of wondering whether Justin would ever trust her again.

Aunt Libby and Mrs. Kelly paid no mind to the reporter. Assured everyone was safe, they took the children under their maternal wings, eager to bathe them and put them safely to bed. Effie launched into her version of their adventure before they'd taken two steps, and Evan broke in with additions and corrections repeatedly before the four were out of earshot.

Chuckling, Alex leaned back against the wagon. "Expect the story as Effie tells it would make a great dime novel."

To Constance's surprise, Justin joined in Alex's chuckle. The angry distance the men had kept between them had evaporated. *What could have happened to change their attitudes so quickly?* she wondered.

The reporter cleared his throat.

At the reminder, Justin lead the small group to the library.

How many scenes the friendly, booklined room had seen in its short existence, Constance thought, lowering herself into a leather chair. Marian and Alexander sat on the couch, Marian's dress a bright splash of blue and gold. The reporter, at Justin's invitation, sat at the desk, while Justin stood beside the fireplace, one arm on the mantle.

Benson pushed up his spectacles. "Let's have the entire story from the beginning."

Marian leaned forward eagerly, her blue eyes outshining the gold buttons on her short jacket. "It all began the day of the train robbery, when Rasmus forced Justin and Constance to marry two days before Justin and I were to wed."

Benson's jaw dangled. "Forced them?"

"Marian!"

"Marian!"

Marian just waved a hand to dismiss Constance and Justin.

Constance darted a glance at Justin. His face was dusky with anger and embarrassment.

Marian was continuing blithely, "I guess God arranged that marriage because He knew Justin and Constance were perfect for each other."

Constance kept her gaze glued to her hands, which were clasped tightly in her lap. Still, she knew when Justin moved from the fireplace to stand behind her chair. Awareness of his presence kept her from hearing much of Marian's story.

Justin, Constance, and Alex had little opportunity to tell their own parts in the story, but by the time Marian was through, Constance saw a blessing in Marian's version.

When the reporter finally left, Constance turned to her. "I don't know how to thank you for your generous act. Now the townspeople will know that Justin didn't purposely. . ." She struggled to find a delicate way to state the facts.

Marian grinned. "Leave me standing at the altar?"

Her directness startled Constance. "Uh, that he didn't purposely break your engagement. They'll know that you have forgiven him, and perhaps they will be able to forgive him, too."

Alexander took Marian's elbow. "Something tells me it's the proper time for us to leave. May I see you home, Miss Ames?"

His gaze caught Constance's for a moment. Was it pain she saw in his eyes? "Good-bye, Mrs. Knight." His voice was unexpectedly rough.

The house was incredibly still after they left. Large as it was, it seemed too small now that Aunt Libby and Mrs. Kelly were upstairs putting the children to bed, and Constance and Justin were left alone.

She watched from beneath half-lowered lashes as Justin returned to the fireplace. Unshaven, eyes set in smudges of sleeplessness, wearing his flannel shirt and corduroys, he looked like a stranger to her. Until his eyes met hers, eyes that had so often smiled into hers, had made her feel beautiful and cherished, and horribly guilty. Her gaze skittered away.

Justin picked up the brass poker and pushed idly at the unlit logs that lay always ready for the match.

"How did you talk Rasmus's mother into showing you the hideout?"

It was a moment before she comprehended his question; it was so far from the topic she expected.

"I—I think I realized what you have always known. Deceit only bears more evil in its wake. I want to follow the One who is 'the way, the truth and the life,' as you do. So I went to Mrs. Pierce with the truth, and hoped that a mother's love would do what was best for her son, and for Effie and Evan."

He put the poker down and crossed the room toward her, his hands buried in his trouser pockets.

Her breath came faster and shallower. He towered over her, dwarfing what little courage she had. She rose quickly. It would be easier to face him on her feet.

"What you said to Marian just now. . ." He struggled with the words. "Instead of being concerned for yourself, your thought was for me. Thank you."

Had Marian's attitude toward his marriage hurt him? Did he wish it was Marian he was married to now? She kept her gaze averted, afraid to see in his eyes the answer to the question she needed to ask.

"Are you still in love with Marian?"

He settled on the arm of the wing chair. "No. I'm ashamed to say I never loved her as a man should love the woman he marries. When I proposed to her,

I didn't know what it meant to love."

He caught her hands and drew her close, pressing his lips to her fingers. "Don't pull your hands away!" He folded them close to his chest. "Last night—was it only last night? It seems a lifetime ago—I was so hurt when I discovered you were an agent, that I didn't think I could ever trust you again.

"Then when Bixby and I went to retrieve the stolen money, he told me that I had been a suspect. That's when I knew everything Marian said about you tonight was true. And I realized what a fool I'd been, raging at what I saw as your deceit and lack of trust. You didn't even know me, it was possible I could be a criminal, yet you moved into my home to protect the children from Rasmus. The trust you gave me is. . .humbling."

"In my heart, I knew you weren't capable of anything so dishonorable as being a partner with Rasmus."

"I said awful things to you last night. It was my pain speaking, but that doesn't excuse me. Can you forgive me?"

She could feel his heart beating beneath the fingers he still held against his flannel-covered chest, and wondered at the knowledge that it beat as erratically as hers. She smiled as she repeated the words he said to her earlier.

"I already have."

He bent his head over her hands.

"I realize the Pinkerton Agency has accomplished much that is good. I admit I don't know how some criminals would ever be brought to justice without the use of deception, though I'd like to think there is a way. I should never have judged you so harshly." He took a deep, shaky breath. "Now that Rasmus has been apprehended, do you plan to return to Chicago and your position as a Pinkerton?"

Was the question as difficult for him as the roughness in his voice indicated?

"That depends. I'd like to fight injustice in the manner a man I know once suggested, by raising children to love our Lord. That is, if—if you want me." Her words quivered into a whisper.

"If I want you!" He dropped her hands to wrap her close in his arms. The ardor of his cry drove away her fears and left her lightheaded with joy and relief.

"Are you offering to stay with me because of your marriage vow?"

She nestled her cheek against the soft flannel covering his shoulder, away from his demanding, suddenly possessive eyes.

"I do believe the vows are meant to last forever. But even if I didn't, I should wish to stay." She dared a laughing glance at his face. "Even without the added inducement of the pony and cart Effie suggested."

"You may have any inducement it's within my power to give." His lips pressed against her neck, sending delightful shivers over her. "Mrs. Knight, I've been waiting a lifetime to hear my wife tell me she loves me. Must I wait longer?"

His husky confession compelled her gaze to his. Tears sprang to her eyes until she could no longer see the hunger in his. "I love you, Justi—"

His kiss smothered the words exultantly.

When he finally allowed her to catch her breath, it was to say unsteadily, "I'll spend the rest of our lives trying to show you how much I love you."

The promise was in his eyes as well as his words. It made her feel cherished.

"We didn't thay prayerth, yet."

Constance jerked away from Justin, spinning to face Effie in the same move. "Why aren't you with Aunt Libby and Mrs. Kelly?"

"They fell asleep," Evan offered.

"Yeth."

"Evan, what happened to your hair?"

Effie pulled herself onto the leather seat of a chair. "I cut it."

Evan nodded, mellow light beaming off the uneven, chopped brown hair. "I wanted it to look like Justin's."

Constance sighed, one hand clutching at the ribbon at her neck. "Oh, my."

Behind her, Justin chuckled. His arms slipped around her waist.

"Something tells me that raising these two will be every bit as challenging as apprehending criminals."

"And every bit as satisfying." She rested the back of her head against his shoulder, smiling at the adorable twins. Contentment slid over her heart. Her family. What a wonderful gift God had given her before she was even willing to acknowledge His existence.

Effie snuggled further into the leather chair.

"Shouldn't we thtart praying? We have lots of people on our litht, you know."

Sweet Surrender

Dedication

To my nephews and their wives,
Brian and Heather Olsen, Chad and Sheri Olsen, and Paul and Randi Olsen.
May your lives be filled with love.
And to Jody Kvanli Capehart, cousin, encourager, writer, friend,
and fellow "sneak-up" artist in our childhood days.

Chapter 1

Alexander Bixby's dress boots clipped against the wooden boardwalk at a sharp, brisk pace, as his heart uncharacteristically pumped faster than his feet. His nails dug into his palms. In a couple of minutes he would be face-to-face with Justin Knight, the man who had married the only woman Alex had ever loved.

He forced his hands to relax, the fists to open, his arms to swing in their normal relaxed fashion at his sides.

After spending months in the bustling metropolis of Chicago, to Alex, River's Edge seemed not only small, but minuscule. The smells of the Mississippi River and the smoke and pine from the sawmills beside it, which gave the town its life, permeated the air. Women and girls who were almost women passed him on the boardwalk. Their walking outfits were nice but not as fashionable as those he saw on Chicago's streets. Boys and girls darted in and out among the adult pedestrians, calling and laughing to each other in the universal manner of children. The horse-drawn trolley car rumbled and swayed past, its bell clanging. The haunting, husky whistle from a steamboat joined with the trolley bell, imitating the music of a town band.

In the distance, Alex heard the train whistle blow as it left town to wind north along the river. His scowl deepened. He wished he'd never arrived on it, or at the very least, was leaving on it now.

Soon he'd see Constance again, be staying in her home with her and Justin. "Lousy thing to ask of any man," he muttered, "that he stay with the woman he loved and her husband." He'd told his Pinkerton superintendent so in no uncertain terms. For the first time in his career, he'd been tempted to disregard an order. Or turn down the entire assignment.

He forced the fists at his sides open again. Unclenched his jaw. *My emotional involvement with Constance and Justin is already affecting my actions on this case,* he told himself, furious. No Pinkerton agent could afford the luxury of allowing his emotions to show. Criminals were often as effective as Pinkertons at reading the telltale signs of body actions.

How could Superintendent Jakes expect him to stay under the same roof with his former almost-fiancée and her husband? His mind swung back to the topic as surely as a compass needle swung north. After months of boring it into his mind, he'd almost convinced himself he'd never been in love with Constance, that what he'd felt for her was warm friendship and regard and nothing—or little—else, and then Jakes ordered him on this assignment. Well, now he'd find out whether he'd been right about his feelings for Constance.

"Something I'd as soon never have to discover," he grumbled through his mustache, turning the corner beside the two-story brick bank building to face unexpectedly bright sunlight. He squinted against its brightness, suddenly blinded.

Something thin and smooth wrapped itself about his legs and yanked.

"What the. . .oof!" A grunt was jolted out of him as he landed with a resounding thump in an indelicate position on the boardwalk. He reached instinctively for the small weapon he always carried.

"Uncle Alex!"

"Uncle Alex!"

His hand stopped on the gun handle. He peered from beneath the brim of his trim gray bowler at the two small bodies charging his way. Relief made his muscles feel as if they were melting. He released the weapon just in time to catch the seven-year-old brunette twins in his arms.

"Aunt Constance said you were coming today!"

"Did you bring us anything?"

"Yes, what did you bring us?"

"Did you catch those old bank robbers you were chasin'?"

"Whoa! Give me a chance to catch my breath and take a good look at you." Alex pushed the girl and boy far enough from his chest to frown playfully into their broad faces, which were covered with freckles and sported snub noses and huge brown eyes. The boy was dressed like a proper banker's son in a belted brown suit with a wide, white cape shirt collar framing his face, and knickers buckled below his knees. Alex would have bet a month's salary—if he were a betting man—that the boy was wishing he could wear long pants like older boys. His brown hair curled in a perfect pageboy, like a knight of old, with thick bangs ending in the middle of his forehead.

The girl's hair was the same rich brunette, but its waves hung far below her dress's lace-trimmed shoulders above leg-o'-mutton sleeves. It was Alex's guess she wanted to dress like a boy as strongly as her brother wanted long pants.

He grinned at both of them. "Yep, I guess you're Effie and Evan, all right."

Four rows of tiny pearl-white teeth gleamed. Effie put a small hand on his gray broadcloth vest and shoved. "Of course we are, silly!"

The tugging on his legs resumed, and he realized it was from the leather lead of a small, white, noisy tornado of a dog. The creature was straining to touch its pink tongue to Alex's face.

Behind the dog, the hem of a woman's white linen skirt waved in the breeze. Alex caught a groan in his throat before it could escape. Fallen in a heap like a schoolboy, and right in front of Constance. Not the way I planned our meeting, he thought. Hope the assignment starts off better than my personal life.

He kicked himself mentally when he realized he was excited at seeing

Constance again, even in his present position. He lifted his eyebrows and smiled. "At your feet as always, beautiful."

His gaze lifted to her face. "You're not Constance!" Disappointment dashed the hope his heart had known for a brief instant. Embarrassment immediately swamped the disappointment.

The woman behind the dog had laughing gray eyes beneath a fringe of the heaviest, longest lashes he'd ever seen. Brown hair touched with gold poufed above her head in the new pompadour style, topped by a wide-brimmed hat of rose chiffon and silk flowers. Was it the hat that gave her complexion that lovely glow? Perhaps it was the laughter that tinged her face so beautifully.

"Indeed, I am not Constance. Even so, I rather like having dashing young men at my feet."

Surprise at her bold retort darted through him. He searched her eyes, but saw nothing but laughing innocence reflected in their depths. Nothing there of the militant 1890s female. "I, uh, I thought you were—"

"Mrs. Constance Knight. I believe we've settled the fact that I am not Mrs. Knight." She knelt down swiftly but gracefully to begin dislodging the dog's lead from his legs.

Her action brought him to his senses immediately. She was trying valiantly to succeed with her task without touching his legs in an unladylike manner, but it was an almost impossible challenge.

"I'll do it." He took the lead from her gloved hands, unwound the lead and handed it back to her.

She stood, pulling the little dog back to stand reluctantly beside her. Laughter still filled her eyes. He felt it drawing an embarrassed smile from him. He became aware of other passersby, who studied him with quizzical expressions and snickers. His embarrassment grew, and his smile faded.

Alex allowed the children to each take a hand and pull him up. He dusted his clothes off quickly while the woman apologized for her dog. "The sun blinded me when I stepped out of the bank, and he just got away from me, I'm afraid."

"That's quite all right, Miss—"

The little girl swung his hand with both of hers, eager for his attention. "That's Miss Amanda. She lives next door to us. We were walkin' her and Thunder to the bank."

"Thunder?" Surely she didn't mean that snippet of fur. It couldn't weigh more than twelve pounds soaking wet.

"Thunder is my dog," the woman replied.

Alex thought irrelevantly that a man would walk across a hundred miles of desert to hear a voice as lovely as hers.

"You are Uncle Alex, I presume?"

"Uh, right." He dragged the gray bowler from his head with his free hand. "Pleased to make your acquaintance, Miss Amanda. . ."

"Miss Mason," she supplied when he hesitated.

He nodded. "Mason." He studied her eyes until she lowered those ridiculously long lashes over her eyes to hide them from him.

"Uncle Alex." Evan tugged at Alex's sleeve for attention.

"Yes, Evan?" Alex gently released his jacket sleeve from the boy's long fingers. If the kids kept this up, one sleeve would be longer than the other before he arrived at their house.

"Are you coming to our house now?" Evan asked.

"Not right away. I have to stop here at the bank and see. . .Justin. I'll come home with him after the bank closes." *What did Evan and Effie call Justin? Their stepfather? Their father? Uncle Justin? Mr. Knight? Just Justin?* Alex realized he didn't know whether Constance and Justin had formally adopted Constance's dead brother's children. But then, he wasn't truly their Uncle Alex, either. He'd been a good friend of their father, and they'd called him Uncle Alex as long as he could remember.

"But that won't be for hours," Effie wailed.

"Yes, hours," Evan repeated.

"Now, Effie, Evan," Miss Mason said in a soothing voice, "it won't be that long. It's already almost three o'clock. Oof!" She lurched forward as Thunder threw all his weight toward Alex once more.

Alex took the leather lead from her. Thunder jumped up against Alex's leg, wiggling so fast and furiously that Alex wondered the dog didn't fall down. While Amanda regained her composure, tugging gently at the sides of her skirt, Alex handed the lead to Evan. "You're the man in the group. I think you'd best handle this wild beast."

Pride straightened Evan's young back as he took the lead, giggling at Alex's exaggerated reference to the dog's size.

"Are you here in River's Edge lookin' for criminals, Uncle Alex?" Effie asked eagerly, her brown eyes huge with hope. "Can Evan and me help?"

"Yes, can we?" Evan echoed. "We've been practicing detectiving."

Alex laughed, shaking his head. Out of the corner of his eye, he could see curiosity fill Amanda's pretty face. Wouldn't do to let these two know about his assignment here. "I'm here to visit you two and Justin and Constance."

"Shucks!" Evan kicked a small stone off the boardwalk into the dirt street.

Disappointment almost dripped from Effie's round face. "We want to be detectives."

Alex patted her lace-covered shoulder. "You've plenty of time for that when you grow up." He wouldn't be a bit surprised if feisty Effie did turn out to be a Pinkerton agent when she was a woman. He put on a sad frown of his own. "Won't you let me stay with you even if I'm not 'detectiving'?"

Amanda gasped, then slid a small, gloved hand over her mouth. Above it, her eyes danced.

Effie and Evan didn't notice. "Yes, you can stay with us," Effie ungraciously agreed.

"Good." Alex knelt in front of her. "Then can I have a hug?"

The abandon with which she threw her arms about his neck and hugged him tightly heated his eyes with unexpected and unshed tears. He returned her hug, patting her back, and clearing his throat. When she pulled back with a smile, he winked at her. Then held out his hand to Evan, who shook it with all the manliness a seven-year-old boy could muster.

"Take good care of Thunder."

"Yes, sir, Uncle Alex."

Alex nodded at Miss Amanda Mason. "Pleased to meet you, Miss Mason."

Her eyes twinkled. "Thank you, Detective Alex."

He darted her a shocked look. Then realization dawned. "I'm sorry. I forgot to introduce myself properly. I'm Alexander Bixby."

She wrinkled her dainty nose. "I find Detective Alex far more intriguing. I find mystery men almost as fascinating as men who fall at my feet." Turning, she glanced over her shoulder at him with a smile that showed she was laughing at him rather than out-and-out flirting. "Come, children. Constance will be wondering what happened to us."

The children obediently turned to accompany her, waving. "Good-bye!" Evan called.

"Good-bye, Detective Alex!" Effie called.

Alex stared after them, then burst out in a laugh. Little Effie had thought the term as amusing as Miss Mason. He watched them cross the street, pausing for a passing delivery wagon emblazoned in bright red with EDWARDS' MEAT MARKET. Shaking his head, he swung his bowler hat around on the tip of his index finger. Miss Amanda Mason was an endearing combination of ladylike manner, innocence, and coquet. His lips stretched in a grin. Found Detective Alex intriguing, did she? Well, Detective Alex found her intriguing, too, in a schoolgirlish sort of way. After knowing Constance Ward. . .*it's Constance Knight, now,* he reminded himself. . .such a lighthearted female wasn't for him. Lighthearted and light-headed to boot, most likely. He'd loved Constance's serene manner. She'd been an intelligent Pinkerton operative, and he'd admired her wisdom. No one could be more different in personality from the love of his life than Miss Amanda Mason.

His smile died when he turned back toward the two-story brick bank building with its tall, deep-set windows. The large doors loomed in front of him like the doors to a black future. Might as well go inside for his meeting with Justin Knight, president of the bank, and the man who'd married Constance. He took a deep breath, squared his shoulders, and pushed open the heavy door.

Chapter 2

Alex stopped inside the door, his gaze sweeping the bank. Looked like almost every other bank he'd been inside, and he'd been inside a lot of them on assignments. The marble floor gleamed in the light of the ornate gasoliers that hung from the ceiling, and magnified every step and word of the young, red-haired clerk, the middle-aged woman he was assisting, and the young man in a suit and derby pacing back and forth behind her. The shining brass-wire lattice rose from dark walnut and separated the clerk from the customers.

Everything looked shiny and bright and new. Alex recalled the bank had been rebuilt after Rasmus Pierce and his cronies blew up the vault and most of the building in a robbery. That had been almost a year ago. It was the assignment to capture Rasmus Pierce that had brought Constance and Alex to River's Edge, and Constance into Justin's life. Rasmus was behind bars now, and Constance was Justin's wife.

Alex took his place behind the pacing man. His experience as an operative had taught him to hide his true emotions well. He clasped his hands behind his back, bobbing his derby up and down, and glanced about in a casually curious manner. He felt his shoulders tighten and tautness ride up his neck. He pressed down his shoulders, hiding the tension he felt at the coming meeting with Constance's husband.

The woman customer left, and the young man in front of him stopped pacing, leaned against the fat brass bar edging the walnut counter, and asked to make a deposit. Alex moved a couple of feet forward. A door behind the teller windows squeaked open, and Justin's firm but cheerful voice clanged against Alex's eardrums like a church bell. Other men's voices responded.

Tension leaped back through Alex's body at the sound of Justin's voice. His jaw clenched. He made himself release it. Was that the way he was going to react during the entire assignment, that angry response to Constance's husband?

Through the leaded windows guarding the area of bank business from customers, Alex could see Justin moving confidently beside two portly, white-haired men who appeared to be in their fifties. The three filed through the door in the walnut base. Justin's step hesitated only slightly when his gaze met Alex's. Alex nodded toward him, and Justin returned the gesture.

Alex watched Justin walk the men toward the door. He's every inch the reserved, competent banker who earns his customers' confidence, Alex thought, watching him take his leave of the men and turn back toward him.

Alex took his hand and they shared a firm handshake. "Justin."

"Alex. It's good to see you. Have you been by the house yet?"

Have you seen Constance yet, he means, Alex thought, noting the guarded look in Justin's brown eyes, a look that betrayed his friendly tone. "No, I thought it best to meet you here." No sense discussing the case in the middle of the bank's public area. No telling who the counterfeiters were. Even that fresh-faced, redheaded clerk could be in on it, or that nervous young man who'd just made a deposit, or that middle-aged woman who'd left a couple minutes before, or the prosperous-looking businessmen Justin had just ushered out the door, or the lovely Miss Amanda Mason, or—well, maybe not her. He couldn't imagine her a counterfeiter or any other kind of thief. Her face revealed her emotions too easily.

Justin waved a hand toward the door leading behind the teller windows. "Why don't you join me in my office?" He led the way. Alex noticed a barely curious look from the clerk. Did he notice everyone who went into Justin's office? He should, but perhaps he was only curious because he didn't recognize Alex as one of the townspeople.

A large mahogany desk was in the middle of the room, a tall wooden chair behind it, and two smaller chairs in front. The wall behind the desk was lined with mahogany bookshelves, leather-bound volumes filling them and giving the room warmth with their brown, red, and black bindings. A comfortable yet functional room.

Justin perched on the edge of the wide desk and waved Alex toward a chair. "Thanks for agreeing to come."

"I was assigned the case." Alex lowered himself into the hard chair, suddenly and uncomfortably aware of the dog hair on his suit, and his wrinkled slacks where the dog's lead had bound him. He was sweaty and a bit sooty from his train travel, and who knew what his backside looked like after falling on the boardwalk—thanks to Thunder again. His clothing didn't compare well to Justin's well-pressed, well-cut suit and vest with its gold watch chain.

"Didn't Supervisor Jakes tell you Constance and I asked for you on the case?"

Alex was as surprised as Justin sounded. "No." He wasn't sure he appreciated their interference in the assignment. Anger ribboned through him. They might have asked him first if he'd be willing to come, to stay in their home, before speaking to Jakes. Didn't Constance know it would be painful for him? It wasn't like her to be so insensitive.

Hope slipped into his chest. Maybe she misses me. He pushed the thought away immediately. She was married to Justin. Both he and Constance believed in the sanctity of marriage vows. If she'd missed him, she would never admit it to him or the world; probably not even to herself. In fact, he was pretty certain if she missed him, she would have asked Jakes not to assign him the case. He forced his attention back to Justin.

"We thought you would be the best person for the assignment," Justin was explaining. "You already know the territory. People know you're a Pinkerton operative, but they also know you're our friend."

Our friend? Alex liked Justin and respected him, but it was a bit too much to call him a friend. Maybe if he hadn't married Constance—time to derail that train of thought. He was here on business. "It's a small town," he said. "It won't take long for people to figure out why I'm here. Can't question people without starting gossip."

"At least you'll have a head start. The counterfeiters have to be stopped."

Alex nodded. "Jakes told me a little about the case. Suppose you tell me what you know about it."

Justin crossed his ankles and linked his fingers together. "Constance will probably want to tell you her version. Being a former Pinkerton agent, she may think of important things to tell you that I won't think of."

Alex nodded again, more sharply this time. Actually, it would be good if Constance was working on the case, but he knew Justin wouldn't allow it. He didn't approve of the deceit inherent in their work, and naturally didn't want his wife exposed to danger.

Constance had been a mighty sharp operative before she'd married Justin. Living here, she'd likely picked up on things she wasn't even aware of yet. He knew from experience that sometimes clues lay hidden in an operative's brain until other aspects of a case made them pop up like a sunken log in a river.

He listened attentively while Justin told him how the counterfeit bills had turned up only occasionally at first, not enough of them to create suspicion. The bills weren't recognized as counterfeit until they showed up at one of the county's banks, including this one. Local businessmen turned them in with cash collections from numerous customers. The bills' denominations were low enough that the businessmen couldn't recall which of their customers had used them to pay for their goods and services, and most of the customers had been people the businessmen had known all their lives, anyway, and trusted. The local sheriff thought they were stray bills that found their way into locals' hands.

Alex rested one elbow on the chair arm, played the tip of his index finger over his mustache, and nodded. "The sheriff made the normal conclusion, and the usual mistake. Counterfeiters often introduce the bills slowly to the community at first, to soften suspicion before they begin dumping the bills in large quantities."

It was Justin's turn to nod. "That's what happened. One week there was an unusually large amount. The sheriff started then to try to track down the source, but he had no success. He wants to talk to you tomorrow about the facts of the case."

"Of course. I want to talk to him, too."

Justin pulled the gold watch out of his vest pocket, stood, and grinned. "I'll be in the doghouse with Constance if I don't get you to the house early enough to say hello before dinner. We're having company for dinner tonight. Sorry to put you to work right away, but we've invited some people I think you're going to want to meet concerning the case: the bank's lawyer, Lance Chase and his wife, and the former owner of a local sawmill, Thomas Mason, and his daughter. Some of the counterfeit money turned up in the sawmill's payroll."

Alex shook his head. "Spread rapidly from there, I assume."

"That it did. You can ask him about it yourself at dinner tonight."

"Do your guests know why I'm in town?"

"No. Like everyone else, we've only told them you are visiting, taking a break from work." He stood up. "Let's pick up your luggage at the depot and head toward home."

Following Justin through the tall, thick door into the sunshine, Alex glanced down at his wrinkled, furry, dirty traveling suit and cringed. This wasn't quite how he'd imagined looking when he saw Constance. His heart felt almost as worn and weary as his clothes looked.

Justin hailed a colorful, horse-drawn trolley that was swinging down the street, its bell ringing cheerfully. The driver braked, and the men climbed on. Justin dropped a nickel for each of them in the driver's tin box and headed for a seat.

Alex sat down across from him, crossing his arms and thinking it felt as if he were headed to his own funeral. Weariness from the train trip from Chicago didn't make his mood any lighter. Still, he'd run all the way back to that city, starting now, if his sense of duty would allow it. He'd committed himself to this assignment, and he prided himself on keeping his promises, even if it meant his heart burned in his chest the entire time from his proximity to Constance.

He swayed with the trolley's rhythm. The horse-drawn trolley wasn't as smooth as the electric trolleys in Chicago, but he'd ridden lots of the less modern trolleys on assignments outside the city, and adapted to its rocking easily. If only he could adapt as well to the thought of staying at Constance and Justin's home.

"Hope you're hungry."

Alex opened his eyes to see Justin grinning at him across the narrow aisle.

"Mrs. Kelly has quite a feast planned for this evening," Justin continued.

Alex forced a smile. "I don't doubt that." He remembered Justin's middle-aged, round, Irish cook's mouthwatering meals. She always made plenty, too, so a man didn't fear walking away from her table hungry. He wasn't hungry now. If he were a betting man, which he wasn't, he'd bet a month's salary that the meal would taste like sawdust. How could a man eat seated at a table with the woman he loved and the man she'd chosen to marry over him?

His stomach burned at the thought of it. It was going to be one miserable evening.

≈≈≈

Amanda laughed, watching Thunder race Effie and Evan up the front steps and across the wide veranda at Justin and Constance Knight's home. The rambling Victorian mansion's friendly demeanor made it the perfect home for children, she thought. Grunting, they pulled open one of the heavy wooden doors with its oval, etched-glass window. Thunder tore inside, trailing his lead, followed by the twins.

"Aunt Constance! Aunt Constance!" Effie's eager voice floated back to Amanda as she entered the house.

"Aunt Constance, we're home!" called Evan in his softer, yet just as eager, tones.

Amanda followed them down the wide hallway, her heels clicking lightly on the black-and-white marble floor. She tilted her head back to look at the ceiling, two stories above. She could never walk through the entryway without admiring the fresco of cherubs and clouds against a robin's-egg blue sky.

She followed Effie's high, excited voice to the kitchen, entering through the swinging door. The wonderful aroma of browned meat met her as Mrs. Kelly lifted a cast-iron Dutch oven from the top of the gleaming woodburning stove and bent her ample frame to place the roast in the oven. At the counter beside the cast-iron sink, Constance was arranging ferns and cut lilies in a tall crystal vase. The flowers' heavy fragrance was noticeable even over the roast. At the same time her aunt listened with amusement to Effie's tale of Thunder tripping Uncle Alex.

"And he's going to be here for dinner," Effie rushed on, "he promised. Can we please have dinner with you and your guests tonight?" She clasped her hands in a prayerlike manner, held them out toward Constance, and squeezed her face into a dramatic plea. "Ple–e–ease."

Amanda pressed the gloved fingers of one hand to her lips and swallowed hard to prevent the laugh gurgling up inside her. She saw Mrs. Kelly's red cheeks pushed into balls by her grin.

Constance's gentle smile grew larger than usual, but she didn't laugh. She cupped the girl's round cheek in one slender hand. "You may."

"Whee!" Effie whirled around and grabbed Evan's hands. Together they danced in a circle, chanting, "We get to eat with the big people. We get to eat with the big people."

"However," Constance continued when they'd quieted down, "when the meal is over and it's time for the adults to visit alone, you are to go right to bed, with no displays of temper."

"Yes, Aunt Constance," Effie assured without hesitation.

"We will, Aunt Constance," Evan agreed.

Effie swung toward Evan. "Let's go to the stable and play with our pony and cart."

They started toward the door.

"Not so fast." Constance's gentle command stopped them. They peered at her with raised eyebrows, questioning. "You may go visit your pony, but don't ride him or attach him to the cart. You'll need to clean up and change clothes before the guests arrive, and I don't want either of you to need a complete scrubbing."

Effie's face fell. "Come on, Evan, let's try to find something clean to do."

Evan called to Thunder, and the three of them hurried from the house.

Constance shook her head, still smiling, and stuck another lily into the vase. "Effie lives every moment as if it's the most exciting of her life and drags Evan along."

Amanda rested her gloved hands on the marble-covered counter beside Constance. "You love the excitement with which Effie faces life, as much as you do the careful way Evan views it. You wouldn't change a thing about either of them, given the power."

"You're right. I do love them as they are. Still, I worry sometimes that Effie's act-first-think-later manner will get both of them in trouble one day."

Amanda watched while Constance completed the arrangement. Constance managed to make the flowers look as though they'd simply fallen into the delightful and balanced bouquet.

Constance is like the flowers, Amanda thought, serene and perfectly balanced. Wherever she is, she brings peace, even with Effie around. Nothing flusters her. Amanda admired Constance more than any other woman she knew. Although Amanda always thought of herself and whirlwind Effie as kindred spirits, she and Constance had become fast friends since Constance had married Justin and moved in next door to Amanda and her widowed father.

They were as unalike in looks as in personality. Constance's thick black hair was worn at the back of her head in a simple but elegant twist that suited her perfectly. Amanda's golden brown hair, which she always thought looked pale and drab beside Constance's, was in the latest style, pinned right on top of her head, with a hair rat giving a soft, poufed effect about her face, so the style didn't appear severe.

"Thank you for taking the children downtown with you, Amanda. Mrs. Kelly and I have had so much to do preparing for the dinner tonight. We've been able to accomplish much more than we would otherwise, without worrying what mischief Effie and Evan were creating."

"I love spending time with them," Amanda said honestly. "I like the way they enjoy life."

"They are certainly excited about Alexander's visit."

Amanda had been hoping Constance would bring up the subject of the handsome Pinkerton detective, so she wouldn't have to be so obvious as to bring it up herself. She gave her attention to slowly pulling off one glove. "Yes, they were all over the poor man in front of the bank."

Constance chuckled, a low, sweet sound. Her green eyes danced. "They and Thunder, from what they told me. Poor Alexander, brought to his knees by a tiny mound of fur, and in such a public place. He must have been mortified."

Amanda grinned at the memory. "He was more than a little embarrassed. Is this the same man you worked alongside so often as a Pinkerton detective?"

"Mr. Pinkerton preferred the word operative. He felt the word detective left an impression of unscrupulous men in the profession," she reminded Amanda.

"You are correct, though, Alexander and I did work together often. Didn't you meet him when he was in River's Edge on the case that brought me here?"

"No, I was in Minneapolis at typewriting school." The town had been full of talk about the case when Amanda returned from her typewriting course. Constance had been sent to River's Edge to gather information about the thief, Rasmus Pierce, who'd grown up in the town. When Rasmus had forced Constance into marriage with Justin, Alexander had been sent to help on the case. In the end, Rasmus had been apprehended, and Constance and Justin discovered they were in love and that marriage suited them well. Amanda thought it terribly romantic. Nothing so exciting had ever happened in her own life. She sighed deeply. "To think I had to be in Minneapolis during the most exciting time River's Edge has ever known."

Constance led the way to the parlor, the crystal vase in her hands. "The most excitement during that time was caused by Rasmus kidnapping Effie and Evan. I can do without that kind of excitement again, thank you."

"Don't you find it difficult, being a housewife, after being a detective. . .I mean, operative?"

Constance set the vase upon a marble-topped, elegantly carved rosewood table in the middle of the room, then stepped back to view the effect. "I enjoyed the years I spent with the Pinkerton Agency, but the joy I find as Justin's wife and raising Effie and Evan make my life as a Pinkerton look drab."

Amanda couldn't imagine feeling that way. Secret identities, disguises, following dangerous men and women, all sounded like wonderful adventures to her. Alexander's dark good looks slipped into her mind, and a smile slipped over her face. She remembered his first comment to her, when he thought she was Constance: "At your feet as always, beautiful." Had there been more between them than a working relationship? Constance had never indicated so, and she was certainly in love with her husband now.

"It must have been interesting working with an operative as good looking as Mr. Bixby."

"Alexander?" Constance looked up in surprise. "I guess he is rather nice-looking, isn't he?"

"Rather," Amanda agreed, dryly.

Constance didn't seem to notice her sarcastic tone. "He is a very good operative. We did have great fun solving cases together."

"Mmmm. I would think so."

This time Constance didn't miss her inflection. Her green eyes widened with shock. "Amanda!"

"Truly, Constance, don't you think it would be more fun to work as a detective, I mean, operative, with an exciting, fine-looking man like Alexander Bixby than to do. . ." she couldn't think of a fair comparison. She flapped her gloves about and frowned. "Well, than to do almost anything with almost any of the men in this town?"

Constance laughed. "Amanda Mason, you had best watch your tongue, or your reputation as a fine Christian young lady will be decidedly smirched."

Amanda wasn't worried. She knew enough not to speak so indiscreetly around anyone but Constance. Constance never carried tales or gossiped. It was one of the nice things about their friendship, the complete trust they had in each other.

At least her suspicion that Constance and Alexander Bixby had been more than friends and fellow detectives appeared incorrect. Constance certainly didn't act like a woman recalling a past love when Alexander's name was mentioned.

She fingered the delicate lace at the edge of one linen sleeve. "Alexander Bixby has to be more interesting than any of the other men in River's Edge."

She already had an image of the man beneath that handsome exterior, thanks to Constance's stories of their work together, an image of a man whose character was built of courage, intelligence, and respect for justice.

"Besides, a woman could do worse than a Pinkerton man. At least she would know his morals are above reproach. You've told me yourself that Pinkerton operatives must not have an addiction to drink, smoking, card playing, or low dives, and must not use slang." Amanda counted the items off on her slender fingers as she listed them.

"That's true. Alexander definitely has the high morals required by his employer. He's a fine man. But. . ."

"He's not married, is he?" Amanda jumped in at Constance's hesitation.

"No."

"Is he engaged?"

"I hardly think so, though I haven't seen him since the trial of Rasmus Pierce, four months ago."

"Surely if he'd become engaged to be married since then, he would have told you so when he responded to the invitation you and Justin sent, don't you think?" Amanda's heartbeat quickened with hope and anticipation.

"Invitation?"

"That is why he's in town, isn't it, because you and Justin invited him to visit you?" She almost stomped her foot in impatience. What was the matter with Constance this afternoon? She was normally very sensible and sharp-witted, but today she was acting more addlepated than Amanda had ever seen her.

Rare, dull red color infused Constance's cheeks. "Yes, of course he is here at our invitation."

Amanda shook her head and pulled on her gloves. "I'd best be leaving and allow you to continue preparing for your dinner party. Obviously your mind is on the preparations, and not on your guests, or at least not on Alexander Bixby." She flashed her friend a teasing smile.

Constance wrinkled her nose in return. "I am looking forward to visiting with all of our guests this evening, including you and your father. You are welcome to stay a few minutes longer. Mrs. Kelly has things well in hand, as always."

"You may not need the time to prepare for your dinner party, but I do. I plan to look my most appealing tonight for the intriguing Mr. Bixby."

"You are impossible, Amanda."

Her affectionate tone told Amanda that the comment was made in warm friendship. Amanda wiggled her gloved fingers in a wave of farewell, and left, already imagining the look on Alexander Bixby's face when she returned tonight in her most fashionable gown. Constance might not find Alexander a distracting man with whom to work, but Amanda had definite plans to be distracting for him this evening.

Chapter 3

Alex stood in front of the long mirror that hung over the low walnut chest in the guest room, and surveyed himself.

Not too bad, he admitted, tugging at his steel-gray suit jacket. A major improvement over the traveling suit he'd arrived in.

He still hadn't seen Constance. She'd been out when he and Justin arrived at the house.

"Buying more fresh flowers," Mrs. Kelly told them. One glance at Alex's mussed outfit brought a look of horror to Mrs. Kelly's round face. "Mercy!" There was a hired girl helping her today, because of the dinner. Mrs. Kelly wasted no time ordering Alex to give the hired girl a clean suit from his traveling case so she could press it for him. Mrs. Kelly also sent warm water to his room. He'd gratefully cleaned himself up, using the porcelain bowl on the walnut washstand and the fresh towels that hung on the stand's narrow brass towel racks.

He leaned forward and straightened the wide, blue and gray striped ascot at his throat. Amazing what a little water and clean clothes could do for a man's courage when it came to a woman. Courage? He snorted, shaking his head. "You're a Pinkerton man. Ever known a Pink to be afraid of a woman who wasn't packing a gun?"

Constance isn't just any woman; she used to be a Pinkerton operative, too, his thoughts reminded him.

He groaned and walked out of the room.

Odors of the evening meal met him, and his stomach growled, in spite of his assurance to it that the oyster stew and roast beef he smelled would taste like sawdust from the guest's sawmill.

He came down the wide curving stairway and through the tall mahogany posts at the bottom, his senses tight, watching and listening for Constance. She wasn't in the wide, elegant hallway. Nor was she in the parlor. His gaze swept the elegant room. Pale gold wallpaper was topped by a wide, hand-painted frieze of blue and gold. Dark blue fabric window cornices topped soft golden draperies over a large bay window. Below them stood a long, graceful rosewood sofa covered in blue damask. Matching blue damask wing chairs sat opposite the fireplace. A red Persian rug covered the floor and softened his footsteps. Fragrance from a vase of lilies filled the room.

Resentment pushed into his chest. Justin Knight had certainly had a great deal more to offer Constance of the world's goods than he, a mere detective, had had to offer. Instantly he felt ashamed of his thought. Constance was not the

135

kind of woman who would marry a man because of his financial status. He probably knew her better than anyone after the years they'd spent working alongside each other. There didn't exist a woman with higher values or a truer heart. Why couldn't he swallow his pride and admit to himself she had simply preferred Justin Knight to himself?

"Alex! It appears you managed to ready yourself before any of my family."

Alex turned to see Justin entering the room. As they shook hands, Justin said, "Constance and I were helping Effie and Evan dress, too. Thought we'd never have everyone ready."

The happily possessive tone in his voice cut into Alex's heart. He was glad the thud of the brass door knocker took Justin away to greet his guests.

Half an hour later, seated at the huge mahogany table in the elegant dining room, Effie smiled up at him with a cat-who-stole-the-cream smile. "I asked Aunt Constance to let me sit beside you, Uncle Alex."

Her pleasure at his company warmed his heart. He gave her a wink that made her giggle. "I'm glad you asked. I don't mind sitting next to the prettiest girl in the room."

She sat up straighter and threw her seven-year-old shoulders back. "This is my best dress."

"Mighty becoming." He took time to actually look at the misty gray silk dress trimmed with deep purple velvet. The sleeves above the elbows were huge, and a ruffle around the neck added to the femininity of the garment. He noticed it hung loosely from the shoulders to hem, and expected the freedom of movement was one of the reasons tomboyish Effie liked the dress so well. "Haven't seen a more fashionable garment this side of Chicago, or in Chicago, for that matter."

Effie beamed. "Thank you." She set her lips in a prim smile, and carefully reached for her crystal water goblet.

He was glad the girl had asked to sit beside him. He genuinely enjoyed her company, but also, she was a buffer between him and Constance, who sat at the end of the table on Effie's right.

He chanced a glance at Constance, who was listening attentively to Lance Chase, the bank's lawyer, who sat at her right. He and Constance hadn't had a time alone to say hello. The guests had arrived and were still in the hall when Constance had come downstairs with Effie and Evan.

Was that a blessing or not? he wondered. *Would we have been more uncomfortable if we'd spent our first moments alone? What would I have said differently? What would she have said differently?*

Nothing, he finally admitted to himself.

Nothing. In spite of the shock of seeing her condition. From her form, gently rounded, it was obvious she was expecting a child.

Her condition hadn't made her any less beautiful! The flowing, dark green silk top she wore brought out the intense green of her eyes. Serenity still sat about her like a calm forest mist. The all-too-familiar twist of pain turned in his heart at the knowledge he had lost all chance of a life with her.

He looked away. The pain was too intense. At least his training in disciplining the outward manifestations of his emotions served him now.

His gaze shifted to the lawyer, who was still conversing with Constance. He supposed Lance Chase would call this conversing, though to Alex it appeared a rather one-sided conversation. The lawyer was explaining the legal effect of bankruptcy to her, in answer to a question she'd politely asked. From his tone, Alex surmised Lance Chase thought Constance's intelligence not quite up to understanding such important matters. Alex's opinion of the man immediately dropped to several degrees below intelligent. Constance was one of the brightest people—not only women—he knew, and any intelligent man would have recognized her intelligence quickly.

The lawyer leaned against the high chair back, hooked his thumbs in the pockets of his gray and black striped vest, and continued entertaining himself with his little speech. Beneath his thinning reddish-blond hair, his facial expression showed that naturally, this was a topic he understood backward and forward, in spite of his audience's inability to comprehend it. Alex swallowed a snort of disgust, and turned to the young woman seated on his left.

He'd been pleasantly surprised to see Amanda Mason among the guests this evening. He hadn't made the connection when Justin had told him that a former sawmill owner, Mr. Mason, and his daughter would be joining them.

He smiled at her, and was answered with an instant smile of her own. He was surprised at the trickle of pleasure it sent through him. *Guess my male heart's been yearning for a few smiles from a woman,* he thought.

Miss Amanda Mason was a woman any man would want a smile from. In her purple gown with darker purple trim—petunia, he remembered Constance calling the color when she commented on Amanda's gown earlier—she was lovely as a sunset. He liked the way lace over velvet circled her slender throat, but he didn't understand why women agreed to wear dresses with shoulders that were so wide an eagle's wingspan would barely compete with them.

"Didn't Effie say you live next door, Miss Mason? I can't believe that I don't recall meeting you when I was last in River's Edge." He saw in her eyes her pleasure at his compliment. "Perhaps you and your father moved in recently?"

"No, Uncle Alex." Her eyes laughed at him from beneath her lashes. "We've lived there for years."

Her use of Effie and Evan's title for him touched that fun place inside him, and he grinned. He hadn't laughed with a woman for a long time. His assignments had kept him too busy to seek out women's company for pleasure, and after Constance's marriage to Justin, his wounded heart and pride had killed his desire to do so.

Effie poked Alexander's arm, and he turned to her, lifting his eyebrows. "Yes, Effie?"

"Do you know what we're going to have for dessert?" she asked eagerly.

"No, what?"

"Angel food cake with whipped cream and strawberries!"

"Angel food cake, no kidding? Must have been named for you." He bit back a chuckle when she giggled and actually blushed.

"It's my favorite," she admitted. "We had it for our birthday party last month, too. Evan's and my party. We're twins."

"Yes, I know."

She smoothed the skirt of her dress with the palms of her hands. "I thought you might have forgotten. Some people do, you know, because Evan's a boy and I'm a girl. Some of the other kids at school don't even believe me when I tell them we're twins."

"I believe you," Alex said in a respectfully serious voice. Then he winked. "I knew you when you were babies in diapers."

Her brown eyes grew wide with embarrassment. "Uncle Alex!"

He leaned close to whisper in her ear. "Shouldn't I have said the word diapers at a dinner party? Maybe I should have asked you for a lesson in dinner-party manners this afternoon."

She giggled up at him, her embarrassment forgotten, delighting in the fun attention of an adult.

A drift of pleasant lavender scent floated past him. Miss Amanda Mason was leaning close, looking past him at Effie. "You look lovely tonight, Effie. Isn't that the dress you wore for your birthday party?"

Effie nodded, smoothing the skirt once again, a pleased smile dimpling her cheeks. "Yes, thank you, Amanda." She looked up at Alex. "Amanda's birthday was last month, too. She's twenty. When is your birthday, Uncle Alex?"

"Very soon, on August fourteenth."

"How old will you be?"

"Twenty-six." He wondered whether Amanda minded Effie announcing her age to an almost stranger. Likely she was too young to worry yet over the world knowing how old she was.

Constance claimed Effie's attention, and Amanda started up the conversation with Alex where they'd left off before Effie told him about the dessert.

"I was in Minneapolis the last time you were here," Amanda continued. "I remember how shocked I was to return home and find Justin married to Constance."

He tried not to grimace at the reminder. "Yes, I was surprised at the marriage, too. I knew Constance and her brother, Effie and Evan's father, in Chicago."

"Yes, Constance told me." She glanced down at her lap, then back up at him with a smile.

He wondered what exactly Constance had told her. Had she told her about them working together for the Pinkerton Agency? Or that he'd proposed to her? He knew Constance wouldn't have given away confidential information.

If Constance were any other woman, he'd be sure she'd told about his marriage proposal. Most women couldn't seem to keep such news to themselves, even when they didn't want to marry the man.

Amanda gave an exaggerated but feminine sigh. "I was especially disappointed upon returning from Minneapolis to find not one, but two Pinkerton detectives had been in the house next door. I couldn't believe I'd missed the most exciting period in little River's Edge's history! Kidnappers, bank robbers, train robbers. Goodness!"

"Well—" The admiration shining from her eyes made him lose his train of thought.

"Yes, Mr. Bixby." Lance Chase's voice drew Alex's attention away from the sweet gray eyes that were gazing at him with such flattering interest. "I understand you are with the Pinkerton Agency."

"Yes." Displeasure tightened Alex's stomach. He seldom told people his profession, but after the case he and Constance had solved in River's Edge last year, it had become common knowledge in the area. It hadn't seemed important then. He hadn't expected to be back in this small town, and what could it matter if the people here knew his profession?

The lawyer drew thin fingers along his thin lips. "Are you here on business?"

Alexander smiled and leaned back, hoping his pose was giving the relaxed impression he intended. "Just visiting. I haven't had a break from assignments since I was last in River's Edge. Nice to have a chance to relax and visit friends."

He could sense Justin tensing at his statement, and remembered how badly Justin hated deceit. Well, it couldn't be helped. Sometimes little lies were necessary when ferreting out criminals. Justin might not agree, but Justin was a banker, not a Pinkerton.

From across the table, Amanda's father beamed at him. "River's Edge is a nice little community. You couldn't have chosen a better place to get away from the tensions of the city."

"Just what I was thinking earlier today," Alex agreed. Mr. Mason seems sincere and open. Doesn't look like he has anything to hide. His detective senses were operating as always, he realized, trying to analyze everyone around him and their responses to every situation. Even when he wasn't on a case, he found himself doing this.

He glanced at Amanda, who was staring at him with curiosity large in her gray eyes, her chin resting on her fingers.

"What a disappointment," she said with an attractive little pout to her lips that teased a smile from him. "I was hoping your presence meant more excitement for River's Edge, since I missed out on it all the last time you were here."

"If you replace the word excitement with danger," he responded gently but with a fatherly warning underneath, "your observation of my last visit will be more accurate."

He noticed Evan, seated on the other side of Amanda, squirm on the tall dining room chair. The boy's brown eyes were as big as his now empty dessert plate. Alex swallowed an exclamation of disgust with himself. *How could I have spoken so carelessly?* he berated himself silently. *How could I have forgotten how frightened Evan was when Rasmus Pierce put a gun to the boy's head and kidnapped him and Effie?*

Constance rose with her usual grace, and said in her soft voice, "I believe it's time for Effie and Evan to get dressed for bed."

"Oh, no!" Effie jerked up straight. Her pained expression accused Constance of a complete lack of justice. "Please, Aunt Constance, can't we stay longer? We've been good."

Alex heard a muffled sound from the other side of him, and he knew Amanda was stifling a laugh at Effie's dramatic expression and plea. His glance caught Amanda's, and they shared a smile.

"You've been very good," Constance agreed with Effie, "but it's already later than your usual bedtime. Say good night to our guests."

"But, Aunt Constance—" Effie began.

"Please, can we stay longer?" Evan pleaded.

"You heard your aunt." Justin's voice held just enough of a touch of fatherly sternness for the children to realize there was to be no more arguing.

With pouts on their round faces, Effie and Evan did as they were told. Alex's heart twinged with a mixture of gladness and regret when Effie threw her arms around his neck and hugged him as hard as she could.

Constance led the children out into the hall. In a minute she was back.

"Aren't you going to help them change and listen to their prayers?" Justin asked.

"They assured me they don't need my assistance." Constance seated herself. "I told them we'd both be up later to hear their prayers, Justin."

The smile she and Justin shared slammed through Alex's chest, and the realization of their love for each other hit him in a new way.

They share not only their marriage vows, he discerned, and their attraction to each other, but love, and a sharing of daily events, and the responsibility and joy of raising Effie and Evan. His gaze slipped to Constance's rounded form. Soon they would be raising their own child together. Constance wasn't only part of a couple that didn't include him, she was part of a family now.

His sense of honor held with the commandment that a man did not covet another man's wife. He'd tried to live by that code since Constance married Justin, and failed miserably. The failure shamed him, even though he didn't think anyone else knew of it, and even though he had no intention of trying to win her away from Justin. Seeing Constance as part of a family deepened his shame and made him more determined than ever to find a way to turn his heart from Constance.

It would have been a lot easier if he hadn't been assigned to this case!

Lance Chase cleared his throat. "I thought perhaps you were here about the counterfeiters, Mr. Bixby."

Alex studied him a moment. Had his eyes narrowed, just the slightest bit? He noticed the comment had drawn the attention of all the others at the table. It was as if everyone was holding their breath, wondering what he would reply. Evidently his assurance that he was here only on a visit had not been convincing. He forced a friendly smile. "Counterfeiters?"

Chase set his elbows on the table, linked his fingers together and leaned slightly forward. "Yes. We've been having some problem with them in this county lately. Isn't that so, Justin?"

A frown creased Justin's forehead. "Yes, it is."

Alex waved a hand slightly in dismissal of the issue. "I'm sure the local law enforcement is handling it."

"Not so well," Chase accused.

"We can't expect Sheriff Tucker and the marshall to solve the case immediately." Irritation edged Justin's voice. "They are competent law officers. I'm sure they will solve the case in time, as Alex has said."

"I'm sure that's true," Constance agreed.

Alex wondered if Justin and Constance felt their statements were close to untruths. If so, he knew they were mighty uncomfortable about now.

Chase shrugged his skinny shoulders. "It wouldn't hurt to get some expert advice, would it?"

"Well, I was hoping to relax a bit here in River's Edge," Alex tried to turn away Chase's insistence. "Get away from the business of detecting for a while."

"But this wouldn't take much of your time," Chase insisted. "I'm the bank's attorney, and—"

"Yes, I know," Alex said sharply. The man didn't know how to take a straightforward no, let alone a hint!

"Justin," the attorney continued, "I think it would be a good idea if you talked this business over with Bixby. Maybe he'll see something Sheriff Tucker and Marshall Fisk have missed."

Alex could see the anger in Justin's face, but true to form, he kept it under control when answering his dinner guest. "I'm sure if the sheriff and marshall want to speak with a representative from the Pinkerton Agency, they will contact the agency themselves."

Of course, Alex had every intention of speaking with the local officers, and Justin knew it, but they hadn't planned to advertise the fact Alex was on the case.

Chase glared at Justin. "We owe the bank's customers a duty, Justin."

Justin pressed his lips together firmly. Alex could almost hear him counting ten and in addition saying a prayer for patience, too. "You are right, of course," he finally replied. "Alex, I'll fill you in on the details later. Of course, there are likely many facts of which I'm not aware. The local law enforcement doesn't normally take me into its confidence." He flashed an indignant look at Chase, then turned back to Alex. "I'd consider it a personal favor if you'd share any insights or suggestions you may have with Sheriff Tucker."

"Glad to do anything I can for you, Justin." Alex hoped Chase caught his inflection on the word you.

"You might want to talk with Mason here, too." The lawyer jerked his thumb toward Amanda's father.

"Me?" Mr. Mason's round face turned redder than the Persian rug on the floor. He stared at Chase as if the attorney had lost his mind.

Likely he's embarrassed to be dragged into the discussion by Chase's poor manners, Alex thought.

"Yes, you."

Alex wondered whether Chase lost cases from treating everyone as if they were less intelligent than himself. Did he treat judges and juries this way?

The crass man was continuing. "After all, Mason, some of the counterfeit money did turn up in the payroll of your former sawmill."

Amanda leaned forward slightly. "I believe former is the important word in your statement, Mr. Chase."

The ice in her words sent a shiver through Alex. Surely even Chase couldn't be immune to the anger in the beautiful young woman's voice! No wonder she was angered. Chase almost made it sound as if he suspected one of her father's former employees at the sawmill to be a counterfeiter or accomplice. *It very well could be so,* Alex surmised, *but then, it could be almost anyone in the town or even county.*

"Yes, well. . .ahem." Mason patted his full lips with his linen napkin. Alex thought the man seemed to be casting about for a way to smooth his daughter's anger and the lawyer's faux pas. "It's all right, Amanda. Lance is quite possibly correct. I doubt I can personally shed any light on the counterfeit bills, but it may very well be wise to ask Mr. Bixby to speak with our accountant about that payroll." He glanced at Alex. "Would you consider it, as a favor to me?"

The request stunned Alex for a moment. He hadn't expected Mason to go along with Lance's pushy suggestion. Still, he wasn't about to turn down the opportunity. Never knew when or where an important clue would show up in an investigation. He'd seen providence, or God, or something step in too often when least expected to pass by any chance to learn more about the situation.

Alex shrugged one shoulder, smiled, and lifted one hand slightly. "As a favor to a friend of the Knights, I'll be glad to speak to the man."

"I will happy to pay for your services, of course." Mason looked surer of himself again.

"That won't be necessary. I don't mind giving up a few hours of my visit here if it will relieve your mind, Mr. Mason."

Mason sighed, obviously relieved. "That's mighty good of you."

"Perhaps you'll give me a tour of the sawmill. I've never been inside one."

Chase bounced a skinny fist lightly off the table, making his crystal water goblet wobble. "See, Justin? I knew Bixby wouldn't mind helping out."

Justin's face darkened. Alex expected the wealthy young banker wasn't accustomed to being spoken to in such a manner. He doubted Justin appreciated it, even though the lawyer had played right into their hands in giving them an opportunity to look into the counterfeiting situation without letting the town know the banker had officially asked for the Pinkerton Agency's help.

"No sense letting expert help go to waste," Chase continued, hooking a thumb in his vest pocket again. "Besides, I'm sure Bixby here is glad to have a chance to get involved. Professional curiosity, you know."

"I do appreciate your willingness to give some of your time to the case, Alex." Justin's voice held the hard edge of tightly controlled anger. "I have to admit, the case has me concerned. Counterfeiters have broken the economy of entire communities. I wouldn't want that to happen here, to my neighbors and the people who trust our bank to watch out for their financial investments and safety."

"Glad to do it. I—"

"OOF!" The swinging door from the hallway opened suddenly into the room. Effie's hands slid down the door, and she fell on her face.

Constance gasped. "Effie!"

"Are you hurt?" Justin demanded to know at the same time.

Alex leaped up, pushing back his chair in the same movement, but Justin and Constance were already crossing the room to the little girl.

Before Justin and Constance reached her, Effie had pushed herself to her knees. She brushed furiously at the front of her dress.

Evan was peering around the doorjamb, eyes wide.

Effie looked over her shoulder at him. "I told you to quit pushing!"

Evan bit his bottom lip, but didn't reply.

With his hands on her upper arms, Justin gently helped Effie stand up. "Are you all right?"

Effie nodded, her eyes snapping with anger.

Constance, kneeling beside the girl, lifted the hem of Effie's dress slightly. "You've torn a hole in your stocking."

The anger drained from Effie's face. Relieved she wasn't hurt, Alex watched her anger be replaced with the sudden realization that she was going to be in trouble in a minute for being in the wrong place at the wrong time. He bit a corner of his mustache, remembering moments just like this from his own childhood.

"Why aren't you and Evan in your bedclothes, and in bed?" Constance asked in the way-too-patient tone every child knows means big trouble.

Effie's face crumbled into a pained expression. She grabbed the knee of the leg with the torn stocking. "I think I hurt my knee."

Amanda seemed to choke. Alex glanced at her, and saw she was stifling a laugh at the girl's convincing whine. She glanced his way, and he winked, sharing in her mirth.

"You were playing detective again, weren't you?" Constance asked sternly.

Detective? What does she mean? Alex wondered.

Evan looked down at his shoes. Effie only wrinkled her face into an even more pained expression. "My knee really hurts, Aunt Constance."

Constance stood, and took each child by the hand. She smiled over her shoulder at the guests still seated at the table. "I'll be down in a few minutes."

The children went with her docilely, not even saying another good night to the guests.

Too embarrassed at being caught in a blunder, Alex guessed.

"Aren't they funny?" Amanda said in a low tone, her eyes still filled with laughter. "I'm glad Constance didn't continue questioning them in front of us, though. It's difficult enough being caught in something you shouldn't be doing when you're that age, without being reprimanded in front of others, don't you think?"

"I do." Alex vividly remembered scenes from his own childhood where the punishment wasn't nearly as punishing as the embarrassment of being publicly chastised. "What did Constance mean, when she accused them of playing detective?"

"They like to sneak up on people, hide, and listen to what they are saying. Justin and Constance discourage it, of course. No amount of explaining has convinced the children that eavesdropping is not proper or kind." Her eyes twinkled at him. "Effie insists she must practice so she can be a detective like you when she grows up, Uncle Alex."

"The girl certainly has the courage for the work." He grinned at the fun that sparkled in her face. Miss Amanda Mason was completely different from quiet, reserved Constance. Amanda wore her emotions on her face and in her eyes with no attempt to hide them from the world. She laughed a lot. He liked that about her.

Escorting her into the parlor for after-dinner coffee, he smiled down at her while she chattered away about her afternoon with the children. *It might be pleasant to spend time in Miss Amanda's company while I'm in River's Edge,* he thought. A woman as lovely to look at and as lighthearted as Amanda Mason might prove helpful in protecting my heart from Constance.

Chapter 4

Smells of coffee, hotcakes, and sausage led Alex to the kitchen the next morning. He discovered Justin had already left for the bank, and Effie and Evan for school. Mrs. Kelly set a place for him in the dining room. Constance joined him with a cup of coffee, having eaten earlier with her family.

He was more nervous than he'd been when assigned to his first case. Now that he was finally alone with her, what did he say? What did any decent man say to the woman he loved, when she was married to someone else, and carrying her husband's child? He cast about for small talk.

"Superintendent Jakes and everyone else at the Chicago office asked me to greet you for them, Constance."

"How sweet! Be sure to give them my regards."

"You're missed there, by everyone." *Especially by me.*

"I think of the people we worked with often. How have you been, Alex?"

"Fine. Had a couple of interesting assignments since we saw each other last." He poked absently at the stack of hotcakes. "I guess you and Justin are going to have a baby." Heat spread up his neck and over his cheeks. It wasn't considered proper to mention the baby, he knew, but how was a man supposed to ignore such a thing?

"Yes, in October."

He glanced up at her. She looked radiant. Because of the baby, Justin's baby. "You're happy with your life here, aren't you?"

"Very happy." She smiled at him sweetly over the rim of the delicate china cup.

"I'm glad." He did want her to be happy; he just wished she could have found that happiness with him. Reminding himself he'd decided not to think about her that way anymore, he tried replacing the thought with another subject. "About this counterfeiting case, is there anything you can tell me?"

"Probably nothing Superintendent Jakes and Justin haven't told you." She relayed what she knew anyway. They both were well aware pieces of important information could inadvertently be dropped, unrecognized by even the most experienced detective.

"You're right; nothing new to me this time," Alex said when she was done.

She placed a hand against the small of her back and stretched, then relaxed against the chair's tall back. "Justin and I are so glad you were assigned to this case. We prayed you would be free of other assignments and able to take this one."

They'd prayed that he would take it? The thought stopped his fork halfway to his mouth. He stared at her, cleared his throat, and rested his fork on his plate. "You prayed about it? That I would take the counterfeiting assignment and come to River's Edge?"

Her low, sweet laugh was so familiar to his memory that it brought a familiar pang of longing for their old friendship. "Of course, Alex. Justin and I pray about all the important things in our lives."

He cocked one eyebrow. "You told me during the last case we worked on in River's Edge that you'd become a Christian. Hard for me to believe the logical mind of yours that I so admired is depending on a force you can't see to assign Pinkerton cases."

Her laugh was more spontaneous this time. "God has handled much more difficult challenges than Pinkerton assignments, I'm sure."

"I recall vividly listening to you argue convincingly to a pastor we met on one of our cases why God could not possibly exist, and why, if one should decide to believe He did exist, He could certainly not take any interest in our personal lives."

Color swept her cheekbones. She glanced into the coffee cup she was holding in both hands. "I was rather awful in what I thought was my wisdom when I was younger, wasn't I?"

"Awful? Hardly that! Nothing I enjoyed more than a good debate with you. Your logical mind was always a challenge."

There was a gentle smile in the green eyes that searched his. "Choosing to believe in God's love for me has changed my life completely, and all for the better. I hope one day you will make the same choice for yourself."

He took a couple more bites of hotcakes and sausages to hide his embarrassment. He didn't mind discussing religion in a theoretical manner; in fact, he rather enjoyed such arguments, expounding on why religions, Christianity in particular, were not realistic ways of life. To have Constance make the discussion personal made him decidedly uncomfortable.

"I—I have to admit I've been rather intrigued by your. . .conversion. I've thought about it more than a few times since I last saw you. You are one of the most intelligent people I know. I've wondered how well your religion held up over the past months to the beliefs you once held against it. I guess this proves it's held up rather well."

"Jesus has a way of doing that."

"Yes, well. . ." Alex pushed back his chair and stood. "I really should be headed to the bank to talk to that husband of yours about the case." He forced a grin. "After all, since God answered your prayers and brought me out here to help with it, I probably shouldn't waste His time."

Constance rose gracefully. She took his arm and started with him toward the hallway. "I'm glad you are here, Alex. Justin has been terribly worried about the counterfeiters. So much so, that I was worried about him. Just knowing you were coming has made him rest better the last couple of days."

If she knew how he'd fought coming, she would probably be insulted. He laid a hand over hers, noticing the softness and delicate shape of hers, remembering the feel of it with another twisting of his heart. "If it eases your mind, and your husband's, to have me here, then I'm glad I came." He knew as soon as he'd said the words that they were true, and the knowledge loosened the tightness about his heart.

He left her at the door, and started down the walk in bright August sunshine. His thoughts drifted back to their conversation as he walked. What he'd told Constance about wondering whether her religious beliefs had held up to the pressures of life was true. He had thought often about her decision to become a Christian. He had always had great respect for her wisdom, and knew she would not have made the choice lightly.

He'd even started attending church when his assignments permitted. He'd wanted to see if he could find a faith as real as hers, but he didn't know how to ask her how she'd found it for herself. Asking something like that, well, it was too personal. It meant exposing too much of the real self he kept hidden, the part of himself he tried to keep safe.

He'd been surprised how the Bible stories and teachings from his childhood came back to him now that he was attending church again. He was comfortable with the moral teachings of Christianity. They went along well with his ideas of justice and right and wrong.

Still, so far church attendance hadn't changed his skepticism of faith. He hadn't found there whatever it was that had changed Constance's life.

"Hello, Uncle Alex!"

He stopped with a start, only inches short of running down Miss Amanda Mason. She smiled up at him from beneath a straw hat the color of ripe peaches. A wide matching ribbon tied in a bow beneath her chin. A dress a few shades lighter gave her already perfect complexion a delightful, healthy glow.

He tipped his bowler to her. "Good morning, Miss Amanda. This is a pleasant surprise. Out for a morning promenade to enjoy the sunshine?" He noticed she hadn't opened her chiffon parasol trimmed with silk flowers that matched her bonnet.

"I have an appointment with Constance's Aunt Libby. She owns a millinery." She touched the brim of her bonnet. "Time to order a new fall hat."

"I remember meeting Libby Ward on my last visit." A delightfully spunky woman, he recalled. "Isn't her shop downtown? I'm headed that way myself, and would be pleased to escort you."

"Why, Uncle Alex, I thought you'd never ask!" With a grin she fell into step beside him.

He pulled at one edge of his mustache. "If you keep calling me that, I'm going to start feeling old and rickety."

"Uncle Alex?" Innocent surprise filled her face. "Why, the word *uncle* shouldn't make you feel old. Now, if I had called you *grandfather*. . ."

He groaned. "Let me quit while I'm ahead, or at least, not quite so far behind." He was only twenty-six. Thanks to Effie's comment last night, he knew Amanda had just turned twenty. Did he truly seem so ancient to her, or was her teasing all in fun? Had his work made him appear old already?

It was pleasant walking through the upper-class neighborhood with its wide, well-kept lawns and fine homes, Alex thought. So restful after his last assignment in a tough part of Chicago. Here toddlers played on sprawling verandas, a well-groomed horse attached to a shiny new buggy and secured to a ring in a fancy wrought iron post waited patiently beside a stoop, milk and meat-market delivery wagons rolled by, the sound of their wheels muted by the wooden blocks laid beneath the pavement, and birds canvassed the lawns for morning worms.

"Tell me about yourself, Miss Amanda. How does a young lady spend her days in the metropolis of River's Edge?"

Amanda nodded and said, "Good morning," to a woman pushing a perambulator. Then giving him a shame-on-you look, she shook a gloved index finger back and forth. "You mustn't disparage our little town, not if you wish to win the trust of people here. They will close up as tight as clams if they think you look down on them and their town, and you'll never get any information from them about the counterfeiting case."

Her voice had a friendly lilt to it, but Alex recognized she was serious about the advice she gave, and recognized the wisdom of the advice, also. "I most humbly apologize, and will take your sage advice to heart."

"Good."

He was glad to see her smile back in place. Come to think of it, she seemed to smile most of the time. The only time he could recall her actually looking unhappy or angry was when Lance Chase's words seemed to insult her father. Was that what made her so appealing, her constant good nature?

He liked the little bounce in her step, too, and the way she lightly swung her closed parasol. Not that she wasn't graceful, but she didn't walk with that almost gliding effect so many ladies carried off, or the lumbering quality of women who couldn't manage the glide. It always amazed him that any woman could walk gracefully wearing pounds of clothing. Amanda Mason was graceful, but walked as if she enjoyed life; like little Effie all grown up.

"I'd still like to know how you spend your days," he reminded.

"I'm sure a recitation of my schedule will bore you, but since you insist—I begin the day going over the menus with the cook, and the day's duties with the maid and hired girl. Then I run errands and do the marketing. In the afternoon I accept or return social calls. Evenings I spend with my father or close friends, when I'm not attending some meeting or other."

"What meetings? What organizations are you involved in?" Alex found he truly wanted to know what this vivacious creature found interesting.

"Church, of course. I sing in the choir, so I attend rehearsal Tuesday nights." She wrinkled her nose in a manner he found delightful. She leaned a degree closer to him. A light lavender scent wafted about him as she confided, "I'm a very poor singer, but it's a small church, and they aren't allowed to turn volunteers away, even for the choir."

He dropped his head back and roared with laughter.

"It's true," she assured him. "The choir director says I have a rather unconventional attitude toward singing. God gave some people more beautiful singing voices than others, but why would He have given the rest of us the ability to sing at all if He didn't expect us to use it to tell Him how much we love Him, or even just to make ourselves happy? Besides, it's much more fun to sing in church than listen to others sing, don't you think?"

He stopped chuckling long enough to say, "I never thought of it in that manner."

She nodded, as though his comment were understandable. "Unconventional," she repeated.

"I have heard people with good voices say they consider singing in a choir a way of serving the Lord."

"Yes, that's what the director says. Those people are chosen to give solos, or duets, or sing in small groups, so their gift does have special opportunities to bless the congregation. I must admit, most people in the audience appear to enjoy it." She gave him a tiny smile. "I've never been asked to sing in a group smaller than the choir."

Alex chuckled again. If there was a God, he suspected the deity enjoyed having this woman in His church. "What other unconventional ways do you help out the church?"

"I'm a member of the Missionary Guild." She sighed. "I'm not much help when it's time to mend clothing or stitch quilts. I try, but I expect the recipients wish I didn't. Their clothes and quilts likely fall apart at the seams I stitched."

"Is there any area of church work in which you excel?"

Amanda propped her gloved fists daintily on her hips. "You needn't laugh at me. It's the heart God judges, not the quality of the voice or stitches, isn't it?"

He disciplined his grin with difficulty. "So I've always heard."

She began walking again, and he fell into step beside her. "Actually, there is something I think I'm rather good at. At least, I hope I am. I teach a Sunday school class for children Effie and Evan's age, and enjoy it very much."

"I would imagine the children love having you for a teacher. I would." He was immediately aware he'd put his whole heart into the compliment. What had come over him? As a detective, he never allowed himself the luxury of relaxing to such an extent. He had spoken without thinking.

"Why, Mr. Bixby, what a lovely thing to say!"

Ah, now it was "Mr. Bixby," not "Uncle Alex." He wasn't sure he liked the change. Had she thought his comment too personal? He cleared his throat and looked away from her as they continued to walk through the residential section. The homes weren't as fine or the lawns as wide here. The smell of the river was stronger, intermingled with the pleasant pine smells from the sawmills that were such an important part of the town's economy. They were meeting more people, men and women, most of whom greeted Amanda and cast curious glances his way. The streets weren't as quiet here, and were busy with horses and delivery wagons and buggies, wheels rattling and horses' hooves thunking on the pavement. He could see that he and Amanda would soon pass the area where homes stopped and the town's business street began. A whisper of regret blew over him. He would prefer continuing his visit with Amanda to beginning his workday.

"Are you involved in organizations other than church?" he asked.

"Oh, yes. There are lyceum meetings with interesting debates each week, and I always attend the meetings of the Women's Christian Temperance Union."

He bowed slightly from the waist. "As every good woman does."

"The Temperance Union's work is very important," she defended. "Don't you think so? After all, as a Pinkerton man, you don't imbibe liquor, do you?"

"I do not." He glanced about them to see who might have heard her comment, and was relieved to see no one near enough. "Where did you learn the Pinkerton Agency doesn't allow drinking men in its employ?"

"Constance told me. She's told me a lot about the agency. Justin has books written by Allan Pinkerton about some of the agency's cases. He's let me borrow them. It sounds so exciting to be a detective. . .I mean, operative."

The admiration in her face and voice filled him with pride. "It is rather interesting work," he admitted, hoping he sounded properly humble.

"Interesting? I should think it would be fascinating work! It would take such courage, such intelligence, such devotion to justice!"

"Well. . ." He glanced down at the sidewalk and shrugged. He definitely agreed with her, but one didn't admit such things outright.

"But it does!" she insisted, evidently taking his reaction as modesty. "One would have to be intelligent to figure out how a crime was committed, and by whom, and how to go about capturing the criminals. Mr. Pinkerton wrote that detectives 'must be men of high order of mind, and must possess clean, honest, comprehensive understanding, force of will, and vigor of body.' "

"He did?" He couldn't help but grin. Imagine her memorizing such a thing.

"I've been reading Mr. Pinkerton's book, The Counterfeiters and the Detectives. It would be such fun to try solve the counterfeiting case here in River's Edge! I've been thinking about it a lot, reading this book and all, and I have some ideas about the case I'd like to discuss with you."

Disappointment swept through him as he gazed down into her eager face. Her eyes were alight with excitement, and her cheeks pink with it. She was disconcertingly lovely. The thought of her putting herself even remotely into danger by becoming involved with a criminal case made his scalp crawl. Why did people always think any untrained person could do detective work?

"Miss Amanda, solving crimes is not a game for untrained young ladies. It is serious work."

The excitement on her face faded to hurt and shock. "I realize that, but—"

"There are no 'buts.'"

At his angry tone, Amanda gasped slightly and took a step backward. A middle-aged man passing by darted a concerned glance at the couple.

Alex pressed his lips together firmly. Amanda's hurt expression cut into his heart. He quickly looked about again to be sure no one else was near enough to overhear them. There wasn't. He lowered his voice anyway, and tried to gentle it somewhat. "I'm sorry. I didn't mean to speak so sharply. Please understand that I would be remiss if I allowed an untrained person to become involved in a potentially dangerous situation."

"But these are counterfeiters, they're not armed robbers or murderers!"

"Any criminal is capable of violence if he fears he's been discovered, or is about to be."

She rapped the end of her parasol on the boardwalk once, smartly. Her gray eyes snapped. "I wasn't planning to arrest anyone. I merely wanted to make some suggestions."

He hardened his voice, hoping to make her understand the seriousness of the situation. "This isn't a parlor game, Miss Amanda. Instead of the danger the counterfeiters pose to your community, all you seem to see is excitement in solving a crime. Stick to your Sunday school work and temperance meetings, and let the professionals handle the criminals."

Her eyes widened. He saw pain and disbelief flash across them, and was instantly sorry he'd been so harsh. "Miss Amanda, I—"

She didn't allow him to finish. The delicate chin, bordered by the peach satin ribbon and bow, lifted, trembling slightly. "From the wonderful things Constance has told me about you, I would never have suspected you could be such a—a. . . man!"

Amanda swung around, her back stiff, and entered the shop beside them, setting brass bells above the door tinkling. He took a step toward the door, intending to follow her. The sight of a window filled with bonnets stopped him. He wouldn't follow the worst criminal into Libby Ward's Fancy Millinery Shop!

Fuming, he turned on his heel and headed toward the bank.

Chapter 5

Anger propelled Amanda to the middle of the shop before she stopped beside a table filled with beautiful creations in the latest French and English styles. Libby Ward, helping the mayor's pleasantly plump wife tie a bonnet just right, glanced at Amanda in surprise.

Amanda forced a smile, then turned her back to the skinny, wrinkled, fashionably dressed milliner. She reached out to touch the brim of a bonnet trimmed with jet-black feathers, feigning an interest in the fashionable hats that usually gave her such pleasure.

How could Alexander have acted so detestably toward her? All she'd wanted to do was make some suggestions, and he'd spoken to her as though she were a naughty child. " 'Stick to your Sunday school work,' indeed!" she muttered angrily.

"Excuse me? Did you say something?" Libby asked from across the room.

Amanda shook her head quickly, gave the milliner a tight smile, and turned back to the display and thoughts of Alexander Bixby. She'd been prepared to like the man from Constance's stories about him. What she learned of the man's character at the dinner party last evening had only assured her that her instincts had been correct. She'd liked the way he handled Lance Chase's ungentlemanly demands, and it had been fun sharing laughter and smiles over Effie and Evan's antics.

This morning she had been pleased to run into him. At first they had been so comfortable and easy with each other. Pure pleasure had filled her from simply being in his company. Her chest tightened. Then he said those nasty things. Did he truly believe she didn't care about the threat the counterfeiters posed to the community?

He needn't have been so cruel. One would have thought she'd said she was going to strap a six-shooter about her best gown, grab a rifle, jump on a horse, and head out of town after a den of thieves!

A smile tugged at her lips. Such vocabulary! Perhaps she had been reading too many detective books and novels after all.

She struggled with herself for a few moments. She could choose to dwell on his unkind comments, and remain angry, or choose to forgive him. The anger would keep up walls that might protect her from being hurt by him again. Forgiving him would make her more vulnerable to him. Was that safe for her heart when she found him so attractive?

Perhaps not, but she was already tired of being angry. Anger took so much energy. *After all,* she thought, as though she had to justify choosing forgiveness, *he did say he didn't want me to become involved because he is concerned for my safety. Even if I think his attitude is overprotective, can I be angry that he doesn't want me injured?*

She felt the tightness in her shoulders relax at her decision. Her gaze scanned the appealing bonnets on the table in front of her with renewed interest.

A moment later, Libby Ward stepped up beside her, a friendly smile on her thin lips. "Looking for something special, Amanda?"

Amanda picked up a French bonnet with the new wider brim and mauve chin ribbons. "Yes, Libby, I am looking for something special." Something that will make Mr. Alexander Bixby, Pinkerton detective, want to investigate Miss Amanda Mason!

⁓❧⁓

Alexander's footsteps thunked loudly against the boardwalk as he stalked toward the bank. Amanda had been so captivating, so delightful, during their walk. How could she have turned unreasonable so quickly? Her last words rang through his brain: *"I would never have suspected you could be such a man!"* He snorted. She'd said it as if being a man was the same as being addlepated. "What does she think I should act like, a rabbit?" he muttered.

A matronly looking woman with a marketing basket over her arm darted him a suspicious look, and stepped closer to the shop they were passing, edging away from him.

He groaned. That was the second time he'd forgotten himself because of Amanda to the extent that he drew undesirable attention from a passerby. He forced himself to slow his walk and stuck his hands in his trousers pockets to appear more casual. His jaw wasn't so easy to relax, but he tried.

He shook his head slightly. How could such a charming young woman as Amanda have such an effect on him? When he'd told himself spending time with Amanda Mason might take his mind and heart off Constance, he hadn't anticipated it happening in such an unsettling, angry manner.

A smile began to slip across his face. What was it she'd said, before that silly female comment about his acting like a man? Something about Constance telling her wonderful things about him.

His smile grew wider. Had she asked Constance about him? Pleasant thought!

"Why—!" He stopped abruptly. *I was so pleased with the possibility of Amanda asking about me, that I didn't even notice she said Constance had said wonderful things about me.* Not long ago, as recently as the previous day, in fact, he would have been delighted to hear Constance had been saying wonderful things about him to anyone.

He started walking again, slower, amazed at his discovery. Did it mean his heart was finally releasing its hold on unattainable Constance? He barely dared hope so. He'd been fighting his disappointment over her marriage to Justin for so long.

Reluctantly, he put his heart's questions behind him and turned his mind to business when he entered the bank.

There was only one customer in the bank. Not unusual, he was sure, for such an early hour. There were three clerks or cashiers in the banking area behind the glass and brass wire that separated them from the customers. The two men not waiting on the customer each glanced up when he entered, but went about their business of counting funds for their cash drawers.

A casual look around showed him the vault doors had been opened for the day. He noticed with approval that the vault was in the safest part of the bank, at the rear end of the banking room near the president's office. The clerks' backs were toward the vault as they stood at their windows.

He stepped up to one of the clerks and asked for Justin. The clerk went to the president's office to announce him, and a minute later the clerk returned to usher him into the office. Justin closed the door behind him so they could talk in private.

"Where do you propose to start?" Justin asked after they'd shared a few friendly comments.

"I'd like to start by talking with the sheriff, but since you said he's out of town until tomorrow, how about if I start here?"

Justin's eyebrows rose in surprise. "Here? At my bank? You think one of my staff is in league with the counterfeiters?"

"It's always possible. A bit risky for a bank employee to plant counterfeit money, but a lot of opportunity."

Justin rubbed a loose fist back and forth beneath his chin, considering Alex's words. "I think my staff are all trustworthy. Naturally, I wouldn't have hired them otherwise."

"Naturally, but many crimes are committed by those we trust. We don't give people we don't trust the opportunity to steal from us."

"Makes sense. What do we do?"

"Tell me a little about each of your staff. Introduce me to them. Tell them I'll be spending some time watching them as they perform their duties, looking for ways you can improve the bank's safeguards. We don't want them thinking they are under suspicion in any way. Probably watch them off and on over a few days to get a better perspective."

"Since we're a small-town bank, the clerks aren't assigned to specific duties. They each perform whatever needs to be done. We've three male clerks, and a young woman secretary."

Alex listened carefully while Justin gave him a little background on each of the staff. A few minutes later when the bank was empty of customers, Justin introduced Alex to the staff and explained why he would be watching them.

Alex tried to keep a friendly, nonthreatening manner about himself as he watched the staff's faces. He didn't notice anything to indicate anyone was suspicious of his motives, but he knew that didn't mean they were all innocent.

An elderly man in a worn but well-cut suit came in to cash in a bond, and the staff went back to work. Before long, the secretary arrived from a trip to the post office. Justin brought the plain, quiet brunette, Miss Sherman, in her Eaton suit, into his office to introduce Alex and make his explanations once again out of earshot of customers. Miss Sherman went back to her desk, outside the clerk's banking area, to sort the day's mail, but she looked a little nervous. *She seems a bit of a shy thing,* Alex thought, *and unmarried.* Perhaps she was nervous only at the thought of having a man watching her perform her duties. Certainly she didn't need to fear undesired attention from him. She hadn't Constance's serene beauty, or Amanda's engaging nature.

Justin supplied Alex with official-looking papers so he could appear to be performing bank business, and not attract undue attention from the customers while he observed the staff at work.

Shuffling through his papers, Alex watched discreetly as the skinny, freckled, red-haired young clerk he'd seen when he'd stopped in the bank yesterday waited on a farmer's wife who was depositing egg and milk money. The woman asked about the clerk's mother, and Alex remembered Justin had told him the man, Lawrence Williams, was unmarried and supported his widowed mother.

Williams's quiet, sober manner was a complete contrast to that of Jack Davis. The sleek, good-looking blond man's loud voice and patronizing manner grated on Alex's nerves. Or maybe it was Justin's comment that Davis was seeing Amanda occasionally that struck such an off-key chord, he admitted to himself reluctantly.

He wasn't certain whether Miss Sherman found Davis attractive or annoying. Her cheeks reddened at the clerk's almost-ungentlemanly, almost-flirting comments, but she lowered her head and her lashes, and Alex couldn't read her expression as the keys of her typewriter tapped away.

He thought the third clerk, Roger Jackson, appeared the kind of man he would like for a friend. In his thirties with thin, curly brown hair and a mustache, he was a responsible, hardworking family man according to Justin. What Alex admired most about the man, though, was the way he treated the customers. No matter the age, the apparent financial or social status, or how grumpy the customer, he treated each pleasantly. His patience in dealing with those who didn't understand financial matters never appeared in the least bit stretched.

Alex reminded himself that the nicest people often made the best embezzlers. He mustn't allow himself to make snap judgments about any of the staff. Not even Davis, he thought, scowling as Davis's loud laughter at a customer's comment filled the bank. He tried to imagine the annoying man with charming Amanda and couldn't picture it.

Amanda. His face relaxed into a smile. As a trained, experienced detective, he couldn't read people easily or solve a case like this quickly. Imagine Amanda believing that after reading a few books on Pinkerton cases, a young girl like herself could evaluate the facts and come up with a proper solution, and do so without tipping off the criminals! He chuckled at the remembrance of her eagerness.

Soon after Alex and Justin returned to the bank from lunch, Mr. Mason stopped in on business. Seeing Alex, he offered to take him over to the sawmill.

"The sawmill payroll situation included the largest dumping of counterfeit bills in the county so far," Justin told Alex in a low voice.

"Yes, yes, it was." Mason shook his head. "Most distressing. Hate that it was associated with the mill I was so proud of for so many years."

"It's also the event which most disturbs me in this crime." A frown furrowed Justin's forehead. "The payroll came through our bank, and my people didn't catch the counterfeit bills."

Alex's senses perked up at that. He'd ask Justin more about it when they were alone.

It was pleasant to be out in the August sunshine, a light breeze keeping the air comfortable and the mosquitoes away. Thomas Mason was a heavyset man, and he breathed hard as they walked along. Alex slowed his pace a bit, looking around them at the buildings and scenery as if that were the reason. "Beautiful little town you have here, Mason."

"Mmmm." The portly, white-haired man glanced about.

Alex wasn't certain whether Amanda's father was agreeing with him or not. He tried again. "The tall bluffs behind the town and on the other side of the Mississippi make this one of the prettiest towns I've ever seen."

"Sometimes what is beautiful can also be dangerous."

"Dangerous?"

"It's not uncommon after a winter of heavy snowfall for the Mississippi to flood. Towns all along the river are damaged then. Here, it can be worse than some other places. The bluffs trap the water, making floodwaters deeper than they would otherwise be in the town, and channeling the river's power."

"I hadn't thought of that. I can see how that would happen."

They walked on a few more steps, Mason puffing beside him, but not as hard as he had been earlier. "Lost my sawmill to the floods once, and had damage to it more times than I like to count. Built right on the edge of the Big Muddy like that. . ." He shook his head.

"Must have been tough. I've never been in a flood. It must be an awful experience, losing a home or a business, or trying to clean one out after the water and mud have swirled through it."

"Minor losses."

The older man's pained tone caused Alex to glance at him sharply.

"I lost my wife, Lila, in one of the floods."

The man's hollow voice and his awful revelation slammed through Alex's chest. "I—I—I'm sorry. I didn't know. I can't imagine how horrible that must have been for you."

"It's a long time ago now. Fifteen years."

From his voice and eyes, Alex knew the years hadn't washed away the pain of his loss. And Amanda's loss. That delightful, barely-out-of-childhood woman had lost her mother when she was only five! An image came to his mind of himself now, as a man, holding that little girl in his arms and comforting her. He wished he could have done that for her. Instead, it was this man beside him who had comforted her. Sorrow for her tightened his throat and made it hard to speak. "It must have been difficult for you, raising Amanda alone."

They were almost to the river now, where the sawmill stood. Mason raised his face and stared at the tall gray bluffs across the river. "Amanda became everything to me; my reason for living, my reason to fight back, to rebuild." He stopped, leaning both hands on his cane, still staring at the bluffs. "She became my greatest strength," he whispered, "and my love for her, my greatest weakness."

Seeing the love and sorrow in Mason's face, Alex felt a great fondness for the man swell up inside him. He laid a hand on Mason's shoulder. "Your wife would have been pleased with the way you raised Amanda."

Mason sighed deeply. "I'm not so sure." He began walking again, toward the sawmill, shaking his head. "But I dearly hope so."

Chapter 6

Alex was rather disappointed in the visit to the sawmill. It didn't provide him with any leads, at least not any he recognized at the moment.

Maybe it will come together later, he encouraged himself, looking out across a wash of logs in the river beside the sawmill. Experience had taught him that things, which seemed unimportant or unrelated to a crime, later often fit into place to help solve the case.

He'd talked to the bookkeeper, a man named Reaves, who had been with the company since long before Mason sold it. He couldn't recall anything out of the ordinary happening the day part of the payroll turned up counterfeit; no strangers in the office or normal people doing anything unusual who would have had an opportunity to switch funds.

Perhaps the switch had happened at the bank. Alex hoped not, for Justin's sake. Justin was sure to feel responsible if it turned out one of his staff was involved in the crime.

Mason, who had been showing him about the mill, walked up beside him. "Logs don't often come down the river anymore. Used to be you could walk across the river when the logs were sent down from the northern forests. Now they're mostly shipped by rail. More efficient, but I miss the old ways." He sighed deeply. "You'll see, Alex. As you grow older, there are so many losses, not all of them large. The little losses add up."

"Doesn't life give you new gifts as you grow older, too?" Alex asked gently, not wanting to discredit the man's experiences, but hating to see him look so sad. "Some big, some little?"

The older man stared out over the logs a moment longer, then turned to Alex. "Yes. Yes, indeed it does. Thank you for reminding me."

They walked home together, Mason telling Alex stories of the town's history, and the town's characters.

When they arrived at Mason's home, Amanda was watering flowers that grew in front of the large, Georgian-style brick building. Alex's heartbeat quickened at the sight of her, glad for an opportunity to speak with her again. Almost immediately apprehension squelched his joy. Would she want to speak with him after the anger in which they'd parted that morning?

At Mason's urging, he started up the walk with him toward the house. Amanda straightened, a tin sprinkling can with roses painted on it in her hands. When she caught sight of them, her wonderful smile filled her face, and flooded Alex's heart.

Don't be a fool, Bixby, he warned himself. *The smile is likely for her father, not for you.* His heart refused to give up hope.

After a few minutes of conversation between Mason and Amanda, asking after each other's afternoon, Mason went inside. "I'm glad you went to the sawmill with Father," Amanda said, going back to watering her flowers. "He told me this morning he was hoping you would go with him today."

"He gave me a tour of the mill. I enjoyed it. I've never been inside one before." It wasn't the mill he wanted to speak of.

"He's very proud of that mill. He put so much of himself into it over the years. It's meant a lot to him, to his employees, and to the community. Have you noticed all the businesses about town that rely on the sawmills? Barrel companies, shingle companies, companies that make gingerbread for houses."

He smiled, pleased at the pride she showed of her father's success. So many young people didn't recognize all the effort and sacrifice it took for their parents to build their dreams. "I did notice. Your father has done a lot for this town. I could tell he is proud of the mill. He's prouder of you."

She looked up at him in surprise, her gray eyes wide.

The innocence he saw there brought back the picture he'd seen in his mind earlier, of himself comforting her as a little girl, and the sorrow he'd felt for that child who became this young woman.

She held the handle of the sprinkling can in both hands. Her gaze searched his face. "Mr. Bixby, I hardly know what to make of you. You can say the nicest things, and then—"

He waited for her to comment on his verbal attack of this morning, but she didn't continue. He cleared his throat. "About this morning, I was hoping for a chance to speak with you."

Caution slipped into her eyes. "Yes?"

Did she think he was about to warn her again to stay out of detective work? "I'm sorry I spoke to you so sharply earlier."

She dropped her gaze. "You were concerned about the danger involved with the case. I understand."

Relief that she wasn't holding his angry words against him sent his spirit soaring. He sat down on the broad steps, and rested his elbows on his knees. "It's flattering when people say they believe detectives are brave and live exciting lives, but a lot of a detective's work is boring."

"That's hard to believe." She sat down beside him, setting the can between them.

"It's the truth. A detective's primary tools are patience and logic."

Her gray eyes danced with fun. "I have patience and logic to spare."

He'd set himself up for that one! "I said they are a detective's primary tools, not his only ones."

"His?" She didn't wait for him to respond to her challenge. "In addition to patience and logic, I have a knowledge of the community which you lack."

Disappointment weaved through him. He wished she would stop insisting on trying to push her way into the case. He found her so refreshing and relaxing to be around. Most people in his life were criminals trying to hide their true nature, or detectives whose jobs depended upon hiding their true selves. He liked Amanda's transparent nature, and found he didn't want her to become like everyone else in his life. If only she would put that silly idea of playing detective out of her lovely head!

He laid a hand gently over hers, barely touching it. He caught his breath at its softness and fragility, and for a moment forgot what he had intended to say. Then he squeezed her hand, once, slightly, and released it. "Please, stay away from this case, Amanda."

Surprise filled the eyes that looked up into his. Her lips parted slightly. She didn't reply, not to promise as he wished she would, or to refuse. She simply studied his eyes, his face, with a curiosity as unveiled as her usual forthright comments.

Her lips looked so soft. He wondered what it would be like to kiss her. He leaned toward her slightly, then abruptly stood up. "Good evening, Amanda."

Without allowing himself a backward look, he walked swiftly toward Constance and Justin's home next door. What had he been thinking? He barely knew Amanda. How, for a moment, could he have considered kissing her? The memory of her sweet, appealing face reminded him exactly why he'd considered it, and he clenched his teeth against a groan. Even if they'd been courting or betrothed, a gentleman didn't kiss a lady on her front steps for the whole world to see. It wasn't even lamplighting time!

Besides, becoming romantically involved with a woman while on a case was not in the least professional. A man couldn't keep his mind on a case and a woman at the same time, and if a detective's mind wasn't on the case, he was asking for trouble.

And Miss Amanda Mason could cause a man a whole lot of trouble.

❧

Amanda watched him cover the walk between the two houses with his long-legged stride. He'd called her Amanda! Not Miss Amanda, but Amanda. She'd never heard her own, familiar name sound so beautiful, so special.

Her hand still felt warm from his touch. She never allowed intimacies from the men in her life, but she had held hands with some. She couldn't remember anyone's touch affecting her as Alex's had.

She could hardly deny to herself that she'd wanted him to find her attractive. Was she interpreting his attentions correctly, or was it only wishful thinking on her part that his touch, his tone of voice, and the look in his eyes had been that of a man sweet on a girl?

Even though she'd taken typewriting and shorthand classes in Minneapolis, she hadn't much experience with men from larger cities. Certainly she hadn't been escorted or courted by men Alexander's age, or men who had seen as much of the world as a Pinkerton detective would have had to have seen. Had Alex intended his touch to be as intimate as it seemed to her, as intimate as she wanted to believe he'd meant it? Or was he only trying again to warn a silly young Sunday school teacher to stay away from his work?

Wrapping her arms around her knees, she looked toward the house next door, where he had disappeared. "Alexander." She whispered the word. "Alexander Bixby. Alex." Would she ever dare call him Alex or Alexander and not Uncle Alex or Detective Alex as she teased him with before?

The beautiful sound of his voice saying her name drifted through her mind, filling her with warmth. She wanted to hear him say it again, and again, and again.

"Please, Lord, let him care for me," she whispered, "if it be Thy will."

So often when she prayed for something she wanted this much, an emotion almost like fear tightened her chest, fear that God wouldn't want her to have whatever she'd set her heart on. As if God's will were anything to fear! As if what He chose to give her wouldn't always be what would make her happiest!

There was no fear this time, only a deep sense of peace, that God meant something very special to exist between her and Alex. The lovely sense of serenity existed all through the evening she spent with her father.

Looking out before she went to bed from between the pale blue velvet draperies that covered her bedroom windows, she viewed the pale golden squares of the winodows of the house next door, and whispered, "Good night, dear Alexander."

❧

The next day, Alex spent the morning with Sheriff Tucker, discussing the case.

The round, middle-aged man had stroked his red handlebar mustache and shook his head in despondence at his lack of suspects. "Checked out all the strangers hereabouts, between me and the marshall. All the likely ones, that is. There's always someone stops uptown during train or steamboat stops. When the first counterfeit bills straggled in from local merchants, figured that was where they were coming from. Thinking that, guess we didn't look too hard for suspects." He gave Alex a sheepish look from beneath bushy red brows.

"Most people would have done the same as you did," Alex assured him. He'd seen local law enforcement officers act this way in the presence of a Pinkerton before, embarrassed they hadn't been able to apprehend the criminals themselves. "With the fake bills coming in only one here and one there, you would have needed a miracle to find the counterfeiters at that point."

Sheriff Tucker's face relaxed a bit. "It was the sawmill payroll that showed us we had a real problem on our hands." The bushy brows met in a frown. "Try as we did to trace that money to someone who might have placed it, we weren't successful."

"I was at the sawmill yesterday. I talked with the bookkeeper, Reaves. Didn't sound like there was much opportunity for the bills to be exchanged after the payroll reached the sawmill."

"That's what we thought."

"Why don't I tell you the story of that day the way Reaves told me? Then you can fill me in on details Reaves left out, or on any place his story doesn't fall in line with what you already know."

"Shoot." Sheriff Tucker leaned forward on his desk to listen.

Alex repeated what he'd learned the day before. Tucker didn't hear anything that didn't agree with what he already knew.

Tucker sighed heavily. "The marshall and I figured someone at the bank might have had an opportunity to switch some bills."

"I've had the same thought. Any luck along that line?"

"None. We've tried watching the bank staff when they're away from work, thinking they might lead us to where the money is being printed. Saw nothing suspicious."

"I'll be doing more checking along that line," Alex assured him. "Are you still watching them outside work?"

"Yes."

Alex nodded. "Good. Justin Knight, too?"

The sheriff's eyes narrowed just a fraction. Alex could see he was weighing the fact that Alex was the Knights' friend against the knowledge of Alex's position as a Pinkerton. "Much as I hate to say it, we have to watch anyone who had a chance to touch those bills."

"Good," Alex said again. "I have complete faith in Justin's innocence, but having him treated by you and your people like any other possible suspect will give proof to others of his innocence."

He hadn't been so sure Justin was a law-abiding citizen when he was here on his last case, at least in the beginning. Now he would never suspect him of a crime. Justin Knight loved justice, hated deceit of any sort or degree. Alex was glad that if Constance had to have married someone else, the man she'd chosen was Justin Knight.

The sheriff's large chest lifted in another oversized sigh. "It's a hard thing when something like this happens in your hometown, when all the possible suspects are people you've always thought were honorable, honest citizens, and friends besides."

"I'd never thought of it from that standpoint," Alex admitted.

꘎

He repeated the statement when he told Constance later of the sheriff's comment. "I never thought of it as being difficult for local law enforcement that way, suspecting friends, the loss of trust in people you've known for years," he admitted. "I only thought of their involvement with their townspeople as impeding their ability to be objective."

"Until living here, I'd never thought of it from Sheriff Tucker's point of view, either," Constance admitted.

The evening meal was over, the kitchen cleaned up, and Mrs. Kelly had gone home for the day. Justin was tucking in Effie and Evan, and Constance was preparing a snack of coffee and cookies for herself, Justin, and Alex.

Alex leaned against the granite countertop, watching Constance grind coffee beans. "You seem very content here. Domestic. Are you happy with life in River's Edge, and with your marriage?" Would she think his question too personal? "Perhaps I shouldn't have asked, but I want. . .I want to know if you're happy."

She quit turning the handle of the grinder and laid her hand on one of his. Her smile was gentle, and filled her eyes. "How could the question be too personal coming from one of my dearest friends? I'm very happy, and it is kind of you to care."

Her comments both relieved him and embarrassed him. He wasn't accustomed to acting sentimental with married women he'd once asked to marry him!

She poured the ground beans into the graniteware coffeepot on the stove, then glanced at him out of the corner of her eye. "Didn't I see you visiting with Amanda Mason on her front steps last evening?"

His embarrassment grew. "We talked for a few minutes after I walked home from the sawmill with her father."

"She and I have become close friends. She's quite delightful, don't you think?"

Indeed he did, but he wasn't about to admit it to Constance. "I'm used to the company of hardworking women like female Pinkerton operatives. Women like Amanda can be frivolous. Not my type."

"Indeed?" Her laughing eyes challenged him. "Did you know she is trained in typewriting and shorthand? She was in Minneapolis learning her skills when we were working on the Rasmus Pierce case together."

"Why isn't she using them? Rather be a social butterfly?"

"Alexander! That isn't like you!"

"Sorry." He was, too. He'd only meant to divert suspicion from his interest in Amanda, not truly insult her.

"The effects of the financial depression of 1893 are still being felt. There are so many family men and women raising their families alone who cannot find jobs. Amanda wanted to work because she wants to feel she is contributing something useful to the community, but felt it wasn't right to take a job someone else might need for a family's survival."

Disgust at himself made him almost angry. He should have realized Amanda's choice would have been made for some such reason. After all, women of Amanda's social standing rarely took courses to qualify them for business. She wouldn't have done so if she were lazy or satisfied to be a social creature unconnected to her community in a meaningful manner. He admired her courage in moving to the city and taking the course. "I know she's not lazy," he admitted, thinking of Amanda's involvement in church work. "Guess I'm just feeling ornery today."

The cheerful sound and friendly smell of boiling coffee made the room feel more welcoming. A light breeze fluttered the sheer curtains at the open window, and a slowly revolving ceiling fan helped disperse the warm air from the woodstove.

"I thought you and Amanda got along pleasantly at the dinner the other night." Constance took some of Mrs. Kelly's sugar cookies from the crockery cookie jar and placed them on a small china plate trimmed about the edges in roses and delicate gold.

He leaned back against the counter, crossed his legs and grinned at her. "Thought we did or hoped we did?"

"Why, Alex, what do you mean?" Her laughing eyes betrayed that she knew the answer. She opened the icebox and removed a jar of cream.

"Constance Ward. . .Knight, are you playing cupid, or trying to?"

She began pouring the cream into a small etched crystal pitcher, conveniently avoiding his eyes, he noticed with amusement. "Does that sound like me, acting the matchmaker?"

"No, it doesn't, but in this case I think it might very well be true."

"Amanda is a dear," Constance admitted.

"You never worried about the state of my heart when we were working together. I think you're only playing cupid now to alleviate your own guilt for breaking my heart." Would his smile take away the sting of truth in his statement?

She turned from the tray she was arranging, and went to stand directly in front of him. He searched her face, struggling to continue smiling. "My dear friend, I don't believe you asked me to marry you because you loved me, but because you are chivalrous and noble."

He snorted. "Me, noble?"

"We worked together for years. You didn't ask me to marry you until my brother died and left Effie and Evan parentless. I believe you thought I needed a husband to help me raise them. Now, isn't that true?"

He didn't answer. He didn't know the answer. Was she right? Had he convinced himself that their friendship was love because he'd felt it his duty to marry her?

She went back to her work, pulling the heavy coffeepot from the burner. "I do think you and Amanda would be a lovely couple, but that special until-death-do-us-part love can only be seen through the eyes of the lover. The only woman I want you to marry is the woman you can't imagine living without."

Her words brought a painful lump to his throat. There had been a time he would have been angered if she'd suggested he hadn't known his own heart, and that he might ever love someone other than her. Now, her words seemed generous, even loving, in the way of a friend. It was a couple of minutes before the lump shrunk enough that he could speak. "You're a good friend, Constance."

The words were true, and he sensed the beginning of new peace entering his life.

Chapter 7

Alex spent the next few days visiting other towns in the county, speaking with their bankers, law enforcement officers, and merchants who had been cheated with counterfeit bills, gleaning what facts he could about the case. Their experiences had been minor compared to River's Edge's sawmill payroll episode.

Way too few facts for a quick solution, he thought, climbing off a railcar into the calm evening quiet at River's Edge, his satchel in his hand.

He waved aside the horse-drawn bus, opting to walk to Justin and Constance's home. It felt good to stretch his legs after being on the passenger car.

He hadn't gone far before he noticed his gaze darting among the people he saw, looking for a certain familiar face, and he laughed at himself. His step picked up, became bouncier. It was Amanda he was watching for, not Constance. The days he'd been away, it had been delightful, vivacious Amanda who had been on his mind. Maybe I'll see her soon, maybe tonight.

At the Knight household that evening, his mind sought for a polite excuse to leave and go next door to call on the Masons, but the Knights kept him busy. First there was dinner, after which Effie and Evan gave him a running account of everything they had done while he was away. Justin told him in an aside as they left the dining room that after the children were in bed, he would like Alex to let him know everything he learned on his trip.

Alex swallowed his disappointment as the evening wore on. *After all, the counterfeiting case is the reason I'm here,* he reminded himself, *not to call on young ladies, no matter how appealing I find them.*

The Knight family devotions reminded him of his dismal attempt to become more spiritual. He watched their faces while Justin read the Scriptures. After the reading, they each took a turn at prayer. They all seemed so content and comfortable with the devotional time, seemed to find the words of the Bible so easy to accept.

Why couldn't religion work for him the way it had for these friends? Going to church hadn't turned his life around. Was it because he wasn't like so many people who decided to accept the Bible's teachings late in life, instead of when they were children? Even when he'd rejected the idea of a God, he'd agreed with the moral aspects of Christianity and Judaism. When he decided to give God a try, he couldn't turn around 180 degrees like Saul who became Paul in the New Testament. Having never embraced any of the sins the world considers major, such as drinking or womanizing, he couldn't relinquish them when he decided to try religion.

Not that I don't realize I'm a sinner, he thought, listening with only half an ear to Justin's comments on the Bible reading. *I've plenty of pride, and I guess God would think I don't mind judging other people much, especially criminals.* He glanced at Constance, who sat with her arm around Effie's shoulders. *As much as I hate the fact and thought I'd never be one to do it, I have coveted another man's wife, though that thankfully seems to be changing.*

After the devotions, Effie hurried over to hug him tightly about the neck. He hugged her back, sadness winding through him at the realization that he was going to miss being part of this little family when the case was over and he returned to Chicago.

When she unwrapped her arms, Effie clapped a hand over her mouth. "I almost forgot! Amanda said to invite you to dinner tomorrow, Uncle Alex."

Amanda invited him to dinner? His heartbeat jumped to double-time, pounding in his ears. He tried to make his voice casual. "She did?"

Effie's head bobbed up and down. "You're coming, aren't you?"

Evan threw himself against Alex's knees. "Please come."

Did Amanda really want him there? Would she issue an invitation through the children? As much as he wanted to believe it, he hardly dared trust the invitation.

"Justin is going to Red Wing tomorrow on business," Constance explained. "Amanda offered to watch the children so I can join him. She said you may join them for meals. If you think you'll do that, I'll tell Mrs. Kelly at breakfast that she may have the rest of the day off."

Disappointment colored his pleasure at Amanda's offer. She'd only asked him as a favor to Constance and Justin. "I'd hate for Mrs. Kelly to lose a day off because of me. I'll be glad to accept Amanda's invitation."

"Yay!" Effie started skipping around the room, waving her arms in the air. "Yay!"

"Yay!" Evan started after her.

Justin grabbed Effie's shoulder and one of Evan's hands. "Enough of that, you young hooligans. It's time for bed."

"Night, Uncle Alex!" the children called, waving to him as Justin led them into the hallway.

"Are we really hooligans, Uncle Justin?" He heard Effie ask. "I like that word!"

Alex grinned and stood up. "I'd better get my daily report written on the hooligans we're after," he told Constance, "so it's ready to post to the Chicago office in the morning. Too bad there's not much progress to report yet."

In spite of the lack of progress on the case, he was whistling as he climbed the wide staircase. He was having dinner with Amanda tomorrow! She might have only asked him out of courtesy, but he intended to enjoy the pleasure of her company anyway.

❧

While Alex was having breakfast with the family the next morning, Amanda stopped over and issued the invitation in person. Anticipation of the evening ahead brightened his day. The memory of her smile when she'd issued the personal invitation that morning stayed with him, pushing into his thoughts while he watched the staff at the bank go through their duties and as he made occasional suggestions to better safeguard the bank's and customer's assets.

Only a smattering of counterfeit funds had shown up in River's Edge since Alex had arrived in town. Was it because the counterfeiters knew he was watching? He tried to spend part of each day he was in town at the bank. If the bank staff was involved, they wouldn't be making any moves while he was watching. Also, if they were intelligent, and most counterfeiters and embezzlers were very intelligent, they wouldn't throw suspicion on themselves by making a major dump of false bills on a day he wasn't watching their activities.

He stopped at the jailhouse to see Sheriff Tucker, and they shared information on the small counterfeiting activity that each had gathered while he was out of town. The sheriff had followed up on a couple of possible suspects, but they had led nowhere.

Alex and Sheriff Tucker had lunch together at the hotel dining room, a noisy time with the railroad travelers crowding in for a rushed meal. Alex wondered whether any of them were counterfeiters making their way casually through the county again and again, dropping false bills and taking real ones in change. From the way Sheriff Tucker watched the crowd from beneath bushy red eyebrows while greeting the busy waitresses with a smile, Alex expected the law enforcement officer couldn't put the counterfeiters out of his mind, either.

Alex did notice that not one of the girls waiting on customers, and not one of the woman travelers, could hold a candle to Miss Amanda Mason when she smiled and her gray eyes sparkled with her love of life that he found so contagious.

Later Effie and Evan were seated in white wicker chairs on the broad front porch, watching for his arrival, when he swung down the sidewalk toward the Mason home. They dashed down the steps toward him, with Thunder a bundle of moving fur at their heels. All three threw themselves on him in a gleeful welcome that warmed his heart.

Effie took one hand and Evan the other, and tugged, hurrying him into the house. He laughed, teasing them by hanging back a bit. "Where's the fire?"

Amanda opened the front door for them. Her smile curled into his heart. What would it be like to come home to a family like this every night? he wondered.

In the front hall, he stopped to greet Amanda, and thank her again for inviting him.

"Father asked me to give you his regrets," she told him. "He is dining with Lance Chase this evening."

"I'm sorry to miss him." Alex meant the words more to be polite than accurate. With one less adult at the table, he'd have more time to talk with Amanda, and that certainly sounded fine to him.

The kids were still yanking on Alex's arms. "Whoa there, Evan. I need a hand to remove my hat for this lady."

Evan released his hand, scowling. "But you have to come inside."

Amanda took Alex's bowler and hung it on the brass and porcelain hat tree hook, while Alex glanced about the paneled hall with a puzzled look. "Thought we were inside, old man."

"I mean way inside." Evan stepped behind Alex and pushed.

"Evan, act a gentleman," Amanda scolded with a smile.

"But he won't hurry!" Effie tried again to pull him forward.

Alex questioned Amanda with his eyes.

She shook her head, still smiling. "I guess they aren't going to let us wait for the surprise."

"Surprise?"

"All right, Effie, Evan. You may take him into the dining room."

"Dinner is a surprise?" he asked, allowing the children to guide him through the parlor toward the door leading to the dining room. "I thought I was invited for dinner."

Effie and Evan giggled. "Dinner isn't the surprise, silly," Effie informed him.

The first thing he noticed about the parlor and dining room is that they were furnished with furniture of the simple lines that had swept the country since the style's presentation at the Columbian World's Fair in Chicago the previous summer. He found the concentration on wood and line instead of curves and overstuffing and flowers restful to the eye, though he knew the furniture wasn't as comfortable to sit on as the Victorian furniture to which the world was accustomed.

The second thing he noticed stopped him in his tracks just inside the dining room door. Paper chains decorated a high-backed chair at one end of the dining room table. A paper crown painted yellow with the words "Uncle Alex" written across it in crooked black letters sat on the china plate in front of the decorated chair. Along the top of a window, paper letters spelled out "Happy Birthday."

Emotion welled up in his chest and closed his throat. No one had made a special day of his birthday since he was Effie and Evan's age. He'd believed he'd stopped caring about such things years ago, believed birthday celebrations were only for children.

"Happy birthday! Happy birthday, Uncle Alex!" Effie and Evan were calling out while jumping up and down.

He dropped to one knee and gathered them in his arms, hugging them close, afraid the tears pooling in his eyes would spill over if he tried to speak.

Chapter 8

Amanda watched Alex wrap an arm about each child and pull them close. His lips pressed together hard for a moment. Then he looked directly into her eyes and whispered, "Thank you."

Were his eyes filled with tears? she wondered, smiling her welcome. She couldn't be certain, for the children immediately reclaimed his attention.

"You're welcome, Uncle Alex," Evan said, pulling back from the embrace.

"Were you surprised?" Effie grinned, her eyes wide with question.

"Very surprised. It's the most wonderful surprise of my life."

Effie tilted her head. "Why is your voice so funny?"

"Guess I have frog in my throat."

Amanda's own throat thickened, and she turned her back to them, pretending to be busy with the flowers on the table. Seeing Alex's face, his eyes, was like looking at a soul laid bare. He might be embarrassed to have her witness him in this state. She doubted he was accustomed to allowing himself to react so strongly and sentimentally, let alone to allowing anyone to see him doing so. Besides, she needed a moment to blink back her own tears.

Effie and Evan evidently didn't recognize Alex's emotions. They laughed at his answer. "Who ever heard of a frog in a throat?" Effie asked.

Alex cleared his throat. "Why else would someone's voice sound as if he were croaking?"

Amanda could tell he was regaining control of his emotions. Swallowing the lump in her throat, she turned to wave an arm toward the decorated chair at the end of the table. "You have the seat of honor today, Uncle Alex."

"Evan and me decorated it." Effie lifted the paper chain that lay across the top of the chair and hung down both sides to the floor. "We wanted to use our favorite colors, but we couldn't find my favorite color, purple, so we used Evan's favorite blue color and my second-favorite color, red. Amanda made glue from flour for us, so we could stick the ends together."

"It's perfect," he assured them.

They beamed. Then Evan pulled out the chair. "Sit down."

"Gentlemen are supposed to help the ladies with their chairs before they sit down, aren't they, old man?"

"Not on their birthdays." Amanda quickly pulled out the chair opposite him and sat down, not even taking time to smooth her skirt. She picked up the crystal bell beside her plate and rang it.

Evan grinned. "Not on their birthdays."

"I stand, that is, sit, corrected." Alex seated himself.

"Don't forget your birthday crown." Effie handed him the yellow and black paper creation.

He set it carefully on his head. "What do you think? Will it replace the bowler?"

Amanda grinned as his gaze met hers. *He is such fun! I'm so glad he is entering into the spirit of this, for the children's sake.* "I don't know if it will replace the bowler, but it should. I've never seen you look more handsome, Uncle Alex. Don't you agree, Effie?"

The girl nodded so hard her curls bobbed on her shoulders.

Amanda's heart seemed to stop when Alex's gaze held hers for a long moment before he turned to Effie. Had she been too bold, saying he looked handsome? She'd thought her teasing tone would disguise the impropriety. He was more handsome than she'd ever seen him, as much because of his attitude toward the children as his looks.

The maid brought in the first course, oyster stew. While she was serving it, Alex raised an eyebrow and studied Effie. "Isn't that your favorite dress, the one you wore to dinner the night I arrived in River's Edge?"

Effie swelled with pride. "Yes. I wore it because it's your party."

"That was mighty nice of you. You look very pretty."

"Hmph!" Evan crossed his arms over his chest. "Amanda made me wear this stupid suit. I told her you wouldn't care if I wore my comfortable knickers and play shirt, Uncle Alex, but she nagged and nagged."

Amanda tried to bite back a laugh, but failed when Alex's laugh boomed out.

"Hard to fight women when it comes to what to wear to a party, old man," Alex comforted Evan. He nodded toward the crystal vase in the middle of the table. "Did you two kids collect these flowers, too?"

Amanda caught his quick glance at her before he looked politely at Effie who was assuring him that she and Evan had indeed put together the bouquet. Amanda shared a smile with him, knowing it was the wilted dandelions, their browning yellow heads drooping over the side of the vase, surrounding the cut flowers from her garden, that told him who had collected the bouquet for him.

The birthday cake was angel food with whipped cream and fresh blueberries. "Mrs. Kelly made it," Amanda told him.

"Mrs. Kelly? Constance gave her the day off."

"When she heard it was your birthday, nothing would do but that she make the cake. She brought it over just before you arrived."

He stared at her as if he were unable to comprehend that a person would do such a thing for him when she had the day to herself to do as she pleased. Wasn't he accustomed to people expressing their affection for him? Amanda's heart clenched at the sad possibility. He was such a dear man! He deserved to have people show him how special he was to them.

"It's time for presents," Effie informed Alex when they moved to the parlor after dinner, with Alex still wearing his birthday crown. "Come on, Evan!" The two ran from the room. The sound of their racing footsteps told him they were headed upstairs.

Alex gave Amanda an amused look. "Presents, too?"

"They made the gifts themselves." Amanda waved him toward a large wooden rocker with a leather seat. "They are most original."

When Evan presented the first gift, Alex repeated Amanda's words. "Most original! I've never had a mud pie for my birthday."

"We wrote 26 on it in tiny stones," Evan pointed out unnecessarily. "That was my idea."

"And a good idea it was. Do I get to keep this?"

They nodded, already turning their attention to the next gift. Amanda took the mud pie from him and set it on a nearby table.

Effie pulled a large piece of paper from behind her. She spread her arms wide so Alex could see it all. "I made this. It's you detectiving. Do you know what you're doing?"

Amanda slid a hand over her mouth while he looked at the drawing of an open door, with a man in a bowler bent at the waist beside the door. Would he recognize Effie's attempt? The girl was not a born artist; she drew rather the way Amanda sang.

Alex placed a hand on each end of the picture, and cocked his head to one side. "Looks like I'm listening to hear a secret."

Amanda breathed a small sigh of relief that he'd recognized it. She wouldn't have wanted Effie's feelings hurt.

Effie's grin couldn't have grown wider. "I knew you'd know what it was. You sneaked up on the people in the room behind the door, doing detectiving."

"Effie and me did detectiving today," Evan informed him.

"You did, huh?" Alex ruffled his hair and looked back at his picture. "I'm going to have it framed, so I can hang it on a wall and keep it forever," Alex assured her. "These are the best birthday presents I've ever had, and the best birthday party, too."

Effie and Evan exchanged grins of satisfaction. Then Effie folded her forearms against the rocker's wide wooden arm. "Amanda helped us with the party."

"That was nice of her." His gaze met hers over the children's heads. His eyes were filled with warmth and gratitude that touched her heart.

Before she could respond, there was a knock at the door. Justin and Constance had arrived back in town and had come to pick up the children.

Alex immediately showed Justin and Constance the children's gifts, and raved about the party. Effie and Evan puffed out their little chests out in pride.

A sweet happiness unlike any she'd previously known filled Amanda as she watched the interaction. Alexander Bixby was a far greater, dearer man than she'd guessed. She'd known he'd be intelligent, honorable, and courageous. She'd admired him for those qualities from the beginning, but it was his love for children and his special way with them that was turning her admiration into love.

Justin and Constance stayed long enough to have a piece of the birthday cake before taking the children home for the night.

Alex lingered behind with Amanda in the hallway after the others left. Anticipation and joy made her heart race. She linked her fingers together loosely and turned to him with a smile she hoped didn't look as nervous as she felt.

"May I stay a few minutes?" he asked. "It's a pleasant evening. We could sit on the porch, since your father isn't home."

"That sounds lovely." How thoughtful of him to suggest a partly public place when her father wasn't home to chaperon. With the children there and the cook and maid waiting on them, it wasn't considered improper for them to dine together, but now she knew their characters would be questioned by the community, and she appreciated his care of her image.

She led the way onto the porch. Golden lamplight shone from the parlor windows. The delicate scent of spirea and the songs of evening insects surrounded them.

She felt his hand at the small of her back. "That white wicker swing looks inviting, don't you think?"

She was glad he'd suggested it, but was too nervous at his nearness to reply, so she merely sat down, leaning against the rose-flowered pillows. When he sat down beside her, she folded her hands lightly in her lap and stared at them. It seemed so intimate, to be sitting so close to each other.

"Thank you for tonight, Amanda. I know what Effie said is true, that you helped with everything."

"It was fun. I enjoyed doing it."

He cleared his throat. She could feel his discomfort, and waited. Was he as nervous as she was? Was he—she almost forgot to breathe at the thought—was he about to ask to court her?

"This party," he started, "well, no one's made anything special of my birthday since I was in knee pants. Meant more to me than I can say. I'll always remember it. Always."

"I'm glad." The words came out as little more than a whisper, and she felt her cheeks warm. Surely he must be aware of how much she cared for him! "I'm glad you appreciate all the children went to in arranging this. They spent the entire day at it. When they arrived this morning, the first thing they did was tell me their plan and ask me to help."

"They are great kids."

The tip of his broad index finger lightly traced a figure eight from her wrist to the tip of her own index finger and back again, sending chills up her spine and a thrill to her heart. "When Constance decided to stay in River's Edge," he began, "to raise Effie and Evan with Justin, and give up her work with the Pinkerton Agency, I couldn't understand how she could do it. Life here seemed so tame after life in Chicago. I think I understand now. The people here are very special."

Her heart caught in her throat. Was he saying that she was very special to him? Special as a friend? As something more? Don't read more into it than he meant, she admonished herself. He's twenty-six years old and has full command of the English language. If and when he's ready to tell you he cares for you, Amanda Mason, he will say it clearly. "That's very sweet of you to say, but there are special people everywhere, don't you think?"

He didn't reply for a moment, only continued the tracing on the back of her hand, the tracing that made it so difficult for her to think clearly.

"I guess you're right," he finally admitted. "Perhaps I just haven't been looking for them. Being a Pinkerton operative, my attention is seldom trained on the sweet people of the world."

"But you do the kind people such a service in capturing criminals. Like the counterfeiters. I was thinking—"

He stopped the tracing on her hand to rest his finger against her lips. "Let's not talk of business tonight."

Her lips felt the heat from his finger even after he'd removed it. His brief touch shocked all words from her mind.

He stood so abruptly the swing hit the back of his legs and stopped. Amanda caught the arm of the swing, surprised at his sudden move. What was wrong?

He took one of her hands to help her up, letting go as soon as she was standing. "I should be going."

Bewilderment shoved away the beauty of the evening they had shared. "Is—is something wrong?"

"It's getting late, that's all." He didn't meet her gaze. "If you'd get the children's gifts for me, I'd appreciate it."

She tried to keep the tears from her eyes when she returned to the porch with the mud pie and drawing. He was standing on the bottom step when she handed them to him.

"I—I meant it when I said I'll always remember tonight."

Amanda swallowed hard and tried to act lighthearted. "I'm glad to hear it, Uncle Alex."

He stepped up to the step below her, placing himself face-to-face with her. His breath was warm against her cheek when he said in a low voice that vibrated through her, "Can we drop the Uncle, Amanda?"

"If—if you like. . .Alexander."

"I like the way my name sounds on your lips, sweet Amanda."

She held her breath, and tried to watch his eyes in the pale light from the parlor. She yearned for him to kiss her, felt herself sway toward him.

He stepped back. "Good night."

She yanked herself back to reality. Disappointment and satisfaction wound themselves together about her when he walked away. "Happy birthday, Alexander."

He turned and grinned at her in the moonlight, setting her heart tripping all over again. "The happiest, Amanda."

It has been my happiest birthday ever, he thought. He wondered whether Amanda was still on the porch, watching him walk next door. Only with great discipline could he keep himself from turning around to see.

Spending the evening with Amanda and the children had been like spending an evening with family. Longing seeped into his heart, seemed to seep into his very bones. What must it be like to return to a family after each assignment, to be with people he knew and who liked him for his true self, instead of whatever person he was pretending to be for the current assignment? What would it be like to be with people who were always their true selves, people he could trust?

Someone like Amanda. The more time he spent with her, the more he liked her. Even after the hours they'd spent together this evening, and with the proof of the party in his hands, he could barely comprehend all the work she had gone to in helping Effie and Evan arrange his party. She had such a giving heart! She made herself more vulnerable to people than anyone he'd ever met.

The more time he spent with Amanda, the more certain he was that he didn't love Constance any longer. Perhaps Constance was right, and he'd only thought their deep friendship was love.

One thing of which of which he was certain, he wanted to spend as much time as possible with Amanda while he was on assignment in River's Edge. Of course, he'd have to be careful not to encourage her affections. He'd come within a fraction of an inch of making the mistake of kissing her tonight! He almost wished he had kissed her. Just once, he would like to know what it felt like to hold her in his arms, and touch her lips with his. A memory he could hold in his heart when he left.

It wouldn't be fair to her. He knew a number of Pinkerton agents with families, but he didn't believe it was right to expect a wife and family to put up with such a life—dangerous assignments, and sometimes assignments where he was incognito and would have to be away from a family for months at a time.

No, he couldn't allow his feelings for her to get out of hand, but surely there could be nothing wrong with enjoying some friendly hours together, could there?

He ran lightly up the stairs to his room. He pushed the switch on the wall, thinking how glad he was Justin's home was so modern, and the ceiling light came on.

The reflection in the swinging mirror on the low chest of drawers opposite the door caught his attention, and he groaned. He stared back at himself, a yellow paper crown on his head. Embarrassment washed over him.

Then he laughed. He'd been almost romancing Amanda with this silly-looking thing on his head, and forthright Amanda, who always spoke her mind, hadn't said a word.

He took it off, holding it carefully in both hands and examining it. It must have taken the children quite a while to make it. He could almost feel the love they had put into it.

He set it on the dresser, and took paper out of one of the drawers to write his daily report to the superintendent about the case. He grinned to himself. He wasn't going to tell his superior he'd been crowned king of River's Edge this evening!

"I feel as wealthy as a king tonight," he told the man in the mirror.

Chapter 9

"Tell me about some of the cases you were on as a Pinkerton agent," Amanda pleaded with Constance the next afternoon when they had coffee and cookies together on the wide veranda that swept around Constance's large, Victorian home, like a beach along an ocean.

Constance laughed at her over the rim of her china cup. "You are as bad as Effie and Evan, always asking for detective stories. Don't you get enough of them in the books you read? I saw you were reading *A Study in Scarlet* the other day. Surely Sherlock Holmes's cases are more interesting than my adventures!"

"Sherlock Holmes is make-believe. Your adventures were true. Tell me just one."

Constance leaned against the tall, rounded back of her wicker chair. "All right. Did I ever tell you about when we were asked to prove a medium wasn't speaking to the spirits of her clients' loved ones at all, but was merely leading those poor souls on?"

"No!" Amanda leaned forward, her mind already racing with questions about the case. "How did you ever get involved in such a case? How could you prove she was a hoax? Wouldn't she have to be awfully clever to fool her customers?"

Constance held up a hand, palm toward Amanda. "One question at a time. It happened like this."

Amanda listened, enthralled, to Constance's story. When she was done, Amanda leaned against the chair back and sighed. "Your life has been so exciting. I do wish I could be a detective."

"It isn't all excitement."

"That's what Alexander tells me." She wrinkled her nose at the memory.

"So it's Alexander now?" Constance's twinkling eyes belied her calm voice.

"Yes." Just his name set butterflies fluttering in her stomach, and the memory of his nearness when he'd said, "I like the way my name sounds on your lips, sweet Amanda." She leaned forward to set her cup on the wicker table between them. "Not that we are anything more than friends, you understand."

"Of course not."

Amanda propped her hands on her hips and grinned. "You needn't sit there with that prim little smile and look as though I'm not telling all. Alex hasn't asked to court me."

Constance set her own cup down, then reached to cover one of Amanda's hands with her own. "Alex is a fine man. I'd like to see my two best friends fall in love, if only for the purely selfish motive of keeping you both in my life. I must

176

warn you, though, that it may not be safe to lose your heart to Alex."

Apprehension dampened the joy of Amanda's memories. "Not safe? Why would you say such a thing?"

"He is a Pinkerton man. Not many are killed or seriously wounded in their work, but there is always that possibility. Married men often ask for assignments that keep them close to home, but it isn't uncommon for operatives to be assigned cases far away, and be gone for weeks or months at a time. I know of an agent who was sent undercover for years on one case. Of course, some operatives change their professions when they marry."

Amanda watched her fingers trace the rim of her cup, hoping to hide the despair Constance's words brought to her heart. "We're only friends. There's been no talk of marriage."

"I'm sorry if I've spoken out of turn. I thought you should understand what Alex's life is like."

"You are my dear friend, Constance. Nothing you could say to me could ever be misconstrued as interference. I'm glad for your concern."

Was there any chance a man like Alex could let himself love her? Certainly she wouldn't want him to give up his profession for her. Constance didn't make marriage to a detective sound appealing.

Worst of all was the knowledge that Constance's warning had come too late. He already held her heart.

❧

When Alex joined the Knights for devotions that evening, Effie sat down on the pale blue velvet sofa beside him and bounced herself along the cushion until she could lean against the back. "Have you framed my picture yet?"

"Not yet, but I will soon."

Evan climbed up on the other side of him, while Constance lowered herself gracefully to an elegant, blue-satin covered ladies chair which Alex thought suited her perfectly, and Justin found a larger, more comfortable chair.

While Justin leafed through the well-worn, leather-covered Bible, Evan picked up on the conversation Effie had started. "Effie and me were—"

"Effie and I," Constance reminded gently.

"Yes," Evan agreed, "we were detectiving today, too, like you in the picture."

Alex grinned at the boy's serious tone. "Did you discover any important secrets?"

Evan shook his head. "We sneaked up on Aunt Constance and Amanda, but they only talked about boring things."

"It wasn't boring." Effie leaned forward to scowl past Alex at her brother. "They were talking about love stuff." She twisted her shoulders back and forth in a little self-conscious dance. "I think Amanda is sweet on you, Uncle Alex."

"Effie! You mustn't say such things!" Constance's voice was uncharacteristically shrill with shock.

"But you told Amanda that—"

"Stop this instant!" Constance warned sharply.

Effie stopped, but Alex could almost feel the girl's conviction that Constance was being unjust ooze from her.

He rubbed a hand over his mustache, past his mouth and chin. His heart had leaped at Effie's statement, thrilled to hear Amanda might care for him, but he was upset for Amanda that the children were reporting what was obviously intended as a private conversation.

"We've told you both a number of times that eavesdropping is not proper behavior." Justin's face looked like a storm ready to happen. "Not for children or adults."

"But we have to practice detectiving." Effie spread her hands wide, palms up. "Detectives have to find out secrets."

Alex took one of Effie's hands in his, marveling at how small and fragile hers was. "You're right, Effie. Detectives have to find out secrets. One of the other important things good detectives learn is not to tell everything they hear. A good detective can keep a secret, too."

She flashed him that smile that always melted his heart. "All right, Uncle Alex. We'll practice keeping secrets, won't we, Evan?"

"Yes." He bobbed his head once, hard.

Alex squeezed Effie's hand and patted Evan's knee. "Good."

"A promise not to eavesdrop would be a good thing, too," Justin growled, opening up the Bible again, "but I haven't managed to extract that from these two yet."

No one said anything while Justin found his place in the black book.

Alex listened carefully to the selection Justin read. He couldn't help reflecting that compared to Justin and Constance's faith, his own seemed as counterfeit as the bills being distributed by the criminals he was tracking.

As a boy, he'd thought a number of his fellow churchgoers were hypocrites. They didn't seem to live by the faith they professed each Sunday in church. Was his faith as counterfeit as theirs? At least he tried to live by the moral teachings of the church, even if he didn't manage to do so perfectly, and even though his faith in God's love for individuals was more a hope than a solid belief.

When Constance took Effie and Evan upstairs to prepare for bed, Alex asked Justin, "Doesn't it bother you that a lot of people attending church appear to be hypocrites?"

"It used to," he admitted. "Finally I realized that I can't tell which ones are true hypocrites, and which are merely imperfect believers like myself. Each of us has different strengths, and different sins which seem to be difficult or impossible for us to conquer."

"I suppose so." The answer didn't satisfy the questions in Alex's heart.

Justin set the Bible on the marble-topped table beneath the large window overlooking the front porch. "Henry W. Beecher said, 'The church is not a gallery for the exhibition of eminent Christians, but a school for the education of imperfect ones, a nursery for the care of weak ones, a hospital for the healing of those who need assiduous care.' "

Alex nodded. Maybe everyone felt as uncertain as he did about his attempts at religion, and only appeared more secure in their faith. Or maybe he felt this way because he was only beginning to explore the world of faith. *Even though things don't feel the way I think they are supposed to, from what that Beecher fellow says, I must be in the right place, attending church again, because when it comes to being a Christian, I'm definitely one of the "imperfect ones."*

Chapter 10

In spite of his resolve to spend time with Amanda, Alex didn't see her again for days. The case kept him busy, though he was no closer to solving it than when he'd arrived in River's Edge. Each time he passed Amanda's house, he watched for her, hoping for a chance to at least say hello and see her beautiful smile. Even during his work, if he was in River's Edge, he was watching for her: among bank customers, among the people on the street, among store customers when he spoke with merchants.

So when he saw her on her front porch on his way home from the bank Saturday afternoon, his heart skipped a beat, and a prayer of thanks even slipped in a fervent whisper from his lips. His step quickened as he turned onto the walk leading to her house.

He could see she was engrossed in something on her lap. She didn't even notice him until he started climbing the steps. The joy in her face when she looked up and saw him made his heart feel as if the sun were shining on it.

"Alex! How nice to see you!"

"Nice to see you, too." An understatement if ever there was one! Effie's comment that she thought Amanda was sweet on him flashed through his mind. He wished now Effie had been even more indiscreet, and told him exactly what Amanda had said to Constance!

In her pink dress, he thought she looked lovelier than any of the flowers that nodded in the bed in front of the porch. Lace edged the neckline which was cut low for a warm summer day. The sleeves with huge shoulders and upper arms ended at the elbow, another tribute to the summer weather. He always thought women's clothing looked most uncomfortable, but he couldn't deny he liked the way the styles accentuated Amanda's femininity.

"First, I want to ask you to come to my Sunday school class Sunday."

His laugh burst out. "Didn't you say your class is for children Effie and Evan's age?"

"Yes, but I'm not asking you to attend as a student, I'm asking you to attend as the lesson."

He laid both hands on his chest. "I am to be a Sunday school lesson? That's rich! A lesson in what?"

"You'll see." Her eyes sparkled with mischief. "All you have to do is show up. Will you come?"

"I will, to satisfy my curiosity if nothing else. What else did you want to ask me?"

"I've been reading this book," Amanda closed the book in her lap so he could see the cover, *The Counterfeiters and the Detectives* by Allan Pinkerton. "I want to ask you some questions."

Disappointment dampened his enjoyment. Had her apparent joy at his arrival been due to her continuing interest in detective work, instead of his presence? The thought sharpened his tone. "Ask me what?"

"To begin with, how do you recognize a counterfeit bill?"

"It takes a trained eye. You look for things people don't usually notice, like the type of ink, signatures."

"Would you show me?"

"No." Teach her how to do something that would encourage her to become involved in the case? Surely she jested!

"Please, Alexander?" She leaned forward, her hands folded on the book in her lap, and smiled up at him so sweetly he almost lost his resolve.

"No."

She leaned against the chair's high back and shook her head. "You can be so exasperating."

He swept off his bowler, dropped into a chair beside hers, and grinned. "So can you."

Her laugh rang out on the summer air. "I'm so glad you think so. At least exasperating isn't boring. Boring is the most dangerous thing a woman can be, you know."

"Rest assured, you are definitely not boring." Would be a lot safer for my heart if you were! he thought.

"I've been thinking. I know you said you don't want me to become involved in the case, but—"

"And I meant it!"

She held up a palm toward him. "Please, hear me out."

"I'm listening." He crossed his arms. When she got done with whatever harebrained scheme she'd come up with, he would tell her again to stay out of the case.

"Truly listen. Don't simply wait for me to quit speaking so you can say 'no' to me again."

He grinned. Had she read his mind? "I'll try." He relaxed against the back of the chair and waited for her to begin. He had to concentrate to focus on her words, instead of how charming she was when she argued so passionately for her cause.

"You might remember I told you I've read a number of books written by Allan Pinkerton."

He nodded.

"Perhaps you recall his theory that the unique aspects of rural areas emphasize the unusual for its inhabitants. Even a farmer's purchase of a new hat or gun was known about the county in a day, Mr. Pinkerton wrote, with the gossip transmitted by farmers and their wives, hungry for the slightest morsel of news about their neighbors."

"I do recall that."

She shifted forward in her chair, her face shining with eagerness. "Small towns are like that, too. It's impossible to keep a secret here. Gossip rages at Sunday school picnics, and the general store, and the lemonade parties that are so popular now. The telephones with their party lines are wonderful ways to spread news! You don't even have to see the person to share the latest gossip."

"And?"

"Don't you see? I can ferret out information for you from local gossip!"

"Ferret out" information? Good grief! She truly has been reading too many detective novels! "Amanda—"

She held her palm toward him again. "I'm not done. I thought maybe we could put together a group of women—trustworthy, churchgoing women, of course—who could listen to local gossip and report anything suspicious to you. Maybe Constance would help, and Mrs. Kelly, Constance's Aunt Libby and—"

"Justin would have my head if I allowed either of those women to become involved. Aren't you aware of his hatred of deceit in any form?"

He could see his comments didn't even begin to daunt her. "Then we'll find other women. I know a number of women I'd trust with my life. Pinkerton believed criminals always revealed their secrets, and that their secrets could be won from them through sympathy and confidence. Certainly if the counterfeiters are from River's Edge, they would be more likely to reveal their secrets to me and my friends than to you." Elbows bent, she held up her hands at her sides. "Who would suspect us? The townspeople have known us all our lives."

He took her hands and folded them together between his own. "Listen to me, Amanda." He tried to keep his voice low and quiet, so she wouldn't misunderstand his concern. "Pinkerton also believed an operative must have the necessary experience in crime and in human judgment to know the criminal in his weakest moment, when he's most likely to reveal his crime. You and your friends haven't that experience."

Her shoulders sagged slightly beneath their huge puffed sleeves. Then she sat forward eagerly once more, her hands still caught in his. "We could still help. Remember what Pinkerton said about the farmer's new hat? We could listen for new things people have purchased, things that they normally couldn't afford. After all, the counterfeiters must want to spend the money they are getting in exchange for the counterfeit money, mustn't they?"

"That would be the natural assumption." Actually, he was surprised at her insight. Watching for people who were spending more money than they could normally afford to spend was a great way to unearth suspects, and not so difficult to do in a town as small as River's Edge. He'd have to remember to ask Sheriff Tucker if he was watching for this.

Still, he wasn't about to let Amanda think she could do something so dangerous. "Have you considered," he asked, "that your friends would not be likely to report any extravagant purchases made by their husbands, sons, fathers, or brothers?"

Her laugh told him she thought he was being silly before her words said the same. "The women I'm thinking of are good church people, and so are their families. These people aren't crooks."

"Crooks would have a difficult time getting away with crimes if they acted like crooks in their everyday life. It's the people we trust most who can and do most easily deceive us."

Her smile died. "I hadn't thought of that. You're right, of course."

Had good sense finally prevailed? *Thank You, Lord!*

Amanda's face brightened again.

His spirits sagged. It looked like she hadn't given up after all.

"There was the most interesting article in the newspaper today, Alex. Perhaps you can use it to help with the case."

At least she had indicated he might use it rather than herself! "Tell me about it."

"It told about some robbers captured in Grand Rapids, Michigan. A hardware store there was losing money to till-tapping. The owners tried a number of means of entrapping the robbers, but all failed." She extracted her hands from his, the better to help her tell the story, he suspected, but he missed her touch. "Finally, they arranged for a camera to be focused on the cash drawer, and an electrical connection was made to the Edison Company's plant to operate the camera. A device was fitted in the cash drawer so that when the till was opened, the electric connection was made, and the camera shot the picture of the burglars. The robbers saw the flash, but didn't see anyone, so they continued with the robbery. They couldn't deny they had been the thieves when confronted with the picture later."

Alex couldn't help laughing. "That is ingenious, but where would you propose mounting the cameras in this case? In the bank, and in every business in town?"

The corners of her mouth drooped. "I guess it isn't practical, is it?"

Perhaps it wasn't such a bad idea after all. He might mention it to Justin. If they could figure out a way to work it at the bank, they might discover if one of the staff there was an accomplice in the case. He wasn't about to mention such a possibility to Amanda. Too dangerous for her to know anything about the workings or possible workings of the case.

"Leave the work to the men who are trained for it, Amanda, please." *Because I couldn't bear it if you were injured, or worse,* he thought. "It's too dangerous for untrained people."

She studied his face soberly. "Is this case truly dangerous?"

"All cases are potentially dangerous, as I told you before."

"Then I hope you will be very careful, Alexander."

His gaze tangled in hers. His heart seemed to swell until it filled his entire chest. He couldn't remember anyone but his fellow agents expressing concern for his safety. Her words and the care behind them made him feel cherished. The emotion was new to him, and he discovered he wanted to feel that way always.

"It's your safety which concerns me, also." Surely she must recognize his sincerity by the huskiness in his voice.

Someone whistling the popular tune "After the Ball" broke in on the world that had seemed to contain only the two of them. Impatient, he turned to see who had invaded this special moment.

Jack Davis! The young man from the bank; the one Justin had said sometimes escorted Amanda. The obnoxious clerk grinned and waved at them.

Alex drew back slightly from his nearness to Amanda. "He is coming for you?" He tried to keep the jealousy that was burning like acid through his chest from seeping into his voice.

"Yes. We—we're attending the lyceum this evening."

Was it regret he saw in her eyes? Regret that she would be spending the evening with Davis instead of himself? Or was it pity, for himself?

Either way, she'd be walking away from here with Davis in a few minutes, and he'd be spending the evening trying not to imagine them together. Should be easy; at least no more difficult than trying to breathe underwater.

He stood up and forced a smile. "Then I'll be leaving. Have a nice evening."

"Thank you." Her eyes hadn't left his face. "I. . .thank you."

The tie between them felt almost physical to him. Did she feel it, too? "Good night." Turning away from her was like prying a spoon out of spilled molasses.

Davis was climbing the steps to the veranda when Alex reached them. His loud, cheerful "Hello, there, Mr. Bixby!" grated on Alex's nerves. He didn't even want to shake the hand Davis held out to him, but he did, for a fraction of a moment. "Evening, Davis." He kept walking, eager to get away from there as fast as possible.

"What do you think you're doing, Bixby, feeling jealous over her?" he muttered, hurrying down the sidewalk. After all, he had no plans to make a claim on Amanda's future. He had his profession to consider! Hadn't he told himself he intended to enjoy Amanda's company in a platonic manner only while on this assignment, to simply allow himself a few hours of innocent pleasure with her?

So much for good intentions!

Chapter 11

Alex was exhausted from lack of sleep the next day when he entered the bank. He'd tossed and turned all night, imagining Davis and Amanda together. Worse than any nightmare, he thought, walking downtown.

He'd been in the area only a few weeks, but already he was beginning to recognize some of the neighbors and businessmen, and they him. As he walked along, he exchanged simple greetings with the children and matrons out for a morning stroll, merchants and laborers and the postmistress on their way to their day's work, and deliverymen he recognized from seeing them pass so often. It had always been an advantage in his profession to be unknown by most people, and he had rather liked his way of blending into the fabric of a community, unnoticed. Now he was surprised to find how pleasant it was to feel a part of River's Edge and its people.

As I was surprised last night by Amanda's quick mind, he thought. From the first, he'd found her charming and fun, a complete contrast from quiet, sedate, serene Constance. One of the things he'd always admired in Constance was her bright, logical mind. He hadn't expected high intelligence to be among Amanda's qualities. *Why?* he wondered. *Because she laughed so easily, because she seemed so innocent?*

Whatever the reason for his error, he knew better now. Her mind wasn't so neatly logical as Constance's, or his own, but it was quick and creative to an amazing degree. He chuckled to himself. For all his attempts to discourage her involvement in the case, she had given him some good ideas concerning it.

He entered the bank with a light heart.

"So that's what it looks like!"

Amanda's voice froze his steps. His head jerked toward the sound of it. His nightmare come to life! She was standing at one of the teller windows, her head close beside that of Jack Davis.

Alex felt jealousy tangling about him like seaweed about a diver, pulling him down, trapping him.

Davis looked up, noticed Alex, and waved. "Morning, Bixby!" His loud voice grated on Alex's nerves, as usual. Alex nodded sharply and dug his fists into his suit jacket pockets.

Amanda looked up with a bright smile. "Hello, Alexander." She held up a bill and waved it. "Mr. Davis is showing me how to recognize counterfeit bills."

The grin beneath Davis's sleek blond mustache showed he was proud of himself.

Fury burned through Alex. How could the bank clerk be such an idiot as to put her in such danger, and so publicly? His glance darted about the bank. At least there didn't appear to be any customers in the bank at the moment.

After he'd warned her to stay out of the case, how could Amanda have asked Davis to show her counterfeit money? Had she no more respect for his experienced warning than to do such an outlandish thing?

He stalked through toward the tellers' area, not even acknowledging Miss Sherman's quiet "Good morning, Mr. Bixby."

His hand closed about the forearm of Amanda's navy blue Eaton suit jacket. "I'd like to talk with you in Justin's office."

Shock widened her eyes and parted her lips as she stared down at his hand.

"I say, Bixby, that's hardly a gentlemanly manner in which to treat a lady." Davis scowled at him.

Alex snatched his hand back, embarrassed that in his anger he'd forgotten his manners. Not only had he treated Amanda rudely, he'd done it in front of Davis, the man in front of whom he'd least wanted to act poorly. "Sorry." He met Amanda's eyes, and wondered if his were as defiant as hers. "Will you give me a minute, please?"

"I think not, Mr. Bixby." Her voice was low and even. Her gaze didn't flicker.

He hadn't thought it possible to become more angry or more embarrassed. He hadn't felt this awful since he was fifteen, and the girl he'd liked had publicly humiliated him by showing all the other girls in class the sweetheart note he'd written her for Valentine's Day, giggling over the words he'd struggled with to express his heart. He'd determined then and there that girls weren't worth the trouble they caused men.

Should have stuck to that belief!

He touched his fingers to the brim of his derby. Unclenched his teeth long enough to say, "I apologize again for my rude manner, Miss Mason." He glanced at Davis. "Is Mr. Knight in his office?"

At Davis's nod, Alex turned on his heel. A moment later he was facing a surprised Justin.

"What makes you look so rough?" Justin asked.

Alex explained, pacing the office while he did so, with an effort keeping his voice low enough that it didn't penetrate the thick wooden door.

His anger somewhat abated after justifying himself to Knight, and he dropped into one of the wooden chairs opposite Justin's desk. Then he told him about Amanda's suggestion of checking on townspeople who were spending more than they could afford. Who better than the local bank president to recognize such people?

Justin could think of no one who was making purchases beyond his or her means. "Let me think on it. Perhaps now I'm aware to watch for it, I'll notice someone doing just that."

When he and Justin were through talking, Alex was glad to see Amanda had left the bank. Maybe by the time they saw each other again, both would have forgiven the other, at least a bit.

❧

At church the next morning, Alex approached Amanda with some trepidation, anger, and an expected rebuff making him uncomfortable. "Do you still want me to come to your Sunday school class?"

The corners of her mouth lifted slightly in a trembling smile. "Yes." She took a deep breath, lifting the lace trim on the front of her lilac gown. "I—I'm sorry I acted so abominably at the bank yesterday. It doesn't excuse me, of course, but your manner embarrassed me."

He hadn't expected an apology! He'd believed he was the one to apologize, and had been determined not to do so. Her gracious, unexpected act destroyed his prideful resolve. "You've nothing to apologize for. I had no right to speak to you so angrily, and certainly not to embarrass you in public."

Her face relaxed into a full smile. She held out a glove covered hand. "Truce, Alexander?"

He hesitated. He wanted complete forgiveness between them. He wanted to forget yesterday had ever happened, but he couldn't. His fingers closed over hers. He kept his voice low, so he wouldn't be overheard by other parishioners. "I'm sorry for the way I spoke to you in public, Amanda, scolding you as if you were a child, but I'm not sorry for wishing you hadn't approached Davis about the counterfeit bills. I wish you'd understand the danger in which you might have placed yourself."

Color swept her cheeks. She tugged her hand away from his. "I am an adult, Alexander." He was relieved her voice didn't hold anger. It was even, and controlled, but there wasn't fury in it. "I weighed the risks you expressed to me, and made my choice. Isn't that a freedom allowed all adults in America?"

"Of course it is."

She was right. She wasn't required to listen to his warnings, even when they were for her own good, even when they were expressed out of his growing affection for her. The realization didn't make him feel any better that she'd disregarded his warning.

"When do you want me to join you for Sunday school?"

Her eyes sparkled with anticipation, and he found himself smiling at the eager way she approached even a simple Sunday school class for children. "I don't want the children to meet you before the lesson begins. After classes begin, come downstairs and wait in the hallway. I'll let you know when it's time for you to enter."

❧

As always, it took Amanda a few minutes to quiet down the children and get them to pay attention at the beginning of class. They squirmed about on their stiff little oak chairs which were arranged in a semicircle, facing the wall. It didn't help Amanda's attempts at gaining attention that there were older and younger groups of children having classes in each corner of the large basement hall that served as the Sunday school room for everyone. Little heads swiveled, checking out the other classes, making faces at a friend or brother across the room, or giggling with the person beside them.

The hour began with roll call, and a recitation of the weekly Bible verse they'd been asked to memorize. Finally it was time for the lesson to begin. Amanda had Evan pass out small slates and a piece of chalk to each of the children. Then Amanda sat down on one of the small chairs, rested her elbows on her knees, and leaned forward with a smile, trying to draw the small ones' attention.

"I'm going to tell you about a special friend of mine. His name is Alexander Bixby."

Effie jerked up straight in her chair, clapping her hands. "Uncle Alex?"

Amanda nodded. "You and Evan mustn't tell anything about him this morning. This is a game. He is going to be the mystery man. Can you pretend you don't know him?"

Effie and Evan nodded, grinning widely.

Amanda started over, moving her gaze from one end of the small class to the other. "My friend's name is Alexander Bixby. Sometimes his friends call him Alex. He's twenty-six years old. He's tall and strong. He has black hair, and a mustache. His eyes are dark brown. Mr. Bixby is a good man. He doesn't lie or steal or hurt people. He is smart, and he can be very funny. He likes children. Why don't each of us draw a picture of Mr. Bixby?"

Chalk scraped across slates as the children began drawing. Occasionally a child would stop to ask a question. "Is he very, very tall?" "How can I make his hair black when the chalk is white?" "Does he have a big nose?" "Is he skinny?" "Is he fat?"

When they were done, she had them each hold their slates in front of them, facing outward. "Which do you think looks most like Alexander Bixby?" she asked. Looking at Effie and Evan, she put a finger to her lips and shook her head, reminding them they weren't to tell. They grinned, bit their lips, and hunched their shoulders, their eyes growing wide with mischievous fun.

Some of the drawings of Alex had curly hair, some straight hair. He was shown with mustaches of every shape and size. One child imagined him with a beard.

Harlan, a quiet little boy whose father had died the year before, pictured Alex holding the hand of a child, and Amanda remembered she had said Alex liked children. That had evidently been the most important thing Harlan heard about Alex. Her heart went out to him. She wanted to wrap love like a large, soft quilt around him to protect him from life's hurts.

A shy girl had drawn a large heart on Alex's chest, and told Amanda it was because she had said Alex was a good man. Many of the children had heard her say he could be funny, and had drawn him with a large smile. The class clown had drawn Alex with his hands on his stomach, his mouth in a large O, with the words "Ha, ha, ha!" printed beside his head.

"Do you want to see what Mr. Bixby looks like in person?" she asked when she had looked at every picture.

The children nodded eagerly, and she sent Evan out to the hall to find Alex. They came back hand in hand. Amanda noticed Alex's uncertain smile and wondered, amused, whether he was finding comfort in Evan's small hand.

Amanda explained that she had described him to the children. He examined their pictures. She liked the way he took time to look at each one, make a comment or ask a question about each, and ask each child's name and smile at them.

How has a man who has spent his life chasing criminals developed such a wonderful way with children? she asked God, then thanked Him it was so. Was one of the reasons justice was so important to this man because he wanted the world that children lived in to be safer and better and more filled with love for them?

When Alex had looked at each picture, Amanda asked him to read the Bible lesson for the day. His shocked look surprised her, but he took the Bible, sat cross-legged on the floor, and read the story of Jesus and Zacchaeus.

After that, Amanda let the children play "ring-around-the-rosy" and "London Bridge." Alex and Amanda played with them. At one point, while they were the "bridge," Alex whispered to her, "I didn't think Sunday school would ever be like this."

She'd whispered back, "You'll understand later."

The children's favorite part of the games was when Alex was caught in the falling bridge. He overreacted to his part in a manner that delighted the children.

When the games were over and it was almost time for class to end, Amanda asked the children to take their seats again and quiet down. It took Alex to convince them to do as she said, though they normally obeyed her much better.

Amanda didn't have the heart to ask Alex to take one of the tiny chairs, so she stood beside him in front of the children. "What do you think?" she asked them. "Is it different to know Mr. Bixby, than it is just knowing about him from what I told you of him?"

"Yes!" they called out, still excited from their play.

"That is the way it is with Jesus. We learn about Him from stories in the Bible, like the one Mr. Bixby read to us today, but it's not the same hearing about Him as it is knowing Him."

The little girl who had drawn the heart on Alex's chest in her slate picture raised her hand.

"Yes, Frances?"

"How can we know Jesus?"

The shy girl's sincere desire to know touched Amanda's heart. "If we believe the things the Bible tells us about Jesus, we can ask Him to be our friend, so we can not only know about Him, but know Him."

Francis spread her little hands. "But, Miss Mason, Jesus is invisible. How can somebody who is invisible be our friend?"

"Does the Bible tell us that Jesus performed miracles?"

Frances and the rest of the children nodded.

"Because we are only human, we can't understand how Jesus can be our friend when He is invisible to us. When He becomes our friend, that is a miracle."

"Oh." Frances frowned.

Amanda tried again. "What do you like about your best friend, Frances?"

A small smile crossed the freckled face. "She's nice. She likes to play the same things I like to play. And she doesn't say mean things to me or about other people."

"So you like her because of the kind of person she is, and not because of the way she looks?"

Frances nodded.

"If you could see Jesus, the way you can see Mr. Bixby, would you like Jesus because of the way He looked, or because of what He is like?"

"Because of what He is like," Frances said. "Because He is always kind. He loves everybody."

"Yes, He does. If we know we like Him no matter what He looks like, does it matter whether we can see Him?"

A slow smile grew on Frances's face. "I guess not."

Amanda folded her hands at her waist. "I'm going to pray and ask Jesus to be my friend. Any of you who believe what the Bible says about Jesus and want Him to be your friend, too, can pray along with me silently. Let's fold our hands and bow our heads."

She waited a moment until everyone was ready. Her heart sounded loud in her ears. Had the children understood what she tried to tell them? Would they open their hearts and pray along with her? She was aware that beside her, Alex was bowing his head and folding his hands, too.

"Dear Lord, we thank You for coming to Earth because You loved us. We love the things we've learned about You in the Bible, and want to know You as we do our friends. Please come live in our hearts and be our friend. Amen."

There was silence in the circle when the prayer was over. Little heads lifted, but no one spoke.

Then the church bells rang, telling the end of the Sunday school hour. The room erupted with the noise of children's voices and children's racing footsteps and scraping chairs. Most of the children hurried from the room, eager to be out in the summer sunshine. A few stopped to say good-bye to Amanda. Effie and Evan were eager to say hello to Alex.

Amanda was most touched when Harlan, the little boy who had lost his father, braved reaching out for Alex's hand when Effie was telling Alex a story about Thunder. Alex turned to the boy with a surprised look. Harlan bit his lip, hesitating, before he said, "I just wanted to thank you for coming, Mr. Bixby."

Alex must have noticed there was something special about Harlan. He gave him his full attention, shaking his hand in a man-to-man manner. "Your name is Harlan, isn't it?"

Harlan nodded, looking amazed and pleased Alex had remembered.

"Thank you for making me feel so welcome, Harlan."

Harlan gave him a shy smile before leaving.

When Justin and Constance had picked up Effie and Evan, Amanda told Alex, "I was surprised you remembered Harlan's name. You met so many children today."

"Pinkerton men are trained to remember names. Besides, there was something special about him, something in his eyes, like a pain that you usually see only in adults who have lost faith in life."

"He lost his father last year."

"Ah. That explains it."

It doesn't explain how a man who believes himself to be a hard-hearted detective who lives by his logic recognizes wounds in the heart of a child, she thought, glancing at him from under her lashes as they straightened the chairs. *Does he also recognize the love that's growing in my heart for him?*

Chapter 12

A little over a week later, Amanda's father left town on business for a few days.

"You're retired," she reminded him when he told her of the trip. "What business needs your attention?"

"Lance Chase has asked me to give a friend of his advice. I'll be home in a couple of days. Will you be afraid, staying here without me?"

She laughed and straightened his wide, striped, satin tie. "With the cook and two maids and Thunder staying in the house? I hardly think so!"

The house did seem quieter, just knowing he wouldn't be in and out for a couple days. She was even glad when the cook announced that morning that the deliveryman from the dry goods store had arrived. "He's brought the monthly bill, Miss Mason. Your father usually sends the money back with him. Shall I tell him to bring the bill back next week?"

"No, Mrs. Brady. I'll take care of it. Please ask the deliveryman to wait."

Amanda glanced at the bill. She didn't have enough money in her reticule to cover it, but her father always kept money in his office.

She opened the side door of the large walnut desk in her father's study and pulled out the top drawer. Inside was a carved box about a foot long and six inches wide. She lifted the heavy cover and smiled. More than enough to meet this bill.

Humming a little tune, Amanda counted out the bills she needed, and closed up the desk. She counted the bills again, just to be sure, as she started toward the door. Her humming broke off abruptly. *Why, how strange!* Moving to the wide windows, she examined the top bill more closely in the sunlight.

Was the ink slightly smudged? Was the color a little bluer than the normal ink used for bills? Her heart beat faster, louder. Where was the line that should be between the mouth and nose on the man's face? Jack Davis had told her that some of the counterfeit bills that had come through the sawmill payroll were missing that line.

She moved the bill closer to her face, and frowned, trying to see the details better. Dread slithered through her. "It's not there. The line's not there!"

She leaned against the window frame, one hand over her mouth, staring at the bill as though by willing it, she could change it, make it normal. She'd never thought the counterfeiting tentacles would reach into her own home!

Bills clutched in her hands, she paced the floor. The dread she'd felt at first was fast changing to anger. "Father's been cheated. 'Gypped' as they say in the detective novels. Who would do such a thing to him?"

She stopped at the window, staring unseeing out at the yard. "How can I find out who did this?" A movement caught her attention. The horse attached to the white, enclosed delivery wagon waited patiently for its master, its tail switching against pesty flies and mosquitoes.

"Oh, my! I'd forgotten all about him." She darted toward the door. Stopping, she stared at the bills in her hand. They certainly couldn't be used to pay him!

She replaced the bills in her father's desk, then hurried to the kitchen to apologize to the deliveryman.

He was chatting with Mrs. Brady and finishing off a piece of her apple pie. Thunder was seated on the floor beside him, his gaze glued on the man, the tip of his pink tongue showing between his teeth.

The room was filled with the wonderful smells of baked pastry, apples, and cinnamon, hiding the smells of the bread which Mrs. Brady always baked first because it required more heat than the pies. Loaves covered with linen towels rested on the counter below the window, curtains fluttering lightly in the morning breeze above them. On the sill, covered with dome-shaped screens, the pies were cooling.

How strange that life seems so homey and normal, she thought, *that Mrs. Brady and Tom don't realize there is anything unusual happening, when someone has stolen from Father!*

She didn't want them to know, either. No sense letting the news be spread about town before her father knew it himself. Besides, perhaps she was mistaken. A sprig of hope bloomed. After all, she wasn't an expert or a detective, she was only a young lady who had been shown a couple points about counterfeit money by a bank clerk. Perhaps the bills in her father's desk weren't counterfeit after all. Perhaps it was only her imagination, set afire from the books she'd been reading, and the knowledge of the counterfeiting ring that was operating in River's Edge.

The realization made it easier to smile at Tom, who had stood hastily upon seeing her enter the room, guilt on his wrinkled face, leaving a couple bites of pie on his plate.

"I'm sorry," she told him. "I can't find enough money to pay you today. Could you possibly bring the bill back with you next week, when Father is at home?"

He agreed amiably, as she was sure he would. Her father was well-known in town. The deliveryman, she knew, had no fear her father wouldn't meet the obligation on the next delivery.

"Please, finish your pie before you leave," she encouraged him. "Mrs. Brady makes the best pie in town, though Mrs. Kelly, next door, might argue that point."

"Thank you, miss."

"Come, Thunder. You don't need any pie."

The little dog took a step toward her, hesitated, looking back at Tom, who still stood beside the white kitchen table. Evidently deciding he wasn't going to win any morsels from the tall, skinny man, he trotted obediently after Amanda.

Amanda managed to keep her smile until she was through the swinging door into the hall. She wrapped her arms across her chest and wandered into the parlor.

Thunder jumped up and curled against her when she sat down on the sofa. "You know better than to be up here," she half-scolded, scratching behind one of his little white ears, but she didn't chase him down. It was comforting to have him beside her. "Maybe Father will remember who gave him those bills, Thunder. I wish he were home, so he could tell us right now. How am I going to stand waiting for two days until he returns?"

The day dragged by. Usually this was the day of the week she spent the afternoon returning social calls, but she knew she wouldn't be able to keep her mind on her friends today. She tried answering social notes, but there, too, her mind kept drifting to the bills in her father's desk.

Hours passed. Questions about the money continued to plague her. Morning slid into afternoon, and afternoon into dinner hour. She could barely eat the fried chicken and mashed potatoes Mrs. Brady set before her.

After dinner, she wandered into the flower garden. Thunder nosed about in the dirt, bottom in the air, tail going a mile a minute, winning a smile from her. If only her own life were as carefree!

Perhaps I'm worrying over nothing, she told herself for the hundredth time that day. "Maybe the bills are real," she told Thunder, as he tossed at her feet a withered walnut he'd dug from the ground, and looked up at her expectantly, waiting for praise.

Effie and Evan's laughter drew her gaze next door. They had their pony and cart out and were preparing to drive it down the alleyway.

"Alexander would know whether the bills are counterfeit, wouldn't he, Thunder? Why didn't I think of that before?" He should be at the Knights this evening. He'd been out of town much of the past week, but Constance had said he was expected back last night.

Surely he wouldn't mind if she asked him about the money she'd found. If the bills were counterfeit, she would be handing him another clue in the case. *That would show him I'm capable of helping him solve the crime, without endangering myself or anyone else,* she thought, excitement building inside her as she hurried toward her father's office.

❧

Walking out on the back steps, coffee cup in hand, Alex spotted Amanda hurrying up her own back steps, Thunder, a bundle of white fur, bouncing behind her. A sliver of disappointment darted through him at lost opportunity. If Amanda were out in her flower garden, it would have been the neighborly thing to do to walk over and say hello. Of course, he could stop over anyway, but it wouldn't seem as casual.

A number of counterfeit bills had shown up in different towns in the county and just beyond, towns along the Mississippi River where it stretched between lower Minnesota and Wisconsin. Pretty little towns like River's Edge, filled with pleasant, hardworking people, who were being cheated out of their hard-earned dollars by one or more counterfeiters. He'd kept busy trying to track down where the different counterfeit bills had shown up in the last couple weeks, and trying to trace them. No success.

He sat down on the top step, balanced his coffee cup on one knee, rested an elbow on the opposite knee and ran a hand through his hair. This case was getting more frustrating by the day! He'd never had a case where at least a small ray of light hadn't shown through after this length of time.

His gaze wandered to the flower garden next door, and he laughed at himself. Perhaps he wasn't looking hard enough for an answer to the case. Perhaps he wanted to prolong it to stay near Amanda.

The case hadn't kept him near her the last couple of weeks. He'd missed her like crazy while he'd been away. An idea had started playing in his mind, one he found quite appealing.

He had a nest egg set aside. Not much chance to spend most of his salary, what with traveling on assignments so often. He had enough saved that he could afford to take a few months off work.

"Uncle Alex! Uncle Alex, watch us!" Effie called.

Alex grinned and waved as she and Evan passed through the drive behind the house, raising a cloud of dust. The children's laughter, the clatter of the cart's wheels, and the light pounding of the pony's hooves chased away the early evening quiet.

That's the way it should be, he thought. *Family makes the hard things in life worthwhile.*

Why had it taken him so long to realize that? Because it hadn't been time for him to experience family before?

Over the rim of his coffee cup, he gazed at the house next door. *Is it time now, Lord?*

The thought of family brought to mind Amanda's wonderful way with children, memories of her with Effie and Evan, and the children in her Sunday school class. It seemed obvious to him that her true gift was the way she won children's hearts, their trust. Why couldn't she see that? Why did she insist on trying to be a detective?

She'll make a wonderful mother one day. Pleasurable anticipation warmed his chest. As the mother of his children? He could see them raising a family together.

The idea he'd been toying with the last few days became a decision. When this assignment is over, I'll tell her how much I care about her. His heart beat faster at the thought, excitement mixed with worry. He'd tell her he wanted to court her, that he'd like to ask for a leave of absence. His nest egg would give him the freedom to do so. The leave would give him and Amanda a chance to know each other better, to be certain whether the feelings he had for her were a love strong enough to last a lifetime.

Until the case was solved, he'd try keep the depth of his affection for her his own secret. It wouldn't be easy, but it was never safe to have it known there was a detective's loved one near on a case. It put her in too much danger. Besides, courting her would distract him too much from the case. No, he'd have to wait, and hope that in the meantime, she didn't become engaged to someone else, like that loudmouth Jack Davis.

Please, God, protect her heart for me if we are meant to be together. The thought surprised his mind so much that he gasped, jerked himself up straighter, and almost spilled his coffee. *Is it possible God planned for me and Amanda to meet, to love each other?*

But if that were true, it would mean that when he came to River's Edge on the last assignment, it had been part of God's plan, and that Constance's marrying Justin had been part of God's plan, and the superintendent ordering him to stay in the Knights' house on assignment had been part of God's plan. It would mean it had been God's plan he'd been fighting like crazy for months.

His face relaxed in a smile. That means God uses even the most painful parts of life to bring us something good. Contentment spread through him until he felt as peaceful as a cat sleeping in the sunshine.

"Hello, Alexander."

"Amanda!" His heart seemed to leap through his chest at the unexpected sight of her. He set his coffee cup down beside him and stood hastily. *I've missed you.* He wished he dared speak the words. Had she missed him, too?

He watched her move across the lawn toward him. She was glancing down at the ground, lifting her skirt to keep it from the grass and dirt. When she reached the bottom of the steps and looked up at him, her face wasn't filled with the joy he'd hoped would be there at his return. Her brow was wrinkled, and her pupils were so large from fear or worry that they almost hid the beautiful dove gray of her eyes.

He hurried down the steps. "Amanda, what's wrong?"

"I'm not sure. That is, it's probably only my imagination, but I—I found something, and I wondered if you would look at it for me."

What could she have found to make her sound so breathless? "Of course, you know I will. What is it?"

She held up a hand that had been partially hidden by the folds at the side of her skirt. Between her fingers with their well buffed nails was a stiff new bill. "This. It doesn't look right to me. Jack said there should be a line between the mouth and nose on the man's face, and it's not there. Does that mean it's c—counterfeit?"

He took the bill and examined it closely. "It's counterfeit, all right. Where did you get this? From one of the stores in town?"

"No, it was in my father's desk. He usually keeps some money at the house."

"Where did he get it?" Alarm began crawling along Alex's nerves. He tried to push it away.

"I don't know. He's out of town and won't be back for a couple of days. There's—there's more money in his desk drawer. I think some of it is counterfeit, too. Do you want to see for yourself?"

"Please."

He followed her across the yard, through her house and into the study, trying to keep from relaying his fears to her.

Mr. Mason's study was a comfortable room. Across from the desk stood two welcoming leather armchairs. In one corner stood a fine walnut screen with intricate carvings.

A small faded picture stood in a pewter frame on the desk. *Amanda's mother?* Alex recalled his conversation with Mason about her, recalled Mason saying he hoped she would be pleased with the way he'd raised Amanda.

Leather-bound volumes lined the built-in bookcases, giving a warmth to the room. But the room's atmosphere didn't keep a chill from running down Alex's spine when he went through the rest of the bills in Mason's desk.

Amanda stood beside the desk with her hands clenched together at her waist, her arms stiff, watching him. Her intensity didn't make his task easier. He felt his own face grow tight as he examined each bill. When he laid the last one down on the desk blotter, Amanda said, "Are they. . .are they all counterfeit?"

He reached a hand out and covered both of hers, hating his answer and what it would do to her. "Yes."

Her eyes flashed. "I was afraid so! I wish he were home so we could find out who gave them to him. How could anyone have cheated a nice old man like Father this way?"

Didn't she even suspect her father might be involved? Alex studied her face. All he could see was indignation.

"I don't know," he said slowly, responding to the question she must have known was unanswerable.

The instinct he'd come to trust through years of experience told him Mr. Mason wasn't an innocent victim, but a part of the counterfeiting team for which they'd been looking. He didn't want to believe it. He liked the man, had trusted him. He wouldn't dare accuse the man to his daughter yet. His daughter!

Dread curled inside him. Surely life couldn't play such a cruel trick on him as to allow Amanda's father to be one of the criminals he was seeking! It couldn't! How could a man be expected to endure such a thing?

Chapter 13

Alex awoke the next morning feeling more tired than when he'd gone to bed. He'd laid awake for hours before falling into a fitful sleep. Was it possible Mason was simply a victim, as Amanda believed? If so, who would have given him that much counterfeit money? Why would all of the bills in his drawer be counterfeit?

He only took a couple of bites at breakfast before heading out. He didn't want to share his suspicions with Justin and Constance yet. It would make them too real. He hoped with a little more digging, he'd find he had misjudged Mason, and that he truly was a victim.

At least, that's what his mind hoped. Inside, there was a kernel of certainty that Mason was guilty. He wished he could ignore it, but he'd felt that same certainty at some point on every case he'd solved, and it had never been wrong. It was like a gift God had given him for his work, as He'd given Amanda her wonderful way with children.

His mind kept wrestling with his inner certainty as he hurried along toward the sawmill. The nearer he came to the river, the more men he saw on their way to work in the mill. They were easy to spot, in their denim work clothes and heavy boots, carrying metal lunch buckets.

He passed the blacksmith shop near the mill, where smoke already rose from the forge, and a horse's tail swished against pesty early morning flies as the blacksmith's hammer rang against a hot new shoe. A teamster, who stood beside a wagon, waiting for the horse, touched his fingers to his worn hat brim as Alex passed. Alex suspected he was one of the teamsters who hauled sawed lumber from mill to yard, and yard to planing mill, where Mason had shown him seasoned rough stock was turned into finished material.

What he wouldn't give to be a teamster or a blacksmith or a lumberman today instead of a Pinkerton man!

Jonathan Reaves, the company bookkeeper, looked up in surprise through his small, oval, wire-rimmed glasses when Alex entered his room off the company sales office. He invited him to sit down, his skinny fingers nervously straightening stacks of invoices and papers on his desk. "What can I do for you today, Mr. Bixby?"

Alex made an effort to appear relaxed. He leaned back in the bow-backed wooden chair opposite Reaves, smiled, rested one ankle on top of his knee. "As you might remember, last time I was here it was at Mr. Mason's request. I was checking on some things as a favor to a friend."

"Yes, yes. I understand Sheriff Tucker has asked you to become involved now, too."

"Yes." Well, the sheriff hadn't been the one to ask him, but they were working together now. It was easier to let the small misunderstanding slide than explain. He almost chuckled at the way Amanda had been right again: small-town gossip did get around.

"And there's something more you think I can do for you? I told you everything I knew last time you were here."

It was impossible to get away from the smells and sounds of the sawmill, even in this office. The smell of fresh pine and buzz of the saws and clatter of horses' hooves and wagons in the yards came through the window and walls, and made the room seem busier than it was.

Alex held up both hands, palms up. "I'm not sure you can tell me anything new. I'm just here going over old ground. Thought maybe there was something you told me before that didn't mean anything at the time, but might now that I know more about the case. Would you go through the mill's employees who were in your office while the payroll was here?"

"Sure." Reaves ran a hand over his bald crown. "Let's see, there was. . ."

Alex listened more impatiently than he hoped he showed. He was disappointed when Reaves didn't mention anyone he hadn't mentioned before. The sheriff had already checked out each of the men Reaves mentioned, and had no reason to believe any of them had been in on the exchange of money.

When Reaves was done with his list, Alex rested his chin on tented fingers, and stared unseeing at Reaves's cluttered desk. Who else was there to ask about? He'd just have to ask all the old questions over again. "Who delivered the payroll?"

"Jack Davis, the bank clerk. Sheriff Tucker came with him, of course, to guard the payroll between the bank and the mill, as he always does."

Jack Davis's name raised Alex's ire, as it always did. He wouldn't mind pinning this crime on him, but in truth he didn't believe he'd committed it. Sheriff Tucker and his men had been watching all the bank staff since the payroll was doctored with counterfeit funds, and Davis had given no hint of being involved. For that matter, he'd watched the staff himself at the bank, and had never seen any reason to mistrust the man.

Sheriff Tucker? Always possible a law enforcement man had gone bad. No other reason to believe it was him, other than that he'd been along when the payroll was delivered to the mill. He'd keep the lawman's proximity to the crime scene in mind, but unless the avenue with Mason petered out, he wouldn't pursue it seriously. Still, there was another question he had to ask before he went on to other suspects.

"Was either Davis or Sheriff Tucker alone with the payroll after it reached your mill?"

The bookkeeper's palms struck the desk, and he leaned forward, eyes wide behind his lenses. "You think one of them might be in on it? Sheriff Tucker?"

"No, no, no. Only double-checking every possibility."

"Well." Reaves rubbed his fingers back and forth beneath his pointed chin. "Can't recall either of them being alone with it. Nope, don't believe they were. Davis carried the bag into my office. Sheriff Tucker stopped for a minute to exchange a few words with Art—that's the man at the sales desk out there—" He pointed through his door to a larger office. "Davis set the bag beside my desk. Said a few words. Nothing unusual, maybe about the weather. Sheriff Tucker stuck his head in the door to say good morning. Then they left together."

"Anyone else in here that morning?"

"Well, Mr. Mason, but I told you that before. Came in right as Sheriff Tucker and Davis were leaving. I remember hearing them greet each other."

"Mmmm." Dismay swelled through him. So Mason was there when the payroll was in Reaves's office. He'd hoped to hear otherwise. "Did you tell me he stopped to visit with you?"

Reaves nodded. "Stops to talk for a bit almost every time he come in, which is a few times a week."

"Have anything special to say that morning?"

Reaves glanced in the direction of a corner of the ceiling, frowning, trying to remember. "No, can't say as he did. Course, it was a busy morning. A couple of the employees I mentioned stopped in while he was here. Mason had a newspaper with him and read that when I was busy with others. There was a customer who came in with a question about a bill, so I was out in the sales office for a few minutes arguing with him about that."

The kernel of suspicion about Mason solidified, making Alex feel nauseous. Mason had been alone with the payroll, had had opportunity to switch funds. It was exactly what Alex had hoped not to hear. Mason could have hid counterfeit bills in his pockets or the newspaper he'd carried.

He tried to disguise his suspicions of Mason. "Did you win the argument or did the customer?"

Reaves's grin spread across his skinny face. "I did. I'm a good bookkeeper, if I do say it myself."

"I believe it. Since you mentioned customers, how about them? Any customers in your office that morning?"

He shook his head vigorously. "No, sir. I don't have many rules about this office, but one of them is that customers aren't allowed in here."

"Good rule." Would be better if his rule was that no one was allowed to be left alone with the payroll. He pushed himself up from the chair. "Well, guess I'll be going. Thanks for your time."

Reaves stood, too. "Sure thing. Sorry I couldn't remember anything new to tell you."

"The truth is all I'm after, and I'm pretty sure you're a truthful man, Mr. Reaves."

Reaves beamed. "That I am. Been looking after the mill's books for twenty years. Always balance them to the penny."

Alex had been certain of that before Reaves volunteered it. It was obvious to him that the man had a passion for doing things the right way.

The knowledge he'd acquired in the little office weighed on him like an anchor as he walked toward the Knights' house. He'd never wanted more to be wrong about a case. *Lord, please, if I'm wrong, show me, before I do anything to hurt Mason or Amanda.*

Since he'd prayed with Amanda and the Sunday school children, he'd noticed a change in himself. At the most unusual times, he found himself talking to God about the things happening in his life. Where his mind and emotions were once filled with skepticism and doubt, there was an excitement at getting to know God, an assurance that God was truly there and interested in what happened in his life.

Amazing how the simple way Amanda had explained the difference between knowing about Jesus and knowing Him had explained the problem he'd been facing in trying to find the Lord. His church attendance had taught him more about Jesus, but he hadn't told God he believed what he'd heard, or asked Christ to be part of his life until that morning in the Sunday school class. If he hadn't experienced it, he would never have believed such a simple prayer could make such a difference in a man's life.

If only a short prayer could change Mason's part in this, assuming his suspicions were correct. Sadness slid over Alex, like a heavy blanket. If he was right, what would this do to Mason's life, and Amanda's, and. . .his own?

He couldn't let himself think about that now. If he did, he'd never do what he must to solve the case.

⁂

That evening, having after-dinner coffee with Justin and Constance in the parlor, Alex told them about the counterfeit money Amanda found in Mason's desk and what he'd learned that morning about Mason at the sawmill.

Justin almost leaped from his chair and began pacing the room, his footsteps muffled in the thick Persian carpet. "Mason involved in counterfeiting? Impossible! I'd as easily believe my own father involved in such a thing."

Alex exchanged glances with Constance. They both knew from their experience with detectives that the most innocent-appearing people could be guilty.

"I must admit," Constance said in her usual calm, low voice, "it's not easy to believe, loving Mr. Mason as we do."

Justin stopped in front of the pale blue velvet sofa where she sat. "Not easy to believe, but you believe it? How can you?" he charged.

Alex admired the way she retained her serenity, though he heard the sadness in her voice. "I can believe it because I've seen over and over again that it is the most trusted people who most easily get away with crimes, and because the evidence is quite convincing, at least so far."

Justin's hands balled into fists at his sides, and straightened again. The muscles in his jaw bulged. Alex could sympathize with him; it couldn't be easy to accept that his friend was a thief. "Have you noticed Mason spending more than you expect him to?"

"You mean, have I considered his spending when looking for someone who may be overspending their means, as we discussed a couple weeks ago? I didn't look at him specifically, but I don't recall any purchases that stand out. Do you, Constance?"

"No."

"You've not noticed anyone else spending more than you would expect?"

"No, no one." Justin seemed to deflate. He dropped down beside Constance.

She reached over and took one of his hands in both her own. The simple act of love and comfort touched Alex with something almost like pain. If only he had the right to comfort Amanda. She would need someone to love and comfort her if his suspicions about Mason were true.

Alex bit the left tip of his mustache, hating to continue, but knowing he must. "And you're not aware of any money difficulties Mason might have?"

"No, none," Justin replied.

Constance shook her head.

From behind the couch, Effie's face suddenly appeared between Justin and Constance. "Mr. Mason doesn't have money troubles. He has lots of money."

Evan bobbed up beside her. "Yes, a whole trunk full."

Chapter 14

Justin jumped to his feet. "How many times do I have to tell you two not to listen in on other people's conversations?"

The children's faces blanched. They stared at him, wide-eyed.

"Justin!" Constance whisper was filled with shock.

Alex saw Justin swallow, press his lips together, then speak again. "I will not have you playing sneak-up or detectives or what ever else you choose to call eavesdropping. Do you understand?"

Effie and Evan nodded. Alex noticed Evan's eyes were bright with unshed tears.

"We didn't mean to make you mad." The boy's whisper shook. His hands clutched the serpentine sofa back.

"And I didn't mean to yell at you," Justin assured him, "but you must both learn to obey. I don't want any more of this behavior, understand?"

"Yes, Uncle Justin." Evan brushed at a tear with the back of his hand.

"Yes, Uncle Justin," Effie agreed. "But—"

"No buts." Justin's eyes flashed, but his voice didn't rise.

Alex had a hard time disciplining a smile. Trust Effie to agree to obey with a qualification!

"Children, come out from behind the sofa, please." Constance's manner was as gentle as always. Didn't anything upset her patience? Alex wondered.

When the children came around to the front of the sofa, Constance took one of each of their hands, and leaned forward. "Will you tell us more about the trunk you saw, the one with Mr. Mason's money?"

"What do you want to know?" Effie asked.

"Well," Constance thought a moment. "Where did you see it?"

"In Mr. Mason's house," Evan answered.

"In his attic," Effie clarified.

Justin sat down beside Constance. "What were you doing in his attic?"

Evan bit his bottom lip.

Effie looked at her shoes, and dug the toe of one into the carpet. "We were playing detective up there."

Justin grunted.

"When was that?" Constance asked. "Evan?"

"On Uncle Alex's birthday. You and Uncle Justin were out of town, so we stayed with Miss Amanda, remember?"

"Yes, I remember," Constance answered. "So when you were playing, you went up in the attic and saw a trunk?"

The children nodded.

"How do you know it was full of money?"

Effie and Evan exchanged glances.

Effie took a deep breath, and let it out in a whoosh. "We opened it. There was so much money in it that some floated out and we had to pick it up and put it back inside before we closed the top."

Constance hugged each of them. "Thank you for telling us."

Effie glanced at Justin. "Are we in trouble?"

"Did you ask Miss Amanda if you could play detective in her attic?"

"Yes."

"Then you aren't in trouble for playing detective at her house that day," Justin said, "but I don't want you playing detective here anymore. Now, say good night to Uncle Alex, and we'll go up and get you two ready for bed."

When Justin and the children had left the room, Alex and Constance began discussing the children's news.

Alex rubbed a hand over his face. He couldn't remember when he'd felt so tired. Was it because he didn't want to face Mason's possible guilt and what it would mean for him and for Amanda? "If that trunk exists, we'll have to check it out."

"I'm sure it's real. The children wouldn't have made something like that up, surely."

"If the money in it is counterfeit—" he didn't want to finish his thought.

"If it's counterfeit, there almost no chance Mr. Mason is innocent."

"Someone is going to have to check that trunk, Constance. It would be easy for you to get in the house without raising suspicions."

She shook her head. "No, Alex. Justin would be furious if I became involved. You know how he hates deceit and how adamant he has been about my staying out of this case."

He'd have to do it himself. Well, he'd had to do plenty of other hard things in his life. "Amanda thinks her father is a victim of the counterfeiters. If we're right and Mason is one of them, it's going to be very difficult for her. Will you," he stopped to clear his throat. "Will you stand by her if the worst is true and Mason is arrested?"

"Of course! She is my dear friend."

"I know. It's just. . ." he didn't know how to finish.

Constance sat down on the ottoman at the foot of the chair he was sitting in. "Are you in love with her?"

Her gentle voice and sympathetic eyes were almost his undoing. He had to swallow twice before he could answer, and then his voice cracked on the words. "I think I may be."

"You can ask to be removed from the case."

He nodded. "I've thought of that, but it's too late to change the important things. Being removed from the case wouldn't remove my obligation to reveal the facts I've already uncovered. It won't change the fact that I will be at least partially responsible for Amanda's father's arrest. How does a girl forgive that in the man who loves her, Constance?"

She didn't answer. He didn't expect an answer. Could there possibly be one? His heart didn't believe so.

❦

Alex struggled for hours the next day, trying to decide how to handle the situation with the trunk. In any other assignment, he'd simply slip into the house and check it out, but this was Amanda's home. It seemed a violation to slip into her house and go through her and her father's possessions without her knowledge. He couldn't ask her to show him the trunk without an explanation. Chicken of him, probably, but he wasn't ready to tell her of his suspicions. There was still a chance that the money in the trunk was real. In that case, there'd be no reason to let her know of his suspicions of her father.

What should I do, Lord? He wished God would send a message in writing. Something etched in stone like the Ten Commandments had been would be nice; something impossible to misunderstand.

He couldn't help reflecting on Justin and Constance's attitude toward his profession and the deceit it so often entailed. Constance had once been one of the Pinkerton Agency's best operatives. Justin hated deceit in any form. After she'd met Justin and changed from an atheist to a believer, Constance didn't like that element of the profession, either.

Why didn't he feel as Justin and Constance did, now that he had decided to become a Christian? Why did he still believe in his profession, in its importance for the fight for justice? He did still believe in it. He did still want to work in it, in spite of the fact that some of the methods operatives felt required to use to discover facts weren't as straightforward as he would like. Someday, he'd like to ask Justin and Constance about it.

In any case, right now he was in the thick of the most distasteful case in which he'd ever been involved.

What would Mason feel when he was confronted? Alex wondered. If Mason were his own father, how would he change the way he handled this case? Not that his own father would ever have become involved with counterfeiters, but if he had, Alex would have wanted him to be treated with as much respect as possible.

How did he do that in this situation, how could he treat Mason with respect and still confront him?

"I don't think he's the gun-toting type," he muttered to himself. "I didn't notice a gun in his desk drawer, either. Probably not apt to try to shoot me, and if he does, I always have my derringer with me. Why not just tell him what I heard about the trunk, and ask him to show it to me? If he refuses, at least I'll have been honest about it, and I can force him then to show me the contents."

It wasn't a solution he'd trust in most cases, but he felt a peace about it this time. When he consulted Constance, she agreed with him. The worst thing about it was waiting for Mason to return from out of town. He was to arrive on the midmorning train the next day.

Knowing Amanda would ask her father almost immediately about the counterfeit money she'd found in his desk, Alex determined he'd be there when Mason arrived home. Would he be able to keep his suspicions from showing through to Amanda? He'd have to find a way.

❧

It was with a heavy heart he approached Amanda's house the next morning when he heard the whistle of the train on which Amanda's father was expected.

Bees were buzzing about Amanda's flowers in their bed in front of the porch. Thunder was asleep in the sun on the steps. Amanda was on the front porch, humming a cheerful tune and arranging a bouquet on a large round white wicker table. Alex thought she looked lovely in her white linen shirtwaist with dainty tucks down the front and tiny blue bow at the neck.

She greeted him with a big smile. "Good morning! Father should be home soon. Did you hear the train whistle? It's such a beautiful morning, that I thought we'd have coffee and cookies out here on the porch when he arrives. Will you join us, or are you only stopping to say hello on your way about your business?"

"I will join you. Thank you for asking." Guilt swamped him as he returned her smile and accepted her invitation. She wouldn't have asked him if she'd known his intentions.

He rested a hip against the white wooden railing above the flower bed and made small talk with her. She chattered away while arranging delicate gold-edged cups and saucers, and a crystal plate with flower-shaped sugar cookies and dark molasses cookies.

She placed an etched crystal cream and sugar set that matched the cookie plate on the table and stood back to view the final effect.

"It looks nice," Alex assured her. "You're a born hostess."

Her laugh was light and free, and the innocence in it cut through him. "No woman is a born hostess, but I thank you for the compliment, just the same." She gave him a playful curtsy. "We should probably let Father relax a bit before I tell him we've discovered the bills in his desk are counterfeit, don't you think?"

He nodded, not trusting his voice.

The three of them did have a nice visit after Mason arrived. Alex knew he was only doing what he must to perform his duty as a Pinkerton, and be responsible to the community whose economic stability was threatened by the counterfeiters. Personally, he'd never felt like more of a rat.

When they'd finished their coffee, and he and Mason had finished off most of the cookies, Amanda brought up the topic he'd been dreading, the bills in the desk.

Alex watched Mason while she told the story in her dramatic way. Mason's hand gripped the arms of his wicker chair. His round face beneath his white hair grew flushed, then paled.

"Who gave you those false bills, Father?" Amanda asked, indignation in every word, when she'd finished with her story.

Mason opened and closed his mouth twice before answering. "Why, I'm not certain I recall. I had quite a bit of cash on hand, as I needed some for my business trip." He pulled out his handkerchief and mopped his face. "Oh, my! I hope I haven't been spreading counterfeit bills around the county the last couple of days!"

He took his pocketbook from an inner pocket of his coat, pulled out the some bills, and handed them to Alex. "What do you think? Are these legitimate bills or not?"

Alex accepted the bills, reluctance in every bone of his body. He looked at each one, then handed them back. "A mixture. Most real; a couple, not."

Amanda gave a little gasp, and covered her mouth with the tips of her fingers.

Alex glanced at her and then away. What he'd found was just what he'd expect if Mason had been spreading counterfeit bills about the county on his trip. His gloom grew deeper and darker. If Mason had followed the practice of most counterfeiters, he'd have paid for items with counterfeit bills that would have required a lot of change for the amount of purchase—change that would naturally be received in the form of legitimate tender.

"My, my, my." Mason shook his head, his cheeks bouncing, his gaze on the bills he was returning to his pocketbook. "It looks like I've either been inadvertently spreading some of the counterfeit money around, maybe some I received with the pile of bills Amanda found upstairs, or I've received some in return for purchases I made on my trip."

More lies? "It would seem so," Alex pretended to agree.

"Well." Straight-armed, Mason rested his hands on his knees. "I hope you and Sheriff Tucker find these counterfeiters fast. I don't care for the way it feels to be cheated out of my money, and I expect no one else in the county likes being cheated any better than I do."

He stood up, smiling at Amanda. "Thanks for the coffee and cookies, dear. They hit the spot after spending the morning on a passenger car. Think I'll walk down by the sawmill and see how things are going before lunch."

Or let a partner in the counterfeiting business know someone might be close to discovering his involvement? Alex stood quickly. "Mr. Mason, there's a business matter I'd like your advice on, if you wouldn't mind giving me a minute."

"Be glad to, when I get back."

"It's rather urgent. I'd appreciate it if we could speak right away."

Amanda laid a hand on her father's arm. "Please, Father, he's done so much for us, speaking to the people at the sawmill for you, and verifying the counterfeit funds I found in the house."

Alex's feelings of guilt grew to giant proportions. He saw the hesitancy in Mason's face and the tension in his body.

"You're right, Daughter. What can I do for you, Bixby?"

"Would you mind if we spoke in private, sir, perhaps in your study?"

Again he saw the hesitancy in the older man, but Mason agreed, and Alex followed him to the study. Amanda gave Alex a happy smile when he passed her. It felt like a knife plunged into his chest. She was completely unaware that, if things went as he expected, he was about to turn her world upside down.

Chapter 15

Mason sat down in a leather wing chair, and waved Alex into one just like it. "Sit down, sit down. Now, what is this urgent business you wanted to discuss?"

Was there a tightness about the older man's smile? Did he suspect the reason Alex had asked to speak with him? Alex slid a hand into a pocket of his Norfolk jacket, and wrapped his fingers around the handle of his derringer, hating the necessity to do so.

"Sir, I wanted to ask you about some more bills that were found in your house."

Mason's eyes narrowed. "More bills? What bills would those be?"

"The bills in the trunk in your attic." Alex spoke slowly, deliberately.

The older man's hands wrapped around the chair arms. "I. . . you—you've been searching my house?"

"No, sir. Effie and Evan found the trunk when they were playing the day Amanda watched them for the Knights. They had no right to open it, of course, but they did. They told me it is full of money."

Mason stared at him, the back of his head pressed hard against the chair back.

"Sir," Alex gentled his voice somewhat, "in light of the other counterfeit bills found in your desk and pocketbook, I must ask to see the money in that trunk. If you will not show me, Sheriff Tucker will demand to examine it."

Mason started to push himself up, his hands on the arms of the chair. Suddenly, he dropped back into the seat. "The money in the trunk. . ." He licked his lips, his gaze darting back and forth, avoiding meeting Alex's gaze. "That money is c–counterfeit."

The sadness that filled Alex's chest slipped into his voice. "I was afraid it would be, sir."

Mason dropped his head into his hands, and moaned. "You've ruined everything. Everything! All my hopes of sparing Amanda the knowledge that I've so little money left. You've ruined everything!"

Alex left the man mired in his self-pity a few minutes. Finally Mason lifted his head and pinned Alex with an angry glare. "I suppose you'll be arresting me."

"Yes, sir." He cleared his voice. "About Amanda. . ."

Mason groaned.

"Would you like to tell her yourself, now, before we go to the sheriff's office?"

He nodded, slowly. "Thank you for giving me that opportunity. There's no way of keeping the news from her."

"No, sir." He stood, and cleared his throat again. "You—you haven't a gun on you, have you, sir? Or in the room?" He wasn't worried for his own safety any longer, but was the man apt to destroy himself rather than face his daughter?

Mason drew himself up, lifting his round chin, and met Alex's gaze squarely. "No. I've no firearms in this house. I may be a thief, but I couldn't physically harm anyone."

"I didn't think you could, sir, but I had to ask. I'll tell Amanda you wish to see her."

"You wished to see me, Father?" Amanda asked a few minutes later when Alex escorted her into the study. "It must be serious, if you can't speak with me on the veranda." Settling into the wing chair opposite him, she laughed lightly.

Alex started to leave the room.

"Don't go, Bixby," her father urged. "You may as well hear this now as later."

"As you wish, sir." Alex walked over by the painted screen that stood in one corner by the built-in bookcases.

A strange, uncomfortable feeling drew Amanda's attention to her father's face. There was a grayness to it she'd never seen before, a shadow that sent sudden fear spiraling through her. "What is it, Father? Are you ill?"

"No, no, I'm not ill."

"Then what is it?" The fear continued to twist through her with hurricane force. What could he tell her that would cause him to look this way?

He rested the back of his head against the high chair back. She thought she'd never seen him look so weary. "Last year was a rough year for me, Amanda. The economic depression about wiped me out. I'd invested heavily in a railroad, one of the hundreds that failed during the Panic of 1893."

Relief washed over her. "Money? That is what you are telling me that is so awful, that we haven't much money anymore? Why, I thought what you had to tell me must be something dreadfully important, such as that you were in poor health."

He rested his forehead in one hand, and closed his eyes. "I should have known you would feel that way. I guess I was blinded by fear, fear that you wouldn't have the financial resources I thought you needed if anything happened to me."

"But nothing is happening. You did tell me you aren't ill, didn't you?"

"That is right, I'm not ill." He took a deep breath. "I haven't told you everything yet, though. When I lost most of my money, I remortgaged the house."

"And you haven't the money to repay it?" She leaned forward, eager to remove that awful weariness from her father's shoulders. "It doesn't matter. We can find a smaller place. Anywhere will be home as long as we are together. I can find a job. I did very well in my typewriting and shorthand courses." She shifted her shoulders in a gesture of pride. "Any employer would be fortunate to have me work for him, if I do say so myself."

A little smile rewarded her teasing comment. "I know he would. Unfortunately, things cannot be resolved so easily." The smile died. "When I couldn't repay the mortgage, I did something very foolish. I became involved in. . .counterfeiting." The last word was a hoarse whisper.

The world seemed to stop. Amanda's heart seemed to stop. Her very breath seemed to stop. *It can't be true! He wouldn't, he couldn't do such a thing! Not Father!*

But he was continuing, saying things she didn't want to hear.

"I couldn't find any other way out. I didn't want you to know how poor I was." He leaned forward and took her hands in his. The eyes that peered into hers looked tortured. "Everything I've ever done has been for you, Amanda, but I never wished for you the notoriety you'll receive now. I never wished for you the shame of being branded a criminal's daughter. I kidded myself that I would never be apprehended, that you need never know, that I was preserving your position and reputation in the community. I'm sorry, Amanda. I'm so s—sorry. Please, please don't hate me."

She leaned her cheek against his. "Hate you? I could never hate you, Father."

It wasn't possible to hate him! But oh, how she wished he understood that a man's character is more important than a man's monetary worth.

Was it possible for a heart to be shredded and still beat?

"I love you, Father," she whispered, her cheek still pressed to his.

A tear slipped through her lashes, slid down her cheek, and mingled with her father's tears.

❧

Weariness weighted Alex's shoulders as he walked up the front steps to the Knights' house that evening. He couldn't remember ever living through a longer day! Surely this day had more than the usual twenty-four hours. *And it's not even over yet,* he thought, poking at himself with sarcasm.

Effie and Evan, chasing hoops with sticks across the yard, called to him. He waved at them and continued on into the house. He hadn't the energy for those two now.

He slipped up the steps to his room, avoiding Justin and Constance. He didn't even feel up to talking with them right now. Maybe later, after he'd written his report and freshened up.

After the confession to Amanda, Alex had accompanied Mason to the sheriff's office, where Sheriff Tucker had taken a statement and reluctantly put one of the town's leading citizens behind bars. At Mason's request, he'd rung up Lance Chase, the pushy lawyer Alex had met at the dinner party his first evening in town.

Alex had spent hours trying to convince Mason to name the others involved in the counterfeiting operation. Lance Chase had joined him in urging cooperation. Mason hadn't given them an inch, not a hint of who the others were.

Before he'd taken Mason into custody, Alex had asked Constance to stay with Amanda. Was Constance still with her? He would have liked to comfort Amanda himself, but even if he hadn't other responsibilities for the moment, he couldn't believe she would welcome his presence, let alone his comfort, considering his involvement in the case.

Remembering her face when her father revealed his crime, his heart constricted. If only he'd been able to save her that pain! If only her father had known his daughter better. How could he not have realized that she would have preferred him to act honorably rather than sell his character to supply her with a certain lifestyle? He knew, deep within himself, that her father's lack of knowledge about her true self hurt Amanda more deeply than his commission of the crime.

It was knowing what her father's confession was doing to Amanda that made his weariness so extreme. The knowledge of her father's guilt, his weakness of character, would change her life forever. Never again would she be the carefree girl he'd met the day he arrived in River's Edge. Never again would she completely trust another person, even himself. Never again would she completely believe that no matter what happened, everything would eventually turn out all right.

From now until forever, whenever she smiled that smile that lit up her eyes with sparkles like sunshine dancing across a blue lake, there would be a piece of her—someday, pray God, a piece that would be buried deep—that didn't smile, that didn't laugh.

And he, Alexander Bixby, was part of her betrayal.

At least he had the case to concentrate on. There were Mason's accomplices to discover yet. That would help him keep from dwelling on the pain that seemed to have taken up residence in his chest.

To think he'd let himself believe that God might have meant him and Amanda to meet and fall in love and marry! Instead, the hope he'd had that they might have a life together, a life filled with incredible joy and contentment, had been blown to bits because he'd simply been doing his job.

What now, God? he asked, sinking into a stiff-backed chair beside the writing desk in his room. He pulled out an ink bottle and pen, and prepared to write his daily report. *What's ahead now for Amanda? For me?*

Not a wedding, that was certain.

Chapter 16

The next day, fear routed Alex's weariness. He hurried into the Knight household after another day at the prison with Mason. This time he was looking for Justin and Constance. When he found them, he broke into his story without preliminaries.

They were on the back porch, watching Effie and Evan with their pony and cart.

Alex paced the porch back and forth. "Spent the whole day trying to get Mason to talk. Nothing. Finally, he told me to leave him alone, that his accomplices have threatened to harm Amanda if he names them." Rage and fear tangled together and poured through him. He stopped in front of Justin and Constance, where they stood at the top of the steps. "We need to do something to protect her."

"Of course," Justin agreed readily. "What do you suggest?"

Alex ran a hand over his face. "I don't know. How can we protect her if we don't know who to protect her against?"

Constance laid a hand on Alex's arm. "We'll invite her to stay here, Alex. One of the three of us will be with her at all times."

A bit of her calm seeped into him. "Thanks."

Constance smiled. "She's our friend, too."

Now that he had a plan, reassurance began to take hold in him. He hurried next door to extend the Knights' invitation to Amanda.

Mrs. Brady answered the door. Her news that Amanda was at choir practice, escorted by Jack Davis, sent fear racing back.

In the Knights' parlor, he waited for her to return, alternately pacing the floor and watching out the window. The windows were open, and a refreshing breeze came through the screens, teasing at the drapes.

"Wearing a trench in the floor won't bring her back any sooner," Justin said.

The amusement in his voice didn't humor Alex. "Maybe I should go to the church and see her home."

Justin crossed his arms and grinned. "That should be a popular move with Amanda and young Davis. They probably wouldn't appreciate a chaperon."

Alex shot him a dark look. As if he needed to be reminded of that! "I'm worried about her safety."

"No one is going to hurt her while she's at church, or on the way home."

"Unless Davis is one of the counterfeiters."

"You're getting paranoid. We've no reason to believe he is one of them."

Justin's right. Alex stared out the window. "Stupid choir practice," he muttered.

Justin laughed, sat down in a pale blue gentleman's chair, and opened the newspaper.

Alex spun around. "Don't you think—"

"I think," Justin interrupted him, lowering his paper, "that we've prayed for Amanda's safety, we have a good plan to protect her, she is safe where she is at the moment, and you should stop worrying so much."

Alex dropped down on a hassock. "You're right."

"Well, see that you don't look too cheerful about it."

"There's something I've been wondering about. Something I've wanted to ask you before, but, well, I never had the courage. Maybe it's more accurate to say I had too much pride."

A puzzled frown creased Justin's brow. "Something about the case?"

"Yes. No. Not exactly."

Justin grinned. "Perhaps you could be more specific."

Alex was nervous enough bringing up this topic. He didn't appreciate Justin's finding humor in his attempt, but he asked him anyway. "I, um, I'm kind of new to this faith stuff, trusting the Lord and everything."

Justin's grin grew larger. "Thought there was something new about you I liked."

Alex grinned back. "After watching you and Constance, the effect your faith has on your lives, I figured God was worth trying." His grin faded. "But I'm wondering about my work. I don't think it's wrong to be a detective. I wish it didn't involve deceit, but that's the way it has to be sometimes. It doesn't bother me so much that I think I need to quit because of it, as you would do in my place."

"Then what is the problem?"

Alex rubbed a fist against his chin. "It's the way I'm reacting to Mason's guilt. I've never felt such sympathy for a criminal and his family."

Justin's grin was back. "I would guess that has something to do with the fact that you're in love with his daughter."

Surprise jerked Alex's gaze to his. "Did Constance tell you that?"

"She did mention it, but it's pretty well written all over you."

Alex snorted. "I suppose it is. But I don't think that's the only reason I'm reacting the way I am about this case. What I wanted to ask you is, do you think my faith is making me too compassionate to be an effective detective?"

Justin laid the paper aside and gave Alex his full attention. "No. I expect the situation is just the opposite, that you will become more effective in your work. Not only will you continue to apprehend criminals, but you will change lives."

"Me, change lives?" That was a bit much!

"Perhaps I should have said God's love working through you will change lives."

Davis's loud, grating voice came into the room on the breeze through the window.

Alex jumped up and took a step toward the door.

"You might wait until Davis says good night."

Alex ground his teeth. As if things weren't going badly enough, he had to wait for another man to say good night to the woman he loved! He dropped back down on the hassock.

What was the matter with him? Amanda had just found out yesterday her father was involved with the counterfeiters. The news was all over town. It must have taken a lot of courage for her to go to choir practice as usual tonight, to face her friends' curious stares and questions. And he was upset because she was walking home with Davis. He should be glad she had a friend, be glad someone was with her to protect her.

I should be, but I guess I've got a long way to go with You, Lord, before I'm that perfect. Thank You for keeping her safe tonight, anyway.

He glanced out the window again.

Justin chuckled.

Alex scowled at him and went to stand at the window. It shouldn't be too long before that smart-mouthed bank clerk left.

⁂

Amanda closed her eyes and leaned her head against the back of the rocker, the most comfortable chair in their parlor. She'd never been so glad to get home in her life!

At the sound of the brass knocker thudding on the front door, she cringed. Who could it be? More bad news about her father?

"I'll answer it," she told the maid she met in the hall. Soon she'd be answering the door herself all the time. If they were as broke as her father said, they couldn't afford household help any longer.

"Alexander!" Impulsively, she reached both hands toward him. Tears threatened when he closed his hands about hers. He was a lifeline in the storm that had taken over her life the last two days. "Please, come inside."

He dropped one of her hands, closed the door, and turned back to her, studying her eyes. "Are you all right, Amanda?"

She dashed away a tear with her fingertips before it could fall. "Just a little maudlin, but trying not to be. My voice wasn't quite up to its usual quality tonight at choir practice. Not one person made a nasty comment about it."

Her statement didn't bring the laugh she'd hoped, but he did smile slightly. "Mrs. Brady told me you'd gone to practice, when I stopped over earlier."

He'd stopped over earlier! How nice to know he cared.

"It couldn't have been too easy, going to practice."

"Oh, it wasn't so bad. No one said anything about Father. Not one word." Her voice caught on a sob. "I'm sorry. I told myself I wasn't going to cry, but you were right. Practice was awful, just awful."

She wished he would put his arms about her, and let her cry her heart out against his shoulder. She should be glad he was even speaking to her. All day her thoughts had alternated between sorrow for her father and what Alex must think of her and her father now. Could a man who loved justice as much as Alex possibly allow himself to care for a woman whose father was a criminal?

His hands closed about her shoulders. They felt warm and strong. "Amanda, your father told me this afternoon that his accomplices have threatened to harm you if he reveals their names."

Her father's accomplices. It sounded so awful, as though his heart must be black with sin.

"He hasn't given their names, of course," Alex was continuing, "but we must be sure you aren't in any danger. Constance and Justin have invited you to stay with them until it is safe for you to be alone."

"No, I want to stay here. Why should I be in danger if Father isn't naming anyone else? Besides, Mrs. Brady and the maids are here. It's not like I'm alone." She'd lost so much the last couple days! She was going to lose this home soon enough; she didn't want to leave it before she had to do so.

"Mrs. Brady and the maids can't protect you the way Justin and Constance and I can. Please, Amanda, for our peace of mind. We are all worried about you."

She pulled back, and his hands dropped from her shoulders. "That's kind of you, but I want to stay here."

"Amanda, you're not being reasonable."

He didn't raise his voice, but she heard the anger and frustration in it. "I don't have to leave my home."

His eyes flashed. "No, you don't. Stay here if you want to. But if you stay here, I'm moving in here, too."

Her jaw dropped. "You aren't serious."

"I couldn't be more serious."

"It would be scandalous! It would destroy my reputation!" What little reputation the family had left. Hopelessness and frustration fed her anger.

"It's your choice." He crossed his arms and waited.

She crossed her arms and glared at him.

Neither spoke. The hall clock bonged nine o'clock and ticked on.

Finally she realized he wasn't going to give up. She brushed past him and started up the stairs.

"Where are you going?"

"To pack a bag!" She hollered the words at him, continuing up the stairs.

"Thank you, Amanda."

His soft words barely reached her. She shoved their sweetness away from her as she packed.

It was much easier to be angry with him than deal with the helplessness she'd felt since her father's arrest. She'd thought before the arrest that Alex was beginning to care for her. What must he think of her now that he knew her father was a criminal?

In two days, she'd lost her father to the consequences of his crime, discovered they had very little money, maybe none, and that they would be losing their home.

And on top of everything else, she'd lost the hope of winning Alexander's love.

Chapter 17

Alex was glad Constance and Justin were waiting for them when they returned. Constance took Amanda upstairs to put away her things, Thunder and Effie and Evan bounding up the steps in front of them.

It wasn't long before the women joined him and Justin in the parlor. They could hear the children's laughter and racing footsteps, and the click of Thunder's nails as he followed them down the hall.

"The children are going to love having Thunder stay with them for a few days." Constance smiled at Amanda. "I'm sure they'll be begging us for a dog of their own soon, though they seem to think Thunder belongs to them as much as to you."

"Dogs belong to whomever they choose to give their hearts." Amanda seated herself in a corner of the sofa, crossed her legs beneath the long navy skirt of her Eaton suit, and her arms over her chest protectively.

Alex's heart went out to her. She looked as though she was trying to curl into the sofa, to find a place of refuge. He wished he could offer her that place that would comfort and protect her.

Please, Lord, heal her heart.

Constance sat near her on the sofa. Justin took the comfortable chair with the ottoman. Alex rested an elbow against the fireplace mantel. He was too restless to sit.

Amanda sat quietly while he, Justin, and Constance discussed the case.

"Could someone have reached Mr. Mason since he was arrested to threaten him with Amanda's safety?" Constance asked.

"Maybe," Alex agreed, "but at first he didn't have the appearance of a man frightened for a loved one's safety. His concern in the beginning was for—" he glanced at Amanda and paused. She'd been hurt so much in the last couple days. There was no reason for him to mention to even her close friends the intimate pain he'd seen on her father's face, the words that told that her father's concern had been that he might have lost her love. "His concern was placed elsewhere," he amended.

Justin leaned forward, elbows on his knees. "Other than yourself and Sheriff Tucker, who has visited him since he was arrested, Alex?"

"The marshall, and his lawyer, Lance Chase."

Justin glanced at Amanda, the question large in his eyes, but he didn't ask why she wasn't among those Alex listed.

Alex thought she seemed to squeeze her arms tighter about herself, and his heart felt squeezed in sympathy for her.

"My father won't allow me to visit him. He doesn't want me to see him behind. . .to see him there." Her voice was tight, and Alex knew she was trying to control the tears that he was sure were constantly threatening to escape. "The judge said that he is in no hurry to set bail, since Father won't name his accomplices."

Alex was 99 percent certain that Lance Chase was one of those accomplices, but he couldn't arrest a man without evidence.

"I suppose there's always the possibility someone spoke to him through the barred window." Constance didn't look as though she thought her supposition likely.

"Anything is possible," Alex admitted. "Maybe we should go over the facts again. Something might jump out at us that we've missed in the past."

They went through the leads they'd followed that had led nowhere. Alex tried to examine each as if it was new to him, and knew at least Constance was doing the same thing. No one in the room found even a glimmer of a new lead in the recitation.

By the time they were done, it was twilight, and evening shadows combined with the adults' moods to create an atmosphere of gloom in the parlor. Alex was glad when Constance walked over to the wall, pushed a button, and the chandelier in the middle of the ceiling chased at least the dark of descending night from the room.

"What has Mason told you so far?" Constance asked him, seating herself again beside Amanda.

"Not enough." Alex hit a fist lightly against the mantle, frustrated. "Nothing at all about the counterfeiting ring; not who is in it, not who has the printing plate, not who made the plate, not who is circulating funds besides himself, not what the plan is for circulating more."

Constance turned to Amanda. "Is there anything your father told you that you may have forgotten to share with us?"

Amanda spread her hands and shook her head. "He didn't tell me anything about the counterfeiters. All he said was that he'd lost his money in the depression last year, so he agreed to join the counterfeiters in order to pay back the new mortgage he'd taken out on the house. If only he'd told me about the debt, I could have taken a job and helped pay it off."

"You mustn't blame yourself," Justin said.

She gave him a tiny smile. "You mustn't blame yourself, either. It's not your fault he couldn't repay the mortgage to the bank."

Justin frowned. "He doesn't have a mortgage with us."

Amanda's eyes looked puzzled. "He does all his banking with you."

"I thought he did," Justin agreed.

Alex straightened. Smiled. The combination of excitement and peace he always felt when a case began to unravel washed through him. "That's the key we've been looking for."

"What is?" Justin asked.

"The lender. The lender is the key."

"If Father didn't borrow the money from Justin's bank, where did he borrow it from?"

"Or whom did he borrow it from?" Alex rephrased Amanda's question.

Thunder came bouncing into the room through the door that was open to the hall. He stopped a moment, studying the room through the fur that hung always over his eyes, spotted Amanda, and trotted toward her. Reaching the sofa, he jumped up beside her.

She immediately drew Thunder into her arms and buried her face in his fur. "You dear! But you mustn't jump up on Constance's sofa."

Justin headed toward the hall. "If Thunder is here, the children can't be far behind."

Footsteps told they were running down the hall, away from the parlor. Alex caught Amanda's laughing glance and smiled with her. The tightness in his chest released slightly. He felt glad she'd found humor for a moment in the children's behavior.

They heard Justin call to the children. A minute later, the three entered the room. Effie and Evan had sheepish looks on their faces that told Alex they'd been caught doing something they weren't supposed to again. He knew it was hard for their parents, but he couldn't help liking their adventurous spirits. Unless he was mistaken, River's Edge's smallest detectives had just struck again.

He leaned back against the wall beside the fireplace and grinned at them. "Why, if it isn't Sherlock Holmes and Watson."

Amanda giggled.

Effie's brows scrunched together. "Who are they, Uncle Alex?"

"Never mind. I'm sure you'll find out for yourself one day."

Justin groaned. "I hope they outgrow their fascination with detectives before that." He glanced at Constance, shaking his head. "They were listening outside the parlor door."

"We were detecting," Evan defended.

Justin gave him a stern look. "What have I told you about that?"

Evan looked down at the floor, his lips in a pout.

Effie didn't even pretend to feel guilty. "I bet it's that mean old Mark-My-Words Mr. Chase that Mr. Mason owes money to. Remember the nasty things he said to Mr. Mason on Alex's birthday, Evan?"

Evan nodded, still looking at the floor.

Alex jerked erect. Each of the other adults did, too.

"What did Mr. Chase say to Mr. Mason, Effie?" Constance asked.

She bit her bottom lip, and studied Constance's face. "You said good detectives don't tell what they hear."

Alex knelt in front of the girl. "That's right, Effie." He struggled to keep his impatience out of his voice; he didn't want to frighten her with his need to know what they'd heard. "Good detectives never tell the secrets they've overheard until the right time. This is the right time."

Effie and Evan glanced at each other. Evan nodded. Effie took a deep breath. "All right, we'll tell."

"It was on Uncle Alex's birthday," Evan began. "We were in Mr. Mason's study, looking for some string to tie up your HAPPY BIRTHDAY sign, Uncle Alex. We heard Mr. Mason and Mr. Chase coming, and we hid behind that tall screen in his office."

Effie took over. "Old Mark-My-Words told Mr. Mason that instead of giving him money he owed him, he could do old Mark-My-Words a favor."

"But Mr. Mason didn't want to do the favor," Evan broke in. "He said he wanted to pay the money back later."

Effie nodded. "Old Mark-My-Words said no. He told Mr. Mason if he didn't do him the favor, he'd take Mr. Mason's home away."

"Oooh!" Amanda clapped her fingers over her lips. Tears glittered in her eyes.

Effie leaned against the arm of the couch beside Amanda. "Is something wrong?"

Amanda shook her head. She squeezed one of Effie's shoulders and smiled—a rather shaky smile, Alex thought. "No, nothing is wrong, Effie. Thank you for telling us what you heard. Did I interrupt you? Do you have more to tell us?"

"No, that's all, I think."

Evan nodded.

"Then it's off to bed for the two of you," Justin told the children. "We'll talk about your detective careers in the morning."

"Yes, sir," Evan said, already looking resigned to the portended end of his career.

"Can Thunder sleep with us?" Effie ignored Justin's remark about her future completely, to Alex's amusement.

When the children and Thunder had climbed the stairs, Justin said, "You'll have to find a way to implicate Chase without the children, Alex. They will not be involved further in this case. They've spent months playing detective. The game has been used to justify eavesdropping, invading others' privacy, snooping through other people's property—it ends here." Turning to Amanda, he grimaced. "I'm sorry, but I cannot allow the children in court."

"Of course you can't." Her voice was low, but Alex was sure she was sincere in her agreement. With her love for children, she would never want to expose Effie and Evan to a courtroom, even if a judge would allow it.

"Now that we know Chase is involved, we'll find a way to prove it," Alex tried to assure her.

Amanda wound a curl around one finger, and stared across the room with a strange look on her face. "I think I know how to do that."

Chapter 18

"Y ou have a plan, Amanda?" Alex asked.

"Yes." Amanda couldn't keep her temper out of her voice. "Don't tell me again to go back to my Sunday school class, and leave the detective work to you, Alexander Bixby."

Alex winced.

She heard Justin's chuckle, and Constance's quiet but shocked, "Alex! You didn't!"

She ignored them and continued, lifting her chin to challenge Alex with her eyes. "My father is involved in this case, and I guess I have a right to tell my plan if I wish."

"Of course, you do," Alex assured her.

Was he saying that because he agreed with her, or because he didn't care to be further embarrassed in front of their friends by arguing with her? Either way, she was going to have her say.

"You might all remember I took shorthand courses."

Everyone nodded.

"It should be easy to get Lance Chase to meet with Father, since Mr. Chase is Father's lawyer. I'm certain I can convince Father to direct the conversation in such a manner that Mr. Chase will incriminate himself. I will hide nearby, and record their conversation in shorthand."

Amanda glanced at each of the others in the room, holding her breath. What would they think of her plan? Would Alex say it was silly? Would Constance?

"Sounds like a clever plan," Justin approved, "but won't you be placing yourself in danger? I doubt your father would agree to that."

Constance laid a hand on Amanda's arm. "I'm afraid a judge may not allow the shorthand notes as evidence, on the basis that you are prejudiced. It could be argued that you are trying to lay blame on someone else to lighten the case against your father."

Frustration poured through her. "But Father has already confessed to the crime. What would he or I have to gain by giving false testimony against someone else?"

"A lighter sentence for your father, perhaps," Constance explained.

"I could hide with you."

Amanda stared at Alex. He was leaning against the wall beside the fireplace, his arms crossed, meeting her gaze evenly. Had she heard him right? Had he offered to help her, rather than ridiculing her plan? "What—what did you say?"

"I could hide with you. That way, I could verify that your shorthand transcript is accurate, and I could protect you in case Lance Chase discovers you there and tries to harm you."

Constance clapped her hands together lightly. "Oh, Alex, what a perfect solution!"

Amanda's gaze was tied with his, her heart filled with gratitude. "Thank you." It came out so softly, she wasn't sure he even heard the words.

Justin cleared his throat, stood, and held out his hand to Constance. "Let's go check on those youngsters. We haven't had devotions yet tonight. Maybe we can read them a Bible story."

Amanda watched them leave, not certain whether or not to be glad for their thoughtfulness in giving her and Alex some time alone. She'd been so angry with Alex tonight, and then he'd acted the opposite of what she expected. It made her ashamed.

She'd almost gathered up enough courage to tell him so, when he spoke.

"I do have a couple of concerns about your plan."

Her gratitude washed away in a wave of indignation. "I might have known!"

"Constance said your notes on the conversation might be construed as too prejudicial to your father's case, and that's true, but the conversation might also strengthen the prosecution's case against your father. I'm afraid we may be asking too much of you, expecting you to take part in this. We could find someone else to take down the conversation."

He'd done it again! She'd expected the worst from him, and instead he had only been thinking of sparing her pain. Her indignation with him seeped away.

"I want to do this, Alexander. I want to help bring to justice the man who drove Father into crime. I know Father is responsible for the choice he made, but Lance Chase tried to tie his hands, and make it impossible for him to choose otherwise."

Alex nodded. "All right, then, if that's how you feel about it. The other problem with the plan is that it would be difficult to put over at the jailhouse. If it's all right with you, I'll ask the judge to release your father to my custody, and we'll arrange the meeting at your home."

"They could meet in Father's study. You and I could hide behind the screen, the one Effie and Evan hid behind when they overheard the Father's conversation with Mr. Chase." It would be wonderful for her father to be out from behind bars, even for a little while. "Do you think the judge will allow him to stay out of prison until his trial?"

"I don't see why not, once he posts bail."

"Oh." Despair came back. The feeling was familiar to her now. Since her father had told her his awful news, she'd only been able to shake despair and sadness for all-too-brief moments. How long would it be like this? Months? Years? Would she ever feel truly happy again?

"Justin and I will see he has the money for bail, Amanda, I give you my word."

"Oh!" She pressed her fingertips over her lips. Alex became a blur as tears filled her eyes. "Oh, Alex, thank you."

He moved closer, pulled out a large handkerchief and handed it to her.

She took it and dabbed at her tears. Then, to her horror, she broke into soft sobs.

In a moment, he was beside her, his arms about her, pulling her gently to his chest. She leaned into him, crying out her despair against his shoulder, abandoning all pretext of being in control of her emotions.

His arms felt like a shelter. Eventually her sobs lessened, but she made no move to push herself away. She wanted to stay there forever, his chest rising and falling beneath her cheek, his breath warm in her hair, his lips touching her hair and forehead in occasional feather-light kisses.

"I'm so sorry, dearest. I'm so sorry this happened to you. I'd give my life if I could change it." The words, whispered against her hair in such a sweet, intimate way, wrapped around her heart.

He pulled back slightly, smoothing her hair and smiling into her eyes. "I was wrong about your staying out of detective work, I think. Your plan is a good one."

Her breathing was still jerky from the aftereffects of her cry. "When—when you told me it could be dangerous being involved in the case, I never suspected this kind of danger. I thought it would be exciting to help solve the case, but if I hadn't found the counterfeit bills in Father's desk, he might not be behind bars tonight. I—I didn't think it would turn out like this."

One of his arms still held her near, and she rested against him, trying to keep from crying heavily again. He continued smoothing her hair back from her face, and she noticed for the first time how she'd mussed it, crying against him. His hand was gentle and soothing.

"Your father loves you, dear. Never forget that. He made a mistake, misjudged the best way to show his love for you. Fathers aren't perfect. He isn't the only father to make mistakes. Some of the most revered men in the Bible weren't perfect fathers, either. Look at David. He made some big mistakes as a father, but his life still touched others in good ways."

Tears formed in her eyes again. Alex was such a dear man! Love for him filled her chest until she thought she couldn't bear it. "I was so afraid you would despise Father when you found he was one of the counterfeiters, and I wanted so much for you to still like and respect him. He is a good man, in most ways."

A tear dropped from her lashes. He caught it with the back of a knuckle, gently. "Of course he's a good man. Look at the wonderful daughter he raised."

She laughed, a jerky little laugh, with sobs still near the surface. The laugh died away, and they were smiling at each other. His face was only inches away, and her eyes searched his.

I love you, Alexander. Her mind whispered the words she longed to say.

Cautiously, she lifted a hand, and laid her fingers gently along one of his cheeks. Her heart hammered erratically. Would he think her too bold, or would he welcome her touch?

He laid his hand over hers, his gaze still caught in hers. He turned his head only enough to touch his lips to her palm, and the sweetness of the moment was so intense she could barely breathe.

His gaze slid to her lips. "Sweet Amanda." The words were a tender whisper. He leaned a fraction closer. She closed her eyes, welcoming his kiss. His lips barely touched hers, then moved away, but she could still feel his breath against her lips. A moment later, his lips touched hers again. His arms pulled her closer, and the kiss deepened, lingered.

Joy, quiet and wonderful, filled her senses. The way he touched her, the way he'd comforted her, surely he must return her love! She'd been so sure she had lost all hope of him loving her. But now—

He pulled back so abruptly the sudden space between them was a shock of cool air. He stood almost before she realized they were no longer only a heartbeat away from each other.

"We've a busy day tomorrow. We'll each need a good night's sleep, and I've a report to write yet tonight."

"Of—of course." What had happened? Why had he pulled away like that? "Are—are you angry with me?"

He stuffed his hands in his trousers pockets, lifted his shoulders and eyebrows. "Angry? No, of course not. It's just that it's getting late."

She could hear Justin and Constance's voices and realized they must be coming back downstairs. She brushed at her mussed hair. The emptiness and pain of despair and lack of hope swamped her again, and she cringed inwardly at their return.

He doesn't love me after all, in spite of his endearments! I've embarrassed him with my touch. Had he seen her love for him in her eyes and broken the contact with her before she could embarrass them both further? He'd only meant to comfort her, and she'd misread his intentions.

She rose when Constance and Justin entered the room, and sent a shaky smile their direction, not meeting their eyes. "Thank you for opening your home to me. I—I find I'm quite exhausted. If you'll excuse me, I'll retire now."

She hurried past them, avoiding looking at or speaking to Alex. Her head was pounding, and her eyes swollen, likely because of that crying fest she'd allowed herself—at Alex's expense.

The pain of knowing he didn't love her was like a vise around her chest, but she wouldn't be sorry she loved him. She wouldn't let herself embarrass him again with a display of her emotions.

In her room, she lit a small lamp on the vanity, and surveyed her unkempt appearance in the mirror. She reached a hand to touch her hair where he'd smoothed it back, remembering the feel of his hand, warm and strong and gentle all at once. No matter how painful it is living without his love, I don't ever want to forget those moments in his arms. It may be all I ever have of his touch. Her heart contracted at the thought, and another small sob slipped out. I want to remember forever the wonder and beauty of it.

~~~

The memory of Amanda in his arms, the hurt look in her eyes when he'd pushed himself away from her, stayed with Alex the next day through all his preparations for the confrontation between Mason and Lance Chase.

"I should have known better!" he'd muttered to himself a dozen times during the day. She was especially vulnerable right now. He'd been surprised she allowed him, the man who'd arrested her father, to comfort her, but oh, so glad she had! No chance she'll want me to be a part of her life when she has her feet back on solid ground again. It wasn't fair of me to take advantage of her now, when her emotions are a jumble.

But he'd wanted to hold her for so long.

The softness of her hair beneath his cheek, her palm against his lips, the light scent of lavender that was part of her, all remained part of his senses. It had been a fool thing to do!

With difficulty, he dragged his mind back to the present. It had been a full day, and it wasn't over. First, he'd gone to the jailhouse to tell Mason that, thanks to Effie and Evan, they knew Lance Chase was one of his accomplices. The truth of it was apparent in the defensive tension that released about Mason's eyes when Alex told him they knew.

Next he'd had to convince Mason of Amanda's plan. The older man had stubbornly refused to go along with it at first. Only when Alex assured him that he would see to her safety during the confrontation, and that she could only truly be safe by putting his other accomplices behind bars, did Mason agree.

Sheriff Tucker had to be told of the plan. He didn't like the sound of it right away. "Putting that young lady in danger like that. It just doesn't sit right."

Only when Alex assured him he'd never be more than a step away from Amanda, derringer in hand, and that Constance would be in the kitchen beside the telephone, waiting to call Tucker when Lance Chase arrived, did he finally agree to it.

"Still think I should be in on it, though. Don't like sitting down here at the office when something like that is happening in my town."

Alex had to talk hard to convince him that the more people there were in the house, the more likely something would go wrong, but convince him he did.

Justin found another lawyer for Mason, and supplied the bail money. Then Justin spoke to a judge, a personal friend of his, and arranged for bail.

When Alex had walked up the front porch steps with Mason, Amanda had flown out the front door and into her father's arms. The scene was too emotional for him to watch, and he moved past them into the house, making conversation with Constance, who had been waiting with Amanda for Mr. Mason's return.

Until the counterfeiting ring were all apprehended, Alex, Justin, and Constance had agreed one of them would always be with Amanda.

After Mason and Amanda had themselves composed once again, Alex went over the plan step by step. They checked the screen, and made certain he and Amanda could not be seen when behind it from anywhere in the study.

Amanda spoke with Mrs. Brady and the maids, explaining that there was special business to be conducted in her father's study. None of them were to enter the study while Mr. Chase was there. They were to go about their usual business, no matter what they heard or how strange events might seem. They gave her puzzled looks, but agreed.

Finally, Mason called the lawyer, told him he'd been released on bail, and that it was urgent they meet at his home immediately. As they'd all expected he would, Lance Chase agreed.

They took their places: Constance in the kitchen, where Chase wouldn't know of her presence, Alex and Amanda behind the screen, Mason at his desk. And waited.

Alex was uncomfortably aware of Amanda as they waited behind the screen. She sat on a stool, her purple and cream striped skirt covering her legs, the heels of her cream-colored slippers hooked over a rung. Her back was stiff as a board from her father's former sawmill, her knuckles white from clutching her pad and paper. The paper wasn't bound; a small pile of separate sheets on top of a strong leather portfolio would have to suffice. Turning pages in a notebook might be too noisy, and draw Chase's attention.

Standing behind her, Alex remembered how she had felt in his arms the night before. He'd almost not had the strength to keep from speaking his love for her. Even now, it was difficult not to reach out and touch her. So close, but forever was between them.

It had been difficult for both of them, preparing for this confrontation. She had been distant when they had to be together for any reason. Not that he could blame her. He'd behaved like a bounder last night, first kissing her, then all but leaping away from her.

His thoughts jerked back to the present at the sound of the brass knocker on the front door. His heart quickened. His senses stood at attention, as they always did when he was at a critical point in a case.

He heard Amanda take a deep, shaky breath. Squeezing her shoulders, he leaned forward so his lips were beside her ear. "This is it! Don't worry. You'll do great, Detective Amanda."

Her shoulders relaxed a small degree beneath his hands. Did she remember that when they first met she used to call him Detective Alex?

Footsteps entered the room. One of the maids announced the lawyer's arrival, but her announcement was obviously unnecessary. The man was already in the room.

"Afternoon, Mason," he said, almost before the maid quit speaking. Alex could imagine the skinny, pompous man with thinning reddish-blond hair standing before the desk, thumbs in his vest pockets.

"Thank you for coming." Mason's voice. "Please close the door on your way out, Miss Anderson."

The door shut. Alex recognized the sound of someone sitting down in one of the leather wing chairs. Strange, sound being the only sense he could use.

Amanda had already begun taking down the conversation. Her pencil scratched softly against the paper as she wrote. Would Chase hear it?

He glanced over her shoulder at the shapes he couldn't decipher, the shapes that had the power to entrap the slimy-spirited little man who preyed on his neighbors for his own gain.

"How did you get out on bail without my help?" Chase asked.

"Justin Knight arranged it for me. He lent me the money and spoke with the judge himself, as they are friends."

Chase barked a laugh. "Lucky for you, having a friend like Knight. Too bad you didn't ask him to give you a mortgage on this place, instead of me."

"Yes, isn't it."

Amanda's pencil stopped moving at her father's low comment. Alex squeezed her shoulder again, lightly. *Steady, dearest,* he thought.

She straightened her shoulders and nodded her head, and he knew she'd continue as she needed to do.

He reached into his pocket and slowly, holding his breath, withdrew his derringer. Best to be prepared.

"That mortgage is one of the reasons I asked you here," Mason continued. "When I couldn't make the payments, you threatened to take away my home unless I helped you place the counterfeit funds, I foolishly agreed to do so. I have kept my part of the bargain, haven't I?"

"Yes. You've done everything I've asked. We've made a tidy little profit already, especially from the sawmill payroll exchange. I'd hoped to get a lot more of the false money placed, but when that Pinkerton man, Knight's friend, showed up in town, I knew we'd have to be more careful for the time being. Thought if I insisted he help find the counterfeiters, and talk with the bookkeeper at the sawmill, you and I would be beyond suspicion. Didn't work that way, after all, at least not for you."

"No, it didn't. I've taken more risks than you or any of your other accomplices."

"You've had good reason to take those risks. You had a lot to lose: a fine house, a good reputation, and a lovely daughter."

Amanda's head jerked up. Alex touched her shoulder lightly. *Easy, darling. Don't let his words upset you too much. Thanks to you, his words are going to be his own undoing.*

"I haven't a good reputation any longer," Mason countered. "If I'd turned down your offer, I'd have lost the house, but kept the reputation and my daughter. A much better arrangement, as I've since discovered."

"You knew the risks. Don't turn crybaby on me, now."

"Yes, I knew the risks, and I took them. I will be convicted of counterfeiting activity, we both know that. I've refused to reveal your name or that of any of the others. Now I want what you owe me in return."

"Which is?"

"I want you to sign the note for the house 'paid in full.' "

Chase's laugh bellowed out. "Fat chance of that."

There was a long silence. Finally Mason spoke. "You never intended to release me from that debt, did you? No matter how many of your dirty counterfeiting exchanges I performed."

"Well, you can't fault a man for wanting to make a profit, can you, Mason? Let's just call the errands you performed for me interest on your loan. As for the principal, mark my words, you aren't going to be needing this place for a while, not while you're in prison. I'm sure you're not intending to tell anyone about me, not when you care about that pretty daughter of yours."

Amanda turned her head sharply. Alex met her flashing gaze. "Isn't it enough?" she mouthed.

He nodded. Guilt stabbed at him. He'd become caught up in the conflict and had forgotten for a moment how Chase's words must be hurting her and her father.

Stepping cautiously so as not to startle Chase before he was safely out from behind the screen, Alex moved to reveal himself, derringer ready in his hand. His heart thumped against the wall of his chest, reverberating in his ears like a racing metronome.

His gaze dropped to the legs of Amanda's stool. Don't trip on them.

He felt her gaze on him. She met it. Fright and anticipation were etched on her young face. He winked. She broke into a smile.

He closed his eyes a moment. Took a deep breath. *This is it, Bixby. Don't botch it.*

The next step took him from behind the screen. Relief washed through him. Chase was seated with his back to the screen. Now if only Mason—

Mason's gaze met his. He stopped speaking in midsentence, staring.

Too late! Alex stepped quickly forward, his derringer pointed in the direction of Chase's chair.

Chase's face appeared around the side of the chair. "What—!" He leaped awkwardly to his feet. Shock and fear and anger chased each other across his skinny face.

"Stop right there, Chase." Alex moved his derringer higher to be sure Chase saw the small firearm. He measured the distance between himself and Chase, careful not to get too close.

Chase's gaze riveted on the derringer.

Chase glared at him, his face turning almost purple with rage. "You've betrayed me, Mason! You'll be sorry."

Amanda swept past Alex, waving her papers in Chase's face. "It's your own words that have betrayed you!"

"Amanda, don't!" Fear tore through Alex. He grabbed for her arm.

Chase grabbed her first, catching her wrist above the hand with the papers. The papers tumbled to the floor, scattering.

She cried out in pain and surprise as he twisted her back against himself.

The sound lanced through Alex. "Let her go!"

"Amanda!" Mason started around the desk. "Chase, let her go!"

Amanda struggled against the man's arm, but he held her fast. Alex could see her eyes were filled with anger, not fear. Chase was careful to keep her between himself and Alex. His gaze on Alex, he reached into a leather bag in the wing chair and pulled out a pistol.

No, God! Alex's heart stood still.

Beside him, Mason gasped. "Chase, no!"

Chase stuck the pistol against Amanda's side. She glanced down. Froze.

Chase's breath sounded ragged. "Now, we're going to do this my way."

Chapter 19

Chase nodded at Alex. "First off, you toss that pony of a pistol out the window. And no tricks. Any calls for help, and Miss Amanda gets hurt."

Alex backed to the window, watching Chase's gun hand all the while. He pushed the window open, unhooked the screen, and dropped the derringer out.

Frustration coursed through him. *Lord, that's all I had to protect Amanda against this man and his gun. You're going to have to take care of her now.* Would the God he'd only recently begun to trust help Amanda? He'd seen enough people hurt in his business to know God didn't always intervene to stop such things.

He darted a glance at Mason. Guilt tore at his heart at the agony on the older man's face. He'd promised Mason he would protect his daughter. Instead, by agreeing to her plan, he'd drawn her into mortal danger.

Chase was backing through the door into the hall, dragging Amanda with him. Her hands clutched the arm he had around her neck.

"Don't either of you try anything," Chase barked, "or the girl gets it."

Alex held up his hands. "We won't."

"Don't hurt her!" Mason's cry was hoarse.

Alex's gaze locked with Amanda's. Fright and pleading seemed to scream at him from her eyes. *Courage, my love,* he tried to send a message back to her with his own eyes. *Do whatever he asks. Don't try anything foolish.*

His hands balled into fists at his side. He'd never felt so powerless!

When Chase and Amanda were fully through the door and into the hall, Alex moved into the open doorway, anxiously watching their retreat, watching for a split-second opportunity to overcome Chase and free Amanda, even now. If it came, he wanted to be ready.

The kitchen door swung open into the hall.

"Hold it!" Chase swung toward the movement. Amanda stumbled and would have fallen if Chase hadn't been holding her so tightly.

Sheriff Tucker stood with his ample frame braced against the kitchen door, a shotgun in his hands, his red handlebar mustache quivering at the sight before him.

Constance stood beside him, a restraining hand on his arm.

Alex had forgotten they were waiting in the kitchen for him to come out of the study with his prisoner. Thank God that Constance was with Tucker! Tucker was a good lawman, but Alex trusted Constance's wisdom. He'd been with her in situations this bad and worse in their years as Pinkertons together, and she'd always acted wisely.

But Amanda had never been the hostage before. That fact changed everything.

"Empty the shotgun," Chase ordered.

Tucker hesitated.

Alex could taste sweat on his lips. "Do as he says, Tucker."

When the sheriff complied, relief loosened slightly the bands that seemed to bind Alex's chest.

"Toss the gun down."

Tucker did as asked.

Chase lifted his chin in a tossing manner. "All of you, into the kitchen."

Constance took a step backward.

"Stop! I changed my mind. Stay in the hall, where I can see you. All of you."

Constance stayed where she was. "Of course, whatever you say, Mr. Chase."

Not a ripple of fear or threat touched her voice; it was as calm as always, her manner as serene. Alex thanked God again that she was here.

Chase backed toward the door. Amanda winced as his arm pressed harder against her neck.

A knot formed in Alex's throat at the sight of her pain. He took an impulsive step forward.

"Stay there!"

He stopped. Panic spread through him like the Mississippi flooding its banks. *Keep calm, Bixby! You're not going to help Amanda by losing control of yourself.*

"Listen, Mr. Chase," Sheriff Tucker started. "Why don't you rethink this? Let Miss Amanda go. Give me your gun. After all, where are you going to go? You're a lawyer. Your face is well-known in these parts."

Desperation peered from Chase's eyes. "There are always places a man can hide."

Would he take Amanda into hiding with him, for protection? Everything inside Alex revolted at the thought. If she kept her head, he might release her when he reached transportation. His gaze sought her face, only to find she was watching him. She gave him a wobbly smile. She was trying to give him courage! It almost broke his heart.

Chase backed against the door, pushed the latch with his elbow, and pulled Amanda out onto the veranda with him.

Effie and Evan's laughter and calling voices spilled into the hallway from the yard.

"No!" Constance took a step forward.

Terror coiled in Alex's chest. He'd forgotten about the children. They were obviously playing outside, but where? Would they have sense enough to stay away from Chase and Amanda?

He shot a glance at Constance. Her face was as white as her shirtwaist, her eyes huge. He held a palm toward her. "Wait!"

The door slammed shut.

Alex darted toward it, Constance at his heels. Through the etched-glass window, it took him only a moment to grasp the situation. Chase was no longer facing the house. He was crossing the veranda, a struggling Amanda still in his grasp. Effie and Evan were playing with Thunder in the yard in front of the house, and apparently hadn't noticed Chase and Amanda yet.

Teeth in his bottom lip, Alex opened the door as quietly as possible and started to slip through.

"Thunder, come back!"

"Thunder!"

The children's voices drew his attention.

A ball of fur was headed across the lawn toward the porch, its lead bouncing behind it. Effie and Evan raced along behind, not able to keep up. Thunder tore up the steps, yipping an eager greeting to Amanda.

"Oh no!" Constance's frightened voice echoed Alex's thoughts.

Chase swore and kicked at the dog.

"Don't kick Thunder!" Effie, still headed across the lawn, called an indignant command.

Chase glanced in her direction. Thunder ran around him and Amanda, trying to get Amanda's attention.

Chase stepped on the lead. Thunder tugged, ran the other direction, entangling the lawyer's leg.

"Stupid mutt! Get away! Ea–a–a–h!" Trying to keep his balance, Chase lost his hold on Amanda. His arms turned like windmills as he teetered at the top of the steps for a moment that seemed like an hour to Alex. Then he was in a pile at the bottom of the steps.

His pistol hit the sidewalk. *Blam!*

Alex was across the porch in a flash, his heart quaking. Had the shot hit the children? It took only a moment to see it hadn't, though it had stopped them. They stood like statues, open-mouthed, staring at the man who was struggling to get to his knees and reclaim his weapon.

Alex reached it first, twirling to point it at Chase. "That's far enough. You all right, Amanda?" He didn't dare take his gaze from Chase.

"Y–yes."

Constance was hurrying across the yard to Effie and Evan. Sheriff Tucker lumbered down the steps and made his way to Alex. He held out a large hand for the gun. "I'll take it from here."

Alex handed him the weapon gladly, freeing his gaze to search for Amanda. She was in her father's arms, hugging his neck tightly.

Where she should be, he thought, relief weakening his muscles. He tried to ignore the disappointment in his own chest that he wasn't the one holding her.

He wanted her in his arms to reassure himself she was all right as much as to comfort her for the ordeal she'd been through.

Selfish thought! Knowing she was safe should be enough. *It is, Lord. Thank You for protecting her.*

❧

Walking into the Knights' parlor for coffee and dessert after dinner that night, Amanda slipped a hand beneath her father's arm. He placed a hand over hers and squeezed lightly, giving her a sad smile. She refused to be unhappy; she planned to treasure every moment they had together before his trial.

Pressing her head against his shoulder, she whispered, "I love you, Papa," slipping into the intimate term she'd used as a child.

His faded blue eyes sparked with a hint of his former self, the self that hadn't betrayed his own values.

When he gets out of prison, we'll rebuild his former self together, she thought. *Or perhaps a new self—stronger, wiser.*

The Knights' maid placed a silver serving tray on a marble-topped table. The silver service gave off a quiet glow in the early evening of late summer.

Effie and Evan had departed for the outdoors with cookies in hand and Thunder trailing at their feet as usual. The room was quiet with the pleasant silence of friends who are comfortable together.

Watching Constance pour coffee from the silver coffeepot into gold-trimmed china cups, a lump formed in Amanda's throat. Constance and Justin had done so much for her and her father! They'd lent money for her father's bail, helped them trap the man who had drawn her father into crime, and most importantly, treated her father with respect in spite of his crime.

Amanda had accepted a cup, the friendly aroma of coffee rising from it, and a dainty, lemon-frosted cookie, when Alex walked in. Her heart leaped at the sight of him.

He met her gaze as soon as he entered the room. It felt as though he was searching for something there. For a hint of her love? She hoped so! She smiled at him, and a smile flickered back at her from his eyes—a weary smile.

Lines that hadn't been there a few days ago were etched in his face, and his eyes appeared even more deep-set than usual, with gray circles beneath them. His exhaustion lanced her heart, since she knew his fatigue had been earned helping her and her father. He'd certainly followed the Pinkerton Agency's slogan, "We never sleep."

"What's the news from Sheriff Tucker's office?" Justin asked.

Alex accepted the cup of coffee Constance offered him, and sat down on the ottoman. His shoulders seemed to sag with weariness. "Chase has hired himself a lawyer. He refuses to give Tucker any information yet about the counterfeiting ring. Usually his cooperation would ensure a lighter sentence, but in this case, I think his attempted abduction of Amanda precludes that. I expect he feels the same, or he'd be talking."

"You're probably right," Constance agreed.

Justin frowned. "Does that mean they still have no idea who else may be in on it with Chase?"

Alex nodded at Mason. "Mason gave the sheriff all the names he knew after he agreed to help us entrap Chase in the study. Tucker's been out arresting them, before they could hear of Chase's arrest and flee."

"None of my bank staff among them?"

Alex didn't need to see the twinkle in Justin's eyes to know he meant Jack Davis. Justin probably thought he'd enjoy putting Amanda's too-frequent escort behind bars.

"No. There are only two others: a man who forged the print for the plates and obtained the ink, and the man who made up the plates and printed the money. Neither of them were people we'd checked out. They'd played it smart, we'd had no reason to suspect them."

"It sounds as though they may have been involved in counterfeiting or forging activities in the past." Constance held out the plate of lemon cookies, and he accepted one.

Alex grinned at her. "You're right, as usual. I went through the Bertillon cards on known counterfeiters before I left the Chicago office for River's Edge. Haven't seen any of the men during our investigation in this area, but one of the men Tucker brought in fits the description of a known counterfeiter."

Mason leaned forward. "What's a Bertillon card?"

Amanda patted his arm and laughed. "Father, you have to expand your reading. A Bertillon card is a way the Pinkerton Agency keeps track of criminals. On one side of the card is a picture of the man."

"Or woman," Alex interrupted.

"Or woman." Amanda wrinkled her nose at him, glad to see a twinkle back in his eyes. "On the back, there is a physical description of the man, uh, person, and other information such as any aliases, where he's been known to live, and crimes for which he's been arrested."

"I've changed my mind." Alex smiled at her over the rim of his cup, which looked especially dainty in his large hand. His smile sent happy tremors along her nerves. "With a little training, you might make a good Pinkerton agent yet."

"I suppose there will be a Bertillon card on me, now."

At Mason's statement, quiet descended on the room. Tears heated Amanda's eyes, closed her throat.

It was Alex who broke the silence. "But we all know there will never be another arrest recorded on that card. The card will yellow with age and crumble to dust from disuse."

Amanda couldn't see his face; it was blurred by her tears. Gratitude warmed her chest. I love this man, she thought. *Thank You for bringing him into our lives, Lord.*

She hoped Alex would find a way for them to speak alone that evening.

Since he didn't approach her, she finally approached him.

"I want to apologize."

Surprise filled his eyes with question.

"About that foolish move I made in the study earlier today," she explained. "I was so angry with Mr. Chase for saying all those awful things to Father and for the way he'd treated Father. When I thought he was captured, I couldn't resist waving those papers under his nose. I should have realized how unwise it was to get close to him. I—I put everyone in danger."

"Anyone can make a mistake." His Adam's apple bobbed and she heard him swallow. "I admit I was frightened for you."

"I know." Her own voice came out in a whisper. This time it was she who swallowed. "In spite of what you said earlier tonight about the possibility I'd make a good detective, I didn't act wisely under pressure."

Adam laughed. "It might be Effie and Evan that Superintendent Jakes credits for solving this case. They were the ones who discovered the money in your father's trunk, overheard Chase blackmailing your father, and if they hadn't been playing with Thunder this afternoon, there's no telling where Chase might be now."

"Or whether he'd have released me, or taken me with him." She pressed her fingertips to her lips, then clasped her hands together at her waist, horror spilling through her at the picture memory replaying in her mind. "When I saw those children in the yard. . .and then Mr. Chase fell and his gun went off. . .and I realized that my foolish action had endangered dear Effie and Evan—they were the longest, most frightful few moments of my life."

He laid a hand above her wrist. She could feel the warmth of it through the lace that covered her forearm. "Forgive yourself. We all make mistakes. Effie and Evan weren't harmed." His hand slid away. "If anyone should feel guilty, it's me. I should never have allowed you to be involved in that plan."

"You couldn't have stopped me. I was determined to have a part in bringing that awful man to justice." She glanced down at her hands, tugged a bit at the lace edging her wrist. "I shouldn't judge him so harshly. There are people already judging Father, without understanding why he made the choices he did, and I hate that people are thinking such cruel thoughts about him."

"I'm sorry."

The huskiness in his words spoke of his sincerity, and healed a little of the wound in her heart. "Father hates that Mr. Chase is going to end up with our house. He built the house for Mother, and she loved it."

"Perhaps a way can be found to save it."

She shook her head. "Father doesn't think that is possible. I don't want to hope for it. There's been too much loss. I—I don't think I could bear it if I put the effort into hoping the house could be saved, and yet lost it."

She saw the worry for her in his eyes, and straightened her shoulders and forced a smile. "I'll be all right, though. I remember when Mother died. Life was so painful. Father kept pointing out the good things, the beautiful things that life still held. Through his example, I learned that even when life is painful, there is still goodness and beauty and that they are stronger in the end than the things which cause us pain."

"He is a good man."

The painful knowledge of what was ahead for her father smothered her. "It wasn't until the last couple of years that I understood how difficult it must have been for him to find beautiful things to point out to me. He loved Mother so. How could he have seen anything but his own pain when he lost her?"

He slid a knuckle under her chin and lifted it gently until her gaze met his. "He told me once that his love for you was his strength during that time. Now you can return the gift he gave you when you lost your mother. You can help him find the good things left in his life."

Wonder spread through her, comforting her like a warm blanket on a cold morning. He had given her something to do to help her father now, something to keep her spirit from withering in pity for her father and herself. "Thank you," she whispered.

His hand fell away as her father and the Knights joined them, but the warmth of his touch and the love she'd felt emanate from him lingered in her heart.

❧

"Gone! He can't be gone!" Amanda stared at Constance, disbelief tumbling through her.

They stood in the Knights' kitchen the next morning. Sunshine streamed through the curtains. Pansies danced in the breeze that tumbled through the window boxes outside the open windows.

"He left on the first train east this morning." Constance looked up from table where she was preparing the day's market list.

"When does he expect to return?"

"I have no idea." Constance tilted her head. A line cut between her brows. "Surely you must have realized he would be leaving now that the case is solved. Superintendent Jakes likely already has another assignment in mind for him."

"But he. . .I thought. . ." *I thought he loved me,* her thoughts completed. Pain worse than anything she'd ever known gripped her. It felt as though someone were tearing a part of her away, leaving a gaping wound in her chest.

Constance laid down her pen. "Didn't he even say good-bye?" she asked slowly. "Didn't he tell you he would write or be in touch with you?"

Amanda shook her head, unable to catch her breath enough to answer.

"Oh, my dear!" Constance rose and came quickly to her, taking her hands.

"You—you warned me. You said not to give my heart to a detective, but I thought. . .I hoped. . ."

"He cares for you, I know he does. Perhaps he needs to work out in his own mind whether he can risk loving you. It is difficult for a detective to have a wife and family."

Or was it that, in spite of his kind words about her father, Alex couldn't love a woman whose father was a criminal? Amanda wondered.

She'd been so sure God meant the two of them to be together. There had been that peace, that certainty, inside her when she prayed about it. A certainty that God had given them the gift of each other's love, that they could heal and grow and learn and experience joy with each other in ways they couldn't with anyone else. But God had given them free choice, too, and she knew He wouldn't force either of them to accept His gift.

Evidently, Alex was walking away from that gift.

She wrapped her arms over her chest, sank to a chair, and let the sobs come.

Chapter 20

Alex left his bag at the train station, crossed the boardwalk platform, and headed toward River's Edge's business district, where the courthouse stood. He tossed one end of his black wool scarf over his shoulder, yanked his derby down to a more secure position, stuffed his gloved hands into the pockets of his long, gray wool overcoat, and bent his head into the February wind that was swirling snowflakes in dervishes through the street.

The weather reflected his mood perfectly. His heart was revolting at the mandatory return to this place where the woman he'd loved and lost lived.

A sharp laugh burst from his lips at the memory his return to River's Edge last summer with similar sentiments, that time because of Constance. This time it wasn't Superintendent Jakes insisting he return, but the courts. The counterfeiters' trial was to begin today.

And this time it wasn't Constance he wanted to avoid seeing, but Amanda. *Sweet Amanda!* The familiar ache in his chest returned. Seldom an hour of any day went by without the thought of her. He'd thought when Constance married Justin, that he'd missed her. He knew now that what he'd felt had been a mixture of hurt pride and the loss of a good friend. With Constance, he'd never felt as if he were carrying an anvil around on his chest.

Wind whipped the end of the scarf back over his shoulder, and the chill swept his chin. He wrapped the muffler tighter. His jaw hurt from clenching his teeth against his memories.

Amanda had responded so sweetly to his attempts to comfort her the day before he left River's Edge last August. He'd been sorely tempted to tell her of his love. It wouldn't have been an act of love to do so. She was too vulnerable. She'd thought she cared for him; that had been apparent in her manner.

He was sure he had known better, and had steeled himself against her. Her father's confession, the confrontation with Chase, everything had happened so quickly. When things slowed down, when she fully realized the part he'd played in her father's arrest and his eventual imprisonment, her love would turn to loathing. He'd seen too many criminals' family members turn their anger against the people involved in bringing them to justice to believe otherwise.

The arguments against his heart were familiar; he went through them over and over in his mind every day. His heart never won. The arguments only made him weary in body and soul.

She'd be at the courthouse. Nothing would keep her from her father's trial, or that of Lance Chase. In front of Amanda and the world, for permanent record, he'd have to tell the world what he knew of Mason's guilt. His chest hurt at the thought of it.

With an effort, he tried turning his thoughts away from Amanda. The next few hours and days were going to be difficult enough. There was no sense in inviting more pain into his life than necessary. Guilt stabbed at his heart. Besides, his own pain was trivial compared to what she would suffer during these trials. If things were different, if he weren't one of the enemy, he could be beside her, comforting her, helping her find strength. As it was, all he could do was pray for her—and testify against the person she loved most in the world.

Hmph! Hadn't been too successful in turning his thoughts from her so far. Typical.

He tried again, making himself bring back mind pictures of the case he'd just completed. He'd been on assignment in northern Minnesota almost since he'd left River's Edge. No place to be in the middle of winter! It had been a difficult, dangerous assignment, and he'd had to rely not only on his wits and his experience as a Pinkerton, but on the Lord as well.

Strange to think now that there had ever been a time when he didn't talk things over with the Lord in his mind the same as a person would with a good friend and trusted advisor. Strange to think there'd ever been a time when he hadn't been certain the Lord was always beside him, as real as any human being, only invisible, as Amanda had explained to the little girl in her Sunday school class last summer.

The assignment had been different from past assignments in another way, too. Knowing Mason had given him new empathy for criminals. His compassion hadn't made him less effective as an operative; it gave him a new understanding of the motives behind men's actions. Justin had been right about that. He'd fight harder now for the prisoner reformation programs the Pinkerton Agency was always promoting.

He came to an abrupt stop in front of the county courthouse, staring through the swirling snow at the massive four-story building of rough stone. It resembled a castle, with deep-set windows, colored glass, even a tall square tower.

Blanket-covered horses harnessed to buggies and tied to rings at the curbside filled the street. Alex grimaced in distaste. He'd testified at enough trials to know what that meant. The public and newspaper reporters would be filling the courtroom.

The courthouse doors were set into a massive stone arch. With a brief prayer for strength and a deep breath, he entered them.

He'd expected to find the halls busy with people, but they weren't. A glance at the large, oak-encased clock on the wall told him that court had already started. He wasn't too concerned. The first part of the day would be filled with jury selection.

Hurrying up the wide steps to the courtroom floor, he pulled off his gloves and brushed snow from his coat. He bounced his derby against his coat-covered thigh to restore its color from white to gray. At the top of the steps, he stopped, staring down the wide, high-ceilinged, marble corridor.

It was as empty as the hallway on the lower floor—almost. Wooden deacon's benches lined the walls. At the end of the hallway was a huge arched window the width of the hall. A woman was silhouetted in front of it. He caught his breath. *Amanda?*

He couldn't be certain. The woman was wearing a gray winter coat that came down over her hips, a maroon skirt below it. The brim and feathers of a small bonnet of the style all women seemed to be wearing this year were outlined against the window. A huge fur muff dangled from one arm.

His breathing erratic, he walked slowly toward her, his Alaskas making little sound on the marble floor. Through the closed doors on either side of the hall, he could hear muffled voices from the courtrooms. When he was halfway to the window, the woman turned and faced him.

"Amanda!"

Her smile was warm, welcoming. "Hello, Alexander."

He'd always loved the sound of his name on her lips! He couldn't stop staring at her. He wanted to remember every detail for the long years ahead without her. "You look wonderful."

She laughed, that delightful laugh he'd loved from the first time he'd heard it, the first day they met. "Thank you, Detective Alex." Her voice was low, but he could hear her clearly; sounds amplified in the cavernous hallway. "Constance told me you would be here to testify."

Testify. The word jolted him back to reality, tarnishing the joy of seeing her. "Yes. Are Constance and Justin here?" Anything to avoid discussing the awful truth of her father's guilt that stood between them.

"Constance may need to be here later to testify against Lance Chase. Right now, she's at home with Effie and Evan and the baby."

He'd almost forgotten the baby. His life had been all too centered on himself and Amanda for the last six months. He'd been undercover on his last assignment and had had contact only with Superintendent Jakes. "The baby is healthy, then?"

She nodded. "A girl. Maria Louise. She's beautiful. Lots of dark hair, like Constance. She's a quiet, sweet baby. She'll probably grow up just as sweet and serene as Constance. Justin and Effie and Evan dote on her."

"I'm happy for all of them." He envied Constance and Justin their love and their family. He'd once hoped he and Amanda might have a life as beautiful.

He shifted his feet, turning his derby in his hands. "Have you been well, Amanda?"

"Yes." She hesitated. "I won't pretend it hasn't been difficult. We haven't long left together before he'll be in prison." Her voice trailed off. Pain glazed her eyes.

The sight of her pain seared him. He reached for her hand, wishing he had the right to draw her into his arms to comfort her. "I'm sorry."

Her lashes batted at tears, glistened with them. "I didn't wait for you to turn crybaby."

She'd been waiting here for him?

"I wanted to thank you."

Confusion made him frown. "Thank me?" Never had a member of a criminal's family thanked him for his part in the arrest!

"For paying off the loan to Mr. Chase on the house."

That was why she was being so friendly. "I was glad to do it."

"I could hardly believe it when Father's lawyer told us. Father. . .he cried. I haven't seen him cry since Mother died." She looked down at her muff, smoothing one hand over the beaver fur.

Alex's heart contracted at the sight of the tears still clinging to her lashes.

"I'll repay you, of course," she continued, glancing up at him.

"There's no need. I never expected repayment. It's a gift."

The black feathers standing at the back of her bonnet wobbled as she shook her head. "We couldn't possibly accept such a gift, though your kindness touched my heart more than I can express. I'm working as a secretary in a real estate firm now. I can't pay much, but I can pay a little each month."

"I don't want you to repay it." Impatience tinged his voice. "But I'm glad you've found work. Do you like it?"

She wrinkled her nose in the delightful way he remembered. "It's not as exciting as detective work, but yes, I do enjoy it. I've considered applying at the Pinkerton Agency in Chicago—as a secretary, not a detective, so don't lecture!"

He grinned. As if Superintendent Jakes would hire a woman as transparent as Amanda Mason for a detective! "You've decided against it?"

"Yes." She caught her bottom lip between her teeth. "I want to be near Father when he is prison, so I can visit him as often as possible."

"Of course." Her father again. He would always be between them. Longing for it to be otherwise constricted his chest. "I—I wish I hadn't had anything to do with your father's arrest. I like him and respect him." He twisted his derby, staring into her eyes, wishing he could speak his love for her. "More than anything in the world, I wish I hadn't been part of hurting you by heading the investigation. I can hardly believe you are still friendly with me after. . .everything."

"Alexander, if you hadn't been in charge of the investigation, someone else would have. The result would be the same. I am the one who found the counterfeit money in his drawer and brought it to you. Effie and Evan found the money in Father's trunk. The guilt isn't theirs or yours or mine. What my father has done is between him and God. I believe Father has asked and received the Lord's forgiveness, as he has asked and received mine, but he still must pay for his part in this crime. I don't blame you."

"If only I could believe you will always feel that way, even after I testify against your father."

"I will always feel that way, and you aren't going to be called to testify against my father."

He stopped fidgeting with his hat. "What did you say?"

"You aren't going to be called to testify against my father. He's pleading guilty."

"But—but. . ." He stared at her, dumbfounded. No one ever pled guilty! Of course, he knew it was possible, but it never occurred to him that Mason would do so.

"It's the way Father wants it." Her voice wobbled slightly, and tears moistened her eyes, but didn't fall. "The prosecutor has agreed to try Father after all the others, so we might have a couple more days together before. . ." A tear dribbled out over her bottom lashes. She dashed it away with her fingertips.

The sight caught at Alex's heart. Before he realized what he was doing, he drew her into his arms. "Amanda, dearest, I'm sorry."

"I know." Her words were little more than a shaky breath against his neck. Her hands rested on his shoulders.

The delicate lavender scent he remembered was still a part of her. It felt so good to hold her again!

"You've done so much for us, Alex. Your kindness when Father was first arrested meant so much for me. And the house—" she paused. Regret slid over him when she pulled back to look into his face, her eyes puzzled. "Alex, are you wealthy?"

Her question jolted a laugh from him. "Hardly!"

"How could you afford to pay off Father's loan on your salary as a detective?"

"I'm usually on assignments like the ones in River's Edge, where my expenses are paid, and I've little time or place to spend my earnings. I had quite a nest egg set aside."

"Didn't you have plans for it?"

His heart quickened at the memory of the plans he'd had. "Yes." He captured her gaze in his. "Before your father became a suspect, I had plans. When the investigation was over, I was going to ask if you'd allow me to court you. If you said yes, I planned to ask for a leave of absence, so we could have a chance to find out if we loved each other. When your father confessed, I gave up all hope you might ever love me."

"You did?" Her hands slipped behind his neck, causing prickles to run along his nerves. Her eyes twinkled at him. "Then why are you holding me in your arms in the middle of a public building?" she whispered.

Was it possible she not only forgave him his part in her father's arrest, but loved him as well? His arms tightened about her. "Is it possible. . .could you love me?"

"I do. I do love you, Alex."

Joy, wonderful, unbelievable, enveloped him. He lowered his mouth to hers. Her lips were soft and warm and welcoming beneath his. When he reluctantly ended the kiss, she gave the tiniest of sighs, leaned her head against his shoulder, and lifted her lips to him again.

Minutes later, he searched her eyes when she pulled back slightly in his arms. "Oh, Amanda, I love you so!"

"I know. I've known for months."

He shook her head at her playfully. "You did not."

"I've known since the lawyer told us you paid off Father's loan." She grinned at him mischievously. "Haven't I told you since the beginning that I'd make a good detective?"

He smothered her chuckle with his kiss.

A Man for Libby

Chapter 1

River's Edge, Minnesota—1895

Look, Evan!" Effie squealed. "This hat would make a great disguise."

Libby Ward chuckled as she watched the eight-year-old girl settle a black hat over her thick, chestnut-brown hair and pull the black net down past her round, freckled face.

"See?"

A boy, who looked identical but with short hair, nodded. "It's perfect for a detective, Effie."

Libby exchanged an amused look with her niece, Constance.

Constance shook her head. "The Troublesome Twins are in their usual form." She walked briskly across Libby's millinery shop, plucked the hat from Effie's head, and set it back on its black cast-iron display stand. "You know Aunt Libby's hats aren't toys. If you must try on hats, look at the children's display. You both need new spring hats."

"It's too nice out in the spring to wear hats," Evan protested.

Effie ignored her aunt's comment entirely. She reached across the table and fingered the delicate black veil. "Did you ever wear a hat like this when you were a Pinkerton detective, Aunt Constance?"

Constance hesitated before replying. "Yes, I'm afraid I did."

Libby grinned. Constance's tone indicated she regretted the truth. She knew Constance was afraid her answer would only encourage the children's already overdeveloped interest in detective work.

"To hide your face from criminals, right?" Effie lifted the hat from its display once more. "Will you buy me one?"

"No." Constance retrieved the hat and replaced it again. "You don't need a mourning hat."

"But how can Evan and me be good detectives without disguises?"

"You've done all too well so far without them. Go look at the children's displays." Constance returned to Libby, looking heavenward. "I fear Justin and I will never cure these two of their infatuation with detective work," she confided when she reached Libby's side.

"I'm sure they'll outgrow it before long."

"Before they are harmed by it, I hope."

The children did have a knack for winding up in the middle of dangerous criminal situations, partly because of Constance's former occupation as a Pinkerton, but Libby tried to reassure her. "It's a small town. There's little crime here."

"Try this one on her." Evan's suggestion was followed by a riot of giggles.

Libby's gaze darted toward the children. Effie was stuffing her most expensive French bonnet onto one-year-old Maria Louise's head. Though it was far too large, the eight-year-old girl was pushing either side of the brim, making certain the bonnet fit as tightly as possible.

"Stop, Effie!" Libby lifted her skirts and started to the hat's rescue. Her heels clicked across the wooden floor as rapidly as a Spanish dancer's staccato.

Effie looked up, her brown eyes wide with innocence beneath her thick brown bangs. Her hands still clutched the hat's brim. "What's wrong, Aunt Libby?"

"What's wrong?" Evan echoed.

Libby propped bony fists on her skinny hips. "You know better than to treat my hats that way."

"Children, apologize to Aunt Libby, right now," Constance demanded.

Evan looked at his feet. "Aw, I'm sorry."

"Sorry." Effie stuck out her chin. Her eyes were dark with the adults' perceived injustice. "But we weren't trying to hurt the old hats. We can't have any fun anymore. You don't let us play detectiving, Aunt Constance, and we can't play with Aunt Libby's hats." She swung out her arms. "What are we supposed to do for fun?"

Constance crossed her arms over her chest and shook her head. "I can barely keep up with you two and your fun times. Why don't you go across the street to Pierce's General Store and see if you can find some licorice sticks while Aunt Libby and I finish visiting?"

Effie's and Evan's eyes lit up. "All right! See you later!" They dashed out of the store, setting the brass bells above the door to ringing.

Libby always found it difficult to discipline her niece and nephew, as she thought of Effie and Evan, though they were truly her great-niece and great-nephew. She didn't feel old enough to be a great-aunt, but she couldn't deny her fifty-five years with Effie and Evan about. As if she needed more confirmation of her advancing age than her reflection in a mirror.

She looked down at Maria Louise in her wicker stroller. The little girl tipped her head back and looked up at the women with a wide-eyed, solemn gaze. The hat had been pushed down past her ears and covered her eyebrows.

Libby looked from the girl to Constance, struggling to keep from smiling. Constance's face showed a similar struggle. At the same moment, the women burst out laughing.

"I thought my corset stays would break from laughing so hard," Libby admitted minutes later, wiping tears of laughter from her face with a lace-edged handkerchief.

"Maria Louise and I had best get over to the general store and see what the Troublesome Twins are into now." Constance removed the bonnet from the little girl's head and handed it to Libby. Maria Louise immediately rubbed both her chubby little hands back and forth over her straight, short brown hair, sending the women into another spasm of laughter.

"We'll see you at dinner," Constance called over her shoulder minutes later, pushing the wicker carriage through the doorway.

Libby stared after them, smiling. *Life is so much richer since Constance and the twins moved here,* she thought. Only two years had passed since Constance married Justin Knight and moved to River's Edge with her brother's orphaned children. A year ago, Maria Louise had been born. Now the most important part of Libby's life centered around the Knight family.

She missed the husband she'd lost five years earlier, but she had a good life. She loved buying, designing, and selling hats. Church and the ladies sewing circle kept her busy socially. Ida Clayton, with whom she shared a home, provided companionship. And for the last two years, she'd been blessed with seeing Constance and the children every day. "Thank You for bringing them here, Lord," she whispered.

She bustled about the room, straightening a hat on a display stand, moving a ruffled, pink silk parasol to better advantage behind a group of ribboned bonnets, placing dainty white gloves with tiny pearl buttons beside a hat trimmed with lace, ribbon, and pearls. A few women stopped in. Some wanted only to spend a little of their afternoon admiring the new spring fashions. One planned to have the ostrich feathers replaced on her favorite bonnet. Another purchased a new spring hat. With her assistant, Miss Silvernail, out for the afternoon, Libby kept pleasantly busy with her customers.

When the rosewood clock on the wall chimed five o'clock, a cloud of regret slid across Libby's chest. She'd need to close the shop soon if she was to arrive at Constance's house in time for dinner. Constance hadn't mentioned that there would be other guests, but Libby was sure an eligible man would join them. All too often lately, such men turned up at Constance's dinners. Always Constance had a reasonable explanation, usually that the man had been doing business with Justin or that she was paying back a favor the man had done for the family. The men were all widowers. So far the guests had included the owner of a local sawmill, a bank officer, the owner of a sash firm, and a pinch-nosed schoolteacher.

Libby wasn't fooled. Constance was trying to find her a husband, or at least a beau. As if a woman of fifty-five needed a beau. Besides, she'd lived in River's Edge all her life. There wasn't a man in town she didn't know. If she wanted a beau or a husband, she'd make her own choice and set her cap for him. Perhaps it was time she came right out and told Constance so. Of course, she realized Constance only wanted her to find a husband because Constance was so happy married to Justin.

"She doesn't know there isn't room for another man in my heart," Libby whispered. "The two who are there fill it to the brim."

Libby's husband, Joshua Ward, had been a fine man. He hadn't been wealthy, but he'd held a respectable position as an accounting clerk in a local sawmill. He'd been well liked in the community. He'd shared Libby's love for the Lord. They hadn't had children, but their fellow church members and neighbors had been like family and still were for Libby. Libby and Joshua had respected and admired each other and shared a quiet, companionable life. Although Libby had loved him, he hadn't been her first love.

"If only Spencer had loved the Lord." The memory of him tightened her chest with longing.

She stopped before the wall mirror in an ornate walnut frame. Was there any resemblance between the reflection in that mirror and the young woman of twenty she'd been when she last saw Spencer?

Libby brushed a stray hair back over her ear. Her hand paused there, beside her face. The face in the mirror had deep wrinkles and faded blue eyes. Her hair was more gray than brown now. Her gaze traveled to her hand. Blood vessels showed blue through her skin. Libby sighed. "Barely a sign of the girl Spencer asked to marry him."

The spring breeze carried inside the scent of the earth awakening and the sound of birds returning to the northland. The last day she'd spent with Spencer had been just such a day. She moved to a window, from which the bluff where they'd picnicked that long-ago day could be seen above the town roofs.

The memory washed over her. . . .

&

"I thought we'd never make it to the top!" Libby hugged her waist. Her side was aching from the climb. Her legs were strong, but Spencer set quite a pace. He'd held her hand the entire way, helping her over the most difficult spots, yet the climb had seemed steep, particularly in the hooped gown, one of her most fashionable—and definitely her favorite. The tight corset didn't make it easy to breathe deeply, but she did like the way it cinched her waist.

She loved pretty clothes. They made her feel attractive. She knew she wasn't the best-looking young woman in town; in fact, she was plain. Her parents had told her so since she was little. "Better be pretty on the inside, Libby," her father would say, shaking his head, "because you sure ain't pretty on the outside." Her mother hadn't thought she was pretty on the inside, either. "You're never going to win a husband, Elizabeth Mann," her mother had flared many times through the years. "Plain of face and plain ornery by nature." Libby tried to be quiet and demure and giggly like other girls, but she couldn't seem to keep her lips sealed on her own opinions.

Spencer laughed and tugged at her hand. "Come along, lazybones. We're not quite to our spot yet. I want to sit at the bluff's edge, don't you?"

"Yes, the view's best there." She stopped, hugging her waist tighter with her free hand. "Let's rest a moment, please."

His arm slid about her waist, and she leaned into him, resting. "Are you all right, Libby?"

She scrunched her eyelids shut and forced a smile. "I've a stitch in my side, that's all. It will go away in a moment." They stood that way for a few minutes, Spencer waiting patiently while the pain subsided. She loved the way she felt cherished and sheltered, leaning against him.

When the pain was gone, they walked across the bluff. The light wind played with their hair and surrounded them with the happy smells of spring's renewing life. At the bluff's edge, they removed the blanket from the basket Spencer had been carrying and spread it out. The picnic lunch was simple: biscuits and ham and dried-apple pie. It didn't matter. The only thing that mattered was that the two of them were together. They had so little time. He'd been away most of the winter, working as a lumberjack in the northern forest. Now that the river was free of ice, he was back in River's Edge and would be working at a local sawmill, eleven hours a day, six days a week. The only time they would have together would be Sundays, like today.

The view from the bluff was spectacular. Beneath them, the wide, blue Mississippi River flowed past. Across the river, the view mirrored the side of the river where they sat: trees, with pale green buds hinting at the splendor of their coming summer dress, climbed three-fourths of the way up the steep sides; from there to the top was a wonderful expanse of limestone, pale yellow in the sunshine. On top of the bluff, trees again reached to the sky. In the valley to the right of where they sat, River's Edge stood bravely on the riverbank.

A long, white, elegant steamboat, its tall black smokestacks trailing streams of gray smoke, made its way northward.

"Someday, I'm going to work on one of them." Spencer circled his knees with his arms. "I'm going to travel the river, see the big cities to the south. No more spending my winters in lumber camps."

Libby's chest clenched. She plucked at a new blade of grass, keeping her gaze on it. "If you work on a steamboat, we'll be apart as surely as when you are at the lumber camp."

She could tell from the corner of her eye that he turned from the river to look at her. "Ah, Libby, don't you know I'd take you along to see the world with me?"

Her gaze darted to his. His voice had been thick with emotion. His eyes were dark with it. He slid a hand behind her neck, then slowly bridged the short distance between them. His lips were gentle, his kiss lingering. With a slight sigh, she responded, leaning against him. His kiss shut out the world. Nothing existed for her but Spencer.

Minutes later, he pulled back, laughing shakily. She understood that self-conscious laugh. Their kisses were too sweet, too intimate, too dangerous. Better to stop.

He laid down on his back, resting his head in her lap. Her huge skirt billowed out around him. "Brought something back from the camp for you."

"Whatever could you have found for me in a lumber camp?"

"Didn't exactly find it. I made it." He reached for his jacket, which he'd taken off when they sat down, and plunged a hand into one pocket. "Close your eyes and hold out your hand."

She did as he asked. A moment later, she felt something hard with a smooth finish in her palm. She opened her eyes. It was a bird carved from wood. "It's beautiful!" She stroked the goose's delicately carved wings and long, graceful neck. Lifting the bird to her face, she breathed deeply. "I can smell the forests where you worked."

"They were beautiful in winter, with snow covering the pines. And the silence! Like a church. I wish I could have shared the beauty of it with you."

They smiled into each other's eyes. Libby was filled with sweet wonder that he should want to share something as simple as a winter scene with her.

Spencer lifted his eyebrows. "Of course, everything about the forest wasn't beautiful. It was mighty cold! And those bearded, swearing lumbermen didn't make the forest any prettier. Nothing like a few days with them to make a man miss a woman."

Libby laughed with him, pleased and a little embarrassed at his implication. She changed the subject back to his gift. "I didn't know you could carve."

"I didn't either. Believe me, this wasn't my first attempt. I whittled a number of them before I made a couple that satisfied me." He pulled something out of his other pocket and held it out. "I wanted one for both of us. I've been told geese mate for life." His voice had dropped. "Once a goose and a gander take a liking to each other, they never part. That's what I want for us: to be together forever."

"I want that, too." Her throat was so tight it hurt to speak the words. He'd told her before that he loved her, but he'd never spoken of their future. She looked down at his dear, wide face, the straight, blond hair that glistened in the spring sunshine, looked into the blue eyes that were watching her. Love filled her chest until there was no more room for it, and it overflowed. She could feel her smile trembling.

"I hated being away from you this winter, Libby."

"Naturally, since you were in the middle of a forest with nothing but trees, men, and snow to keep you company."

He drew her hands down until her arms circled his head. He held his goose beak-to-beak with the one in her hands, moving it slightly back and forth in a teasing, flirtatious motion. "Won't you tell me you missed me a little bit?"

His low, intimate tone sent shivers through her. She could feel his breath against her hands. She tried to keep a teasing tone in her own voice. "I missed you a big bit, Spencer."

"I knew it!" His free hand clasped one of hers. He grinned up at her, triumph sparkling in his eyes.

"You are abominable!" She tugged at her hand, and he released it, laughing.

"Tell me how you missed me."

She shook her head, her long, fashionable, pale brown curls swinging against her cheeks. "I will not."

"Then I'll tell you what it was like missing you." He curled his fingers around hers, cradling her hand against his chest. He closed his eyes. "Lying in my bunk at night, I'd see your face. I'd go over it in every detail, remembering the softness and sweet smell of your hair, those blue eyes that blaze when you're upset with me, your cute, pointed chin, and the line of your throat above your high-collared gowns." He smiled, as if he enjoyed the memories. "Mostly, I remembered your smile and how soft your lips were when I kissed you good-bye when I left for the lumber camp." He touched his lips to her fingers. "Did you do that, Libby?" he asked in a whisper. "Did you think about me that way while I was gone?"

Heat spread up Libby's throat and over her cheeks. "Yes."

"Good." His smile widened.

"You're impossible." She tried unsuccessfully to draw her hand back.

"It's only the two of us here. You don't have to act like there's a prim and proper chaperon listening. We can speak the truth to each other without embarrassment. Isn't that the way it should be?"

"I–I don't know."

His eyelids flew open. "You don't think we should tell each other the truth?"

"Quit mocking me. Of course I think we should speak the truth, but proper manners require certain things be left unsaid until—" She pressed her lips together firmly. She'd already said too much, as usual.

"Until what? Until people are married to each other?"

Libby kept her gaze trained on the wooden geese on Spencer's chest. "Well, yes."

"How do people know they want to marry each other if they don't tell each other what they feel before they're man and wife?"

She didn't have an answer when he put it in those terms. She felt his gaze burning into her. Finally, she could ignore it no longer and reluctantly turned to meet it.

His gaze claimed hers. "Will you marry me, Libby?"

Chapter 2

Libby's heart smashed against her ribs. Her hands froze on the wooden goose. *Did he really ask me to marry him, or did I imagine it?* she wondered. She couldn't tear her gaze from Spencer's.

"Libby?" His blond brows slipped together. Uncertainty clouded his eyes. "I love you, Libby."

"I love you, too," she whispered.

Her answer routed the doubt from his eyes. "Is that a yes to my proposal?"

"I want to marry you, Spencer, and spend the rest of my life with you."

A grin filled his face. He sat up so quickly the wooden geese that had rested on his chest tumbled to the ground. "Come here, my future wife."

She allowed him to draw her into his embrace, returning his kiss, but his arms weren't the same as they'd been earlier. The world didn't disappear. Instead, worry over the way Spencer would react to the rest of her answer made the embrace bittersweet.

After a few minutes, he pulled back far enough to look into her eyes and smile. "Mrs. Spencer Matthews. Has a nice sound to it, don't you think?"

"The nicest." Her throat hurt so much that she could barely get the words out.

"Let's get married this summer. I don't want to wait a day longer than necessary to begin our life together."

Her laugh sounded more like a sob to her. His eagerness touched her. How blessed, to be loved this way! "Don't you think that's a little soon?"

"Why? We love each other." He raised his eyebrows. "Your parents won't object to me, will they?"

"I hardly think so." Her parents were surprised any men were interested in her. That Spencer wanted to marry her would surprise them but surely not offend them.

"I suppose you're worried it will take awhile to plan the wedding."

"No." She took as deep a breath as her corset allowed. "Spencer, you know how important my faith in Jesus is," she began.

He nodded. "Sure. You don't think I'll ask you to give it up? I might not share your faith, but I have to admit, it's one of the things I like and admire about you."

She took both his hands in hers. "I love you, Spencer, but I can't marry you until you believe in Jesus, too, and He is the most important part of your life."

He stared at her. He looked as stunned as though the earth had stopped spinning. "You can't mean that."

Libby bit her lips and nodded.

Spencer yanked his hands from hers. "I may not believe in your God, but that doesn't make me too dirty to marry, does it?" He was yelling now. "Faith in God isn't something a man can whip up just because a woman wants him to!"

Libby winced. "I know."

"What makes you so much better than I am, just because you believe what somebody wrote a couple thousand years ago?"

"I don't believe I'm better than you, Spencer."

He hadn't waited for her reply. He was still yelling, bouncing his fingertips off his chest. "What about me is so awful that you can't abide the thought of marrying me?"

"Nothing." Misery ribboned through her at the hurt her words had caused him, at her inability to take the words back and heal the wound.

"Didn't I stop smoking and drinking for you?"

She nodded.

"What more can I do to prove how much I love you, to prove I'm a good man? What does it matter what I believe about God if my actions are good?" He didn't wait for her to answer. He went on with similar arguments until he appeared to run out of words.

It was then Libby tried to explain. "It's my faith that makes me who I am, Spencer. My values are determined by my faith. My strength in hard times is supplied by my faith. My faith is a beacon light when I don't know which way to turn. It's my guide. How can two people travel through life together if they don't have the same guide?"

"Travel with that invisible guide, if that's your choice. God won't give you a home or a family like I would. His arms won't be around you when life hurts and you need a shoulder to cry on. He won't be there beside you, telling you He loves you every day, like I would. You think He's more important than a man who loves you—you just spend your life with Him, Libby Mann!"

"I'm not saying I won't marry you, Spencer. I'm asking you to wait, until. . ."

"Until I believe in your God? In a God you believe doesn't want you to marry a man you love, a man who loves you? What kind of God is that to believe in? If you won't marry me unless I believe in an ornery God like that, you won't ever marry me, because I don't want your God in my life." Spencer turned on his heel and marched toward the path that led down from the bluff.

"Spencer, come back!" Tears heated Libby's eyes, but she could still see he wasn't returning. She sank to her knees, heedless of the grass and dirt. Her chest felt like it was in a vise. "I didn't mean to hurt him, Lord," she whispered between sobs. "Please, bring him back!"

She'd always known, of course, that she shouldn't have allowed Spencer to court her when he didn't share her faith, but she'd been so attracted to him, right from the beginning! At her request, he'd given up the awful-smelling cigars and the liquor with barely more than a murmur of protest. "I always believed he would eventually believe in You, Lord. I still do."

Yet that belief didn't stop the pain. She tried to push away the fear that Spencer might never return, but the fear only grew, filling her stomach and heart and mind.

Libby turned from the window and walked slowly across the shop, stopping in front of the walnut-framed mirror. Spencer hadn't returned. Not that day, not ever.

Three days later, when she'd heard the rumor about Spencer that was flying around town, she hadn't believed it. Two days after that, walking down the short, dirt main street, she'd met Spencer with a young woman clinging to his arm. Color had darkened his face when Libby's gaze met his. Then his gaze had darted away, but not before she saw the shame in his blue eyes. That was when she knew the rumor was true. That was when her world changed forever. That was when her heart was torn open to never fully heal.

After leaving her on the bluff, Spencer had come back to River's Edge and gone on a drinking spree. While drunk, he'd eloped. Before long, he and his new wife left town.

At first, Libby had thought she would surely die. After months passed and it seemed her heart hadn't begun to heal, she had to cling hard to the Lord's promises in Psalm 40 to keep from wishing she could die. "I waited patiently for the Lord; and he inclined unto me, and heard my cry. He brought me up also out of an horrible pit, out of the miry clay, and set my foot upon a rock, and established my goings."

The pain in her heart had made it seem the Lord hadn't heard her cry. When the pain seemed unendurable and she was crying out to the Lord asking how Spencer could have married someone else and taken away all chance they would spend their life together, she would repeat the verse, reminding herself that eventually God would lift her out of that terrible place and life would be good again.

After a year had passed, she began to see a glimmer of that good place. At first, there were only a couple hours a day she could make it through without crying. When the time came that she could make it through an entire day—not every day, but some days—without crying, she knew she would live to see the promise fulfilled. And she knew that even when she hadn't been able to see the light, God had been healing her heart.

She'd learned she could live through anything, leaning on Christ, who had promised never to leave her or forsake her. From that point on, she gave up the right to mollycoddle herself.

Even in the midst of her pain, she knew that how Spencer left didn't matter. Unless he had chosen to believe in Christ and follow His teachings, she and Spencer couldn't have had a life together anyway.

She prayed for him every time she thought of him. Had her prayers been answered yet? Had he ever come to believe?

She wondered, as she so often had, whether he was still alive. His family had left River's Edge soon after he and his wife had moved. Was his wife still alive? Where were they living? Did they have children?

"Thirty-five years!" she whispered. How could her heart still yearn for him? If she'd married him, their marriage wouldn't have been anything like the one she and Joshua had shared. That love had been good and strong but different from the love she'd shared with Spencer.

She studied her reflection. *It's not the face of the young girl Spencer proposed to,* she thought again. Her hair wasn't worn in the fashion of 1860, with dangling curls beside her ears. Now a curly fringe of bangs topped her wrinkled face, and the rest of the graying hair was caught back in a high bun.

"Well, what can a woman expect after fifty-five years of living? The body is meant to get older. Doesn't the Good Book tell us that gray hair is a sign of wisdom?"

I don't feel wise, she thought. *Wiser about a host of things than when I was twenty, but not wise. Sometimes I think there's more things I don't have answers to today than back then.*

Spencer's face flashed into her mind, that dear face that would always be twenty-three years old to her. "One thing I know; I would give him the same answer today." She saw the pain and fury fill his eyes and face as they had that day, felt his pain and fury scorch her heart once more. She had wanted so deeply to marry him. "How could I say yes, Lord, when he didn't share my love for You? What kind of life could we have had together when we didn't share a trust in You?"

She sighed and turned her back on the mirror. If she didn't hurry, she'd be late for Constance's dinner. She felt as though she were dragging her heart along behind her when she carried the hat the children had been playing with into the back room, where Miss Silvernail would change the ribbons the next day.

She'd barely entered the room when the bells above the front door jangled. Impatience shot through her. After wallowing in sad memories, she was in no mood to wait on a last-minute customer. Habit formed from years of running her own shop came to her aid. She took a deep breath, straightened her shoulders, and went back into the shop.

A man her own age or older, wearing a jacket trimmed in gold braid, stood just inside the door, glancing about the room with the bewildered expression she saw on most men's faces when they entered her hat shop. His skin was weathered and wrinkled, his thick hair and bushy eyebrows were white with a tinge of dark gray. A trim, gray-and-white beard framed his wide face.

She smiled and forced friendliness into her voice. "May I help you, sir?"

The man jerked about, staring at her without answering.

She laced her fingers together in front of her and tried again. "Is there something I can help you find?"

The thick eyebrows met. His gaze searched her face until she wanted to wiggle in discomfort. "Libby?"

Her heart dropped to her toes. She'd recognize that voice anywhere. "Spencer!"

Chapter 3

Libby had dreamed of this meeting for over half her life, and now that Spencer was here, she couldn't think of a word to say. All she could do was stare at him, drink in the wonder of his presence, experience the joy flooding her.

Reality tempered her joy. *He wouldn't be in a women's hat shop if he weren't looking for a bonnet or accessories for a woman in his life,* she reminded herself. *At least I know he's still alive. Thank You, Lord!*

Spencer dropped his own black, braid-trimmed hat on a table amidst an assortment of dainty spring bonnets and started toward her, holding out both hands. "Libby! How good to see you again." His deep voice rumbled across the room. Delight filled his creased and tanned face.

His height and broad shoulders dwarfed everything in the room, though Libby admitted to herself that even if that weren't the case, he was the only thing she would see.

She allowed him to take her hands. They were swallowed up in his. She was vaguely aware that his hands were calloused. With a start, she realized that, with the exception of Constance's husband, no man had touched her ungloved hands since her own husband had died, five years ago.

It wasn't only his voice that hadn't changed. His smile was the same, as were his blue eyes. To Libby's dismay, she found they had the same effect on her they'd had when she was twenty.

He squeezed her hands and grinned down at her. "How are you, Libby?"

"Fine. I'm fine." That sounded inane, even to her own ears.

"You look grand."

She tugged at her hands, recalling all too vividly the view in the mirror only minutes earlier. He released her hands immediately. *He's older, too,* she reminded herself silently, trying desperately to reassure herself. *We've both aged, and we look it. Nothing to be ashamed of in that. Silly to worry what he thinks of my looks, anyway. He's married to someone else.* Still, she did worry. A hand went to the lock of hair at her temple that was always falling out of place.

"Um, your boat must have landed in town." She pressed her lips together to keep back a groan. Another silly comment.

"Not exactly." He stuffed his hands into his trouser pockets and leaned back against a display table, looking entirely at ease. "The boat I came upriver on docked here. I'm retired." His eyes widened. "You knew I was a steamboat captain!"

Embarrassment warmed her cheeks. "I. . . Someone mentioned it years ago."

The twinkle in his eyes increased her embarrassment. She turned to the counter behind her and unnecessarily readjusted a French bonnet on its cast-iron stand. "Did you wish to purchase a gift? For your wife, perhaps?"

"No, Libby."

She heard his footsteps cross the wooden floor and stop behind her. Her heartbeat quickened at his nearness. In an attempt to slow it, she closed her eyes and took a deep breath.

"I didn't come to purchase a gift." The intensity in his voice sent shivers down her spine. "I came to see you."

Libby's eyelids snapped open. Her heart raced out of control, rejoicing in the knowledge that he'd wanted to see her. Her mind screamed that his coming was wrong, as was her joy in seeing him.

"My wife died three years ago."

Relief that he wasn't being unfaithful left Libby suddenly weak. She held on to the counter's edge for a moment to steady herself. "I'm sorry." Taking a deep breath, she turned to face him. "I truly am sorry."

"Margaret was a good wife to me. I did my best to be a good husband to her."

"I'm sure you did. I would expect nothing less." Libby tried to ignore the pain in her chest, ashamed to be jealous of the woman who had shared his life and had left it so soon.

The blue eyes she remembered so well studied hers. "Even though I was a faithful husband, we both know why I married her."

Libby stared at her hands. They were clasped together so tightly the knuckles were white.

"I stopped to see an old friend today. He told me that your husband is dead, too."

"He died five years ago."

"I'm sorry." Spencer cleared his throat. "I wouldn't have come here today if he was still alive. You know that, don't you?"

Libby nodded, still staring at her hands. Of course, she believed him. He'd never before looked her up when his boat stopped at River's Edge.

He rested a hand over her clasped ones. She caught her breath sharply, marveling at the gentleness in his touch.

"Will you have dinner with me? I want to hear all about your life, everything you've done in the years since I left River's Edge."

In the years since you left us, she silently amended his words. "I have another obligation."

"Tomorrow evening, then?"

She smiled, aware her lips were trembling. "That would be nice."

"Shall I pick you up here, about this time?"

"Yes, that will be fine."

His hand still covered hers. He seemed reluctant to leave, and she was certainly reluctant to see him go.

Slowly, he slipped his hand away. "I'd best be going or I'll make you late for your engagement." He took a couple steps backward. "Until tomorrow."

"Yes, until tomorrow." Tomorrow! What promise that wonderful word held!

He picked up his gold-trimmed hat from the table where he'd dropped it. In the open doorway, he stopped, staring across the room at her, smiling. Then, raising a large palm held up in a silent good-bye, he left.

Libby collapsed back against the counter. He'd returned! "Why has he sought me out after all this time, Lord?" Her thoughts spun. So many questions, but three stood out boldly from the rest: Was he planning to live in River's Edge? Would he want to court her again? Most important, had he come to a faith in Christ?

The clock on the wall struck six-thirty.

"Oh, my!" Libby hurried into the back room and slung her elbow-length cape over her shoulders. Stopping in front of the wall mirror in the shop, she pinned her hat on with shaking fingers.

She almost dropped the key when locking the front door. *How will I ever keep my mind on conversation at dinner tonight?* she wondered, her heels clipping on the boardwalk. *It will be easier if I'm mistaken about Constance's intentions in inviting me and it's only her family this evening.*

Tomorrow! Tomorrow! Tomorrow! The word rang through Captain Spencer Matthews's mind like a church bell pealing news of hope and cheer. *This time tomorrow, we'll be together.* He'd daydreamed about that time for so many years that he could barely believe it was almost here.

He moved along the boardwalk, smiling and nodding to complete strangers, wanting to shout his good news. He chuckled. Best wait for that until he'd received what he came to River's Edge for—Libby's hand in marriage.

What if she says no? The words crept into his mind. He tried to push them aside. He wouldn't accept the possibility she would refuse him.

Of course, there's that faith stuff she holds so dear to get past. Another thought he tried to push aside. Over the years, he'd come to believe he'd been a fool to allow her faith to keep them apart. Surely she would have realized, too, that she'd been wrong to think such a thing should separate them. We're both too old and wise to let silly superstitions push away love.

The early evening skies were bright as day. Usually he was glad for springtime's longer days. Today he was eager for night to come. The sooner it came, the sooner tomorrow would arrive. Of course, there'd be all those hours to live through tomorrow until he could call for Libby, but—he shrugged, chuckling at himself.

The sight of his hotel brought sour memories. He'd awakened in a hotel the morning—or rather, afternoon—following his marriage to Margaret. His head had been pounding and his eyesight blurred, but he'd recognized the woman in his room and had enough sense to demand what she was doing there.

The feeling of desolation he'd experienced when Margaret said she was his wife washed over him again now. At first, he'd insisted she was lying. He'd stopped that when she showed him the marriage certificate. Hopelessness such as he'd never known before or since had swallowed him up whole. In one foolish move, he'd changed the entire course of his life. He'd cut himself off forever from Libby.

Or at least so he'd thought until today.

His steps quickened. Life had given him a second chance. *This time, I won't throw away our future,* he thought. *This time, I won't stop asking Libby to marry me until she says yes.*

Chapter 4

As Libby had feared, another single man had been invited to dinner: Pastor Daniel Green, who had moved to town a few weeks earlier. He must have arrived at the Knights' only moments before her, as he was still in the wide, walnut-paneled entry hall when she arrived.

It could have been worse, she admitted silently. They'd met at church, of course, and she knew him to be a pleasant, easy-going man. Certainly there wasn't a better-looking man her age in River's Edge. Except Spencer. The pastor was a slender man. His dark hair had less gray and his face fewer lines than most men his age.

Libby unpinned her hat, removed it and her cape, and handed them to Constance, wishing she could simply leave and go home. She tried to overcome her frustration and resistance. It wouldn't do to spoil Constance's dinner party by acting standoffish.

"It must be difficult, moving to a town where you don't know anyone." *He probably has a month's worth of invitations already, from people like Constance, who are eager to introduce him to their unmarried friends. He must find the presence of an unexpected and marriageable dinner guest as unpleasant as I. I've only Constance trying to marry me off. He'll have most of the matrons in River's Edge trying to find him the proper mate.* The realization tempered her distaste of the situation and made her more tolerant.

"It's easier for a pastor than for most people, I think," he answered, "though it was easier to move into new communities when my wife was alive. The church members always draw a pastor into the community quickly."

Constance turned from the hall closet and slipped an arm through Libby's. Starting for the parlor, she explained to Pastor Green, "I married Justin and moved here from Chicago two years ago with my eight-year-old niece and nephew after my brother and his wife died. Aunt Libby took us under her wing. We're the only family either of us has left. I'd like her to move in with us, but she insists on living in her own home with her friend, Mrs. Clayton." Constance gave an exaggerated sigh. "So we must settle for Aunt Libby's presence at dinners whenever she can work us into her schedule."

Her words further eased Libby's tension; perhaps the pastor wouldn't think her a manhunting female after all.

Racing steps caught the adults' attention. Constance shook her head. "I apologize for the children. I admonish them numerous times daily to walk, not run, in the house, but the admonitions fall on deaf ears."

Libby smiled. "I believe the children, Effie especially, are simply so excited with life that they can't bear to move through it at a pace as slow as a walk. A wonderful way to approach life, don't you think?"

"I do, indeed."

Libby liked the way the pastor greeted the children warmly and included them in his conversation while they visited with the Knights in the parlor.

It was only a few minutes before the maid announced dinner and they moved into the formal dining room. The chandelier sparkled above the elegantly appointed rosewood table. Cream-colored velvet draperies and satin-striped wallpaper lent a tranquil atmosphere.

As owner and president of the local bank, Justin Knight was adept in social graces, for which Libby was never more grateful. Instead of trying to carry on a conversation with the pastor, she allowed Justin and Constance to do so.

While they talked, her mind drifted back to the unexpected meeting with Spencer. Her heart quickened at the thought of him. His smiling eyes filled her memory. Watching Pastor Green, she couldn't help but compare him to Spencer. They were nothing alike physically. She was sure they were nothing alike in personality, either.

They were barely into the main course when Effie piped up. "Did you hear about the ghost?"

The word "ghost" effectively brought a halt to the adult conversation. Everyone turned to stare at her. Effie's grin spread across her wide, freckled face. Libby slipped her napkin over her mouth to hide her smile at Effie's evident self-satisfaction.

Justin set down his fork and frowned. "What's this about a ghost?"

Effie leaned forward. Her brown eyes danced with excitement. "Evan and me heard about it at Pierce's General Store this afternoon."

Evan's head bobbed emphatically. "A bunch of people were talking about it."

Effie's voice dropped an octave and trembled. "There were strange, moving lights on the bluffs north of town last night." She lifted her fingers just above the edge of the table and wiggled them.

A shiver ran down Libby's spine. *Stop it!* she admonished herself. *You don't even believe in ghosts!*

"Don't be silly." Justin's voice sounded hoarse. "Pastor Green can tell you there are no such things as ghosts. Even if there were, lights on the bluff are no sign of ghosts."

"He's right," Constance agreed. "Why would ghosts need lights? If there were lights on the bluff, it's because there were people on the bluff."

"But they were on the side of the bluff," Effie explained, not willing to let go of her ghost theory so easily.

"That's right." Evan jumped in, his voice eager, his brown eyes huge. "People might walk on top of the bluff, but they wouldn't walk on the sides of the bluff, at night, would they?"

He's right, Libby thought. To try to climb the bluff's steep walls at night or walk the few crumbling paths along them in the dark would be a fool's mission. She was sure similar thoughts were flashing through Justin's mind, as he hesitated before answering Effie.

"Maybe it was just a traveler, staying overnight in one of the caves."

"Why wouldn't he stay in a hotel?" Effie asked.

"Maybe he didn't have enough money," Justin answered, a bit lamely.

Effie picked up her fork and went back to her dinner. "I think it was ghosts."

"Me, too." Evan dug into his meal, imitating his sister as usual.

Libby wondered uneasily what Pastor Green thought of the children's talk of ghosts. He hadn't said a word, and if he disapproved, his face didn't reveal the fact.

Justin changed the subject, speaking of a newspaper article that reported a continuing upswing in the nation's economy. Pastor Green followed Justin's lead, and soon the adults had forgotten the subject of ghosts and were discussing the wonderful recovery the country was making from the financial depression that had started two years ago.

"I'm not educated in things of the financial world like you, Mr. Knight," the pastor said. "Still, I enjoy reading the articles arguing the benefits of a silver standard as opposed to a gold standard."

"That's what the ghost is looking for." Effie didn't bother looking for the adults' reaction this time. She just took another bite of roast beef.

Justin carefully set down his fork. Libby expected he was counting to ten. "What is he looking for?" His voice was tight with exasperation.

Effie looked up, raising her eyebrows beneath her thick bangs. She swallowed her bite. "Gold, of course."

"Oh, Effie, really." Constance shook her head.

"It's true." Evan straightened up in his chair. "That's what the people at the store said."

Justin closed his eyes and opened them again. "What would a ghost need with gold?"

"The gold belongs to him," Evan informed him.

"How can gold belong to a ghost?" His frustrated voice, even more than his words, revealed his belief that all this talk was foolishness.

Even if Justin's faith didn't encourage him to not believe in ghosts, Libby thought, *his practical banker nature wouldn't let him believe in them!*

Effie spread her hands palm up on each side of her plate. She looked at Justin as though she couldn't believe he could be so simple. "It belonged to him before he became a ghost, of course."

"That's right," Evan supported his sister again. "He hid it in a cave in the bluffs before he died."

"Who hid it before he died?" The question slipped out before Libby thought.

"The captain of that old steamboat that ran up on the sandbar below the bluffs last month," Effie answered.

Evan nodded.

"Where did you children come up with such an implausible story?" Constance asked.

Effie frowned. "What's im–implaws. . ."

"Implausible," Constance finished. "It means not believable."

"We told you," Evan reminded her. "At the general store."

"When the boat got stuck," Effie explained, "the captain was afraid people would steal the gold, so he hid it. After he hid it and came back to the boat, he got sick. The men who worked for him tried to help him, but they couldn't, and he died."

Evan broke in. "But before he died, he whispered something. The men couldn't understand all of it—"

"But they heard the words gold and bluff." Effie's voice was thick and low and trembly.

Libby shivered, even while scolding herself for reacting so strongly to Effie's storytelling skills. She remembered Captain Hollingsworth's death the month before. His heart, the doctor had said. The steamboat was still sitting on the sandbar. It had been one of the first steamboats on the upper Mississippi this year, arriving almost during rather than after the spring thaw.

Constance rose. "I believe we've had more than enough of this ghost business for one evening. I want you two to go upstairs and get dressed for bed."

Evan's mouth dropped. "But we haven't had dessert yet!"

Effie crossed her arms and leaned back in her chair, glaring. "It isn't fair! We were just telling you what people said."

"Mrs. Kelly can bring your dessert to your rooms." Controlled Constance was firm, unflustered, as usual. "Justin and I will be up to hear your prayers later."

"But—" Effie started.

"Now," Justin ordered. "And no 'detectiving.'"

Libby hid another smile. Detectiving, or eavesdropping, on the Knights' guests was the children's favorite pastime.

I wonder if Spencer would like Effie and Evan. Libby thought. When they were young, she'd enjoyed watching Spencer with his siblings and neighborhood children. He'd never shooed them away but played and teased and laughed with them whenever they came around. *But he's almost an old man now. Maybe he doesn't care for children any longer.*

After warm hugs and good nights all around, the children headed off to bed.

"I do hope you don't think we raised the children to believe in ghosts, Pastor." Constance looked apologetic.

He gave her an easy smile. "I didn't hear anything that sounded as though you or your husband were encouraging their belief. Besides, the children heard the story from adult townspeople. It isn't easy to teach children to know when to believe other adults."

Libby was pleased with his reply.

The conversation moved on. Libby put on a polite smile and let her mind drift to Spencer. Though Pastor Green was a pleasant man, she wasn't in the least interested in knowing him better. How could any man compete with the excitement of seeing Spencer again?

Libby was glad when Justin offered her a ride home. She had been wondering how she would turn down the pastor's offer to walk her home, if he should make such an offer, as Constance's bachelor dinner guests normally did.

Libby breathed a huge sigh of relief when she closed her front door. The dinner was behind her, and her own home was dark and quiet. Ida, her housemate, had retired for the night.

Upstairs, Libby slipped into her long, white, cotton nightgown and climbed into bed, pulling the wedding-ring quilt, which had been a wedding gift from her church's sewing circle, up under her chin. Finally, she was alone and could let her thoughts drift uninterrupted to Spencer.

She found herself having one conversation after another with him in her mind, asking him all the things she'd wanted to ask through the years and hearing him declare his undying love for her.

"Stop it!" She sat up suddenly and pressed her hands over her ears to shut out the words that seemed as loud inside her head as if they'd actually been spoken. "I mustn't think these things. He only invited me to have dinner because I'm an old friend." At least, that was all she dared let herself think. If she allowed herself to hope it was something more and it wasn't, there would be so much pain to endure!

"Besides," she whispered into the night, "we don't know each other anymore. We may find we don't even like each other now."

In her heart, she didn't believe that was possible. She didn't dare dwell on her greatest question: Had Spencer ever come to believe in the God she loved so well?

Chapter 5

Libby stuck a pearl-tipped hat pin into the dainty spring bonnet atop her head and studied her reflected image with anxious eyes. The fashionable hat was darling. She'd seen one just like it in the latest issue of The Ladies' Standard.

She dragged a bentwood chair from the workroom. Climbing onto it, she tried to view her full form. The image in the mirror was of the beautiful brown moire satin gown—at least, the portion from just below her bust to just above her knees. "Why didn't I think to ask Spencer to meet me at my home, where I have a full-length mirror? Maybe I should go next door and use the dress shop's mirror."

She shook her head resolutely. Her housemate, Mrs. Ida Clayton, owned that shop. When she'd told Ida she had a dinner engagement, Ida had assumed it was with the Knights. Libby hadn't corrected her. She wasn't ready to discuss Spencer's reappearance.

Libby gave her attention back to her gown. The mirror reflected her small waist, accentuated by the brown satin bow, and narrow lace wrists topped with tiny brown bows at the bottom of leg-o'-mutton sleeves. She bent at the waist to view the top of the gown. Smiled in satisfaction. Creamy-white Venetian lace rippled over her shoulders and circled her neck.

Is it too fancy? she wondered. She didn't want Spencer to think the night was too important to her, but she simply couldn't bring herself to wear one of her working dresses to dinner. She'd brought the dress along to the shop this morning, after perusing all the gowns and shirtwaists and skirts in her closet. The last hour the shop had been open she'd been hopelessly inattentive to her clients, fearful she wouldn't have time to change before Spencer arrived.

She took a deep breath. "Still covering yourself with beautiful gowns, the same as when you were young, hoping their beauty will make up for your plain features, aren't you? You'd think after fifty-five years of living, you'd have learned you are an ugly duckling and won't ever become a beautiful swan."

Ducklings never grow into swans, a voice in her head seemed to say, *but they become beautiful ducks, and that is what they are born to become.*

Libby shook her head. The wrinkled, skinny face in the mirror wasn't beautiful, no matter what fairy stories and silly voices in her head said.

The brass bells tinkled merrily. Libby swung to face the door, grabbing the chair's back to keep her balance. "Spencer!"

"Evening, Libby." He crossed the room in a few large steps. "May I help you down?"

He acted as though it was perfectly normal for a woman to be standing on a chair hunched over a mirror. Though his hand was a strong support, she felt clumsy climbing down from the chair. It was mortifying, him coming in on her that way, when she'd spent so much time hoping to make a good impression on him. Her cheeks stung with embarrassment.

He didn't appear to notice. Still holding her hand, he swept her with his gaze. "You look lovely, Libby."

Her embarrassment turned to pleasure. He'd always had that rare quality in a man of noticing a woman's attire. "Thank you." This time, her tone was warm. "You look quite the gentleman yourself."

His chuckle shook his broad chest and brought a twinkle to his eyes. He fingered the silk ascot at his neck. "You needn't look so shocked. Steamboat captains have plenty of gentlemen passengers to show us how we're expected to dress as landlubbers."

Flustered, she didn't attempt a reply. She knew, of course, that captains were the steamboats' hosts. He must have entertained many wealthy, prominent people in his time. Did he think her hopelessly unsophisticated and inexperienced in travel? "I'll get my cape and gloves."

When she turned from locking the shop's front door, he reached for her hand, and drew it through his arm. Her heart pounded madly, walking with him down the boardwalk toward the tall brick hotel where they would dine. Though she could tell he was shortening his steps for her, she took two steps to his one. She didn't mind; she was normally quick-paced.

Self-consciously, she returned smiles and greetings from surprised townspeople they met on the way. It felt good to walk with Spencer so intimately. Good but scary.

Is it safe, spending an evening with him? It was a question she'd been avoiding for twenty-four hours. Would the evening ahead open all the torn places in her heart that had taken so many years to heal?

The small town was fortunate to have a lovely dining room that catered to the traveling public brought by the steamboats in the past and railroads today. The room looked especially attractive to her this evening. Fine walnut chairs upholstered in maroon velvet and linen-covered tables filled the room beneath a crystal chandelier. Fine art in ornate frames decorated the walls, covered in stripes of pearl and rose.

The waitress smiled at her knowingly after leading them to their table. Libby resented her look, yet was glad she seated them far enough from other guests for private conversation.

When Spencer had ordered steak dinners for them, the time came to face each other and actually talk. Libby's gloved fingers played nervously with the linen napkin in her lap. There were so many things she wanted to ask him, she didn't know where to start! She needn't have worried. Spencer had questions of her.

"Do your children live in River's Edge, Libby?"

"I have no children."

Sympathy darkened his blue eyes. "I'm sorry. I can't imagine you without children. You always loved them so."

"When Joshua and I met, I was working as an assistant in a small millinery department in a local store. Joshua knew I enjoyed the work. He agreed I might continue it until we began a family." She looked down at her lap. "The children never came."

"I'm sorry." His voice was a hoarse whisper.

Was he remembering the times they'd spent with his younger siblings when they were little more than children themselves? Libby put on a smile and lifted her face. "Did you and your wife have children?"

"Two boys. Fine, strapping lads. Henry and Alexander. They're grown now, with families of their own."

"You're a grandfather?"

He nodded, grinning. "Two boys and a girl so far."

Delight for him filled her. "How wonderful for you! I can picture you bouncing a baby on your knee."

"The children have me wrapped around their little fingers, I shamelessly admit."

She smiled. "I've a nephew and two nieces in town who have me in the same position. A rather nice place to be, isn't it?"

"That it is. I'm glad you have children in your life."

"I am, too. God has been good to me. My niece, Constance, moved to River's Edge two years ago and married the banker, Justin Knight." She told him about Effie and Evan and the baby, Maria Louise. Tales of Effie and Evan's attempts at "detectiving" filled the time with shared laughter until the steaks were served.

"Where do your boys live?"

"In St. Louis, queen of the steamboat cities." His smile faded. "Margaret and I moved there when we left here."

Libby looked down at her plate. "That makes sense. You always loved the river. You must have enjoyed being a steamboat captain."

"That I did. I didn't start out as a captain, of course. Must have held down most every position there is on a boat, including that of the lowly cabin boy. I kept my dream in mind, and eventually, I owned my own boat. During the War Between the States, it was a boom time for steamboaters. Troops and supplies were shipped by steamboat, so many were built to handle the demand."

"Did you fight? I thought about you every day of that awful time, wondering if you were involved in battle."

Light leaped in his eyes. "I wasn't a soldier, but it wasn't always safe working a steamboat."

I shouldn't have betrayed myself so, Libby thought. It had been inappropriate, but she'd spoken without thinking.

"Unlike the railroads, steamboats could often bring needed weapons and ammunition and other supplies almost to the battlefields, if the battlefields were near rivers. We carried so many troops and supplies that many steamboats were attacked. Some were even blown up."

"Yes, I remember."

"Were many local men killed in the war?"

"Too many." She shared with him what had happened to men he'd known, young men with whom they'd gone to school, men she'd socialized with at dances and picnics, men she'd worshipped with in church, men who left on steamboats for Fort Snelling and she'd never seen again, and others who returned home with useless limbs.

Libby brushed her fingertips across her forehead, trying to brush away the memories. "Long after the war, I heard you'd landed in town on a steamboat. Joshua and I had been married for years by then. Still, when I heard you were alive—" She studied his face, reexperiencing the wonder of that day. "I thanked God for keeping you safe through the war."

To her surprise, Spencer looked almost stricken. "It never occurred to me that you would worry so over me. If I'd known, I would have found a way to let you know I was all right."

She pulled her gaze from his. "It's likely better that you didn't." Again she'd spoken beyond the borders of delicacy, but she wasn't sorry. The memories had built up inside her for so many years, with no one with whom to share them! She was fiercely glad she'd been given the opportunity to let him know she'd kept him in her prayers during that awful time.

She watched her fingertip slide gently over the etching on her crystal goblet. "What did you do after the war, Spencer?"

"No one calls me Spencer anymore. My children call me Father, my grand-children, Grandfather, and everyone else calls me Captain. I like hearing my name on your lips."

Flustered, Libby couldn't meet his eyes. She was glad he didn't press the sweet talk.

"After the war, steamboats could be had for a song. Still, seemed like a heap of money to me, but I managed to buy a good little boat. It wasn't the best time to be making money steamboating, but I hired the best men I could afford and treated my clients well. Slowly, my business grew into a small packet company. It served me well. Henry and Alexander are running it now."

"I often wondered which boats you captained."

"But you never asked anyone which boats were mine." His voice was low. His gaze kept a firm hold on hers. "Because you couldn't have met my boats at the landing, any more than I could have visited your shop."

Her heart lodged in her throat, beating furiously. She tried to swallow it, gave up, and forced her words around it. "No, I couldn't." She dragged her gaze from his with an effort. "I loved my husband. We had a good life together." It was suddenly terribly important he know that.

"I'm glad, Libby. I always hoped your life was happy. My marriage turned out better than might be expected. Margaret and I were both a bit wild at first, I suppose, but after Henry was born, we settled down. Margaret turned out to be a good mother and faithful wife. Yet I must admit," his voice dropped, taking on a teasing quality, although she heard the seriousness beneath, "I also hoped there would always be a place for me in your heart, as there is for you in mine."

She continued staring at her plate, biting the edge of her lip, thrilling to his words.

"Is there such a place, Libby?"

Slowly, she lifted her eyes to meet his gaze, feeling shy and awkward, and nodded.

His smile made his face look young.

Libby couldn't remember much of the rest of the meal.

Walking home by the mellow light of the gaslights, her arm tucked securely in his, Libby felt wrapped in intimacy. Their conversation was filled with "Do you remembers." Libby rejoiced in learning which memories of their town and friends and of their times together Spencer had carried in his heart through the years.

When they reached her home, he asked if she wouldn't sit with him in the porch swing awhile. She was thrilled he'd asked, that he wasn't ready to leave her. The spring evening was quite cool, but she didn't want him to think she needed to go inside. She wasn't ready to invite him in to meet Ida, and neither was she ready for him to leave.

A moment later she realized she had nothing to fear on that count. She shivered slightly as she sat down.

"Are you cold, Libby?"

"No."

He sat beside her, slipped his arm around her, and drew her into his embrace. "Is that better?" he whispered, just above her ear.

It was such a delightfully youthful ploy! Libby muffled her laugh against his shoulder.

His broad fingers were warm and firm and gentle beneath her chin, urging her to lift her face. She complied willingly, anticipation tearing away her breath, barely able to see the details of his face in the darkness. Then his lips touched hers, and seeing didn't matter.

His kiss was as familiar as though they had kissed yesterday, tender and warm and sweet and lingering. She gave herself to the beauty and joy of it.

When Spencer finally pulled his lips from hers, it was to whisper, "Ah, Libby, I've missed you so!"

Libby couldn't remember ever being so happy.

His lips touched her brow, her temple, her cheek, leaving warmth in their path. When they reached her lips again, it was many minutes before he released hers.

"I came back to River's Edge because of you, Libby."

Her heart stopped, then barreled on again. "You did?"

"I'd hoped for a glimpse of you, or news of you, at least. When I heard of your husband's death. . . I'm truly sorry for your loss, but, forgive me, when I heard you were a widow, my heart near leaped from my chest in hope."

She held her breath, waiting for him to continue.

"We've lived more years than we're likely to see again." His arms tightened about her. He rubbed his cheek against her hair, almost dislodging her hat. She didn't mind—enjoying the closeness. "I've lived without you for thirty-five years. I don't intend to spend the rest of my life without you."

Surely he couldn't be proposing after such short reacquaintance! Libby licked her suddenly dry lips. "What—what do you mean?"

His chest moved with his soft chuckle. "Is my intention so obscure? I intend to marry you, Libby."

I'm dreaming. It must be a dream, she thought. His lips, warm against her temple, assured her otherwise. She drew a shaky breath. "I believe your years as a captain have accustomed you to giving orders rather than asking favors. Haven't I anything to say about your intention?"

He again slipped his hand beneath her chin and urged her face upward. His face creased into deep smile wrinkles. "Yes. You can say, 'Yes, I'll spend the rest of my life with you.'"

Her heart yearned to repeat those wonderful words, but her faith and the discipline that was such a part of her came to her rescue. "We can't leap into matrimony without becoming reacquainted."

"There may be details we don't know about each other, but hearts don't change. I know your beautiful heart is the same as when we were young."

"And your heart, Spencer. Has it remained the same?" She could barely breathe as she voiced the question she'd been afraid to face. "Or have you come to believe in Christ?"

Chapter 6

Spencer Matthews's face stiffened. So, Libby was putting God between them again, after all. After the warm, harmonious evening they'd spent together, he'd hoped she'd put aside that silliness. He wished he could ignore her question, but he knew that wasn't possible. "No, I'm not a Christian."

Libby put her hands against his chest and gently pushed herself away, just far enough so she wasn't leaning against him. Fury and frustration raced through him. He grasped her shoulders. "Libby, is it truly important?"

"Yes. Unless we share the same faith, the same love for the Lord—"

"I remember your arguments." His tone, short and curt, made her wince. "I haven't forgotten a word of our last conversation before I left River's Edge."

"I'm sorry. I didn't mean to hurt you." Her voice was so low he could barely hear her.

"Think of the way we fell so easily into comfortable companionship." He leaned toward her. She drew back slightly. He stopped. Pain lanced through him that she would act as though he were repulsive simply because he didn't share her faith. He forced the anger from his voice. "You didn't act as though you believed we were wrong for each other a few minutes ago, before God was mentioned."

"I—I allowed my joy at seeing you to cloud my judgment."

His stomach clenched at her words. "Do you realize how much it hurts to be treated as though you think my embrace is a sin?"

"I'm sorry," she whispered, burying her face in her hands.

He wanted to draw her into his arms once more, but didn't wish to experience the pain of another rebuff. Instead he covered her hands gently with his own. She didn't resist when he took them from her face, though she gasped lightly when he pressed a kiss to her fingers. "I've spent thirty-five years missing you. After this evening, I can't believe you haven't missed me, too."

"I have missed you. You've become a permanent part of my heart."

"Then can't we put aside this silly religion talk and believe the love we have for each other, which has lasted through this long separation, will overcome the difference in our faith?"

She didn't answer. He wanted to believe it was because she was trying to convince herself he was right, but he was sure it meant she wouldn't say yes.

He tried another tactic. "If you married me, just think how much time you'd have to try to convert me."

It brought a smile. "If I nagged at you about your faith every day, you'd soon tire of me."

Now he was the one without an answer. Likely he'd find it tedious to deal with the issue daily. "There has to be a way past this stumbling block."

Libby stood, tugging her hands from his. "There is no way around it. It was lovely seeing you again. Thank you, for dinner, and—and for letting me know you are alive and well."

"Libby—"

Hearing a sob, he stood and reached for her in one movement. He was too late. His fingertips brushed her short cape as she turned away. She rushed across the porch and through the front door into the small frame home.

Spencer stared at the closed door, unable to comprehend at first that she'd left with no intention of returning. Finally, he stalked down the steps and headed for the hotel.

"This isn't the end, Libby," he muttered. "I've learned a thing or two about getting what I want in life. I want you, and I'm not giving up until you're Mrs. Spencer Matthews."

❧

Libby turned up the flame on the kerosene lamp Ida had left on the table just inside the door. Pressing one hand to her mouth to keep her sobs from waking Ida, she carried the lamp to her bedroom.

She quickly removed her gloves and cape, laying them across the back of a small oak rocking chair. She poured water from the rose-patterned pitcher on her washstand into the matching bowl and splashed the cool water over her face, then dabbed at it with a lavender-scented linen towel.

It didn't help. The tears still came. Libby dropped onto the side of her bed. Crying! She hadn't cried in years, not since the months after Joshua died.

"I've been a fool!" she whispered. "I thought my days of passion were behind me. I'm a mature woman, not an inexperienced girl. How could I have let my guard down, letting him kiss me, with no thought of the consequences?" She groaned and flopped back on the quilt-covered bed. "Let him? I welcomed it!"

It had been wonderful. She relived the beauty of the minutes spent in Spencer's arms. With difficulty, she finally pulled her thoughts away. It had felt so right to be in his embrace again, but it hadn't been right. "I guess I wanted those minutes, Lord, wanted those kisses to remember for the rest of my life. It wasn't fair and wasn't wise for either of us. Now I'll likely miss him more than ever."

With a sigh, she went to the bureau and removed her hat, setting it on the lace-covered bureau top. Something caught her eye. She picked up a wooden goose. Holding it in one hand, she stroked its smooth feathers. A moment later, she picked up its twin, remembering Spencer telling her all those years ago that geese mated for life, that he wanted them to spend their lives together forever, too.

When she'd changed into a soft, high-collared flannel nightgown, she moved one of the birds to her nightstand before climbing into the high bed. Sleep didn't come. The evening played itself over and over in her head. "Thank you for giving me this chance to talk with him, Lord, and find out what his life has been like. Please, don't give up on him. Keep working on his heart, so he might know Your dear love and that of Your Son. Not so we can be together. . ." She paused. "Well, that would be nice. No use pretending otherwise when You know my heart better than I do. Still, even if we can never be together, I want him to know the peace and joy of believing in You."

She snuggled her cheek further into her feather pillow. The pillow was soft and comfortable, but she preferred Spencer's shoulder.

A tear slid over her wrinkled cheek and dampened the pillow.

≈≫

Spencer stalked down the longest dock at the landing, the weathered boards bouncing beneath his feet. At the end of the dock, he sat down, his legs swinging over the water, his hands gripping the dock's rough edge. The current that he knew flowed mightily beneath the smooth, black ribbon of water was nothing compared to the current of anger and despair that stormed through him.

He'd come to the river as he always did when upset, hoping the familiar smells, the regular sound of lapping water, and the moon's wavering gold path would calm him.

He leaned against the large wooden post beside him, letting the evening's events scroll through his mind. Most of it had been wonderful. Just to have the right to sit across from her at a meal, to watch her eyes light up with laughter or soften with a memory, or her gaze skitter away from his when the emotion between them grew intense was a wonder.

His excitement had grown through the evening as he'd realized it truly was the same Libby he'd known all those years ago who looked out from behind the older face. A wiser, more experienced Libby, but the same beautiful spirit. Her spirit had always made her beautiful to him; it always would.

Libby's sweet, lily-of-the-valley scent lingered about him. She'd felt just as he'd remembered in his arms, her kiss was just the same, just as sweet. She'd responded so willingly to his kisses that he'd been certain she'd say yes to his proposal.

"I don't understand how you could say no." He stared at the water, rippling quietly past, but it was Libby's face he saw, her eyes radiant with what he'd thought was the joy of being together again. "So few lovers are given a second chance. If you have to believe so strongly in God, why can't you believe that He brought us together again, instead of believing He wants to keep us apart?"

In the many times he'd imagined this night through the years, it had never ended this way. Instead, Libby had spoken her love for him and agreed eagerly to spend the rest of their days together as his wife.

He wrapped his arms tightly over his chest, trying to ease the burning ache within. "Oh, Libby, will I ever hold you again?"

≈≫

Libby managed to eat breakfast with Ida and walk to their business establishments together without mentioning Spencer. Eventually she'd tell Ida everything, but she wasn't ready to yet. It was difficult enough to keep her emotions in check as it was.

In her shop, Libby didn't find it as easy to keep Spencer from her conversations. Every woman who walked through the door had heard of her dinner with Captain Matthews and wanted to know the details.

They didn't hear the details from Libby. No, she assured each one, he's not a suitor, only an old friend. Yes, he had been a steamboat captain. Yes, he does cut a fine figure for a mature gentleman. No, he's not married.

At noon, Libby went into the back room to partake of the simple lunch she'd brought from home, while Miss Silvernail watched the shop. As usual, Ida joined her. She bustled into the back room, her ample hips bouncing, her hat looking as though it would slip from her graying-brown hair any moment.

"Libby Ward, how could you deceive me so?"

"Whatever do you mean?" Libby hoped she appeared innocent. She sat down on the stool behind the worktable and opened her small tin lunch pail.

Ida propped gloved hands on her hips. Her brown eyes flashed. "You know very well what I mean. Who was that man you had dinner with last night? Customers have been asking about you all morning. Between you and the strange lights on the bluff, the women have been so busy prattling that they've barely made a pretense of shopping." She stopped to take a breath, then accused, "I thought you had dinner with the Knights."

"Uh, no, not with the Knights."

"I know that very well now, as does the rest of the town. Who is he?"

"Ida, please sit down. I feel like a wayward child being interrogated by her teacher."

Ida plumped herself down on a wooden work stool.

Libby sighed. Besides, Ida loved anything that hinted of romance. She devoured, not just read, the romantic serials in the newspapers. "I meant to tell you eventually. It was Spencer, Captain Spencer Matthews."

Ida's lips formed an O. Her eyes widened. "The man you turned down when you were just this side of girlhood."

"The same."

Ida leaned forward eagerly. "What is he doing in town? How did you happen to have dinner with him?"

Libby answered in a few short sentences. She didn't tell her of Spencer's marriage proposal. Ida was her best friend, but it was too much to hope Ida could keep such a spicy tidbit from the town's gossip circles.

"Are you going to see him again?"

"I don't think so," Libby admitted. It occurred to her that she didn't even know how long he would be in town.

"But an old beau! It must be a tempting prospect."

Tempting was certainly the right word.

Ida opened her own lunch pail. "If we put our heads together, we can find a way to convince him to escort you again. I know! Why not invite him to the pie supper the Women's Temperance Union is giving Wednesday evening?"

"I've no intention of pursuing him."

Ida gave a snort of disgust. "Anyone would think you weren't interested in marrying again. You won't pursue the captain. You've turned down invitations from all the marriageable men with whom your niece has tried to pair you. I wish I had a niece so concerned with my matrimonial status!"

"Would you like me to ask her to arrange a dinner companion for you?" Libby tried to look innocent.

Ida waved a plump finger in front of Libby's nose. "Don't tease me about something as important as a man!" She pulled a sandwich and a piece of cake from her lunch pail. "If you're not interested in the captain, will you introduce me to him?"

Libby only smiled and went back to her lunch.

The afternoon brought more curious friends to the shop. Libby began to wonder whether the local newspaper would insert an item in their social column: "Seen at the River's Edge Hotel Dining Rooms on Tuesday last, Mrs. Libby Ward, proprietor of Mrs. Ward's Fancy Millinery Shop of this town, and Captain Spencer Matthews, distinguished retired steamboat captain and former owner of the Matthews' Packet Company."

She was relieved and pleased to see Constance enter late in the day. "How good to see you, my dear. Are you shopping, or did you stop to say hello while on your other errands?"

"I admit, I only stopped in to see my favorite aunt."

"How nice."

"I've been hearing rumors about you." Constance crossed her arms over her black-and-brown walking suit and gave Libby a look that Libby recognized as a pretense of severity.

Libby straightened the cream-colored silk roses on a blue bonnet's brim. "It's impossible to keep anything in this small town a secret, especially if you're a widow doing something as outrageous as having dinner with a man."

Constance laughed. "At the town's best dining room, with a distinguished gentleman, if the rumors are to be believed. Hardly secretive behavior."

Libby's cheeks warmed. "If we'd had dinner in private, people would have put a nasty complexion on it. As it is, they merely feel free to ask nosy questions." Her shoulders had tightened and her voice grown shrill. She made an effort to relax. "I suppose I shouldn't feel so put out. I've enjoyed gossip as much as the next woman. I even repeat it to my customers, telling myself I'm only carrying on pleasant conversation about friends with my customers. Perhaps this is meant as a lesson to me."

"You never carry malicious gossip. It's only natural to be interested in our friends' and neighbors' lives." Constance leaned against the table. "I'm not going to let you change the subject so easily. Here I've been trying, discreetly, to encourage you to begin seeing someone, and all along you had your eye on someone else."

"That's not exactly the way it was."

"Do I know him?"

Libby shook her head.

"Perhaps I'm leaping to conclusions. As a former Pinkerton agent, I should know better. Is he only a friend?"

"Well. . .he's not a potential beau."

Constance looked disappointed, but she didn't ask any more questions about Spencer. She appeared to be thinking something over, so Libby straightened a display of gloves that the day's clients had mussed and waited for Constance to decide whether to share what was so obviously on her mind.

Finally, Constance took a deep breath and straightened her shoulders. "I fear I owe you an apology."

Libby laughed, honestly surprised. "I hardly think so!"

"Oh, I do. I'm sure you've noticed that there have been other guests lately at a number of the dinners I've invited you to share with us."

Libby pulled a long, white glove through her fingers. "I noticed."

"I did have legitimate social or business reasons to invite each of them," Constance hurriedly assured her, "but I admit I've tried to play matchmaker." Her shoulders slumped. "I shouldn't have interfered in your life that way. It's just that I'm so happy with Justin. I want you to have someone with whom to share that special kind of love."

"I knew that was the reason behind your invitations to the unmarried men."

"It was meddlesome."

"Yes, but I knew it was done in love, so it was easy to overlook."

"Thank you." Constance lifted her shoulders in a shrug. "I make an awful matchmaker, anyway. How could I have thought for a moment of exposing you to an evening in Mr. Copperfield's company?"

They laughed together at the memory of the stern, pinch-nosed school-teacher who had been one of the male dinner guests.

"I have to admit," Constance began, "I did think something might grow between you and Pastor Green. You seemed so comfortable together."

"Most of the men you arranged for my dinner companions were nice men, Constance, but Joshua and I had a wonderful marriage. I'm not willing to accept any man into my life just to be married again." It was only part of the truth. She wanted to tell Constance about Spencer's place in her heart, the place he contin-ued to fill, even though there was no hope they could share a future. She searched her mind for the right words and her heart for the courage.

Constance picked up a small black purse covered with jet beads from the display behind them and played with it idly. She caught her bottom lip between her teeth, then released it and rushed in. "Don't you ever get tired of life's strug-gles? Don't you wish sometimes there were someone there to share the load, help with money, make some of your decisions for you, that sort of thing?"

"Humph!" Libby jerked her chin into the air. "Of course I do. I'm human, aren't I?" She pounded an index finger in a rapid staccato on the oak display table. "But whenever I start feeling those collywobbles, I remind myself of the married women I know who can't spend a penny or attend a church social without their husband's approval. Then I hie myself up and get busy putting together a new bonnet or scrubbing the kitchen floor or making a cake for a busy young mother." She shook her head vigorously. "There are worse things in life for a woman than supporting herself."

Constance's eyes sparkled with laughter. "I should have realized you didn't need and wouldn't appreciate my help in deciding whether to bring a man into your life, let alone in choosing one. You run your life so capably."

Libby stared at her, pleased. "Do you think so?"

"Of course." Constance made a sweeping motion with one arm. "Look how well you run this store. The women think you're a wonder when it comes to creating hats and keeping them in fashion. And don't think I've forgotten that you intended to raise Effie and Evan after their parents died. That's why I first came to River's Edge, to bring the children to you from Chicago. If I hadn't met Justin on the train and married him, you'd be raising them now, and doing a wonderful job of it, I'm sure. Oh, yes, Aunt Libby, you're a strong woman."

"Other people have said that. I don't feel strong." She shrugged. "Difficult times come into everyone's lives. The longer one lives, the more of them one experiences. The way I see it, when things seem overwhelming, there are only two choices: give up or keep on going. If one gives up, there isn't any hope for a brighter future. What is strong, then, about choosing to keep going? What is there to do but keep going?"

"Sometimes putting one step in front of the other to keep going takes all the strength one has."

"Life hands everyone material with which to create their lives. No use complaining if you receive calico while another receives silk. You make do with what you have. Some mighty pretty gowns can be made from calico, and they're much more practical than ones made from silk, if I do say so, loving beautiful clothes as I do."

Her words to Constance about not needing a man to support her or lean on were true, but how did a woman stop longing for the arms of a man she loved or wanting more than anything to share his life? She was well aware not all women had the resources to support themselves as she did and understood that it was for that reason society found it acceptable for women to remarry late in life. Women at my age are expected to act mature, not giddy with love like a young woman.

She lifted her chin, suddenly determined to get past her embarrassment and tell Constance about her girlish infatuation with Spencer. "There's something I want to tell you—"

The door opened to the usual accompaniment of the bells and sounds of the trolley and horses and wagons in the street. Libby's hand flew to her throat. Spencer!

Their gazes met across the room and held. Then Spencer turned away, pulling off his hat. He stopped in front of a display of leghorn bonnets trimmed with ostrich feathers, looking as though he was considering a purchase.

Constance's eyes danced. "I'd best leave and let you wait on your customer."

"He isn't a customer. He's the gentleman with whom I dined last evening." Libby took her hand. "Come. I'd like you to meet him."

They stopped across the table from Spencer. He looked up, waiting for Libby to speak.

"This is Mrs. Justin Knight, the niece of whom I've told you. Constance, this is Captain Spencer Matthews."

Spencer bowed slightly from the waist. "Mrs. Knight. It is indeed a pleasure to meet you."

Constance smiled warmly. "And I you, Captain." Her gaze swept his coat and the braid-trimmed hat in his hand. "I assume you captain a steamboat?"

His gaze darted to Libby. She shifted slightly in discomfort. *He's thinking I haven't told Constance about him,* she realized.

"Yes. Retired," he answered.

"Will you be staying in River's Edge long?" Constance asked.

He glanced at Libby, then back at Constance. "I'm not certain. I've some business to transact. I'll be staying until the contract is signed."

Does he truly have business, or is he referring to a marriage contract? Libby wondered.

"My husband owns the local bank," Constance was telling him. "I'm certain he'd be glad to assist you if there's anything he might do to help you conclude your business successfully."

"That's a mighty kind offer, Mrs. Knight." He beamed, shifting his gaze to Libby. "Isn't it?" His smile grew larger.

Marriage contract, Libby decided, her heart quivering. "Very kind. However, I doubt Justin will be able to help with the type of business which you have in mind."

Constance glanced from one to another uncertainly. "I'd best be going. I left Effie and Evan at Perkins's General Store. No telling what mischief they've gotten into by this time. Good day, Captain." She kissed Libby lightly on the cheek. "I'll talk with you later."

Libby's heart started beating faster as Constance left her alone with Spencer. Why had he come?

She hadn't long to wonder.

"Will you have dinner with me again this evening, Libby?"

Chapter 7

Libby pressed her lips together hard. She hadn't thought Spencer would come around again! Now that the opportunity was before her, she wanted desperately to spend another evening with him. *Didn't you learn anything last night? Where could another evening with him lead but to more misery?* she warned herself.

She took a deep breath. "I don't think that would be wise, Spencer." *It wasn't exactly a no,* she realized, berating herself for her weakness.

His eyes darkened. "What harm could come from sharing a meal?"

She didn't answer. It wasn't the meal that worried her.

"I want to see you again, Libby. There's so much we haven't discussed. Have dinner with me, as friends."

She spread her hands. "You don't wish to be only friends, and there's nowhere beyond that for our relationship to grow."

"Last night left me with the impression I'm not the only one who wants more than friendship between us."

"I told you—"

"I'm not thinking of your words, but of your actions."

Libby looked away in embarrassment.

"Caring for each other is not something of which to be ashamed." His voice was low, almost pleading.

"I'm not ashamed of the. . .caring. It isn't wise to act on our feelings when we can have no future together."

He placed his large palms on the table and leaned toward her. "That isn't an ending that's written in blood. You can decide otherwise."

Libby linked her fingers together in front of her and forced herself to look him squarely in the eyes. Would he notice her chin trembling? "I've chosen to decide we cannot have a future together if we do not love and follow the same God."

Spencer glared at her. He whipped around. His boots clipped smartly against the wooden floor. He didn't turn for a last look as he went out the door.

Libby shook all over with the effort it took to keep from running after him. Was this the last time she'd see him; his back to her, walking away in anger, the same way he'd left her thirty-five years ago? *Is that why You brought him back, Lord? So I would live through this all over again?*

Shame instantly dampened her self-pity. She'd been thankful God had let her know Spencer was still alive. She was no less thankful for that now, in spite of the pain she was reliving. "Help me trust You, Lord."

Captain Spencer Matthews stormed past the quiet business establishments, dodging townspeople on the boardwalk. If some of them remarked on his pushy manner or looked askance at him, he didn't notice.

Fury at his helplessness poured through his veins like liquid fire. Libby wasn't giving them a chance, and there wasn't a thing he could do about it.

He headed for the landing. He wanted to be alone, where he could think. *If there's anything I've learned in life, it's that anything is possible.* Hadn't being a steamboat captain only been a dream at one time? And owning a steamboat? Now his packet company owned several. *To win Libby over, I just need a plan.*

Ideas always came easier to him on the river. He stopped at a small frame building at the landing to rent a rowboat.

The wiry man of about thirty with dark hair and a short, scraggly beard named the price, then leaned his elbows on the wooden counter while Spencer dug out his money. "You the retired steamboat captain I been hearin' is in town?"

Spencer nodded sharply. "Guess that must be me."

"I'm a steamboat man myself. Name's Adams. 'Course, I'm not a captain." The man grinned lazily. "I'm just fillin' in time, workin' here on the docks. Me and my pal took a trip up here to visit friends. We planned to catch the paddle wheeler we work on, the Spartan, when it made its first trip north for the year."

Spencer laid a bill on the counter. "Thought I heard the Spartan hit a snag down near New Orleans and was laid up for repairs."

"Yep. So my pal and me are still waitin'."

"Too bad. Maybe you can get work on another steamboat until the Spartan's ready. Always work available for experienced men."

"Think we'll wait around these parts till our boat's ready. We're pretty fond of the Spartan."

"May I have my change?" He was beginning to feel all too conspicuous in the small town to which he'd been so eager to return. He was accustomed to passengers telling him their life story, but not strangers on land. Right now, he was in no mood for small talk.

Relief settled over him as he stepped into the rowboat. The hotel clerk had told him this morning about a steamboat that had run aground upstream a month ago, right after the ice went out on the river. It was still there. He was curious to see it. He might as well head in that direction now.

Rowing was more work than he'd remembered, but he enjoyed the challenge. It helped cool his anger to spend his energy physically. The familiar sound of water lapping against the boat, the gentle rocking, and the fishy odor of river water all helped calm him.

He was soon beyond River's Edge. Bluffs, dense with spring-greening trees at their base and majestic with sheer limestone cliffs on top, bordered his water road. While he rowed, he studied his problem.

The first step in trying to solve a problem, he'd learned, was identifying it, stating it clearly. "The problem is Libby's refusal to accept me unless I become a Christian," he told a gull that landed on the stern.

The gull lifted its wings and let out a raucous cry, then settled down to fix him with its beady stare.

Spencer repeated the problem out loud. "So the solution is to change Libby's mind." He grimaced. "That should be easy. About like pushing a steamboat upstream by hand." One thing about Libby, it was always a challenge trying to change her mind about anything.

Memories of friendly debates they'd had as children drifted through his mind, bringing a smile, but no solution.

"Okay, Captain, start again." He heaved a sigh, dug the oars deeply into the muddy water, and repeated the problem slowly. "The problem is Libby's refusal to accept me unless I become a Christian."

He stopped rowing, his hands resting on the oars. "Unless." Was that word the key?

He shook his head hard. It wasn't like a man could create faith in God just by deciding to do so. "But maybe I don't have to create faith. Wouldn't hurt me any to become a regular churchgoer. Might be hard to keep my skepticism to myself and listen to some of those sermons, but if it meant Libby would let me court her, it would be worth it."

He dipped the oars into the water once more. After all, how hard could it be to pretend to be a Christian? Follow the Ten Commandments. He did that anyway, for the most part, all except that first one. How did it go again? He couldn't remember exactly, something about believing in God, or trusting Him, or honoring Him. If a man went to church and kept the rest of the commandments, who would know if he followed the first one?

His plan began to form. He'd begin attending church this Sunday. Might even join Sunday school. Ask the pastor about joining the church.

It wasn't as if he hadn't set foot inside a church since he'd left River's Edge. Margaret had convinced him their boys needed to be brought up attending church. He'd grudgingly agreed. At least the church would give the boys a moral compass. On the rare Sundays he was at home instead of on the river, he'd attended with the family, though in so doing he felt a hypocrite.

Let's see. Step Two. He'd have to settle in River's Edge for a while if he planned to win Libby back. And he intended to win her back, no matter how long it took. Nothing he had to be back in St. Louis for, anyway. His boys were handling the family steamboat company admirably.

He'd get to know Libby's friends, join in social engagements where she'd be present. No doubt that would include a lot of church socials. He chuckled. At least the food was usually good at those events.

Having a plan lightened his heart. He threw his weight into the rowing and belted out a river song he'd learned in his early days of river boating to the accompaniment of creaking oars. The song carried across the water to the bluffs on either side of the river and bounced back to him:

> *Timber don't get too heavy for me,*
> *And sacks too heavy to stack,*
> *All that I crave for many a long day,*
> *Is your loving when I get back.*
> *I'm working my way back home.*

> *Now Paducah's laying 'round the bend,*
> *Now Paducah's laying 'round the bend,*
> *Captain, don't whistle, just ring your bell,*
> *For my woman'll be standing right there.*
> *I'm working my way back home.*

As he finished the song, he rounded a bend and spotted the steamboat, stranded on a sandbar far to the side of the main channel.

He shook his head. He knew firsthand how treacherous it was to navigate a river. A good pilot, familiar with the river's bends and twists and shallows, was more valuable than gold to a steamboat captain. His own favorite pilot hated the stretch of the Upper Mississippi between Minnesota and Wisconsin. "During low water," he used to say, "my paddle wheels raise clouds of dust."

"Water's not too low this time of year," the captain muttered. Winter runoff always caused spring flooding, with the resultant high water. Invariably, it also changed the river's bottom. "Must have been what happened here. Channel changed since the pilot's last run, and his charts weren't current. The hotel clerk said the boat ran aground at night."

The usual attempts to grasshopper the boat over the bar with spars and derricks hadn't worked. The boat hadn't been carrying much of a load, so even after the cargo was unloaded with the assistance of dockhands from River's Edge, the boat hadn't risen far enough to free it. Some tugboats had been sent out from River's Edge to try to pull the steamboat off the bar, without success. The next day, the captain, who'd owned the boat, died.

Likely if the boat had been owned by a packet company, as so many were, the owners would have continued attempts to free the boat. As it was, the townspeople decided to wait, hoping spring rains would raise the water level enough to float or pull the boat off the bar. So far, that hadn't happened. If it didn't happen soon, they'd try using hoses to wash out the mud beneath the boat.

"At least the boat's bottom can't be damaged too badly. If it were, the back end of the boat would have sunk to the bottom by now."

Spencer nosed his boat up beside the steamboat, watching for the sandbar. He could just make out the top of the bar beneath Big Muddy's waters. It was too low, however, to beach his rowboat on it.

He rowed around the boat, examining it. It was an older stern-wheeler, badly in need of fresh paint. The boat was small compared to some of the elegant steamers. There were only two decks below the texas, where the captain and other officers' cabins were located, and the pilothouse that topped the boat like the top tier of a cake. "Jennie Lee" was painted in bold black letters along the side of the pilothouse. He recognized the name of the inauspicious boat. Every captain worth his salt knew the names of all the steamboats that plied the same rivers as his own boats.

Spencer headed around the back of the boat, circling the paddle wheel. "What the—"

A rope hung from the wheel, its end drifting in the water.

Spencer rowed closer. Maybe the rope was left by people trying to free the boat. But when he examined the rope, he could tell it hadn't been in the river that long.

Using the rope to secure his boat, he scrambled onto the paddle wheel. Grunting, he finally made it to the lower deck. "Never was my favorite way to board a steamer," he muttered, wiping his hands on his trousers.

He walked past the boiler room and along the empty cargo deck toward the bow. Locating a stairway, he climbed to the second deck. He opened a couple stateroom doors for quick looks inside.

He swung open the double doors to the dining hall and snorted in disgust. The furnishings, obviously once fine, were shabby. Brass trimmings were tarnished with age. The draperies were almost transparent from sun damage. The boat was old, but that was no reason to let it fall into this kind of shape.

Letting the doors swing shut, he mounted another flight of stairs. The captain's safe was usually kept in the captain's quarters in the texas.

He opened the door to the captain's quarters. His gaze swept the richly paneled room. A large, round, walnut desk stood in the middle of the room. Behind it, two brown-haired children, a boy and a girl, obviously brother and sister, about eight years old, stared at him with huge eyes.

The captain's jaw dropped.

The children's jaws trembled.

The girl summoned her courage. "Are—are you a ghost, mister?"

Chapter 8

A ghost?" The words exploded from Spencer's mouth. "Of course not! What kind of fool question is that?"

The girl's knuckles, gripping the edge of the table, were white. "W–well, you're dressed like a captain, and the captain died on this ship."

"It's a b–boat, Ef–Effie," the boy corrected her, never taking his gaze from Spencer.

Why, they're terrified of me, Spencer realized. He sat down and forced his voice to sound calm. "I'm Captain Spencer Matthews. I was a steamboat captain, but—"

"W–was?" Effie asked. "B–before you died?"

"Of course not!"

Effie took a step backward, landing her against the wall. The boy followed. Spencer swallowed hard. "I'm not dead. I've never been on this ship before, alive or dead."

"P–promise?" the boy whispered.

Spencer laid a hand over his heart. "Promise."

"How did you get here if you're not a ghost?" Effie asked.

"I have a rowboat tied up at the paddle wheel." He saw the girl begin to visibly relax, her shoulders lowering half an inch. "How did you two get here?"

It was Effie who answered. "We found a log washed up against the shore. We pushed it into the water and laid on top of it, paddling with our hands until we got out here."

Spencer felt his face drain of blood. "Don't you know how dangerous that was? You could have drowned!"

"We didn't. Anyway, you can't boss us around."

He ignored that. At least Effie must be losing her fear of him if she could talk back in that sassy manner. "Did you tie the rope to the paddle wheel?"

They nodded.

"Where did you get the rope?"

"We brought it from home," the boy answered. "Because the first time we saw the boat, we couldn't find a way to get out to it."

Effie nodded. "We tied the rope to a branch on our log, so we could get back to shore."

"But the branch broke," the boy interrupted, "and the log floated away, so we're stuck here."

Spencer was glad to see the thought of being stranded was beginning to frighten the boy more than the idea that Spencer might be a ghost. "I'll take you to shore in my rowboat."

Neither of them looked very comforted by his offer.

"Where do you two live?"

"River's Edge."

"What are your names?"

They didn't answer.

He smiled. "I told you my name." He looked at the girl. "I heard your brother call you Effie."

Her eyes widened again. "How do you know he's my brother?"

"I'm guessing. You two couldn't look more alike if you were twins."

"We are twins," the boy said. "My name is Evan."

"Effie and Evan." Spencer grinned. "I should have known. Libby told me all about you."

"You know Aunt Libby?" Evan asked.

Spencer nodded. "I knew her long before either of you were born. I lived in River's Edge then." He recalled the stories Libby had told him about the children. "Were you playing detective when you boarded the boat?"

Effie's eyes flashed. She planted her hands on her hips. "We don't play detective, we practice detecting!"

Spencer wiped a hand over his mouth and beard, trying to wipe away his grin. "Sorry. My mistake."

"You needn't laugh!" Effie stomped her foot. It made an ineffectual "thud" on the wooden floor. "We've helped Aunt Constance find criminals before."

"Aunt Constance was a Pinkerton before she married Uncle Justin." Evan's voice was thick with pride.

"One of the criminals Aunt Constance caught was a real mean man named Rasmus Pierce." Effie hunched her shoulders, narrowed her eyes, and screwed up her round face in an attempt to look tough. "He hid money he stole from a train in some caves in the bluffs."

"So your aunt Libby told me." Spencer crossed his arms over his chest. "Did you find any clues to a crime on board?"

"We aren't trying to solve a crime on the ship," Effie told him.

"Boat," Evan corrected again. "We want to find out about the lights in the cliff."

"Oh, yes." Spencer nodded. "I heard about them in town. Isn't it hard to see the lights during the day?"

"We figured the ghost wouldn't be out in the daytime," Effie explained reasonably.

"But when we got here, we saw the log," Evan said, "so we decided to explore the boat first."

"And then we got stuck here," Effie finished.

"I see. Well," he pushed himself to his feet, "I think we'd better head back to town. It's going to be dark soon, and your family will be worried about you."

The bluffs cut off the lowering sun's last rays, casting shadow along the path of the three traveling the river back to town. The children huddled together on one seat beneath Spencer's coat while the captain rowed. His muscles complained of the unexpected strain of two long rowings in one day, and he was thankful the trip back was with the current.

Once in River's Edge, Spencer walked the children to their home in the most elegant part of town. The frame house was a huge example of all the curves and curlicues of Victorian architecture, set on a large lot.

He reached for the brass knocker on the front door. Before he could grasp it, Evan had the door open. Uncomfortable at the idea of walking into a stranger's home without an invitation from the adult owners, Spencer stood uncertainly while the children entered, but only for a moment. Effie looked back at him from the other side of the threshold. "Come on." She grabbed his hand and tugged.

Her sweet gesture caused his tough old heart to twinge. They stepped inside together.

Although he'd already made note of the elite neighborhood, the elegance of the home startled him. The hallway was wide, paneled in walnut. A stairway, with a fine Oriental carpet quieting treads, curved upward at one side. The ceiling, two stories above, was covered with a mural of sky and clouds and cherubs and edged with gilt.

It took only a moment to take everything in, which was all the time he had. Libby and Constance rushed into the hall between two large open doors from the parlor.

Constance dropped to her knees, sweeping the children into her embrace. "Thank God, you're safe!"

The children hugged her, then leaned back in the arms that still circled them. "Of course, we're safe," Effie assured.

Evan nodded vigorously.

Libby stood behind Constance, her hands gripped together. Her gaze met Spencer's. In it he read questions, relief, and gratitude. He smiled, hoping to reassure her that all was indeed well.

Constance wiped a tear from her cheek, stood up, and crossed her arms. "Where have you been?"

Effie shrugged. "Playing."

Evan nodded again.

Constance glared at them with the frustrated concern Spencer recognized from similar events with his own boys. "Do you realize we've scoured the town for you? Justin and the stable boy and neighbors are still looking for you."

"We're sorry." Effie clasped her hands behind her back and watched the toe of her shoe as she dragged it back and forth on the carpet.

"Where were you?"

"Detectiving," Evan answered.

Constance shook her head. "You know your uncle Justin doesn't want you playing detective. Where were you 'detectiving' that you were unable to get home in time for dinner?"

Effie pressed her lips together, still watching the toe of her shoe. Evan watched her shoe, too. *Guilt is written all over them,* Spencer thought, yet he didn't feel it was his place to make their explanations, at least not unless he was asked to do so.

He noticed Libby was looking more worried as the children's obvious sidestepping continued. The thought flashed through his mind, *What would it have been like to raise children with her? How would the two of us have handled together the everyday challenges of child raising?*

"Well?" Constance demanded.

"We were detectiving by the river," Evan muttered.

"The river?" Color drained from Constance's face. "After all the warnings you've had against playing there?"

"We were careful," Effie insisted. "Can't you tell? We're fine."

"The riverbank is not a play area, especially at night." Constance wagged a finger in front of their faces. "I don't want to hear of you going anywhere near the river, ever again, without an adult. Do you hear me?"

The children nodded, staring at Constance wide-eyed. Spencer remembered Libby telling him of Constance's serene nature. He wondered whether she'd ever before spoken to the children this sharply.

"Spencer," Libby said, standing beside Constance, "how did you happen to bring the children home?"

"We met on the river."

Libby spread her hands, looking confused. "How did you know who they were?"

"We introduced ourselves." He wasn't certain how much to reveal. *It's important Mrs. Knight know the risks the children took today, but I'd rather the children told her.*

Now Constance was looking at him curiously, her head tilted to one side. "At the landing?"

"No, ma'am." He hesitated, watching the children. They were watching him, their gazes wide and anxious. He lifted his eyebrows. "Do you want to tell her, or should I?"

Effie heaved a sigh, lifted her arms from her sides, and let them drop back. "I guess I will."

Spencer smiled at her encouragingly. He well remembered from his own youth the terrors of revealing the tasting of forbidden pleasures.

Effie turned back to Constance. "We wanted to do some detectiving about the ghost and the lights on the bluffs."

"You remember," Evan interrupted. "The ghost of the steamboat captain."

Constance tapped her fingers against her arm. "I remember."

287

"Anyway," Effie continued, "we went to the bluffs. But then we decided maybe we should look for clues on the steamboat first."

Libby lifted her fingers to her mouth. "Oh, my!"

"That's where we met Captain Matthews, on the steamboat," Effie concluded. "Then he took us home in his rowboat."

Spencer almost chuckled. What a master of deception! She'd managed to tell the truth without telling the whole truth and without lying.

Constance looked at Spencer. "Is that all?"

He clasped his hands behind his back and rocked back on his heels. "I think the question you need to ask next is, how did they get out to the steamboat?"

Effie snorted and crossed her arms over her chest. "Oh, all right! We paddled out on a log."

Constance sat down hard on a hall chair. Her face went white.

Libby grabbed the back of the chair with one hand and rested the other on Constance's shoulder. "You could have drowned!"

"We didn't," Evan reminded his aunts.

Constance took a deep breath. Spencer could see her struggling to regain control.

The front door opened, and a man walked in. His face was the picture of despair and fear. Spencer realized immediately he must be Justin Knight. He was about five feet, eight inches, with broad shoulders and wavy brown hair. He looked vaguely familiar.

Justin glanced at Spencer in surprise, then turned his attention to the children. Relief washed his features with joy. He dropped to his knees, held out his arms, and the children rushed into them.

Then the story had to be told again. Constance repeated most of it. By the end, Justin looked grim, and Spencer expected the children would receive a tongue-lashing and strict punishment before the evening was over.

Deciding he had more than overstayed his welcome, Spencer moved toward the door, thinking to slip away without being noticed.

"You wouldn't leave without allowing me a chance to thank you, sir, surely." Justin crossed the hallway with his hand extended.

Spencer took it. "I only did what any other man would do." He leaned forward so his voice wouldn't carry to the children. "If I might be so intrusive, I suggest you keep in mind your own youthful escapades in determining their punishment."

Justin looked startled. Then he grinned a bit sheepishly. "I'll do that, sir."

"Is your father by any chance Albert Knight? You're the spitting image of him."

"Yes, he's my father. Did you know him?"

Spencer laughed. "Did I! You might ask him about some of our early adventures together."

"I wish I could. He's been dead a number of years now. Mother, too."

"I'm sorry." Spencer felt that wave of loss he always felt when he heard of the death of someone he'd known. "I haven't seen him since I left River's Edge as a young man, but I have fond memories of him."

"Thank you." Justin laid a hand on Spencer's shoulder. "If you're going to be in River's Edge for a few days, I hope you'll have dinner with us one night. I'd love to hear some of your stories about Father."

Spencer couldn't keep from darting a grin at Libby. "Thank you, Mr. Knight. I'll take you up on that offer." *Things couldn't have worked out better,* he thought. *This is the only family Libby has left. She can't avoid me if I become friends with them. He was sure he'd enjoy each of them even if it weren't for Libby, but he recognized a gift when he saw one.*

The encouraging turn of events made him bold. "Mrs. Ward, if you're planning to leave soon, I'd be honored to escort you home."

He noticed the way her lips pressed hard together, and the amused look Constance gave her, before she finally agreed to his offer.

Things didn't continue as well as he'd hoped. Libby had little to say on the walk home, although the way was quite long. They passed from the elite neighborhood to an older neighborhood with simpler homes.

At her home, she climbed the two wooden steps to the porch, then turned to face him. They were almost the same height now. "Thank you, Spencer, for bringing the children home. You—you may have saved their lives."

He heard a stifled sob in her voice and laid a hand on her arm. It was true; he may have saved their lives. No telling what would have happened if the children had tried to get back to shore by themselves. Still, he didn't want to frighten Libby further. "They're good kids."

"I think God brought you to that steamboat at just the time you were needed. Don't you, Spencer?"

"Maybe."

Libby smiled, evidently pleased at his admission of the possibility. "Good night."

Wouldn't you know, he thought, disgusted, as he left. *I bring the kids home, and she gives God the credit!*

Chapter 9

Sunday morning Libby took her usual place in church, third pew from the front, with Constance's family. "I enter church at the end of a hectic week feeling like a dusty, battered old hat," she'd once told Constance, "and leave feeling clean, newly blocked, with fresh trimmings, ready to face the world again."

This morning more than usual she'd come seeking renewed strength, but her mind strayed constantly to Spencer and memories of Sundays when they were young. In spite of his disbelief, he'd attended church regularly out of respect for his parents' faith. The town had been younger than she and Spencer, and the church had been the center of social as well as spiritual life.

His parents were sincere Christians, Lord, she prayed silently. *I know they tried to bring Spencer up to love You. Why didn't they succeed?*

Libby felt a tug at her sleeve. With a start, she realized everyone was standing. Effie was trying to balance the small hymnbook open in one hand while urging Libby to stand with the other. Libby hurried to oblige her.

Effie looked around restlessly while they waited to begin singing. Suddenly her freckled face lit up with a smile, and she gave someone a discreet wiggle-her-fingers wave.

Libby glanced over her shoulder to see who had caught her attention. Spencer!

She stumbled over the words of the hymn, causing Effie to glance at her curiously. She barely heard the preacher speak the words of the final blessing that always added special peace to her spirit as she left the service.

Libby fiddled with her pocketbook while people filed from their pews. The Knight family made their way into the aisle, exchanging greetings with friends.

"Captain Matthews! Wait!"

Libby looked up at Effie's call and saw Effie and Evan wiggling through the slow-moving church members to reach Spencer.

Constance stopped at the end of the pew. "Aren't you coming?"

Libby forced a smile and joined her. As they started down the aisle, women and children stopped constantly to smile at Maria Louise or chuck her under the chin and croon, "She is so-o-o cute."

Libby glanced down the aisle. *Oh, no,* she thought. Spencer stood at the end of a pew, just off the aisle, a few rows down. The children were chattering away with him, and Justin had stopped to greet him. *I won't have any choice but to speak with him. If I don't, Constance will surely ask why I've ignored him.*

Her heartbeat quickened as they approached Spencer. He looked distinguished in his suit, his hair and beard neatly trimmed. She noticed other women their age casting curious looks his way.

Her thoughts were a jumble of questions. *What is he doing here? Is he here to see me? I'm sure he hasn't become a Christian since last evening!*

"I hope you'll join us for the men's Bible study classes," Justin was saying to Spencer when Libby and Constance reached them.

"Thank you, I will." Spencer looked past Justin's shoulder and smiled at Libby. "You're looking especially lovely this morning, Mrs. Ward."

Libby's heart dropped to her stomach and bounced back to her chest. Her shoulders tightened, and her fingers clenched her pocketbook tightly, as if her body were bracing to protect her emotions from him. "Thank you." Her voice sounded stiff.

A moment before, she'd wanted to ignore him. Now she was perversely glad she'd worn her new spring outfit. A tiny turquoise blue bow topped the small silk jabot at her neck, and a large, jaunty bow of the same turquoise was tied at the cream-colored gown's waist.

Spencer turned his attention back to Justin. "I'll stop at the bank tomorrow morning, then, to discuss the purchase."

Libby's cheeks warmed. She felt as though she'd been rebuffed. *Quit acting like a silly schoolgirl,* she scolded herself. *No reason he should give you all his attention. Besides, didn't you tell him you didn't want to see him?*

"Now that you'll be living here," Justin was saying, "you'll have to come for that dinner we talked about."

His words hit Libby like a bolt of lightning. "Living here?"

Justin rested a hand on Spencer's shoulder. "The captain is buying the beached steamboat. He plans to live on it while he refurbishes it."

Spencer's eyes danced with fun and challenge as they met Libby's.

Libby's knees felt like melted butter. She grabbed the edge of the pew back beside her with one hand.

"Oh, boy!" Effie jumped up and down, the huge white collar on her robin's-egg-blue silk dress moving up and down, too, like a graceful white wave beneath her long brown curls.

"That's great." Evan climbed up on the pew while he spoke, so he could get closer to Spencer. "Can we visit you on the steamboat?"

"Yes, can we?" Effie seconded.

"Children, where are your manners?" Constance reproved mildly.

"I mean, please, can we?" Effie corrected.

Constance shifted Maria Louise to one hip, slipped a hand over one of Effie's shoulders, and pulled Effie gently back against her skirt. "It isn't polite to invite yourself to visit a busy man like Captain Matthews."

"On the contrary, I consider it a compliment that this pair of fine youngsters would like to spend time with an old codger like me."

Libby's heart warmed at his words, but her knees were still trying to recover from the news that he would be living in River's Edge.

Constance's smile showed her pleasure at his kindness toward the twins. "Perhaps we can arrange a time for them to visit you when you come to dinner. Would this evening be convenient?"

"Can't think of anything I'd rather do tonight, ma'am."

"Good. Will you join us, Libby?"

Libby blinked, startled. She should have expected the invitation. After all, she'd been the one to introduce Constance to Spencer. She didn't have the emotional strength to spend an evening in his company, even with the Knights. "Ida and I plan to dine together." It was a weak excuse, but all her brain could invent on a moment's notice.

Constance's green eyes narrowed slightly, but to Libby's relief, she didn't comment.

Spencer winked at Maria Louise. The little girl giggled, her face alive with laughter. "I have a granddaughter your daughter's age, Mrs. Knight."

"Would you like to hold her?"

Delight spread over Spencer's wide, rugged face. "May I?"

Maria Louise leaned toward him, holding out her arms with a baby's simple, straightforward trust.

Does that trust touch adults so because we've all lost the ability to trust completely through the years and long for it back? Libby mused.

Maria Louise appeared perfectly content in Spencer's strong arms. She poked a finger into his beard, staring curiously at the place her fingertip disappeared.

Even as she laughed, Libby's heart swelled with pain. It looked so natural, Spencer holding a child against his chest, his craggy, worn face so close to the fresh, new one, his attention completely taken up in her. In that moment, she glimpsed in the man she loved the father she'd never seen in him as a young man. *Thank You, Lord, for this memory. I'll always treasure it.*

He was reluctantly handing Maria Louise back to Constance when Pastor Green came up the aisle from the door, where he'd been greeting members as they left, and stopped beside Libby.

Justin introduced him to Spencer.

"Welcome to our church, Captain." Pastor Green reached to shake hands with Spencer. "I hope you'll join us again."

"I'll be living here for a while. You can expect to see me every Sunday."

Pastor Green beamed. "That's good news."

Warning bells went off in Libby's head. What was Spencer doing, saying he would be in church every Sunday and agreeing to attend the men's Bible study?

"Mrs. Ward, may I speak with you a moment?"

"Of course." She allowed the pastor to take her elbow and lead her a few feet away.

He came right to the point. "The Women's Temperance League is having a pie supper Wednesday night to raise money for their cause. Would you allow me to escort you?"

Her first inclination was to say no. He was a nice man, but she felt no attraction to him. He was one of the men with whom Constance had paired her at dinner, the one whom Constance had felt most certain would attract Libby. Libby had been relieved when he hadn't followed up the dinner with an invitation.

From the corner of her eye, she saw Spencer watching her. Perhaps if she appeared to welcome another man's attentions, Spencer would quit trying to talk her into marriage.

"I'd enjoy attending the dinner with you, Pastor." Even if she wasn't interested in a romantic relationship with him, she was sure he'd be a pleasant companion for the evening.

A grin split his smooth, slender face. "Wonderful! Shall I stop for you at six?"

When she rejoined the Knights, Constance whispered, "I couldn't help overhearing. Are you going to the WCTU dinner with him?"

Spencer turned from chattering Effie to stare at Libby.

He heard, she thought. She hesitated in answering Constance. She wanted to discourage Spencer's attentions, yet she hated hurting him. Finally, she nodded.

Constance squeezed her arm. "I'm so pleased. He's a very kind man."

"Yes, he is." Libby suddenly and nonsensically wanted to cry.

Spencer frowned. Libby thought she saw a shadow cross his eyes. She wanted to reach out to him, to ask him to forgive her for allowing another man to court her.

Mentally, she shook herself. Wasn't this the reason she'd accepted Pastor Green's invitation, to discourage Spencer? So why did she feel so awful?

When they left the church, they found a number of people in informal groups on the lawn, visiting in the spring sunshine. Libby heard the words *bluffs, lights, dead captain,* and *ghost* repeatedly. The mystery was still the talk of the town.

Mr. Copperfield, the unpleasant, pinch-nosed schoolteacher who had been one of Constance's dinner guests, broke away from three other men and made his way to them. He greeted Libby and the Knights. After he and Spencer were introduced and shook hands, Copperfield pressed his thin lips together in the manner Libby recognized meant someone had breached his list of do's and don'ts. Immediately she scolded herself. The man's ethics and morals appeared high, as they should be, especially for a teacher and leader of children. It was only his attitude of self-appointed judge that she found distasteful.

"A number of church members are planning an outing this evening to the bluffs." Copperfield's voice dripped disapproval. "Carriage rides to see ghosts are hardly appropriate entertainment for Christians."

With an effort, Libby pushed down her anger at this newcomer's insult to her friends. She grudgingly admitted he was right. "I agree with you, but if they believed in ghosts, would they go looking for them? Wouldn't they be afraid of them? I think they are only curious about the lights, which I must admit are unusual. I've lived here forty years, and this is the first time I've heard of lights on the sides of the bluffs."

"Me, either." Effie crossed her arms over her Sunday gown and glared at him.

"Me, either." Evan imitated her, adding a definitive nod for good measure.

Libby disciplined a smile. The children had only lived in River's Edge two of their eight years.

Justin smiled, too, shaking his head. "I've lived here all my life, and I admit it's the first I've heard of such lights."

Copperfield pressed his lips together again. "I've tried to tell people the lights are likely nothing more than the reflection of lanterns from trains or carriages on the opposite bluffs, but people seem to prefer the ghost explanation."

Justin nodded. "Undoubtedly there is a reasonable explanation that does not include ghosts. Perhaps in viewing the lights, someone will discover the true explanation."

"Of course they will," Libby agreed.

The lines in Copperfield's strictly disciplined face relaxed slightly, and Libby knew he was relieved to find someone who agreed with him.

Effie tucked her hand into Spencer's. Libby saw her eyes challenge Copperfield. "The captain is living on that old steamboat."

Copperfield looked at Spencer in surprise. "Is that true?"

Spencer met his gaze calmly and nodded.

"Have you seen any ghosts?"

"Not a single apparition."

Effie scowled up at Spencer. "What's an ap—ap. . ."

"Apparition," Copperfield snapped. "It means a ghost. If the captain lives out there and hasn't seen any, then there's no reason for you to believe in them, is there?"

"It's no reason not to." Effie tossed her curls. "Ghosts can be invisible if they want."

"Yes," Evan agreed.

"Children." Constance's voice held a warning note.

Ruddy color spread from Copperfield's shirt collar up over his face. Libby had the feeling he could barely suppress his rage. She was sure he wasn't accustomed to children standing up to him. She wondered whether the children really believed in ghosts or whether the idea simply intrigued them. She wouldn't be surprised if Effie took the stance she did only because she'd taken a disliking to Mr. Copperfield. Effie never had been one to meekly accept another's opinion, regardless of age.

Spencer rested a hand on Evan's shoulder and slid his arm around Effie's shoulders. Libby had the distinct impression he was warning Copperfield that the children had an ally, although she couldn't see any such warning in his face.

Copperfield turned away from Spencer and the children. Libby could see anger flickering in his eyes. "Would you attend the WCTU dinner with me later this week, Mrs. Ward?"

Libby almost sputtered in surprise, both at his abrupt change of subject and at the fact that two men had asked to escort her within minutes of each other and both in front of Spencer. It was a moment before she could make her thoughts and tongue work in unison. "Thank you, but I have an escort for that evening." She was glad it was true and that she needn't resort to Mr. Copperfield's company to discourage Spencer.

Surprise and displeasure crossed Copperfield's sharp features. He bowed slightly from the waist in a gesture Libby thought more a dismissal than a sign of respect. "Another time, perhaps."

"Yes," she murmured, not knowing what else to say. *Not if I can help it,* she added silently.

He walked stiffly away.

Libby avoided meeting Spencer's eyes, though she imagined his gaze burning into her.

Constance glanced at her over Maria Louise's shoulder. Laughter danced in her eyes, but she didn't embarrass Libby by remarking on the invitation.

Effie wasn't as reserved. "Thank goodness!" She plunked her hands on her barely there hips. "Who would want to go anywhere with Old Sour Lemons?"

"Effie!" Constance stared at her in horror.

"Effie!" Justin repeated, anger filling the one word.

A laugh burst from Libby's throat before she could stop it. The nickname was so appropriate.

Spencer was chuckling, too. Had he had the same initial reaction to the man, Libby wondered?

She caught Constance frowning at her and stifled her laughter. "We mustn't speak of others that way, Effie," she said, trying to get back in Constance's good graces.

"I don't see why not," Effie argued. "Old Sour Lemons doesn't speak nice about people, especially kids."

"We treat people as we would like them to treat us," Constance reminded her. "That isn't always the same as the way we think they deserve to be treated. Remember the Golden Rule?"

"Yes." Effie's shoulders lifted in an exaggerated sigh. "But I think people should treat me by the Golden Rule before I have to treat them by it."

"If everyone waited for others to be the first to be kind," Spencer said, "no one would live by the Golden Rule. That wouldn't be a very nice world to live in, would it?"

Effie thought a moment. "I guess not. But I still don't like to be nice to people who aren't nice to me first."

"Unfortunately, most of us feel just like you do, Effie." Spencer's gaze met Libby's. The sadness she saw in his eyes made her stomach feel hollow.

Chapter 10

The week that followed seemed unbearably long to Libby. Knowing Spencer was in River's Edge made it impossible to concentrate on her work. It was difficult to carry on conversations with her customers. Her mind drifted constantly to Spencer.

With every ring of the bells above the shop door, her heart leaped with the hope that Spencer had stopped to see her. Not once was it Spencer who set the bells tinkling.

Again and again she berated herself for wanting him to stop by. She was a bundle of conflicting emotions. Not only was she confused about Spencer, she was also upset with God and feeling guilty over her anger with Him.

"Why are You allowing me to go through this, Lord?" she cried one night in the privacy of her bedchamber. "Wasn't it enough that I saw Spencer marry someone else, that I must spend my life without him? Having him near again, knowing I can be his wife if I choose is too difficult! I've done as I believe You wish, refusing to marry him. Isn't that enough? Why must I live through the torture of having him near?"

After she'd sobbed until there were no more tears, she turned to the Bible, seeking comfort. She opened to Psalm 40. "I waited patiently for the Lord; and he inclined unto me, and heard my cry. He brought me up also out of an horrible pit, out of the miry clay, and set my foot upon a rock, and established my goings. And he hath put a new song in my mouth, even praise unto our God: many shall see it, and fear, and shall trust in the Lord."

A small wave of surprise rippled through her. These were the verses she'd clung to all those years ago when Spencer had eloped with Margaret. Back then, as tonight, she had thought the pain unendurable. Many times the pain had been so intense that she couldn't believe God could relieve it, ever, but she'd repeat the verses anyway and tell herself she believed God could take her out of that horrible place and give her a new song.

"And He did," she whispered, hugging the Bible to her chest. "I never forgot Spencer, but life became good again, filled with the love of friends, and family, and Joshua. God helped me before. He'll help me again."

She slid beneath the quilt, still clutching the book, and waited for sleep.

❧

Pastor Green's company at the Women's Christian Temperance Union pie dinner was more pleasant than she'd anticipated. He was easy to be around. Though politely attentive, he didn't fawn over her.

The most uncomfortable part of the evening was the knowing looks from the townswomen: the raised eyebrows, the sly grins, the whispered comments. *It would be bad enough if I wanted to be courted seriously by him,* she thought, *but it's worse knowing I'm only with him to discourage Spencer.*

The next day, townswomen again found their way to the millinery. Libby spent her time dodging questions about Pastor Green—she couldn't think of him as Daniel, as he'd requested—rather than selling hats.

"Such a nice man!"

"Yes," Libby would agree. "Did you notice the latest confection, the hat with the silk buttercups and lace-trimmed brim in the window? Just arrived from New York."

"You two looked so comfortable together."

"The pastor is an easy man to talk to," Libby would reply, keeping her tone brisk and businesslike. She'd pick up a hat from a display and hold it up for the woman to admire. "This style would look lovely with that fetching spring suit I saw you wearing at church Sunday."

The woman would glance obligingly at the hat, perhaps even try it on. "He seemed very attentive."

"He is a gentleman. This style is very becoming to you."

"He looks younger than the man you were with last week, but I'm not sure but what the other man looks more distinguished."

"They're both nice-looking men. Unfortunate that men haven't the opportunity to wear bonnets, isn't it? Amazing what the right style bonnet can do to emphasize a woman's beauty."

"Yes," the woman would agree absently. "It isn't often a widow your age has two such charming men courting her."

Knowing truth lay behind such comments didn't make them easier to swallow. Libby would grind her teeth to keep her replies bordering on polite. Often she'd turn her back on the customer, pretending to be busy with a display or selecting a hat and murmuring something unintelligible.

"I expect both would make responsible husbands." Eventually the comments always came around to marriage.

"I'm sure they would. However, as I'm not planning to marry either of them, I must continue to run the millinery. Did you notice this cute little item with the silk daisies?"

"Oh, I don't see just what I'm looking for today. I'll be back in a week or two and see what you have then that's new."

At six o'clock on the day after the pie dinner, Libby said good night to her assistant, Miss Silvernail. While she was preparing to close the shop, Ida joined her from the dress shop next door for their walk home.

"I didn't make a single sale today," Libby complained, checking over the special-order bonnet Miss Silvernail had completed trimming. "Even asking their opinion on the mysterious cliff lights didn't sway the so-called customers from their prey, meaning me. I felt like a rabbit with a flock of hawks after it."

"I don't think hawks hunt in flocks, dear." Ida picked up an ostrich feather from the trimmings table and pulled its softness across a palm. "Probably didn't make any sales because of your charming manner."

Libby set down the hat, frowning at Ida's tone. "Why do you say that?"

"When the women didn't get any news from you about Pastor Green and that handsome captain, they came to my shop."

Libby groaned.

Ida chuckled. "Really, Libby, you should know better than to speak to Mrs. Keyes as you did."

Mrs. Keyes, the judge's wife. "Oh, Ida, you should have heard her, going on about 'poor old widow women' being like 'beggars who shouldn't be choosers' and how fortunate I was to have two men interested in me when there are younger, prettier, and wealthier widows available in town. It was disgusting."

"It's nothing we haven't heard before. To tell her 'at least the men I'm seeing have a choice with whom they'll have dinner.'" Ida clucked her tongue and shook the ostrich feather in Libby's face. "That was a bit much, all but saying her husband had to put up with her company."

Libby brushed aside the feather. "She deserved it, the old busybody."

"Yes, but you know better than to treat one of your best customers that way."

There was an all-gone feeling in Libby's stomach. Ida was right, of course, but she'd hoped Mrs. Keyes hadn't understood the insult. "How angry is she? Do you think she'll try to keep her friends from frequenting my shop?"

"Well, she's definitely insulted, and she is an influential woman in town."

Libby dropped her head into her hands.

"She's also a proud woman," Ida went on. "Once she's thought about it, I doubt she'll want friends to know what you said. I expect her anger would be mollified considerably if you offered her a good price on that darling peach French creation in your window. It will go perfectly with the dress she ordered from me this afternoon."

Libby lifted her jaw angrily. "That's the most expensive hat in my shop!"

"Angry words can be costly, can't they?"

Libby grabbed her cape from the wooden wall peg and threw it over her shoulders.

"It's hard to keep angry words inside, though," Ida went on in a lowered, softened voice, "when what people say is true, and we don't want to face it, isn't it?"

Libby stopped with her hand on the handle of the workroom door. Was that why she'd lashed out at Mrs. Keyes, because what she said was true? No. "What she said was cruel."

"So is the truth, sometimes. She was right. If I can't say it, who can? Neither of us will ever be young or pretty again. You're fortunate your niece introduces you to marriageable men and that the captain and Pastor Green are interested in you. I haven't had a decent man offer to escort me anywhere in years."

"There's more to a woman than youth and beauty."

"Men aren't inclined to look at the inner woman first."

"The decent men you mentioned will look at the inner woman eventually. Besides, having a man in one's life doesn't necessarily make life better."

Ida sighed deeply. "Easy for you to say, with two men courting you. You may not want to be married again, but I do. I like doing for a man. I don't expect passion." Ida's cheeks grew cherry red at her reference to the private side of marriage. "I only want a companion."

Libby bit back her immediate retort. Ida had never made it a secret she wanted to remarry. If that was her friend's desire, who was Libby to belittle it? She tried to smooth the ripples of anger from her voice. "I admit, I liked doing housewifely things for Joshua, but I don't know that I'd like doing them for just any man. I don't want to settle for a loveless marriage of convenience."

"I guess I'm not so picky. I've been widowed going on twelve years now. I don't want to grow old alone."

Libby slipped her arm through her friend's. "What are you talking about? Neither of us is going to grow old alone. We have each other, haven't we? If that's not fine companionship, I don't know what is."

Chapter 11

Y oo-hoo! Captain Matthews!"
        In the pilothouse where he was oiling the paneling, Spencer peered
out the window. "What—" Who would be calling for him?
"Yoo-hoo!"

On the shore stood Effie and Evan, waving their arms above their heads for all they were worth.

He leaned through the open window and waved. "Hello!"

Evan placed his hands about his mouth to form a megaphone. "We came to see you!"

"Wait for me there. I'll pick you up in the rowboat."

When they were all back on the steamboat, he showed them about. They'd already been over most of the boat on their "detecting" visit, but this time Spencer explained different parts of the ship to them.

In the captain's quarters, Spencer scowled at his desk. He didn't remember leaving the papers in such disarray. He'd found them in the hidden panel in the wall behind the desk. Nothing there but old captain's logs and river charts. Still, uneasiness rippled through him, like a breeze causes ripples across otherwise calm water. On the first deck, he'd seen a lantern he hadn't recalled leaving out of place. In the dining hall, he'd found a bandanna that wasn't his.

Either strangers have been on board, or I'm getting addlepated in my old age. Had people from River's Edge been rummaging about the boat? It was surprising so little had been ransacked in the time the boat had been stranded. He knew of abandoned boats that had been stripped, their furnishings becoming parts of people's homes and businesses. He tried to shove away his uneasiness and gave his attention to the children.

The children's favorite spot was the pilothouse, at the very top of the steamboat. From there, they could look out in any direction.

Both pretended to work the wheel, which was taller than they were. "I bet you drove steamboats," Evan said confidently.

"Sometimes," Spencer admitted. "Most of the time, the pilot was at the wheel. The pilot is the most important man on a steamboat."

"Not more important than the captain," Effie said.

Spencer nodded. "Yes, he is. The pilot has to know all the turns and quirks of a river. If he doesn't, the boat can end up jammed on a bar like this one." He pointed out the front window. "See that tall staff at the very front of the boat?"

Evan nodded.

"That's called the jack staff. It's right in the middle of the boat's bow. The pilot uses it to guide the boat."

"Wow!"

He showed them some of the tools of the pilot's trade inside the pilothouse. They acted as though they'd been shown a toy chest.

"Can I blow the whistle?" Evan's brown eyes were large with hope.

"Me, too!" Effie jumped up and down.

Spencer grinned. All youngsters asked to blow the whistle on their first visit to a pilothouse. "All right, but only once each. Remember, whistles are the way steamboats talk to other people on the river and on shore. Don't want to confuse anyone."

After the great event, Evan turned to him. "What do you do out here all day, since you can't steer the boat anyplace?"

"Clean. Polish wood and glass and brass."

"Can we help?" Effie begged.

Spencer chuckled. "You want to clean an old boat?"

"It would be fun cleaning out here," Effie assured him.

"Yes," Evan agreed. "May we?"

"If your aunt and uncle agree to it, I'll be glad to have your help."

"Where do we start?"

"You can start by polishing the bell on the end of the texas."

Effie frowned. "Isn't Texas a state?"

"Sure is, but on a steamboat, the texas is the level below the pilothouse. The captain and officers have cabins in the texas." He grabbed some rags and polish. "Come on out, and we'll take a look at that bell."

The bell was huge, like all steamboat bells. Its brass was dulled from age and the elements. Spencer shook his head in disgust. He'd never allowed things to be so poorly maintained on his boats.

"Wow! This must be as big as the bell in the church steeple." Evan slid a palm over it in admiration.

Spencer showed them how to polish it. He was quite sure they would tire of helping him long before the bell was shining again. It was so nice out in the spring sunshine that he decided to help them instead of continuing his work in the pilothouse.

Evan's comments brought his thoughts back to the church and from there to the preacher. Not that his thoughts needed much encouragement to lead in that direction. He'd been picturing the preacher and Libby together all week.

His gut tightened at the thought. It was becoming an all-too-familiar sensation. He'd been so surprised Sunday to hear the preacher was escorting her to a function that he could have been knocked over by the proverbial feather.

How could I have been such a fool? he berated himself for the twentieth time since Sunday, while Effie and Evan chattered away as they worked. *Why didn't I suspect some other man would be trying to stake a claim on her? Her husband's been dead five years; she's long past the required mourning period when other men would refrain from courting her. The amazing thing isn't that other men are interested, but that a woman as fine as Libby hasn't remarried by now.*

Not just one man was interested. There were at least two. The preacher and Old Sour Lemons. He grinned. *Can't quite imagine Libby with that last one. Looked like he hadn't a funny bone in his entire long, thin body.*

But the preacher had him worried. He was just the kind of man Spencer would expect her to like: respectable, friendly, educated, and worst of all, he shared her faith.

He rubbed the bell furiously, wishing he could rub the picture of the smiling preacher and Libby out of his mind.

"Are you coming to church tomorrow, Captain?" Effie asked.

"Expect so, since tomorrow's Sunday."

"I like going to church. 'Specially since we got the new pastor."

Spencer's ears perked up. "New? When did he come?"

Effie shrugged. "A couple months ago."

"Did, uh, did he and your aunt Libby begin courting right away?" He was almost ashamed of himself, trying to get information about Libby from the children. Almost, but not quite. *All's fair in love and war,* he reminded himself.

"I'm not sure." Effie scrunched her eyebrows together as though trying to remember. "But the pastor came to dinner at our house one night when Libby was there."

The knot in Spencer's stomach tightened. "Is your aunt Constance happy about your aunt Libby and the pastor courting?" He remembered the smile Constance gave Libby on hearing the two would be attending that pie dinner Wednesday night.

Effie shrugged. "I don't know."

"Me, either," Evan said.

He'd struck out on that attempt. He'd almost gone to that pie dinner, but in the end, he hadn't had the courage to see Libby with another man. Hadn't talked to Libby all week, either. Trouble with a woman running a hat shop was that a man had so little excuse to stop into the store, and since she'd refused to allow him to court her, he felt he needed an excuse. Now if she ran a general store, or was a postmistress, or—

"We did hear Aunt Constance tell Uncle Justin something about Aunt Libby the other night when we were detecting," Effie interrupted his thoughts. "She said she wanted Aunt Libby to find a man who loved her, because love was life's true treasure, or something like that." Effie stopped rubbing the bell and looked at him. "Do you think love's a treasure, Captain?"

He ruffled her hair and smiled at her. "I sure do, Effie. The greatest treasure."

"Even greater than the ghost captain's gold?" Evan asked.

"Even greater than that."

"I'd sure like to see those ghost lights." Effie stared up at the tall limestone bluffs that rose above the steamboat. "Too bad you haven't seen them, Captain."

"Told Copperfield I hadn't seen a ghost, not that I hadn't seen the lights."

Both children whirled to face him, wide-eyed, their mouths open. "Where were they?" Effie asked.

Spencer pointed out the window behind Effie. "On the side of those bluffs." He pointed out the back window. "And on the bluffs down there." Then he pointed toward the Wisconsin shore. "And over there."

"All those places?"

He almost laughed at the disappointment that hung on Effie's face. "All of them."

Effie and Evan exchanged frustrated looks.

This time Spencer did burst into laughter. "From your long faces, anyone would think you were planning to search for the gold yourselves."

Evan's gaze jerked to him. "Who, us?"

"Yes, you two." A chill ran along Spencer's nerves at Evan's guilty face. He laid a hand on one of each of their shoulders and bent over until his face was level with theirs. "I know you two are ace detectives, but climbing around those bluffs can be dangerous. I don't want you two doing that. Understand?"

Effie looked at her shoes. He felt her wriggling beneath his hand. "We understand."

He looked at Evan. "You, too?"

Evan nodded.

"Good." Relief loosened his stomach muscles.

The children glanced at each other and grinned. Bells tinkled ever so softly in Spencer's brain. He ignored the sound. He didn't believe the children would flat-out lie to him.

Effie looked at Spencer with wide-eyed innocence. "Are you going to look for the treasure? You could probably find it, since you live right here."

Spencer looked up at the cliffs. "Nope, I'm not going to look for that treasure." *The treasure I'm after is worth a whole lot more,* he thought, *just as Constance said.*

⁓⁓

That morning, Libby could no longer face her nonbuying, too meddlesome customers. Besides, thoughts of Spencer made her too restless to work. She left the shop in Miss Silvernail's care and went to visit Constance.

The downstairs maid led her to the backyard, where Constance was watching one-year-old Maria Louise and their little white fluff of a dog roll about together in the new spring grass. Maria Louise's squeals of delight brought a smile to Libby.

Constance greeted her warmly, then asked the maid to prepare coffee and a plate of cookies. "I've missed seeing you the last couple days, but I didn't want to take Maria Louise out in the rain we've been having."

Libby assured her niece that she understood and sat beside her on the quilt Constance had spread over the grass. "I simply had to get away from the shop."

"What happened? You usually love your time there."

Libby explained about the customers.

Constance smiled gently. "I know it seems they are prying into your personal affairs, but most of them are interested because they care about you."

"I know." Libby sighed. *If Spencer were a Christian and I could welcome his attentions, perhaps I would enjoy their bantering questions, she admitted to herself.*

Constance gave Libby's hand a quick squeeze. "Now I'm going to be nosy. Tell me if you wish me to mind my own business. How was your evening with Pastor Green?" Her usually calm green eyes couldn't hide her curiosity.

"Pleasant."

"I'm glad. I do think he is a very nice man."

Thoughts darted about Libby's brain like a badminton shuttlecock. She was bursting to tell Constance the truth behind her acceptance of Pastor Green's invitation, but would she feel too vulnerable if Constance knew the truth?

"We enjoyed the captain's company at dinner last Sunday," Constance was saying. "He told us you knew each other when he was a young man."

Libby's heart started beating louder than a trolley car bell. *Did he tell Constance and Justin about the love we shared and how he married Margaret?* Before she could ask what he'd said, Maria Louise and Thunder tumbled onto the quilt.

Libby slipped her arms around Maria Louise's chubby waist and pulled her onto her lap. Maria Louise let out a squeal. "Good morning, Angel," Libby said in her ear.

The little girl stopped struggling, turned around, and gave Libby a hug. The immediate and complete acceptance in the chubby arms and soft cheek warmed Libby's heart. *What business have I to feel sorry for myself, when there's so much love in my life?*

The maid announced the coffee was ready, so Libby, Constance, and Maria Louise moved to the wide porch, which swept gracefully around three sides of the house. They relaxed in fan-backed white wicker chairs beside a round wicker table. Delicate chintz cups and saucers, matching coffeepot, cream pitcher, and sugar bowl, along with lace-edged tea napkins, lent an atmosphere of elegance to the simple repast.

Maria Louise sat on Constance's lap. It took a few minutes to convince her Thunder didn't need a chair of his own. Milk in a miniature mustache-style cup with two handles and a large sugar cookie kept Maria Louise busy while the women visited. Neighbors waved and called greetings as they strolled past, some pushing carriages, some with young children in tow.

Constance's conversation went back to the captain's visit. "He told the funniest tales of boyhood pranks, or perhaps I should say young manhood pranks, he and Justin's father pulled together. At least, I found them amusing. I expect neither of their mothers found them humorous."

A smile tugged at Libby's lips. "You're right. Spencer's mother always said she despaired of his becoming a worthwhile, respectable citizen. I recall one April Fools' Eve, Spencer and Justin's father changed the signs on the businesses after dark. When the owners went to their shops the next day, the barber found the shoemaker's three-foot-high wooden boot above his door, the barber's pole was in front of the church, the bakery was behind a real estate sign, a lawyer's finely scripted sign was over the saloon door, and the saloon's sign was over Mrs. Pickering's Dining Room and Tea Parlor. Mrs. Pickering was a vocal teetotaler."

They laughed together, picturing the mix-up on the frontier town's winding, dirt street.

Maria Louise joined in the laughter. A grin of tiny pearl teeth dimpled her cheeks. Both hands hit the table, palms down, causing the coffee cups to dance, the silver teaspoons tinkling a merry tune on the saucers. Constance and Libby grabbed the cups to steady them and laughed all the harder at Maria Louise's sheer enjoyment of life.

"What a wonderful sense of humor the captain must have," Constance said, when everything was orderly again.

"Yes, he always did."

"Did you know each other well?"

He didn't tell her, then, she thought. She took a sip of coffee, trying to decide how much to tell. *Why not the whole truth? I'm tired of spending energy trying to hide the past.* "We were in love." She lifted her chin and looked Constance in the eye.

Constance's expression softened. "I'm not surprised. His voice changes when he speaks of you."

"It does?"

"Yes."

Libby shifted on the seat cushion. "Having a former Pinkerton agent for a niece is downright uncomfortable at times. You see right through people."

Constance smiled. "Do you still care for him?"

Tears heated Libby's eyes. "Yes."

Maria Louise, tired of sitting with boring grown-ups, slid from her mother's lap, then stretched her arm out as far as it would go toward the sugar bowl. Constance gave her one sugar cube for Thunder, and the girl sat down beside the dog, happy once more.

Constance turned her attention back to Libby. "So that's why you weren't excited to spend an evening with Pastor Green."

Libby nodded. "One of the reasons."

"Why did you agree to his invitation at all, if you care for Spencer?"

"I wanted to discourage Spencer."

Haltingly, Libby started to explain. Soon the whole story tumbled out. "So you see, I can't marry him because he isn't a Christian."

"Perhaps he'll have a change of heart. I wasn't a Christian when I met Justin, either, remember."

"I'd forgotten."

"You mustn't give up on him, Libby."

"I know. I keep praying for him, but I can't marry him." Libby twisted her napkin. "Do you think I'm a foolish old woman, that I should settle for a good man I don't love?"

Constance's laugh danced out on the spring breeze. "Of course not!"

"Some people would."

"Some people are born old, with no sense of adventure or romance."

Libby smiled, more relaxed than she'd been since Spencer walked into her shop more than a week ago. "I was so worried you would think badly of me if I told you about Spencer. Instead, you've made me feel better."

"I could never think badly of you!"

"Sometimes, I feel guilty. I loved Joshua, but I've never forgotten Spencer. The thought has even crossed my mind that by allowing Spencer to come back into my life, God is punishing me for wondering about Spencer while I was married to Joshua."

"Oh, Libby!" Constance reached for Libby's hands. "Neither you nor the captain were unfaithful to your vows. I know you gave Joshua all the love that was in you while you were together."

Libby had to swallow twice before she could respond. "When Joshua asked me to marry him, I thought he was a wonderful gift from God. We were happy together, but the love I had for him was different than the love I have for Spencer."

"We never love two people exactly the same way. I'm sure you and Joshua were gifts to each other, for a season. That season is over. You mustn't feel guilty for caring for the captain or for anyone else."

"Learning how to live without Spencer all over again is hard."

Constance squeezed her hands. "I'll be praying for you and for Spencer, too."

Maria Louise threw herself against Constance's knees. "Up, Muvver, up!"

Constance drew her into her lap.

"Where are Effie and Evan?" Libby asked. If the twins were anywhere in the vicinity, she was sure she would have heard them by now, unless— She sat bolt upright. "They aren't playing detective again, are they?"

"Eavesdropping on us, you mean? No. They're off playing somewhere."

Libby leaned against the fan back, relieved. Sneaking up to hear adults' conversations was one of the twins' favorite ways of playing detective. It wouldn't do at all to have her confession about Spencer spread about town by those two little detectives-in-training.

Chapter 12

Two weeks later, Spencer pounded a nail into unpainted lumber. The sweet smell of pine filled the room in the church basement.

"That should be it." He stood back to admire the bookcase. "What do you think, Daniel?"

Pastor Green, hands on his hips, black sleeves rolled up to his elbows, grinned. "It looks great. Thanks for the time you've given to make it. The Sunday school teachers and children will thank you, too. They haven't had anywhere to store their books and teaching supplies."

"Didn't do it by myself. We did it together."

Daniel ran a hand through his long, dark hair. "Nice of you to say so, but I know my talents as a carpenter will never put a true carpenter out of business. If it weren't for you, the bookcase would have remained nothing but a wish."

"Only the paint job is left. Have you bought the paint? Sooner we get started with it, the sooner we'll get done."

Before long, they were painting the shelves, Daniel starting at one end and Spencer from the other.

Spencer's thoughts, as usual, strayed to Libby while he worked. His plan hadn't been working out. He'd thought by becoming involved in the church, he'd see a lot of Libby. All he saw was her back during the weekly service. Instead of spending time with Libby, he was spending time with the other men in town at things like the men's Bible study.

The only times he saw Libby other than church were the times she dropped in at the Knights' while he was there. He stopped by whenever he had a pretense. He was enjoying getting to know them. Unfortunately, whenever Libby found him at their home, she left as soon as possible.

Spencer decided since the church wasn't giving him more time to spend with Libby, at least he could find out more about his competition. He had. To his dismay, the more time he spent with Daniel, the more he liked and admired him. The man was not only sincere in his faith, he was intelligent, compassionate, and got along easily with everyone. He knew Daniel was about the same age as himself and Libby, but Daniel had a youthful air about him, both in looks and manner.

Instead of encouraging himself by getting to know Daniel, Spencer was losing his faith in his own ability to win Libby's hand. *How can she help but fall in love with Daniel?* he asked silently, looking at the other man spreading white paint over the boards. *He believes in everything she believes in.*

Daniel looked over at him with a grin. "I do believe God sent you to us, Captain."

Spencer grunted. "I hardly look like the answer to anyone's prayers."

"Don't be so sure. Most of the church men are too busy to help with projects such as this."

"They're busy earning a living for their families. I'm retired."

Daniel laughed. "That doesn't mean you're sitting around whistling and whittling. You've told me how much work is involved in fixing up that steamboat. Besides helping with the bookcases, you've added a spark of life to the men's Bible study. When I came here, the group, though loyal, seemed to have fallen into a boring pattern. Your questions have livened things up, made the men think a bit about their faith again."

Spencer wondered what Daniel would think if he knew those questions weren't inspired by his desire to strengthen and understand his faith, but by his lack of faith and opposition to it. "I never could handle the idea of a God who's so weak He's threatened by a few questions from lowly humans." That, at least, was true.

"Me, either. I know we can't find the answers to all our questions. Some things we just have to trust God is handling, even when it looks to us like everything's a mess. Since He made us, He must realize we don't understand everything and that we'll have questions."

"Ever afraid your questions will pull you away from the faith, Daniel?"

"Now that's a scary question for a preacher to answer!" Daniel's eyes filled with laughter. "Pastors have been dismissed for lesser things than answering a question like that honestly."

Spencer shrugged. "Don't answer if you don't want to."

"When I've admitted to myself I have questions and have sought answers to them, I've usually grown stronger in my faith, not weaker. I do, however, have a list of things I sincerely hope the Lord will explain to me when we're all together for eternity."

Spencer laughed with him.

"As for being dismissed," Daniel went on, "I don't worry about things like that. I live as my conscience and, I believe, God's Word dictate. I've not yet been dismissed by a congregation. If such a thing happened, I'd trust God's hand was in even that."

Spencer's brush stopped. "You believe God is involved in everything that way?"

"I know there are some Christians who believe God's hand is in everything, as I do, and those who think He is only involved in the things we perceive as good. Most people wouldn't perceive being dismissed as a good thing. But what if I needed exactly that in my life in order to become open to a change I needed to make in my beliefs? Or what if the Lord had been trying to tell me it was time to move on, and I wasn't hearing Him or was resisting what He was trying to tell me? If I stayed, I might prevent just the man the congregation needed at that time from taking the position." He shrugged. "Maybe it doesn't work that way, but I think maybe it does."

"Sounds a lot like predestination."

"I don't think it's the same. God brings us to certain places in life, but we always have free choice in how to react in those situations. Our reactions determine where we go and how we grow next."

Spencer nodded. *At least he agreed our choices determine our destinies.*

"No, it's not predestination," Daniel was continuing, "so much as it is truly believing Romans 8:28: 'And we know that all things work together for good to them that love God, to them who are the called according to his purpose.' Too many of us give lip service to that verse, but don't believe it in our hearts."

Doesn't sound like it applies to people like me who don't love God, Spencer mused. *So Daniel believes God brought me here at this time. If that's true, I wonder why. Maybe so He could punish me for not believing in Him by letting me watch Libby marry this man who does believe in Him? If that's the way this God loves, I don't want anything to do with Him.*

Libby had said God had brought him to the steamboat at just the right moment to rescue the twins. If she and Daniel were right about things, was it possible the twins would have died if he hadn't come back to River's Edge?

A moment later, he snorted in disgust. What was he thinking? He didn't believe this silly God stuff. He was here for one reason only: to win Libby's heart back.

"Coming to the hymn-sing tomorrow evening?" Daniel's question broke into his thoughts. "It'll be held in the park behind the church. The members tell me there's usually a good turnout."

"I hadn't thought about it. Are you escorting Mrs. Ward to it?"

Daniel grinned. "Yes, I sure am."

Spencer's stomach felt tighter than a wet knot. "She's a wonderful woman."

"That she is."

Spencer cleared his throat. "Do you believe she's one of the reasons God brought you to River's Edge?"

Daniel met his gaze calmly. "Might be."

"How will you feel if she marries someone else? Will you trust that even in that, God is in control?"

Daniel's eyes narrowed slightly. "Why do you ask, friend? Are you interested in her yourself?"

Spencer hesitated. It was one thing to tell Libby his intentions. It was quite another to tell the man who appeared to have the advantage in her affections. His determination hardened. He was here to win Libby. He believed in speaking the truth. He nodded once, sharply. "I am."

Daniel studied him for a minute. "Thank you for your honesty." He walked over and held out his hand. "May God's will prevail."

Spencer shook his hand and nodded, trying to appear calm. His stomach turned over. If there was a God, Spencer didn't think it likely He was on Spencer's side. He wasn't at all sure he wanted God's will to prevail.

⁓⊛⁓

The next morning, there was a guarded look in Daniel's eyes when he greeted Spencer at church. Spencer didn't blame him. He felt the same way.

He was pleasantly surprised when Effie and Evan begged him to sit with their family during the service. As Justin seconded their invitation, Spencer joined them.

His spirits soared when he found Libby was already waiting with Constance for the rest of the family. He tried to ignore the fact that she didn't look as pleased as he felt. In fact, she looked trapped.

Effie and Evan insisted on sitting one on either side of him. He'd have preferred sitting beside Libby, but as Libby sat on the other side of Effie—at Effie's insistence, bless her—he considered himself fortunate. He smiled broadly at her over Effie's head and was pleased when she responded with a smile of her own, though she immediately disciplined it and looked away.

When Daniel turned to face the congregation at the front of the church, his face was calm and welcoming. Spencer suspected he was the only one to catch Daniel's short pause when he caught sight of Spencer sitting with the Knight family. Daniel's gaze darted from Spencer to Libby and back again.

Spencer tried to play honorably and not grin, but he failed miserably. He couldn't resist smiling and feeling smug. Daniel needn't know Libby preferred that Spencer sit elsewhere.

He didn't envy Daniel, trying to keep his mind on his sermon while watching Spencer seated with the Knight family. He wouldn't want to be in his shoes.

Spencer was surprised to find his own attention caught by Daniel's sermon. He was speaking on the question Spencer had brought up to him the day before, whether God was involved in the ordering of everything in our lives. He listened carefully, wondering whether Daniel, who had answered his questions so respectfully yesterday, would speak of people who did not agree with his views disrespectfully today, when he had his image to uphold before the church members. His own respect for Daniel increased when the man didn't change his view in front of the church.

"Whether my beliefs on this are right or wrong," Daniel said, "I find that in believing God has a reason for everything He allows to happen in our lives, I am more open to asking what it is God has to teach me in each situation, rather than railing at Him for allowing it or making excuses for my own choices."

Following the sermon, Daniel announced the hymn-sing would be held that evening. Spencer was surprised when he next heard Daniel tell the congregation of Spencer's help in obtaining the wood and building the bookcases.

Spencer rubbed a palm over his beard. *This man makes it harder and harder to dislike him. I hate to admit it, but if he wins Libby's heart, she'll have a good man.*

Not that I intend to let that happen!

After church, Effie clung to his hand. "Can we invite Aunt Libby out to see the steamboat, Captain? Evan and I have told her how we've been helping you. We want to show her what we've done."

Spencer glanced at Libby. Her face was a pretty rose color in embarrassment. "Mrs. Ward is always welcome on my steamboat."

Libby's color deepened.

Effie whirled around to face Libby. "You'll come, won't you?"

Say yes, Spencer urged silently, not taking his gaze from Libby's eyes. He could see the struggle she was going through inside. *Say yes.*

Finally, she nodded. "I'd love to see what you and Evan have been working on so hard."

"When?" Effie asked.

"How about right after church?" Spencer asked. "We can catch some fish and have a cookout."

"Or maybe I can pack a lunch," Libby said dryly.

Spencer laughed, happiness filling him. "Might not be a bad idea, just in case."

Daniel was friendly when he and Spencer shook hands at the church door, but he still had a guarded look in his eye. "It's not over yet," he succinctly reminded Spencer with a smile.

But things are looking up, Spencer thought, walking down the steps with a twin skipping on either side of him. *Things are definitely looking up.*

Chapter 13

Spencer had obtained a rope ladder, which hung over the side of the steamboat for easy boarding. At least, he found it easy boarding that way. The twins thought it an adventure.

Libby found it humiliating. The twins, who had been the first to scurry up the ladder from the rocking rowboat, stood on the lower deck, urging her upward. Spencer was right behind her, urging her forward, assuring her in his calm, low rumble that she could manage it just fine.

She wanted to push him off the ladder into the river.

She didn't dare. It would have meant hanging onto the ladder with only one hand. It was all she could do to lift her hands one at a time to move up each rung.

It wasn't like her to be frightened of anything, but she'd never climbed a ladder where the rungs sank beneath one's feet, over water, in an ankle-length skirt, with the man she loved but couldn't have right behind her. She tried to forget she didn't know how to swim.

I should never have agreed to come out here, she scolded herself, *but I couldn't turn the children down.*

Effie and Evan grabbed one of her arms when she reached the top, trying to drag her over the edge. With their help, she heaved herself onto the deck and sat, breathing hard from the unusual exertion and—she hated to admit it—from fear, her arm feeling like it had been pulled from the socket, while Spencer climbed aboard.

She was glad she'd worn her brown suit with the jet black lace today. Any woman who spent her day climbing ropes onto dirty steamboat decks couldn't afford to wear anything pastel and frilly!

"Have you ever been on a steamboat?" Effie asked her.

"Oh, my, yes. Back when Spen—the captain—and I were your aunt Constance's age, everyone traveled by steamboat if they wanted to go any distance at all."

"What if a town wasn't built on a river?" Evan looked smug. "Then people couldn't go there on a steamboat."

"Most towns were built on rivers because it was easier to travel by river than to build roads."

"What about the railroad?" Effie asked.

"Weren't any railroads in this part of the country when River's Edge was built." Spencer put his hands on his hips and looked out over the river. "There weren't any railroads in Minnesota for a good ten years or so after the first settlers started River's Edge."

Effie and Evan frowned. They didn't look like they believed Spencer. "We came here from Chicago on a railroad." Effie looked as if she thought her comment would change Spencer's mind.

Spencer looked down at her. Libby wondered if it was sympathy she saw in his eyes when he answered. "I imagine you did. There aren't any rivers running from Chicago to River's Edge, more's the pity. Nothing compares with the romance of steamboat travel." He cleared his throat and rubbed his hand across his bearded chin. "Maybe we should show your aunt Libby around the boat before we go fishing." Spencer held out a hand to help her to her feet.

Once Libby was on her feet, Effie and Evan each reached for one of her hands. "Come on!"

Though Libby's heart warmed as always at their care for her, regret spread through her when she removed her hand from Spencer's to take the children's hands. She wondered, her breath coming more quickly at the thought, *Did our touch transport him back to when we were young and in love and all our dreams seemed possible?*

Spencer smiled at her over the children's heads. "Maybe we can find some places you haven't seen on a steamboat before. Let's show her the engine room first, twins."

The huge, wood-fired boilers didn't impress her nearly as much as the small galley, tucked into a tiny space near the boilers. "Imagine trying to prepare meals for an entire boatload of people in this small space," she said, shaking her head.

"You have to see the dining hall." Effie led the way up the sweeping staircase to the next level. "That's the prettiest part of the whole ship."

"Boat," Evan reminded her forcefully, rolling his eyes.

Effie ignored him. "Hurry!" She ran down the deck, past the closed stateroom doors, toward the double doors leading to the dining hall.

Libby had seen many steamboats' dining halls, also called social halls or saloons, but she was curious to see this one. They were always elegantly decorated.

"Don't get your expectations up too high," Spencer spoke from beside her. "The prior owner kept up the parts that kept the Jennie Lee afloat and running, but he didn't spend any money taking care of the rest of her."

Effie and Evan each held one of the double doors. They playfully bowed when the captain and Libby entered.

"O–o–oh!" A sense of sadness and disappointment swept through Libby when she saw the room. It had obviously never been one of the more elegant ones on the river, but it had been lovely once. Spencer had been right; it hadn't been cared for.

She walked slowly down the middle of the long room, her steps noiseless on the once-thick carpet. She stopped beside a round walnut table with inlay, and ran an index finger across the top. The wood was scarred and water-stained.

Gold-and-maroon-striped velvet on the side chair was threadbare and torn. The matching curtains at the window above the table were almost transparent in places.

Libby jumped slightly when Spencer spoke from behind her. She'd become so involved in the state of the room that she hadn't realized how close he was. "Do you think I'm a fool for wanting to refurbish her?"

"No." She shook her head but didn't turn to face him. "I understand that you would want to see her restored to her original elegance. Loving riverboating as you do, it must be painful to see a boat neglected this way. But it will take a lot of work."

"Yes, it will, but I have the time."

Effie climbed up on the side chair, her weight on her knees, her palms on the table. She grinned at Libby, her eyes wide with excitement. "See? Isn't it the prettiest room?"

"Yes, dear."

"Captain Matthews is going to let us help him wash the windows and polish the brass candlesticks and lights in here." Effie looked puffed with pride.

Libby looked at Spencer and lifted her eyebrows. "How nice of him."

Spencer shrugged his shoulders and spread his palms in a what-could-I-do look. "They offered to help. Wasn't that kind of them?"

"It was," she admitted.

"It's fun to work on the steamboat." Effie slipped off the chair and continued down the length of the room toward the stern.

The others followed. Libby saw that the floor-length, maroon velvet curtains that separated the men's from the women's areas were in better shape than the window drapes. She reached out to take their softness in her hand, remembering the days she'd traveled by steamboat. Then the women's area had been carefully guarded to protect women from the gambling and from the men who drank and smoked cigars in the men's saloon.

As they left the room, Evan tugged her toward another sweeping stairway. "You have to see the pilothouse. I think that's the best part."

When they entered the room, Evan went directly to the brass-bound wooden wheel. "This is where the pilot steers the boat."

Libby smiled at the obvious. "I see."

"Captain Matthews says the pilot is the one who steers the boat, not the captain," Evan elaborated, "except sometimes. I want to be a pilot when I grow up."

Effie gave an exaggerated sigh and rolled her eyes. "You can't be a pilot, Evan. We're going to be detectives, remember?"

Evan gripped the wheel tighter and stared out the window over the bow of the boat. "I'm going to be both."

Effie shook her head. "Boys will be boys."

Spencer coughed. Libby caught his laughing gaze and tried to swallow her own amusement.

Effie swung her arms wide. "The captain already did a lot of work in here. See how shiny all the brass things are?"

"Yes." Libby glanced at the brass lanterns and chandelier and the brass-ringed cords hanging from the ceiling. "Everything looks like new."

Spencer beamed.

Libby caught her hands behind her back. "I think perhaps this is Captain Matthews's favorite part of the boat, too, don't you, Effie?"

Effie grinned. "Yep."

Evan turned from the wheel and pointed to the cords, which were too high for him to reach. "Do you know what these do?"

"No. I've never been in a pilothouse before." Libby smiled at Evan. "Do you know?"

He nodded and stuck out his chest proudly. "The pilot pulls this one to stop the engines in an emergency. He pulls this one to call the captain. This one blows the whistle."

"Very impressive."

"Every steamboat's whistle sounds different," Evan explained importantly. He pointed to a long wooden tube sticking out of the floor near the wheel. "Do you know what this is?"

"I couldn't even guess."

"The pilot talks to the men in the engine room through it." Evan could barely reach his face to the top of the tube. "Hello, down there!" he called. He swung around. "Hey, Effie, why don't you go down in the engine room and see if you can hear me?"

"Okay!"

Spencer caught her shoulder as she turned to dash from the room. "Not so fast! Let's do that another time. We still have to catch our lunch, you know. I'm getting hungry, aren't you?"

Soon they were on the bottom deck. Spencer brought out some long bamboo poles. "Found these on board." He indicated a pail filled with mud. "Want to fetch out some nightcrawlers for me, Evan?"

"Sure!" Evan dropped to his knees beside the bucket and dug his hands into the mud without a moment's hesitation.

Libby cringed at the sight. She almost felt that mud beneath her fingernails.

Soon they each had a pole over the water. Libby was glad Evan had put the nightcrawler on her hook.

"It's so peaceful. No wonder you like living here." Libby looked out over the water. The river looked deceptively calm. She knew the currents in the middle were strong, in spite of only a few ripples on the surface. *Like the currents between me and Spencer,* she thought. *Always there under the surface, no matter how hard I try to deny them.*

Spencer smiled at her. "Remember the first time we went fishing together?"

Laughter bubbled up inside her at the memory. "It was my first time fishing ever. You made me put on my own worm and take the fish I caught off my hook."

"As I remember it, I tried to make you take the fish off, but you screamed bloody murder when you touched a fish for the first time."

Effie giggled. "Aunt Libby, you didn't!"

Evan joined in her laughter.

"Then she wanted me to throw 'the poor things,' as she called them, back in the water so they wouldn't die," he informed the twins.

"He expected me to prepare them for lunch," she defended herself. "I didn't know anything about filleting a fish."

The twins chuckled together.

"Your aunt became a good fisherwoman eventually."

Libby bowed her head in acceptance of the compliment.

"Do you still like to fish, Libby?"

It was a moment before she answered. "This is the first time I've been fishing since—since you moved away from River's Edge." She shrugged. "There were always other things that needed doing, and then, Joshua, my husband, didn't care to fish." *Besides, there were all those sweet, funny memories of the times we spent together fishing,* she thought.

"Tell us stories about when you were little," Effie urged them.

"How old were you when you came here?" Evan asked. "Were you about our age, eight?"

"Oh, I was much older than you, fourteen or fifteen."

They told the children what life had been like in the early settlement when they first came to River's Edge.

The children listened, fascinated, their interest broken only when pulling in the numerous fish they caught. They soon had enough for a meal. Spencer retrieved a cast-iron skillet and a coffeepot. "The stove in the galley is too large to prepare such a small meal. We'll cook over an open fire on shore, instead."

So Libby climbed back down the rope ladder, her heart in her mouth, certain she'd land in the Big Muddy instead of in the rowboat. Thanks to Spencer's strong hands at her waist as she climbed, that didn't happen.

On shore, Spencer led them to a small circle of rocks where Libby could see there had been numerous fires. Obviously he had cooked many meals here. The children helped him gather kindling. He stirred the ashes until the coals caught the kindling, then laid on larger pieces of wood. Soon the fire was going. While it burned down to cooking height, he filleted the fish. The children went off down the shore to play, with strict orders to stay out of the water and off anything floating in the water or hanging over it.

Libby spread her shawl on a fallen log near the fire and sat down, leaning her elbows on her knees and watching Spencer. "Thank you for being so wonderful with the children, Spencer."

He glanced up at her. "Nothing to thank me for. I like them."

"They like you, too."

"Effie reminds me of you—spunky."

For a couple minutes, silence stood between them. Libby noticed the sounds of the river lapping the shore, the breeze brushing the bushes along the base of the bluff behind them, birds and gulls talking as they looked for food.

"I used to wonder what it would be like, Libby, raising children with you, watching you love our children, watching them love you." Spencer's voice was low, unusually soft.

Her insides filled with a sweet aching. Tears sprang to her eyes. She pressed her lips together to keep the pain inside. *If I tell him I've wondered the same things about him, it will only encourage him to believe I might change my mind and allow him to court me.*

She watched him place the fish in the skillet, rake some coals to the edge of the fire, and set the skillet on a cast-iron spider over the coals. It gave her time to wipe the tears in her eyes discreetly away with her handkerchief and get her emotions slightly under control.

With the skillet safely over the coals, Spencer washed his hands in the river, dried them on his clean handkerchief, and came to sit beside her. His nearness caused even more turmoil inside her.

"Won't take long for the fish to fry. Suppose in a couple minutes we'll have to call for those mud-nosed tadpoles, as river men would call the twins." His smile told her he didn't think of the children in such uncomplimentary terms, yet she knew he didn't expect or want her to let the term go by without comment.

"What a terrible thing to call children, Spencer Matthews! Why, it almost sounds like cursing."

"Cursing? It's a term of endearment. I should know. On a riverboat, a man hears a lot of cursing. Lots of river sailors swear like you never heard before, even in the early days of River's Edge." He brushed sand from the knees of his pants. "Whenever I'd catch myself using such language, I'd remember you scolding me for using it when we were children."

His voice had dropped to that level that vibrated through her so intimately. She wished he would quit doing that! It did disastrous things to her resolve.

"Remember how you used to do that, Libby?"

She nodded.

"You were always so good. Your goodness made me want to be a finer man."

"You were always a fine man, Spencer."

"Not so you'd notice. A fine man doesn't get drunk and elope with a woman he barely knows."

She hadn't an answer to that.

"I gave up drinking after that. Figured if I could mess my life and Margaret's up so bad after one episode, I didn't need it in my life."

"I'm glad." She was glad, too, that she'd been given the gift of finally knowing it. She looked down at her lap, twisting her handkerchief. "You messed up my life, too, that night."

He enveloped one of her hands in his own. "I'm sorry." He took a long breath, and she was surprised to hear the breath shake. "But if I hadn't married Margaret, you wouldn't have married me anyway, would you?"

It was true. She wouldn't have married him unless he became a Christian. Still, she wished things wouldn't have ended that way between them, so abruptly, so irrevocably.

"In all the years since I left River's Edge, I've tried to be the kind of man you'd respect. Margaret and I saw to it that the boys were raised in the church, and I attended services when I could. I've tried to live by the Golden Rule, loving my neighbors as myself."

"I believe you love goodness, Spencer, but that isn't enough. The Golden Rule ends with loving our neighbors. It starts with loving God with all our heart and soul and mind and strength."

His calloused, worn hands cradled hers. It was as though she could feel his love flowing from his gentle touch. She knew she should pull away from him, but it was so beautiful to feel this loved.

"How can I love God more than anything else when there's you in the world to love, Libby?"

With a small cry, she pulled back. "You mustn't love me more than God!"

Spencer gave a snort of disgust. "Truly, Libby, you can be the most mule-headed woman at times."

"Mule-headed!"

"Now, stop your sputtering. Yes, mule-headed. I admit, most of the time I like that about you. I wouldn't be interested in any weak female who doesn't know her own mind. But when you get to talking about God, there's no reasoning with you."

Libby opened her mouth to retort, but before she could, he continued.

"Why would I love a God who kept us apart? I've been angry at Him for thirty-five years, and I sure don't see any reason to stop now!"

Libby stared at him, one hand at her throat, stunned at his anger.

He glared back, his chest heaving.

Effie and Evan's laughter and the sound of their feet running along the shore broke into the stillness that lay between Libby and Spencer.

Spencer moved to the fire and bent over the skillet, turning the fish with a long stick. Libby opened the wicker picnic basket she'd brought and removed plates and silver with shaking hands. They weren't shaking anywhere near as fast as her heart.

Libby smiled and nodded as Effie chattered away, displaying a round, river-polished stone, but all the while, Libby's mind was reliving the words between her and Spencer.

Suddenly, a thought occurred to her. *How can he be angry with You if he doesn't believe You exist, Lord?* In the midst of her confusion and anguish, a sliver of hope poked through. *Is it a start, a place faith can take root and grow, or am I grasping at straws? Don't give up on him, please, please don't give up on him!*

Chapter 14

*A*t least the children don't seem to notice the tension between Spencer and me, Libby thought, watching them trailing their hands in the water over the sides of the rowboat on the way back to River's Edge.

Effie and Evan were chattering away about their plans for future picnics and walks along the bluffs, apparently not realizing the adults' lack of response.

Seated in the bow, Libby had to look past Spencer, who was rowing, to see the children. She was thankful his back was to her. *I couldn't bear to look into his stony face all the way back.*

"Captain, what's it like to be old?" Evan asked, still watching his fingertips forming a "V" in the water.

Spencer snorted. "Old?"

Libby pressed her fingers to her lips.

"Humph. Guess I do look old to you," Spencer responded.

"Of course," Effie agreed. "Don't you think you look old?"

Libby's sudden coughing spasm caused her to almost miss his reply.

"Depends on who I'm comparing myself to." His oars dug into the river again. "Getting older means my mind and heart become like a scrapbook of memories. The older I get, the more memories I have; memories of places I've seen, things I've done, and the best memories, of people I've known and loved."

Libby's heart swelled with love for him. *What a lovely way to answer a child. What a lovely way to look at growing old.*

Effie smiled mischievously. "Are we in your scrapbook?"

"You sure are. I hope I'm in yours and Evan's, even when you're as old as I am."

"You will be," Effie assured him.

Evan nodded decisively. "Absolutely."

And in mine, always, Libby added silently.

They passed another rowboat, headed in the opposite direction. The woman in it waved cheerfully.

Libby waved back, surprised to see her. She didn't recall that family spending much time on the river.

For that matter, there seemed an inordinately large number of rowboats out. "Are there always this many people on the river?"

Spencer grunted. "More every evening. Some are fishermen, but I suspect most are out to see the lights. A number of people have stopped to ask if they can watch from the Jennie Lee. I said yes to the first few but started turning them

319

away as the numbers grew."

"I had no idea people's interest had developed into. . .this."

"People come out by land, too, as Old Sour Lemons said. They'll build a town out here pretty soon," he joked.

At the landing, a wiry young man with an unkempt, scraggly beard met their boat. "Howdy, Captain." He caught the rope Spencer tossed to him and secured the boat to a dock pillar.

"Hello, Adams."

"I'll watch out for your boat while you're in town. With all the folks headin' out to see the lights, almost have to post armed guards out here."

"Thanks."

"I hear you're working on that old steamboat. I was wonderin' if you could use some help?"

"I hadn't considered hiring anyone. I've been enjoying doing the work myself, just idling time away."

Libby thought Spencer looked rather impatient with the younger man.

"P'rhaps you'd think on it?"

"Sure."

Libby looked back over her shoulder at the man as they left the landing. "Do you know him, Spencer?"

"Met him when I rented a rowboat. Name's Adams. He's waitin' for the steamboat he works on to arrive upriver."

Spencer walked them to the Knight house, then insisted on walking Libby home. She wished he hadn't. It was an uncomfortable walk. *The air is so thick with tension, we could eat it like oatmeal if we had spoons,* she thought.

When they reached Libby's house, she was surprised to see Pastor Green having coffee with Ida on the front porch. She stopped short at the gate that opened to the lane leading to the house and clapped a hand to her throat. Dismay spiraled down through her. "Oh, my!"

Spencer grasped her elbow, bending his head toward her. "What? What's the matter?" His voice was filled with concern.

"N–nothing."

Ida spotted them and waved. "Hello!"

Pastor Green grinned and waved, balancing a cup and saucer in one hand.

Libby tried to smile and returned their greetings.

Spencer stiffened. "Guess I should have realized the problem right off. It's Daniel, isn't it? You're upset he's here with your friend."

"Yes. No. I mean. . ." It was so embarrassing to admit! She went through the gate, turning around to face him as she closed it. Her hands gripping two of the boards, she leaned forward and whispered, "I'm late. I forgot that he is escorting me to the hymn-sing. What must he think?"

Without waiting for an answer, she turned and hurried up the walk.

Pastor Green had risen and started across the porch. With her attention on him, Libby was shocked to hear Spencer's voice behind her.

"Evening, Daniel. Enjoyed your sermon this morning."

Libby whirled. "I thought you'd left." Immediately she wished she could swallow the words. Pastor Green must think her extremely rude.

Spencer ignored her and held out his hand to Daniel, grinning.

Daniel shook it. "Captain."

Why is he looking at Spencer so strangely? Libby wondered. Usually the pastor was engaging, trying to put others at ease, almost always smiling.

Ida bustled forward. "I was beginning to think you'd fallen in the river, and instead of attending a hymn-sing, we'd be dragging the bottom for you."

Libby scrunched up her nose in distaste. "Pleasant thought." She turned to Pastor Green. "I am so sorry. I'm afraid I lost track of time. We had a fish fry, and then we had to take the children home, and—"

"It's all right. I'm sure the people have started without us." He gave her his smile, trying to ease her discomfort, as usual. "Not only do they not need me to praise the Lord in song, they are probably glad to enjoy some hymns without my tone-deaf voice."

Ida laughed as though it were the only joke she'd heard in her lifetime.

Libby smiled politely.

"You'll want to freshen up a bit, I believe, before leaving for the hymn-sing." Ida made shooing motions with her plump fingers. "Don't worry about the men-folks. I'll keep them company until you get back." She smiled widely at the pastor and Spencer. "More coffee?"

Libby made her way slowly to the door, looking back over her shoulder at the group. Discomfort niggled at her. *Why didn't Spencer leave? Surely I made it clear that I'm attending the hymn sing with Pastor Green.*

Still, she couldn't help smiling as she hurried up the stairs to her room. Ida, she knew, was enjoying herself immensely entertaining the men.

Libby's uneasiness over Spencer's presence followed her to the hymn-sing. When she'd returned to the porch after freshening up, Ida had cheerfully informed her that she and Spencer would be accompanying Libby and the pastor.

Before they reached the park, they discovered that Pastor Green had been right about the group beginning without them. They could hear the wonderful words of "Amazing Grace" floating through the early night air blocks away. When they arrived, they saw the choir director was leading the group.

Pastor Green led Libby, Spencer, and Ida to the front. Libby felt as if all eyes were upon them. *I dread the questions and comments this will raise from tomorrow's customers! Maybe I should offer to answer one question for every hat that is purchased. That should raise my sales.*

Seeing them arrive, the director motioned Pastor Green to the front. He apologized easily without explanation for being late, said he hoped everyone would enjoy the evening, and gave the direction back to the director. Then he rejoined Libby.

Twilight had given way to darkness. Gas streetlights, torches, and handheld lanterns lent light to the singers and cast the trees about the park into deeper shadow. *It was a nice atmosphere, a nice change of place in which to worship,* Libby decided.

Libby could remember when the townspeople had planted the trees. There had been hardly any trees in the town when her family moved here.

Her memory wandered. She knew if she looked around the group, she'd know almost every face. Many of them were old settlers, like herself. Most of the rest were their children or grandchildren. She knew the stories of most of their lives, knew the businesses they'd started, the dreams that had thrived, the ones that hadn't, had seen young love grow deeper in marriages, had seen hearts broken, like her own.

Together, these people had built this town, made it what it was today. She was part of them, and they were part of her. It was special, feeling she belonged to something larger than herself. In a way, as much as she disliked the interest the townspeople were showing in her escorts, she felt she was betraying her friends by allowing the pastor to escort her, as if her very behavior was a falsehood. *I must tell him I can't see him anymore,* she decided.

Her decision made, she turned her attention back to the hymns. She did love singing, especially hymns. She could tell the pastor did, also, though the comments he'd made about his voice back at the house weren't much of an exaggeration.

She saw Constance and her family across the crowd and smiled at her. As her gaze swept the crowd, it met Mr. Copperfield's. His scowl showed he wasn't pleased she'd attended with Pastor Green instead of himself. Libby was glad she wasn't attending such a happy event with such an unhappy man.

Spencer stood on the other side of Ida, but Libby could hear his voice booming out on the familiar verse, "Oh, how I love Jesus!" Her heart crimped at the sound. *If only it were true!* she cried silently.

Why had he come tonight? She hoped he hadn't asked Ida to accompany him, at least not in a manner that would indicate he intended the evening to be more than friends spending time together. She didn't for a moment believe he was interested in Ida, and she didn't want her friend's feelings hurt.

She was sure he hadn't come because he loved to praise the Lord; not after the conversation they'd had on the beach.

It was becoming increasingly difficult to have him near. She wasn't sure how much longer she could bear seeing him and knowing they couldn't be together. Perhaps eventually his love for her would dissolve when he realized she would not change her mind, perhaps realize for himself that their love couldn't survive if they didn't share their faith. She didn't want that to happen either—for their love to actually die.

She glanced at him over Ida's head. How often in church as a young woman and again during the last few weeks she had imagined them standing together in church, worshipping the Lord from their hearts. If only it could be true. If only—

Her heart continued the prayer it had started so many years before.

⁂

Spencer bent into the movement of the oars. The current had been getting stronger the last few days. The river was slowly rising, too. Both were to be expected. It was normal for the river to crest the middle of May in this part of the country, give or take a week. Unless he was mistaken, the Jennie Lee would be ready to float off the sandbar in a week, maybe a week and a half.

His mind drifted back to Libby, as it always did, as faithfully as a compass needle pointed north. It had been fun at the hymn-sing tonight, but he would have enjoyed it more as Libby's escort.

He grinned into the night. It had done his heart good to see the uncertainty in the pastor's eyes when he'd come up the walk with Libby, especially after the beating that heart had taken from Libby earlier in the day.

He looked up at the stars. "Why do I keep handing my heart over to her to slice up? You'd think I'd learn. She does it every time. But I know she loves me, I know it. I can see it in her face. Everything about her betrays her love, but she won't speak it. Instead she keeps trying to push me away. I don't understand. How can a love for You be so strong she won't go against her beliefs and marry me?"

He snorted. There he went again, talking to that God he didn't believe in.

It was beautiful out on the river tonight, with the moonlight shining off the limestone cliffs. He rounded the bend and saw the lights of the Jennie Lee. He didn't light the entire boat, but he always made sure there were enough lights burning that other boats would see her. Not only darkness was a threat; mornings on the river were often foggy. The Jennie Lee was grounded out of the usual travel lanes, but still, one couldn't be too careful. He wondered for the fiftieth time what the pilot had been thinking to be sailing so far out of the usual steamboat path when the Jennie Lee hit the bar.

He hoped the spring crest would free the Jennie Lee before some large debris carried by the high water hit her. At least there shouldn't be any danger from log floats. Back when he and Libby had been courting, it was common to pile the huge cut pines in the forests up north on the frozen river during the winter and float them down to the sawmills at places like St. Anthony and River's Edge. Why, he could remember when a man could walk across the Mississippi hereabouts on logs.

His glance slid along the bluffs on either side of the river. No mysterious lights in sight. Of course, on such a brightly lit night as this, lights might not be necessary.

The light watchers had apparently given up for the night. He hadn't seen many boats out on his way home.

He was pretty well convinced that Effie and Evan were at least partially right in their beliefs about those lights. Someone was searching for something, and the dead captain's rumored treasure was as likely a goal as anything. There were plenty of tales of hidden and lost treasure along the length of the Mississippi. But he hadn't a doubt the searchers were made of flesh and blood. He'd never heard of a lost treasure tale that didn't bring out people looking for an easy way to wealth. He shook his head at the thought of it. It didn't sound like the easy way to him.

Once on board, he started around the lower deck, taking his usual check of the boat before retiring. He grinned, laughing at himself. "Old habits die hard, I guess."

Entering his cabin at last, he stretched, looking forward to the comfort of bed. His foot struck something, and he stumbled, hearing a crash.

In the light of the moon coming through the open door, he saw an unlit tin lantern lying on its side, a pane of glass broken. The hair on his neck rose to attention, sending a prickly sensation along his nerves. Slowly, he knelt down and righted the lantern. It wasn't his. He hadn't set any lanterns inside the door. He didn't even have any tin lanterns on board; they were all brass.

Was whoever left it still on board? His mind raced through the path he'd just taken through the boat. He'd thought he'd looked at everything, into every room, but he knew there were hundreds of places a person could have hidden.

Why did they leave their lantern behind? he wondered. Maybe they'd forgotten it because they hadn't needed it on deck in the moonlight. What were they looking for? That question wasn't so easily answered.

Well, sleep is out of the question until I convince myself I'm alone on board. He glanced about his quarters, looking for something easy to carry that was heavy enough to serve as a weapon in case he needed one for self-defense. He settled on an old spyglass.

Keeping as much as possible to the shadows, he made his way along the texas, looking into each stateroom. Nothing.

He'd checked the pilothouse last thing before entering his own quarters on his first check, so ruled out the need to look there again. Taking each step as quietly as he could, he made his way down the steps to the next deck, his heart in his throat. It would be easy for a man to hide beneath the stairs and attack him before he even knew he was there.

Quit imagining things! one part of his brain ordered. *Pretty soon you'll have yourself believing in Effie and Evan's ghost.*

It's not imagination, it's caution, another part of his brain assured him.

Neither voice stilled the fear rippling through him.

He was gripping his spyglass so tightly the muscles in his hand were cramping. He changed hands, flexing the fingers in his right hand.

He took a deep breath when he reached the bottom of the stairway. Swung his head quickly to the left, then the right, but saw no one leaping to attack him. His breath whooshed out in relief.

For a moment, he looked around uncertainly. Which way should he go first? To the left or right? Maybe the wisest move would be to see whether there were any boats alongside the Jennie Lee. There hadn't been when he'd returned, at least on the side nearest shore, where he'd tied the boat at the bottom of the rope ladder.

His senses were heightened. His ears hurt from trying to hear anything unusual. The sound of the river lapping against the boat's hull was louder than normal. Every ordinary creak of the boat made him want to jump.

He took a long look up the deck, studying each shadow, waiting to see if any of the shadows moved. Tightening his hold on the spyglass, he moved quickly to the railing and looked over. Nothing but water.

He glanced again in each direction. Behind him. Nothing stirred.

Swallowing the lump of fear in his throat, he began searching the passenger deck.

By the time he'd completed the search, poking his head into every nook and cranny he could think of that could possibly hide a man, his chest hurt from the many times he'd held his breath. He'd found nothing, but he wasn't reassured by his search. It had taken over an hour. It would be easy for a person, or more than one, to have slipped back to an area he'd already searched.

So what should I do? Leave my own home? It was tempting to climb into his rowboat and leave, he had to admit, but he wasn't going to give into his fears that easily.

What were they looking for? He still didn't know the answer to that question. It was well known in town now that he lived on the boat. It was probably just a common thief who left the lantern.

Or Effie and Evan's treasure hunter.

More likely, it was left by some of the light watchers. A lot of them had asked to come aboard the Jennie Lee, where they could watch in comfort, as he'd told Libby. Matter of fact, more than once he'd found people who had boarded in order to find him and ask permission to stay. He wouldn't be at all surprised if some of them had taken advantage of his time in town to use the boat.

The possibility eased his fears enough that he headed up to the texas and his quarters, but it was almost dawn before he fell into a fitful sleep. It was the first time since he'd decided to return to River's Edge that he fell asleep with something other than Libby on his mind.

Chapter 15

B ye, Captain!" Effie waved, starting off for the path that led to the top of the bluff.

"Bye, Captain! Thanks for everything. We had a great time." Evan waved and headed down the narrow, barely visible path through the scrubby growth at the bottom of the bluff. Thunder, their neighbor's little white fluff of a dog, trotted at his heels.

"Good-bye!" Spencer stood on the narrow beach, watching them, frowning, until they were out of sight, hidden by the thick underbrush between the break in the bluffs.

Worry crawled through his stomach. Should he have let them go alone? Why not? Hadn't Constance and Justin said they might walk home alone? The path, though overgrown here, was well known to the townspeople and well used. It led to a dirt road by which people often came out to picnic. They should be safe. "Something just doesn't feel right."

Quickly, he checked the rowboat to make sure it was pulled up far enough onto shore and hauled out the anchor and wound the anchor rope around a tree, to be doubly sure the boat wouldn't float off. Then he turned and started toward the path.

"Captain Matthews! Hello!"

He turned toward the river and voice in surprise. He wasn't expecting anyone.

A young man waved from a rowboat out near the Jennie Lee. "Hello, Captain!"

Spencer squinted, trying to make out the face. "Why, it's Adams."

The man was obviously heading toward shore. Spencer waited impatiently. He looked over his shoulder toward the path, eager to join the children.

Adams nosed the bow of his boat up to shore and jumped out into the shallow water, paying no mind that the water went over the ankles of his boots. Spencer grasped the nose of the boat and hauled it further onto shore.

"Thanks." Adams's skinny fingers settled on his lean hips, and he looked toward the bluffs, his constant smile in place. "Nice. Must be like ownin' your own piece of river, livin' on a river queen and havin' a piece of shore to rest on whenever you've a mind to."

"I like it," Spencer admitted, cautiously, "even though my river queen's a bit shabby."

"That's what I'm here 'bout. Wondered if you'd thought any 'bout my offer ta help out."

Spencer rubbed the back of his neck. "Have to admit, I haven't."

Adams shrugged his shoulders up about his ears in a manner that reminded Spencer of a turtle trying to decide whether to hide or stick its neck out. "Is that a no?"

"No. It meant exactly what I said. I haven't thought about it."

Adams nodded, his head bouncing. "Well, guess that's good. You see, it's like this. I got to thinkin', maybe if I helped you out with the boat, you'd let me stay on board." He shook his head, still grinning. "You know how it is. Stay on land too long, I begin to feel like my bones clank."

Spencer's mouth tugged in a smile. "Yes, I do know."

"I'm a hard worker. I'll be glad ta help you just for a bed."

Spencer hadn't any doubt the man was a willing worker. He'd seen him about the docks often enough, and he'd never appeared to be shirking or lolly-gagging. "I'm sure your help would be worth more than a bed."

Adams gave a sharp little nod. "Thank ya."

Spencer studied the wiry man's eyes. *No reason not to hire him, I guess. Could sure use the help.* "All right. I'll show you what I'd like done. If you still want to stay on after that, we'll talk about pay."

Adams's grin widened. "Thank ya. That sounds good ta me."

Spencer had the absurd impression that Adams's grin was as permanent as a rag doll's. He turned for a last look at the path the children had taken. They had quite a head start on him. He'd probably never catch up to them now. Still, he wavered for a moment. Should he head after them?

"Captain?"

It's likely too late. I'm being a paranoid old man. What harm could come to them along the path on the road to town? He swung around. "Let's head out to the Jennie Lee."

An hour later, he and Adams had worked out an agreement, and Adams had started back to River's Edge to retrieve his few belongings. Spencer looked out the pilothouse window toward the bluffs, unease drifting into his chest like smoke, definitely there, but intangible, unable to be grasped. *Why can't I shake this silly fear?*

The limestone bluffs stared back at him, mute.

The lights had danced along those bluffs again last night. The children had stayed overnight with him on the boat. They'd been fascinated by the lights. It had rained the last three days, but the storm had moved off just in time for Effie and Evan's visit. The sky last night had been clear and starlit.

Before the lights came out, the children had asked him to tell them stories of other hidden and lost treasure along the Mississippi. He'd enjoyed the telling of them, embellishing them as he had when his own children were small. Between his stories and the lights, he'd thought the children would never calm down enough to sleep.

"Should have known better. My own boys would have reacted the same way when they were Effie and Evan's age."

He'd seen the lights too many times not to have wondered about them. *Are they from lanterns carried by people looking for the rumored treasure? Maybe those who are carrying the lanterns are trying to attract attention from the areas where they are concentrating their search.*

Of course the lights were carried by humans. No doubt in his mind about that. But who?

River's Edge was a small town. Surely if the treasure hunters were residents, someone would notice them missing every night, or tracking limestone around on their boots, or sleeping all day because they'd been working all night.

"Could be newcomers or strangers in town," he mused. "Maybe bachelors, men whose actions no one would notice."

That man who had asked Libby to the pie dinner, the one she'd turned down, the one with the crimped face, was a newcomer and a bachelor. "Old Sour Lemons," he remembered, grinning. "Almost wish he was courting Libby. Sure would have a lot more faith in my ability to win her away from him than from Daniel."

Daniel. Another newcomer and unmarried. Spencer considered the possibility. Shook his head. He couldn't imagine Daniel clandestinely climbing the bluffs looking for treasure.

Of course, the river and railroad brought strangers to town every day. The treasure hunters could be one of a hundred men or more, he guessed. He snorted. "Why waste my time on it? Treasure hunters aren't thieves. If they want to climb about on cliffs at night, who am I to say they shouldn't?"

A movement toward the bottom of the bluff near where the path disappeared into the underbrush caught his eye. He scowled, trying to make out the form that was emerging. "What! Surely not!"

He grabbed the spyglass. Peered through it. It was. "Libby! What's she doing here?"

His heart took off like a pheasant routed from hiding during hunting season. She was actually coming to him, without the children prodding or any coercion, for the first time since he came to River's Edge.

He raced out of the pilothouse and down to the texas. Did he dare let himself hope she came to let him know she cared?

He threw himself against the railing. "Libby! Stay there. I'll take the boat and meet you!"

Spencer made the trip from the texas to the rowboat in record time. He fumbled with the knot securing the rowboat to the paddle wheeler, wasting precious minutes with it. When he arrived at shore, after much too much time according to his heart's calculations, he slipped the boat along the exposed roots of a tree, where he could jump out quickly without getting soaked.

Libby stood silently, watching him tie the boat to the tree. Spencer thought she looked great in her navy blue walking suit and prim straw hat with matching navy blue ribbon about the crown.

He was beside her in a few strides, feeling as though his grin couldn't grow any wider. He reached for her hands. "Libby, what are you doing here?"

"I came for the children. Are they on the boat?"

His chest felt like a band had been bound around it. "They left for home over an hour ago. Constance and Justin had said they might walk home. They took the path up the bluff to meet the road into town. You must have come by the same path. Didn't you meet them?"

She shook her head. Her eyes were wide with fear. Her hands clutched his. "Constance decided she would feel better if someone met the children and took them home. She and Justin couldn't come, so they asked if I would. I took the carriage as far as possible and the path the rest of the way." She glanced down at her feet, and Spencer's gaze followed hers. Limestone mud from the bluff path caked her high, buttoned boots and colored the hem of her skirt.

Her gaze slid back up to meet his. "Where can they be?" Her voice cracked on the whisper.

He couldn't bear to look into the terror in her eyes. His arms slipped around her. He pressed her cheek against his shoulder and touched his lips to her hair. "Shhh, dearest. It will be all right. We'll find them."

He squeezed her tightly, trying to will strength and hope into her, then took one of her hands in his. "Come on. We'll follow the path. They must have turned off to explore somewhere. You know Effie and Evan. If an adventure calls, they'll answer."

She followed along, one hand trying to hold her skirt back from twigs and sticky weeds. Her quick steps kept up with his long strides. "You—you don't think they've gone looking for the dead captain's hidden gold, do you?"

It was exactly what he thought. Wished he didn't. "I guess we'll find out."

The path was still almost level with the ground about it and had only begun to rise, when he began to call. "Effie! Evan!"

Libby joined in. "Effie! Evan! Where are you?"

Soon the path began to climb. It had developed over the years by people following the easiest way down to the river from the top of the bluffs, so it was not too narrow or difficult to walk in most places. Spencer soon realized why Libby's shoes were so mud-covered. The rains had left the path soaked and slippery. The mud almost oozed about his shoes, clutching at each of his steps. Even so, he could see in the mud where Libby had slipped and slid along the steeper parts.

"Effie! Evan!"

He or Libby repeated the call every few moments. He turned to smile reassuringly at her over his shoulder and squeeze the hand he still held. Her fingers were clutched about his like a vise wrapped in soft cloth. She was holding up well.

"Effie! Evan!"

"Yip! Yip! Yip!"

He stopped. Listened so hard it felt like his ears were growing. Had he imagined it? "Did you hear that?"

"Hear what?" Libby asked.

Imagination, or wishful thinking that he'd heard Thunder's high yip. He tried to push away his disappointment and kept walking. "Effie! Evan!"

"Yip! Yip! Yip!"

"I did hear it!" He stopped so suddenly that Libby walked right into him. He felt her clutching his coat to keep from slipping. "Did you hear it that time?"

She shook her head.

"I thought I heard Thunder."

He watched her, standing still as stone, listening. Nothing. "Effie! Evan!"

"Yip! Yip! Yip!"

Libby's eyes widened. Joy flooded them. "I heard him!"

"They can't be too far. Thunder wouldn't have left them." They started up the path again, faster, calling, then listening. A couple yards farther along, another sound joined Thunder's barking, a sound that sent fear pumping through Spencer's veins.

"Help!"

Let it be my imagination, he prayed.

"Effie! Evan!" Libby called.

"Shhh!" Spencer turned around and clasped his hand firmly but gently over her mouth. *She doesn't hear it,* he realized. "Listen."

He saw the question in her eyes and looked away. He didn't want to see the fear in her eyes when she heard. Made himself look back. He wanted to be there for her, needed to be there for her.

"Yip! Yip! Yip!"

"Help! Help!"

Her eyes widened and filled with fright. He slid his hand from her mouth. "Effie?"

He nodded.

"O—o—oh!"

"We're right where we should be. The awful thing would be if we weren't where we could hear them."

She took a trembling breath. Nodded.

Spencer knew what he said was true, but he wished the words brought him more relief from fear. Why didn't they hear Evan calling? "Come on, let's find them." He squeezed her hand.

Her smile quivered.

His heart ached for her. Was she, too, silently wondering about Evan? He made a megaphone of his hands. "Effie! We're coming! Keep calling!"

She did. The calls changed from "Help" to "Over here!"

After what seemed several lifetimes, Spencer spotted a place where someone had slid off the path into the scrubby woods. He pointed out the signs in the mud to Libby and led the way into the trees.

The branches were thick and low. They had to push their way through them. Spencer was careful not to let any whip back and hit Libby. He thought he spotted signs others had passed that way; broken branches, the fallen leaves of years pushed slightly to one side here and there, as if a step had slid in them. He continued calling as they went and breathed easier as Effie's voice grew louder.

"Up here! Look up!"

They did. At least twenty feet above them, just at the height where the tree-tops began to hide the limestone cliff faces from view, he saw her.

Effie was evidently lying down. Spencer could see her fingers over the edge of the ledge she was looking over. A grin burst over her face. "You found us!"

"Thank God!" Libby clutched Spencer's arm with both hands.

Thunder peeked over the edge. "Yip! Yip!" Backed away.

"I knew you'd find us!"

Spencer wished he'd been as sure. "Are you all right? Have you been hurt?" he called. *Find out about her first, then ask about Evan,* he told himself.

"No, but we can't get down. Evan's over there. He can't get to me, either." She pointed to her left.

Spencer's gaze followed along the narrow ledge that ran in the direction she pointed. *Must be how they got where they are,* he realized. But where was Evan?

"I don't see him." Libby's voice was thick with worry.

He placed a hand over hers, where she still clutched his arm. He moved through the trees in the direction Effie had indicated, trying to watch the cliff as he walked.

He stopped abruptly. Blood drained from his heart.

Instinctively, his arms circled Libby, drawing her against his chest to shield her from the inevitable pain and fright.

Evan stood on the narrow ledge as if his back were glued to the cliff wall. On either side of him, the ledge had slipped away. No more than two feet of ledge was left.

Chapter 16

"Oh, no!" Libby's horror-filled whisper squeezed Spencer's heart unbearably. His arms tightened about her. "Evan is safe for now. We'll get him down." *Or I'll die trying,* he promised both of them silently. "No wonder we haven't heard him calling."

"He's probably too frightened to let out a breath."

Evan seemed to be looking in their direction. Spencer wasn't sure whether or not he could see them through the trees. He sensed Libby was about to call to Evan. "We don't want to startle him."

He felt her nod against his shoulder.

He took a deep breath. "Hi, Evan!" he called, trying to keep his voice light and friendly. "Your aunt Libby and I are here. We see you, tadpole! Don't you worry, now. I'm going to get you down. Okay?"

Evan's head barely moved in a nod.

Libby wrapped her hands around one of Spencer's arms again and leaned her head against his shoulder. He felt her shake as she took a breath, and he leaned his cheek briefly against the top of her head, keeping his attention on Evan.

"Give us wisdom, Lord," he heard her whisper, "and keep Evan safe."

Anger surged through him. *I'm the one who has to save Evan, not God!* He tried to push his fury away. Through his years as a steamboat captain, he'd learned that anger had no place in an emergency; it only clouded good judgment.

"Evan," he called, "I'm going down to the rowboat to get a rope. I'll go as fast as I can, I promise. You're doing fine up there. Your aunt Libby's going to stay right here and talk to you until I get back. Okay?"

Again, Evan's head barely moved. "H–hurry!"

Spencer barely caught the word, but his heart constricted at the sound of it. "I'm leaving right now, Evan!" He looked down at Libby. "Talk to him. Talk about anything. Let him keep hearing your voice so he knows he's not alone."

"I will." She released his arm. The terror in her eyes made him want to take her in his arms again and make the fear go away, but the only way he could make it go away was to get those kids down safe.

"You're a strong woman, Libby. You can do it." He turned and started running back the way they'd come, crashing through the trees. *Can Evan hear all the racket I'm making? I hope so. Hope he knows it's the sound of help coming as soon as possible.*

By the time he'd reached the main path, his face and hands were covered with scratches from the branches he'd pushed through. Somewhere he'd lost his hat. He slipped and slid down the path to the river. A couple times he'd thought he'd lose a boot to the mud.

Things weren't any easier at the rowboat. He spent many frustrated minutes trying to undo the knot securing the anchor so he could take the rope back up the hillside. He considered going out to the Jennie Lee to try to find a rope, but the rowboat's anchor rope was long and strong, just what he needed.

By the time he got back to Libby, his chest burned and his legs ached from the unusual exertion.

"Captain Matthews is back," Libby called to Evan when Spencer came into her sight.

"Hi, Evan!" Spencer tried to make his voice cheerful. "You're doing fine up there. You've got a better view than any pilot in a pilothouse."

She looked at the rope, then met Spencer's gaze. She looked anxious. "What are you going to do?"

"I don't know yet." Trying to get his panting under control, he stared at the cliff and the trees about them. None of the trees were close enough to Evan or Effie to be of any help. The cliff walls were sheer and treeless. "Don't see how we can get to the kids from here. We'll have to see if we can get to them from up above."

"But how can you do that? The ledge is gone, and it's a straight drop from the top to where the children are."

"I know. We'll have to see what's up there that we can turn to our advantage. How's Evan doing?"

"He's terrified."

"Effie?"

"She's all right. There's a cave behind her, she says, so she isn't in imminent danger like Evan, though she can't climb up or down, either."

"Need to check some things out, Evan," Spencer called. "We won't be talking to you for a couple minutes, but we're still here. We won't leave without you and Effie, I promise."

Spencer headed back toward Effie, trying to study the broken ledge through the trees. If he could somehow reach the cave, maybe he'd be able to find a way to reach Evan from there by an outcropping or by still-intact pieces of ledge.

Nothing looked promising. He tried to ignore the hopelessness that was creeping into his brain and heart, dulling his ability to look for solutions. *Pull yourself together. Giving up won't help.* Maybe he should send Libby back to River's Edge for assistance. It was a long way, but she'd said she'd left the carriage up on the bluff near the road, and—

"That's it!"

"What's it?" Libby held a branch aside as she moved to his side.

"The carriage! I'll tie the rope around myself, tie the other end around the harness shaft. I'll climb down to the kids from the bluff, and the horse will pull us up."

Libby's face went white. "That sounds dangerous."

"Not as dangerous as leaving Evan on that eroding ledge." His steps quickened. "I'll need you to come up top with me to lead the horse."

He stopped again below Effie and called to her that they were going up top. "Be sure to let Evan know, in case he can't hear us."

"Are you leaving?" Effie yelled.

"Not a chance." Spencer could hear the fright in her voice. *More like barely disguised hysteria,* he thought. Not surprising, though he knew there wasn't much that frightened that spunky girl. "I think I'll be able to reach you and Evan better from the top, that's all."

"Why don't you sing some of your favorite songs, Effie?" Libby suggested. "Maybe 'Oh, How I Love Jesus.'"

"Okay."

As he hurried toward the path, Spencer could hear her sweet young voice singing out words that sounded absurd to him under the circumstances: "Oh, how I love Jesus, because He first loved me."

As soon as he came out on top of the bluff, his eyes searched the small clearing. On the far side, the horse, still attached to the carriage, was tied to an oak. "Sweetest sight I've seen in all my years." He glanced at Libby. "Will you get the horse? I'll let the kids know we're here and see if I can find a good place to lower myself over the edge."

She bit her lip, looking worried at his words, but she nodded and started off in a run.

She must be exhausted, he thought, moving along the edge of the bluff, *but she's still running. Must be love for the kids fueling her.*

The horse was young, strong, and best of all, not skittish. "He's from Justin's stables," Libby told him.

He was relieved. He'd expected a horse from a public stable. Usually rather docile animals, but no telling what to expect in strength or willingness to perform some unusual stunt such as he was about to ask.

Quickly, Spencer checked the carriage and its boot.

Libby shifted anxiously. "What are you looking for?"

"Anything that might help us out in the rescue attempt." All he found was a lap robe and a short carriage whip.

Giving up his fruitless search, he started preparations for his climb. He attached one end of the anchor rope to one of the wooden shafts connecting the horse to the carriage and tied the other end around himself, using a strange cradle-like configuration. The rope went around his waist, through his legs, around one thigh, through his belt buckle, back through his legs and around the other thigh. He grinned at Libby. "At least I've learned how to tie a few good knots during my years as a river man."

She almost smiled.

He explained what he wanted her to do, guiding the horse. Fear passed over her already-pale face, followed by determination. She squared her shoulders and looked him right in the eye. "I can do that."

He touched his fingers to her cheek. "I never doubted it. We're going to get those kids up here safe and sound, Libby. We're going to do it together."

She nodded. "Together."

Spencer checked the knots fastening the rope about him one last time. Not that he thought it was necessary, but he didn't think Libby would appreciate it if he was looking her in the face when he asked his next question. "Can I have your petticoat?"

There wasn't an answer. Didn't appear to be any movement, either. At least, the hem of her skirt, easily visible to him, hadn't risen an inch. He glanced up. "Is that a no?"

Her face was no longer pale. "I–I'm not wearing a petticoat." She lifted her skirt about six inches. The bottom of ruffled and bowed pantaloons peeked out cheerfully, though wearing a muddy facial after Libby's trips up and down the bluff path.

He couldn't contain his grin. "Great. Those will do even better. Take them off, will you?" He turned his back.

"Here," she said a minute later. "What—what are you going to do with them?"

"Might need something extra to secure Evan to me," he answered, tying them around his waist.

When he was done, he laid his hands on Libby's shoulders. "Ready?"

She bit her lip and nodded. "Be careful."

He fought back the desire to take her in his arms and kiss her, just in case things didn't work out the way they were supposed to work out, but he didn't want her to sense his fear. He knew that would only make things harder for her.

He settled for giving her a wink.

The thought flashed through his mind that in addition to praying for Evan and Effie, she'd be praying for him while he attempted to rescue the children. It didn't comfort him, but he suddenly understood that her prayers were a way of loving him and the children, a way for her to go beyond her ability to physically help and protect them.

Back at the cliff, he called down over the edge. "I'm coming down, Evan. You don't have to look up. You'll know when I get there."

The thought of stepping back over the edge of the cliff, even with a horse tied to the other end of the rope, was more frightening than Spencer wanted to admit to himself. He hadn't done this in years. Not, in fact, since he'd been a young man and used to slip down over cliffs along this same line of bluffs with his friends—more than thirty-five years ago!

When I came back to River's Edge, I wanted to recapture some of my youth, but this is ridiculous!

"Ready, Libby?"

Standing with her hand on the horse's harness, she nodded.

He took a deep breath, gave Libby a grin, and stepped back into space.

Chapter 17

Spencer lowered himself down, heart in his throat. He could hear Effie, still singing. A reminder he would be doing this again if. . .no, when, this first mission was accomplished.

He'd told Libby to keep the horse a few feet back from the edge. The horse wasn't lowering Spencer; it would instead be used to pull him and Evan back up. Still, whenever the horse moved, Spencer would drop a couple of feet or be yanked up a couple of feet unexpectedly, sometimes swinging hard against the cliff wall. By the time he was almost to Evan and had called to Libby to stop, his hands were already torn and bruised from the rope and rock.

He saw in a flash it wouldn't be wise to add his weight to Evan's on the remaining piece of ledge. Instead, he walked himself down the wall until he was alongside Evan. "How's the Jennie Lee's future pilot?"

Huge brown eyes beseeched him. "I w–want to g–get down!"

"That's why I'm here. I won't leave without you, I promise." Spencer steeled himself against the boy's terror and the sob-like shaking in his voice. He could see traces of tear trails on Evan's cheeks.

"I'm s–scared!"

"That's all right." Spencer tried to reassure the boy while analyzing the situation. "You've done just what you should. You stayed put, waited for help, didn't move around too much. When a man does what he should do, even when he's scared, he's brave. I'm proud of you, Evan. Now, just let me take a good look at things here, and then we'll get started."

"O–o–kay."

He could feel the boy's eyes watching every move of his eyes. Spencer disciplined his face not to show his emotions. He didn't want the boy to see his fear.

Evan was still pasted to the wall. Couldn't be closer to it if he'd been sculpted from it, Spencer thought. Discouragement washed through him. He'd hoped to find a way to secure Evan to himself with Libby's pantaloons, but he could see there wasn't any chance the boy would move his body far enough away from the cliff wall that he could fit the pantaloons around him.

"Here's what we're going to do, Evan. I'm going to step in front of you on that ledge. As soon as I do, I'm going to pick you up. I want you to put your arms around my neck and hold on tight. Then wrap your legs around my waist. Got it?"

Evan nodded.

Spencer knew they'd need to act quickly. He wasn't certain that little piece of rock would hold his weight as well as Evan's, even for a minute. As soon as his boots touched the remaining ledge, he slid both arms to one side of the rope and reached for Evan's waist.

The sound of pebbles bouncing down the cliff below them sent terror spiraling through him.

He yanked Evan up and against his chest. Felt the boy's arms squeeze his neck and the skinny legs wrap around his waist. Evan's chest shook against his own.

Spencer leaned forward until Evan's shoulders were against the wall again. "I'm going to tie you to me before we start up. To do that, I'll have to let go of you for a minute."

"No!" Evan's hold grew impossibly tighter.

"You'll be safer when I'm done. Just hold on tight to me with your arms and legs. Don't let go, no matter what happens."

He felt Evan's nod against his cheek.

Spencer undid the knot at his side. *If that ledge goes before I finish tying him—*

He didn't let himself finish the thought.

Sweat slid down his forehead, stinging his eyes with salt, while he slid a pantaloons leg between Evan's back and the rope. "Hear your sister singing? She has a good voice."

He tried to keep casual talk going to calm Evan somewhat. "Guess you know how the Jennie Lee feels now, stuck on that sandbar unable to go wherever she wants."

The ledge began to shift beneath his feet. His hands stopped. His heart leaped to his throat. He tried to swallow it. Tried again. "How about when we get her off that old sandbar if you and I take her out on the river and I let you take the wheel?"

Voice creaked like an old riverboat in a storm, he thought in disgust, knotting the pantaloons legs to the rope where it was tied about his own waist. With the completion of the knot came a sliver of relief. In case something happened, the pantaloons might give him an extra few seconds to grab the boy and react.

"All done. Ready to go up?"

Evan nodded.

Spencer dropped back his head to call to Libby.

The ground moved beneath his feet.

His stomach turned over.

A moment later, he and Evan dropped through space, coming to a jolting halt six feet below where the ledge had been. Evan's scream rang in Spencer's ear.

Help us, God! I can't save him alone! The words roared in his mind. His arms clenched about the boy. He swung his body to catch the brunt of the blow as they smashed against the cliff. A small shower of dirt and rubble poured over them. He slipped one hand behind Evan's head. "It's all right. I've got you."

A heart was racing faster than floodwaters on the Mississippi. Spencer wasn't sure whether it was his or Evan's. Both, he decided.

"Spencer? Evan? Are you all right?"

"We're fine, Libby."

"What happened?"

He ignored her question. "Evan and I are ready to get back up top. Start moving the horse back, slowly."

Even with the horse doing most of the work, it was a long way back up. Spencer kept constant vigil, trying to keep Evan from colliding with the wall.

When they were finally on top, Spencer and Evan collapsed in a pile on the ground. Evan broke into quiet sobs. Libby raced over to them, dropping to her knees, and throwing her arms around them.

A moment later, she was yanking at the knot in the pantaloons that held Evan to Spencer, comforting Evan with soft chatter. Spencer stayed where he was, panting, watching her. Her eyes glittered suspiciously, but she wasn't crying.

His heart swelled with love of her. *You are some woman, Libby.*

He couldn't rest for long. There was still Effie to rescue. After examining the rope to be sure it hadn't been dangerously damaged and checking the knots to ensure they were still secure, he prepared for the next descent.

The ordeal wasn't nearly as trying this time. He and Libby and the horse all knew what they were doing. The ledge in front of the cave where Effie was located appeared strong and secure.

When he landed on it, Effie threw herself against him, wrapping her arms about his waist, almost knocking him off into space. "Captain!"

Steadying himself, he hugged her. "Hi, there, tadpole."

Thunder jumped about, yipping a greeting.

"Ready to go back up top, Effie?"

She let loose her hold and grabbed one of his hands. "First, I want to show you what I found in the cave."

Spencer's laugh boomed out, releasing the tension he hadn't realized had built in his chest muscles. *Trust Effie to be more concerned with adventure than with her own safety! Why, she doesn't appear frightened one whit.*

Effie frowned, touching a row of ruffles on the pantaloons legs tied about his waist. "What's this?"

Briefly, he explained. Then he called up to Libby that Effie was safe and unharmed and that they wouldn't be ready to ascend for a few minutes. He turned to Effie and chuckled. "Did you find the captain's treasure?"

Her brown curls swung as she shook her head. "No."

They didn't have to go far. Just inside the mouth, behind a boulder, she pointed at a jumble of items. "Look!"

Spencer looked. "Picks, chisels, shovels, lanterns, tin buckets, ropes, matches, gunnysacks, even a blanket."

Effie wrinkled her nose. "The blanket's dirty and stinky. I thought I'd bring it out to sit on while I waited for you, but it was too awful."

He peered back into the low-ceilinged cave. Too dark to see anything. He could use the lanterns at his feet to explore further, but he hadn't the desire. Obviously, whoever was responsible for the lights people had been seeing along the bluff cliffs had stored things here. If he weren't exhausted from rescuing Evan and the need to get Effie safely back to the top of the bluff, he might be more inclined to look further into the cave.

He rested a hand on her shoulder. "Quite a find, Effie, but what do you say we get back to the top? Libby and Evan will be worrying about us."

Before heading back out to the ledge, he grabbed the rope from the treasure hunters' pile.

Back outside, Spencer looked out toward the river. He could barely see it through the trees. Treetops would almost completely hide the ledge and cave from view from the river or the opposite bank.

He explained to Effie how he planned to tie her to himself and how the horse would pull them back up. The idea of sliding up a cliff at the end of a rope didn't seem to disturb her a bit.

"Okay." She leaned down and picked up Thunder, who licked her nose. "We're ready."

He hadn't counted on this. "We can't take Thunder, tadpole. It's too dangerous."

She set her mouth in a manner that left no doubt of her intent. "Then I'm not going, either."

Spencer crouched down beside her. "You can't stay here. You know that."

"Neither can Thunder."

She's as stubborn as Libby. "I'll come back for Thunder after you're safe on top. He'll be safe here until then."

"I want to take him with me."

"I know that, Effie, but what if he slipped?"

"I'll hold him tight."

"Thunder might get scared and wiggle loose from your arms, even though I know you'd do everything you could to hold on to him. You don't want him to fall, do you?"

She didn't answer. Her eyes filled with tears but remained defiant.

"It will be safer for him if I come back for him alone, Effie."

"You won't drop him?"

"I won't drop him."

"Promise?"

"Promise."

Slowly, she knelt down, hugged Thunder tightly, and released him. "Be good, Thunder. Captain Matthews will be back for you in a few minutes." She dropped a kiss on Thunder's forehead, and he rewarded her once again with two quick little licks on the tip of her nose.

Thunder's whine followed them all the way up the cliff.

It wasn't long before Effie was in Libby's arms.

"One more trip," he told Libby.

He could see she didn't like the thought of him going back over the edge for a dog, but after a glance at the children's faces, she didn't argue. When he was back at the cave, he retrieved a gunnysack from the treasure hunters' stash. Thunder objected to being stuffed into it, but Spencer thought he had a better chance of not dropping the dog if he carried him in this manner.

The trip was successful. Effie and Evan, already recovering from his ordeal, fell on the dog as soon as Thunder crawled out of the sack. The little pink tongue worked as fast as the tail in telling the children how glad he was to be with them again.

Joy filled Libby's face as she watched them tumbling about each other.

Just seeing her like this is worth everything it took to save those kids, Spencer thought.

Her shining gaze turned to him and she reached for his hand. "Thank you."

He knew her heart was in those two simple words. He could feel it. She knew he would have rescued those children even if they weren't related to her, even if he didn't even know them. But he understood, too, how important it was to her that they were safe.

He squeezed her hand. "We did it together."

Once the four tired, muddy people and the muddy, still-wiggling dog climbed into the carriage and started toward River's Edge, Spencer asked, "How did you two find that ledge and cave? They're pretty well hidden by the trees."

"Last night we saw lights on the cliffs from the Jennie Lee, remember?" Effie asked.

Spencer nodded.

"Well," she continued, "we watched carefully. Then today, we tried to remember where on the cliffs we saw the lights. We tried to find that place. We had to climb around in the trees and rocks a lot, but finally, we found that ledge."

"We knew there were caves in the cliffs," Evan said. "Bandits have hidden things in the caves before."

"Yes," Effie interrupted. "So we just followed the ledge to the cave. Or at least, Thunder and me did. The ledge broke before Evan got to the cave." She gasped and turned quickly in her seat. "Evan, I almost forgot to tell you what I found in the cave!"

It took several minutes for Effie to tell Libby and Evan what she found, as she embellished the telling in her usual dramatic storytelling manner.

"Of course," she concluded, "it would have been better if we'd found the treasure or the treasure hunters."

Libby gasped.

Spencer reached for her hand. He knew what she was thinking; that if the treasure hunters had been there, they might have endangered the children further. "They weren't there," he reminded her in a low voice, not meant to carry to the children in the backseat.

"What?"

"Nothing, Effie."

Effie hung over the front of the seat between Spencer and Libby. "At least we proved one thing."

"What's that?" Libby asked.

"It's not a ghost carrying those old lanterns around. A ghost wouldn't need real lanterns, would he?"

"No, he wouldn't," Libby agreed. "Constance and Justin will be glad to know you found out it's people and not ghosts."

The children were quiet for a couple minutes. Finally, Effie spoke up in the most insecure tone Spencer had heard from her yet. "Do you think we need to tell Aunt Constance and Uncle Justin what happened?"

Spencer looked down at his chest and lap. The color of his clothes was barely discernable through the mud. He saw Libby's gaze following the same path, her eyes twinkling.

"Oh, yes, Effie." Libby smiled. "I don't think you can hide this one."

~&~

A couple hours later, after delivering the children home and explaining the situation to Justin and Constance, Spencer and Libby left the reunited family. Justin had kindly allowed them the use of his carriage for Spencer to take Libby home. Even in its confines, Libby was self-conscious about her mud-splattered appearance as they drove through town.

Don't be silly, she scolded herself. *The children are safe. What does it matter what people think of the way I look?*

She glanced at Spencer out of the corner of her eye. She'd been terrified she'd lose the children and Spencer, too, out on those cliffs. *Thank You, Lord, for saving them.*

Her glance dropped to his hands, which held the reins lightly. His hands were torn and bruised, dried blood mixed with mud covered them. Her heart contracted. All that painful damage caused by saving her niece and nephew.

She reached out and grasped the reins. "I'll drive."

He gave her a curious look. "I can drive."

"I know, but you needn't. I shouldn't have let you drive all this way with your hands as they are. They must hurt awfully."

He let her take the reins but didn't reply immediately. Finally he said, "They're beginning to throb. I didn't notice too much at first."

"When we get to my place, we'll wash and bandage them."

The sound of the carriage wheels and the horse's hooves and the noise of children playing in the early evening filled the silence between them for a few minutes.

They were only a couple blocks from her home when he cleared his throat. "I prayed up there, Libby, trying to save Evan. For the first time in thirty-five years, I really prayed."

Joy and hope flooded her. The energy the day's events had sapped came roaring back. She turned to meet his gaze. "You did?"

"I did. But you know something? You and I were the only ones helping that boy. I didn't see God reaching down to help out."

Pain replaced the joy that had filled her moments earlier. What could she say to him? He'd cried out to God on that cliffside. Even so, he wouldn't admit to himself that God had given him the wisdom and strength to save Evan, that God had left that little bit of path for Evan when the rest of the path slid down the bluff.

But he'd prayed. The words whispered through her mind. Somewhere, deep inside, beyond his logical mind perhaps, he'd realized he needed God's help.

She pulled the carriage alongside the carriage stoop in front of her cottage, driving carefully. She didn't drive often; she walked most places.

"I see Daniel's here again."

At Spencer's comment, Libby looked past him to the house. Ida and Pastor Green sat on the front porch. Libby lifted the watch set in a sterling silver heart pinned on her bodice and groaned. "I invited him to dinner tonight. I'd forgotten all about it."

"There was a time I would have found that encouraging. You're late for another evening with Daniel, and I'm escorting you while he waits."

She darted Spencer a dirty look. Her gaze and her attitude were stopped abruptly by the sad look in his eyes and his equally sad, small smile.

"Daniel is a good man, Libby. I don't see how you could do better. You should start treating him with more respect."

Without waiting for an answer, he climbed down from the carriage, then turned to help her down.

Libby felt as though burning coals filled her stomach. Her emotions were in a jumble. She was in no mood to answer all the questions she knew Ida and Pastor Green would pose when they saw the state of her and Spencer's clothing. All she wanted was to finish this discussion with Spencer.

What did he mean, saying those things about Daniel, Lord? She was terribly afraid he had meant he was giving up on her, giving up on the dream of them. Of course, she couldn't marry him, anyway, if he didn't love God, but. . .if he was giving up on them, was he closing the door forever on God, too? *I don't want him to close the door on either of us!*

Chapter 18

A couple days later, Spencer stepped into the Jennie Lee's dining hall to check on his hired help. Adams's lean body moved rhythmically while he scrubbed the salon walls with a brush and hot, soapy water.

"You're doing good work, Adams."

Adams stopped his rhythm to grin at him. "Glad to do it. Not exactly the kind of work I'm accustomed to, but I kinda like helpin' ta bring this lady back ta her old good looks."

Spencer smiled. "Me, too." Men who love boats and the river are always alike beneath the skin, he thought.

He wandered out onto the deck, noticing along the way the myriad of things that needed shining or cleaning or repairing or painting. Good thing he'd hired Adams. Sometimes he regretted having someone else on board. Never knew when the man would walk in on him. Still, he couldn't get any work done by himself right now.

He lifted his bandaged hands, rested the backs of them against the railing, and looked out over the river. Rope burns, blisters, and cuts and scrapes from the cliff rocks had turned his hands into swollen, useless appendages. It would be a week or so, the doctor said, until they lost their tenderness to the point he could get along without the bandages.

He was stiff all over, too. "Move like an old man," he complained.

Leaning against the railing, he sighed deeply. The familiar refrain of the river running past the Jennie Lee accompanied his memories of that day on the cliff. He'd relived that day more often than he'd like to admit, both waking and sleeping.

The story of the day's events had spread through River's Edge faster than water flows over a dam. He was considered the town's local hero. He snorted. A hero wasn't anyone but someone who did what needed to be done. What alternatives did a person have? It was almost humiliating, being treated as if he'd done something special. Did people think he and Libby could have left those children to try to save themselves?

He'd been deeply shaken by the events of that day. Even fighting wild river currents and storms, he'd never felt so helpless as when he saw Evan on the side of that bluff.

Something different shook him now that Evan and Effie were safe. As a riverboat captain, he'd relied on his own knowledge and logic to save himself and his boats and passengers through the years. *This time, I know You intervened, God.*

He wasn't ready to admit it to anyone else, especially to Libby. He could barely admit it to himself and God yet.

"So, where do we go from here, God?"

Later that day, he dug out the Bible he'd seen before in the captain's quarters. He couldn't remember the last time he'd opened a Bible. Probably back before he married.

"Humph! Was nothing more than a fool kid. Now that I've a few years on me, I've learned how little I knew about just about everything back then. Why should I have thought my beliefs about God were any more accurate than anything else I believed then?"

When he finally located the book, he took it outside, settled himself in a wooden deck chair in the sunshine, and opened it up. He'd been in church enough times throughout his life that he wasn't completely ignorant of the book. "Maybe I'll start with John. That's where that verse pastors are always quoting, John 3:16, is from: 'For God so loved the world, that he gave his only begotten Son, that whosoever believeth in him should not perish, but have everlasting life.'" He was a little surprised at the ease with which the verse he'd memorized as a boy came back to him.

He started at the beginning of John. He was still reading when Adams came up two hours later.

"How about if I catch some fish and prepare some lunch for us, Captain?"

"Thanks. I have some bread in my cabin we can have with the fish."

Loaves and fishes, he thought, amused, as he watched Adams leave. Then he turned back to the book. "Don't remember the Bible being this interesting when I was a youngster," he murmured.

He couldn't get enough of it. For the next few days, he was reading it every spare moment—and he had a lot of spare moments.

Adams was helping all over the boat now. On Friday, Spencer looked over some of the work he'd done and was pleased with it. "This isn't one of the most elegant paddle wheelers," he told Adams, "but it must have been a beauty when it was new."

"They always are, aren't they?" Adams agreed. "How about if I wash and wax the floor in your quarters? It was lookin' pretty bad last time I was up there."

"That's a good idea. By the way, I heard the Spartan has headed north. Should reach here in a few days."

"That's good news."

"I'm sure you'll be glad to get back to your old boat, but I'm going to miss your help around here."

Adams grinned his lazy grin. "Thanks. Water's risin' every day. Expect it'll be high enough soon to let the Jennie Lee float free. Found another place to beach her?"

"I'm going to try to rent a place at the landing in River's Edge."

Adams nodded. "Well, I'd best get started on that floor." He headed off.

Spencer walked about the boat, pleased with all that had been started on his restoration project.

"Must be how You feel about us, God." He'd fallen into the practice of talking to God often now, both out loud and silently. "I used to think religion was nothing but a theory and acts and rules, but it's not. You reach out to us and offer to repair the battered places in our souls, like I'm trying to repair this boat." He looked around and took a deep breath. "Well, God, I believe in Your Son, now, like John 3:16 says we must. I'd like You to come into my life and fix my battered places."

Libby wasn't surprised to see Spencer at church Sunday. He'd been there every Sunday since he arrived in River's Edge. But she hadn't forgotten his words about God not helping to save the children. A wave of hopelessness washed over her when she saw him sit down at the end of the pew beside Evan. *Please, Lord, don't give up on him,* she prayed again.

Effie stood up and moved from between Evan and Libby to the other side of Spencer. Libby and Constance shared a smile at the girl's actions. The children had taken to Spencer from the start. The events of the day on the cliff had given him a permanent place in their hearts.

Though the service was starting, the children were whispering eagerly to him. Libby could guess what they were saying. They wanted to spend the afternoon at the steamboat.

The introductory music stopped, and Libby could hear Effie's plea.

"We'll bring the lunch to thank you for saving us," Effie told him. "It's all ready. We brought the picnic basket. It's in the carriage. All you have to do is say yes."

Spencer's eyes twinkled. "Yes." Then he pointed to the front, where Pastor Green was speaking, indicating the children should stop talking.

Evan and Effie grinned at each other over Spencer's lap. Then Effie looked at Libby and formed her fingers into an "O," signifying everything was okay for the picnic.

After the service, the children hurried to Libby's side. "Captain Matthews said we can go to the Jennie Lee for a picnic. Let's hurry."

"Am I invited, too?"

"Of course!" Effie assured her. "It's a thank-you picnic for saving us, and you helped."

"She sure did," Spencer agreed.

Libby returned his smile. "The bandages are off your hands."

"Yes. They're still sore, but I can do most everyday things now if I'm careful. I can't row, though. That's too demanding."

"How will we get to the boat if you can't row?" Evan's voice was thick with disappointment.

"Adams, the man who is living on my boat and helping me out, rowed me into town for church. I'm sure he won't mind rowing us back out."

It was a pleasant trip out to the boat. She hadn't felt so relaxed around Spencer since he arrived in River's Edge. Something had changed. He seemed more peaceful, more settled, not as determined to push his way onto her. *Is it because he's given up on us, Lord? Please, don't let it be that!*

Once they'd boarded, the children's attention turned to the subject that had interested them for weeks.

"Have you seen any lights on the bluffs, Captain?" Evan asked.

"Not since you two found the cave. Expect the treasure hunters haven't been able to get to their lanterns since the ledge is broken."

The children, restless as ever, wanted to move around a bit before they ate. "Can we go to the pilothouse?" Evan begged. Spencer gave permission, and the twins headed for the pilothouse. Libby and Spencer watched them run down the deck, laughing.

"You look especially nice today, Libby. I like that hat."

"Thank you." It was a new little number that she especially liked. A feminine, low-crowned derby style with a wide green ribbon that matched her outfit around the crown and tied in a large bow at one side. Two pheasant feathers stuck perkily out of the bow.

"Would you like to see how much work has been done on the place since you were here last?" Spencer asked.

Libby nodded. "Very much."

The dining hall looked worse than before, with the drapes down. The brass, however, shone. "I need to paper this room," he told her. "Haven't chosen any yet. I'm not very good at things like that."

"I'd be glad to help you select some, if you'd trust my judgment."

"Of course I trust your judgment." Hands in his trouser pockets, he surveyed the long room. "A lot of decorating to be done. We'll need new draperies, upholstery, rugs, and likely things I'm not remembering. It will mean not only deciding on fabric, but hiring someone to make the items." He turned to her. "Would you help with those, too?"

She hesitated. She'd never decorated anything but her small home and her millinery shop. To decorate the hall sounded like such fun, but it also seemed an intimate thing to do for him and would require them spending a lot of time together. She loved spending time with him all together too much. It was time she put a halt to it.

"I'm sorry, Libby. I forgot for a moment that you have the shop to run. You don't have time to take on my projects."

Perhaps it was safer to allow him to believe his interpretation of her hesitation was correct than to destroy his friendliness this afternoon with the truth. The end result would be the same. "I will help with the wallpaper if you still wish it. Also, I can suggest someone to help with the rest."

They talked for a few minutes about colors and styles that he liked.

"What are you going to do with the Jennie Lee when you're finished restoring her?" Libby asked. "Surely you aren't going to live on her the rest of your life. It's a rather large home for one person."

Immediately she wished she could bite back her words. It sounded as though she were suggesting he ask her to marry him again!

If he thought so, he pretended not to notice. "I wasn't sure what I'd do with her when I started. Guess I thought my company—my sons' company now— could use another boat, though with the growth of railroads, steamboat travel is down to a trickle. Nothing to be done to turn the tide of progress back. Travel by rail is faster and, of course, tracks can be laid where rivers don't run."

"The change to railroads is too bad, I think, at least for passengers." Libby ran a fingertip along a brass bar that added a decorative point to the wall. "Steamboat travel is so much more luxurious and relaxing."

"I think so, too."

His voice had that gentle quality to it that it so often had when something they shared was discussed. Libby liked the way shared beliefs about even something this simple made her feel a warm connection with him. *I can only imagine how close we'd feel if we shared a faith in Christ.*

"The last few days," Spencer was continuing, "I've been thinking about the decline in steamboat travel. I'd like to put the Jennie Lee back in service, catering to people who want to enjoy the more leisurely form of travel for relatively short distances on the river; maybe from Prairie du Chien to St. Paul, for instance. It's a small boat, as paddle wheelers go. It would be a good size for that kind of service. What do you think?"

"It sounds like a lovely idea."

"Or maybe I'll move back to St. Louis and run the boat from there. The running season is pretty well year around below St. Louis."

Libby's blood seemed to freeze at his words. *Leave? I might never see him again!* Frustration at her ambivalence made her impatient with herself. Hadn't she just told herself she should stop spending time with him? But to never see him again! *Lord, I'm not ready for that.* Would she ever be?

"Be near the boys and their families in St. Louis, too," Spencer said.

"Yes. It's good to be near family. I wouldn't want to be away from Constance and the children." Her lips felt numb. All of her felt numb.

"I've discovered I'm not very good at this retirement business. Guess that's why I took on this project with the Jennie Lee. I could keep my hand in with the packet company I started if I chose, but I believe it's important for my boys to learn to run the business themselves. They're going to have some rough years ahead with changes in travel, but learning to make it through rough times is what makes a man."

What rough times is he thinking of from his own life? Libby wondered. *Those of his personal life or those from his business life that I don't know about?*

He took her elbow. "There are some changes I'd like to make in the captain's quarters, too. Would you mind looking at it with me and seeing what you think of my ideas?"

She nodded, still numb from his news, and allowed him to escort her out of the dining hall and toward the cabin.

The captain's quarters were quietly elegant. The rich paneling and walnut furnishings made it a beautiful room, in a manly sense. To Libby, it seemed a room in which Spencer would feel completely comfortable.

Although she'd seen the room before when Spencer had given her and the children a tour of the boat, she was looking at it with different eyes now that Spencer wanted her advice on making changes.

She stopped before the huge walnut desk and leather chair. On the desk lay an open Bible.

Spencer was talking, spelling out his dissatisfactions with the room and his ideas for changes. The words didn't register to Libby. The Bible had all her attention.

Has he been reading it? After all the times he's railed against God and my faith in Him, why is he reading it? She couldn't reconcile the act with the man she knew. A tiny flame of hope flickered in her chest. *You haven't given up on him, have You, Lord? Thank You!*

Would Spencer be upset if she asked him about the open Bible? She couldn't remember a time they'd discussed faith when he hadn't become irate. She didn't want to ruin their camaraderie this afternoon, but she could barely stand her curiosity. She screwed up her courage.

"Spencer," she said, interrupting his comments on window coverings, "have you been reading the Bible?" She rested her fingertips on the open pages.

He hesitated. "Yes."

Her heart hammered fiercely. "Why?"

Spencer jammed his fists into his jacket pockets. "Remember that I told you I prayed up there on the cliffs when I was rescuing Evan?"

"Yes." She remembered, too, that he'd been adamant that only the two of them, and not God, had helped the children.

"I guess that was the start of realizing I need Him."

Her heart leaped.

He went on, explaining that he'd been reading the Bible all week and that he'd asked God to take over his life. "Reading the Bible, I discovered I'm not the white knight I've always thought. It's true enough that I don't swear or womanize or steal or kill or even drink since my marriage. I always thought that meant I was a good man. But since asking God to restore me to wholeness, I've begun to realize there are many rotten parts of my nature, just as there are often rotten boards in less obvious places on a boat that need replacing. One of the most rotten boards in my own constitution is my pride, my belief in my self-sufficiency."

Libby's heart sang with thankfulness and joy. Her prayer of thirty-five years had been answered!

Spencer moved closer to her. He leaned one hip against the desk. His fingers played with the pages of the Bible, and his gaze watched them.

"You look troubled, Spencer. I would have thought accepting the Lord into your life would give you peace." *Didn't he accept You after all, Lord?*

"When I returned to River's Edge, Libby, and you told me you still wouldn't marry me if I didn't share your faith, I decided to pretend I shared it. My plan was to join the church, become involved in it, and eventually let you think that through the church, I'd become a Christian. But it didn't work that way."

"What do you mean?" She wasn't sure she wanted to know, but she couldn't bear not to.

"In the end, I didn't seek God because of my love for you after all. I sought Him because I recognized I need Him."

Relief dissolved the niggling doubts. She laid a hand over his fingers, where they rested on the Bible's pages. "That's the way it should be, Spencer. It's the only way it can be."

He lifted his gaze to meet hers, and she gave him her biggest smile. "I'm so glad for you, Spencer."

He seemed at a loss for words.

"Oh, I almost forgot!" Libby dug into her drawstring handbag. "I meant to give it to you after church, but when the children invited us to picnic with them, I forgot." She pulled the item out, its weight and smoothness familiar to her hand. "This is something you forgot, years ago." *Will he recognize it?* she wondered, laying a small wooden goose in his hand.

He did recognize it. She could tell by the emotions that were working across his weathered face. "The goose. You kept it all these years."

"I kept both of them. The other's still at home on my bureau."

"They're a pair." His voice was low and quiet. "They're meant to be together."

"Do—do you want the other one, too?" She hoped not. She had always treasured that special gift.

"No. No, Libby. You keep it." He set the goose on his desk. "Thank you for bringing this one back to me."

The cabin door banged open.

Libby jumped at the sound. She relaxed instantly when Effie and Evan rushed inside.

Evan collapsed into the desk chair. "We're hungry. Can we eat now?"

"What's for lunch?" Spencer asked with a grin.

Effie ticked the items off on her fingers. "Fried chicken, biscuits, strawberry jam, and chocolate cake. We don't need a fire to cook anything, so can we eat on the boat?"

They ate in wooden deck chairs. The children thought it great fun.

"Tell us more stories about lost treasure," Evan begged.

Libby met Spencer's laughing eyes and knew they were thinking the same thing. "I should think you and Effie would have had your fill of treasure stories after your adventure."

"We didn't find any treasure," Effie reminded them, "only tools and stuff."

"Yes," Evan agreed. "Please tell us more stories."

"All right." Spencer swung his feet over the side of his deck chair. He rested his elbows on his knees and leaned forward. "There's a story old river men tell about a race between two paddle wheelers back in '37." He grinned. "That's even before I was born. Below St. Louis, the Ben Sharrod overtook The Prairie. Well, The Prairie didn't want to be passed, so they stoked their boilers and the race was on."

The children forgot their food and listened to his tale, wide-eyed.

He's as much a storyteller as Effie, Libby thought in amusement. But she wasn't interested in lost treasure. With the children involved in Spencer's story, she allowed her mind to explore the issue that had been nagging at her since Spencer shared his new faith with her.

Why had he waited to tell her about his faith until she asked about the open Bible? Why hadn't he told her at the first opportunity? He knew the only reason she had ever given for not marrying him was that he didn't love God.

Has he decided he doesn't love me after all, Lord? she asked silently, not sure she wanted to know the truth. It had been difficult enough to face the prospect of life without Spencer even when she knew he didn't share her faith and she was sure they would never marry. She was glad for his faith, but her heart sank at the thought that he might not love her. Somehow, it seemed more difficult to accept knowing he had turned to God, that now they could share the most important part of their lives together.

But he hadn't brought up the subject of marriage today. Even when she had given him the goose, he had said the two geese were meant to be together, but he didn't say, as he had when he showed her the geese the first time thirty-five years ago, that Spencer and she were meant to be together, too.

Why, he even spoke of possibly moving back to St. Louis! Leaving River's Edge. Leaving me! The thoughts brought tears to her eyes. She tried to blink them back. It wouldn't do to cry in front of the children. She couldn't stop the burning lump that filled her throat.

She watched him now, his face animated in telling his story. The children hung on his every word.

He was part of all of their worlds now.

"One of the survivors of the explosion of the Sharrod was found fifteen miles downriver."

"Fifteen miles?" Evan's eyebrows raised.

"Fifteen miles," Spencer assured him. "He was traveling from Louisiana upriver to open a bank. He'd had with him one hundred thousand dollars in gold in two strong boxes."

Evan gasped.

"What happened to it?" Effie asked.

Spencer shrugged, lifted his hands, palms up, and leaned back in his deck chair. "It's at the bottom of the Mississippi. It was never found."

"Wow!" Evan's eyes were still huge.

"Wow," said a voice behind Libby's chair.

She jerked upright and turned to see who it was. "Oh, hello, Mr. Adams." Libby wondered who the burly, redheaded man with him was. The plaid flannel shirts and heavy denim trousers the men wore were in sharp contrast to the Sunday outfits Libby, Spencer, and the children were wearing.

"Something you and your friend wanted, Adams?" Spencer asked pleasantly.

Adams grinned his easygoing grin. He moved casually to stand behind Effie's chair. His hands gripped the back of it behind Effie's head. "Matter of fact, there is, Captain. Too bad about that gold at the bottom of the Mississippi you were talkin' 'bout. But my friend here and me, we're more interested in the treasure the Jennie Lee's captain left behind. We were hopin' you could lead us to it."

"Me? I don't know anything about that treasure."

Adams nodded, still smiling. "Figured you'd say that. Problem is, I don't believe you. Maybe you want ta think 'bout that answer." As calmly as though he were reaching for his handkerchief, he pulled a pistol from behind his waist and pointed it at the back of Effie's head.

Libby went cold all the way to her bones.

Chapter 9

Fear flooded Spencer. He clenched the arms of the deck chair. His mind felt like a cotton ball. *God, help us!* he cried silently.

The burly man behind Libby pushed back his jacket and pulled out another gun. He said nothing, only pointed the pistol at Libby.

Spencer could only stare in horror. *This can't be happening!*

Even Effie seemed frozen to her chair, her gaze glued to Adams's gun. *Thank You, God! This is no time for her usual daredevil manner.*

Evan's eyes were as large as the paddle wheel. His face was pale as a winter moon.

Adams leaned his forearms on the back of Effie's chair, the end of his pistol dangling perilously close to her head. "Now, what were you sayin', Captain?"

Adams frightened him more than the man beside him. Adams still wore that friendly, good-old-boy smile. His friend had the cold, hard eyes one would expect from a person in this situation.

Spencer forced words past his tongue, which seemed to have swollen in his fear. "What makes you think I know anything about the former captain's treasure?"

Adams shook his head slowly. "Captain, you disappoint me, thinkin' I'm so lackin' in brains. Who'd be stupid enough to fix up this old boat without an ulterior motive? Got to thinkin' 'bout all the time you were spendin' out here. Figured you were lookin' for that dead captain's gold. Now, see, I signed on here to help you so I could get a better look-see on board. Figured Jake here and me could find the treasure ourselves. We didn't want ta resort ta the guns unless it was necessary."

Adams went on to tell all the places he'd searched on the boat while working for Spencer. Spencer paid scant attention to his words. His mind was racing.

He'd wasted his life living for himself instead of the Lord. Now that he'd asked the Lord into his life, would everything end here, for himself and Libby and Effie and Evan? It mustn't!

Show me what to do, God! He sent the plea heavenward.

When there was a break in Adams's story, Spencer spoke up. "If you thought the treasure was on board, why have you and Jake been searching the cliffs at night?"

As usual, Adams was the one who answered. Jake still hadn't opened his mouth. "Well, truth be told, Jake and me didn't think 'bout the possibility it might be on this old boat at first. Took you movin' out here to make us see that.

Just in case we were wrong, we kept searchin' the bluffs, too." He waved his pistol back and forth between Effie and Evan in a manner that sent blood pounding through Spencer's veins. "That is, till these two wrecked the path to the cave."

"The rain wrecked it, not us."

Effie's indignant protest made Spencer's hair stand on end in fear for her. "Quiet, Effie!"

His sharp reproval brought a darting glance from her. She shifted slightly but said nothing.

"I always figured the late captain's treasure was nothing more than a rumor." Spencer tried to stall for time. How could he make a treasure materialize when he had no idea if it even existed? How could he fight off these men without a weapon? "There's certainly stories in abundance of treasure lost and hidden along this river, from the beginning of it to the end of it."

Adams cocked back his pistol hammer. He kept the gun aimed on Effie. "You were sayin'?"

Libby gasped.

Don't get hysterical on me, Libby! The memory of her steel nerves during the rescue of the children gave him a sliver of comfort. If a woman had to be in this situation with him, he was glad it was Libby. *Steady, Libby. Keep your wits about you.*

Adams straightened his arm until the pistol's nozzle was less than an inch from Effie's forehead. He didn't say a word—only kept smiling at Spencer and then raised his eyebrows.

Blood pounded in Spencer's ears. "All right, I'll tell you!"

The words were out before he even thought.

Adams moved the pistol back but kept it aimed at Effie. "Thought you might."

Now what? Spencer cast about for an inkling of an idea to get them out of this nightmare.

"Well?" Adams encouraged.

"He ain't goin' to tell us." Jake's voice was almost a growl. "Mebbe we should show him we mean business."

Spencer flung out an arm. "It's in the captain's quarters!"

Jake finally smiled. "Now that's more like it."

Adams shook his head. "I searched the captain's quarters. Didn't see nothin' that looked like treasure."

Spencer felt like his mind was throwing out fishing lines in every direction, looking for an answer to convince Adams he was telling the truth. "The treasure's not there. It's a map."

"Didn't see no maps, neither."

"It was in with some river charts," Spencer assured him quickly.

Jake and Adams exchanged grins.

"Let's go see it." Adams made a motion with his pistol. "All of you get up, slowlike. Don't try anything brave."

They stood up. Libby started to slip an arm around Effie's shoulders.

"Now, don't be doin' that, ma'am," Adams warned. "You and the captain lead the way. The two younguns will bring up the rear with Jake and me."

Libby's gaze searched out Spencer's. The fear in her eyes almost made him wild. *Remember our God,* he encouraged her silently.

Evan's legs were shaking so badly that Spencer wasn't sure the boy would be able to walk.

Spencer forced his voice to be calm. "Don't worry, tadpoles. Just do as the men tell you."

He found his own legs weren't working too well as he moved toward Libby. His knees had no more thickening than the strawberry jam they'd had with their biscuits for lunch. He had no idea what he was going to do once he got to the cabin. His only hope was that he would spot something there or along the way that he could use for a weapon.

"Hold it!"

At Jake's bark, Spencer and Libby stopped. *What now?* Spencer thought in despair.

Jake undid his belt and yanked it off. He handed his pistol to Adams, then approached Spencer. "Put your hands behind your back."

Spencer followed orders, and Jake used his belt to fasten Spencer's hands together. Spencer's heart dropped to his boots. Now what chance did he have of saving them?

Next the men began belting Libby's hands in front of her. The flame of Spencer's hope died back even more.

Libby winced as Jake pulled the belt tight.

Effie stamped her foot. Her hands were balled into fists at her side. "Don't hurt my aunt Libby, you old mean man, you!"

The men only laughed at her.

"It's all right, dear," Libby assured her. "They didn't hurt me."

That's my girl! Spencer thought. His hope began to lift again. With Libby and Effie's courage to inspire him, he couldn't give up yet.

They passed along the deck and up the steps to the texas.

Maybe it wasn't so smart after all, heading for the cabin, Spencer thought desperately. *If we'd stayed on deck, there'd at least have been a chance a passerby would spot us. There are always a lot of people out fishing and pleasure-boating on a nice Sunday afternoon.*

Too late to change his mind now.

Inside the cabin, Spencer cast about for something, anything, to help them.

"Well, where's this map?" For the first time, he heard impatience in Adams's voice.

Nothing to do but stall for more time. "There's a hidden panel in the wall above the desk, beside that picture of a ship in a storm."

Jake stuck his gun in the waist of his trousers and examined the panel.

Nothing happened. He grunted. "This a trick?"

Spencer explained how to open it. While Jake worked at it, Spencer cast about for something, anything, to help them. When the panel was open, and Adams and Jake discovered there was no map, it might all be up for them. If the thieves shot them and left them in the cabin, it might be weeks before their bodies were found.

Nothing looked helpful. His heart sank like an anchor.

Don't give up yet! As long as you're alive, there's a chance. You have to save the twins! His glance slid to them.

He'd expected to see the fear that had been on their faces while on the deck. Instead, they were exchanging conspiratorial grins. He swallowed a groan. What now? He wanted to warn them not to do anything foolish, but he didn't want to draw the men's attention to them.

"Eureka!" Jake hollered as the panel slid open. He began pulling out the contents and piling them on the desk, right on top of the open Bible. Spencer knew the papers were mostly old river charts and journals.

Adams stepped behind the desk, keeping the pistol trained on the group, trying to glance at the papers. Jake began going through them. Adams couldn't resist giving a little more of his attention to the pile, too.

Effie dashed toward the open cabin door. She almost lost her balance the last couple feet, sliding on the floor Adams had waxed earlier in the week, her arms flailing.

Evan was right behind her. He almost ran into her. His hands on her back steadied her.

Spencer almost yelled at them to stop. Caught the yell back just in time. Glanced at the desk. All the men's attention was on the pile of papers. *Please, God!* It was all the prayer his mind could form in his fear for what would happen to the children if the men saw them.

Effie had her balance back. She and Evan started again.

"Hey!" Jake let out a bellow. "Stop those kids!"

Chapter 20

Swearing, Adams started after them.

Spencer watched with his heart in his throat. Adams's gun pointed wildly in one direction and then another as he raced across the room.

"Run, Effie! Run, Evan!" Libby screamed.

Effie was through the door. Spencer saw the hem of her dress disappear as she took off down the deck.

"Help! Help!"

She's yelling at the top of her lungs, bless her!

Adams was almost on top of Evan. Spencer held his breath, silently urging Evan to hurry. Adams lost his footing on the slippery floor and landed on his bottom. He reached and caught Evan's jacket just as Evan reached the threshold. They fell in a heap on the floor.

Jake let out a stream of oaths and pushed aside the desk chair, leaving his search to help Adams.

Libby swung her belted hands and shoved the pile of papers onto the floor in front of him.

Jake slipped. Only by grabbing the desk did he manage not to wind up on the floor like his partner.

"Let me go!" Evan was struggling to get away from Adams. His feet and hands were pounding the outlaw with a vengeance. "Let me go!"

"Stupid kid!" Adams tried to subdue Evan while dodging the blows and hanging on to the gun.

Spencer threw himself on top of Adams. He landed with a thud that knocked his breath away. Adams tried unsuccessfully to heave him off and still hold on to the boy and the gun.

Adams's gun arm was behind Spencer. Spencer strained his neck to look over his shoulder. "Oof!" He reached for the gun. Too far away. He grabbed Adams's arm and hung on until Adams yanked so hard Spencer thought his shoulders would come right out of their joints.

He let go and rolled backward over Adams's gun arm. *If I can't get the gun, at least I can keep him from using it.* He was face-to-face with Adams now, and Adams wasn't smiling any longer.

"Stop!" Jake's voice roared through the room.

Spencer glanced up. Jake was standing only a couple feet away, his pistol pointed at Spencer. The sense of failure washed through Spencer.

"Get up."

With an effort, Spencer started to roll off Adams's arm.

"Yipes!"

Jake's gun dropped to the floor.

Libby bent and grabbed it. Trained it on Jake.

Jake, holding his gun hand with his other hand, took a step toward her.

"Stop." Libby took a step back, cocking the pistol's hammer.

Jake looked at her uncertainly.

"Think I won't shoot?" Libby's gaze was steady and so were her still-belted hands. "When you and Adams have been threatening Effie and Evan?"

Jake's shoulders sagged in defeat.

Still on Adams's arm, Spencer grinned. *I'd stop, too, if she used that tone, even without a gun pointed at me.*

"Let go of Evan," she commanded Adams.

Adams released the boy.

"And the gun," she added.

Adams let go of the gun. Spencer could feel Adams give up, as the thief's muscles lost their tension.

"What did you do to Jake?" Spencer asked Libby.

"Stuck my hat pin in his gun hand."

Spencer chuckled. "Evan, pick up Adams's gun." He didn't want to chance the outlaws getting the drop on them again. "But be very, very careful. Don't touch it near the trigger. Hold it in both hands."

When Evan had done as he was told, Spencer explained to him how to lower the hammer. "Now, take it out on deck and lay it down."

Evan stepped through the door onto the texas deck. "Hey, there's people coming on board from a rowboat!"

"Effie's calls for help must have been answered," Libby said.

Spencer smiled at her across the room, across the two men who had held their lives and the children's in their hands, and thought, *My cries for help were answered, too. How did I ever think I was self-sufficient for all those years?*

Spencer rolled off Adams's arm and struggled to his feet. Evan began undoing the belt that tied his hands together.

They could hear people outside, hear their footsteps running up the steps.

Adams dragged himself to a sitting position. "Could we just see the map? Would you show it to me? We deserve that much after all the trouble we've been through to get it, don't you think?"

Spencer grinned. "There is no map. Far as I know, there never was. I was just stalling for time."

Adams groaned and dropped his head into his hands.

The fishermen Effie had haled helped Spencer tie up Adams and Jake. Then one of the fishermen went into town for the sheriff. When the sheriff had left with Adams and Jake, the fishermen rowed Spencer, Libby, and the twins back to town, where Spencer and Libby brought the children home.

Effie and Evan could barely hold themselves to Spencer and Libby's slower pace. When they reached the block on which they lived, they raced ahead, eager to tell Justin and Constance how they'd help capture the treasure hunters.

There was nothing for it but that Spencer and Libby stay for coffee and straighten out the children's embellished story. Before Spencer left to walk Libby home, Constance invited him to stay with them overnight if he couldn't find someone to take him back to the Jennie Lee.

Blossoming spring trees and flowers filled the air with fragrance as Spencer and Libby walked to her home in the twilight.

"You're rather quiet this evening, Libby."

"It's been quite a day."

"That it has. You were incredible."

"Me?"

He laughed. "Yes, you. If you hadn't stuck Jake with that hat pin, no telling what might have happened."

His praise warmed her heart. "This is the third time you've rescued my great-niece and nephew. You are the one who is incredible." She shook her head, unable to find the words she wanted. "I don't know how to thank you."

"There's nothing for which to thank me."

"But that's what is so. . .overwhelming. That it is so much a part of you to be that kind of man."

Spencer chuckled. "Justin and Constance probably don't see me through your eyes. I expect whenever they see me coming up the walk, they tremble with dread, knowing their children have been up to something life-threatening again."

"It does seem their lives go from one traumatic event to the next with surprising speed, doesn't it?"

"If my two boys had sought out trouble the way Effie and Evan do, I'd have been an old man by the time I was thirty."

"You will never seem old to me." Libby scrunched her eyes shut. She had spoken without thinking. The words were true, but after this afternoon, she wasn't at all certain whether he still cared for her beyond friendship.

"Nor you to me, Libby." He took her hand and drew it threw his arm. Her heart began beating erratically.

"Will I find Daniel on your porch this evening, Libby?"

"I hardly think so." The cool evening air didn't keep her cheeks from burning at the memory of the numerous times she'd forgotten or been late for evenings with Pastor Green because she had been with Spencer.

"He's a good man, Libby."

"So you've said before." She snatched her arm back. Just because he might not want her himself didn't give him the right to push her off on someone else. "I do wish people would stop trying to shove men at me. I'm perfectly capable of deciding for myself whether to have a man in my life, and if so, whom."

"Of course, you are." His voice sounded shocked. "It's just that Daniel is a good man and—"

"Ooooh!" Her hands formed into fists at her sides.

"He is. You two have so much in common. How could you help but be happy with him?"

Libby stamped her foot and whirled to face him. "It would help if I loved him. Maybe you think I'm too old for that to matter. Lots of people think so. Well, I don't. I can support myself and take care of my home by myself. I don't need a man around unless I love him."

Spencer chuckled and held up his hands in a gesture of surrender. "All right, all right. It's just that you've always believed it so important that the man you marry shares your faith, and Daniel certainly does."

Frustration ran through her with all the turbulence of the Mississippi in flood season. She wanted to tell him that he was the man she loved, he was the man she wanted to marry, but silly convention didn't allow a woman such freedom. "Pastor Green isn't the only man who shares my faith. It would be a mighty small religion if he were."

Spencer guffawed. "That it would."

Libby started down the sidewalk, her heels sounding smartly against the boards.

Spencer hurried after her, grasping one of her shoulders. "Hold up. What's going on, Libby?"

She swung her arms out from her sides, her drawstring purse swinging wildly. "Why didn't you just tell me that you had asked God into your life? Why did I have to find it out almost by accident?"

"Is that what this is all about?"

She looked down at the pointed toes of her Sunday slippers, not willing to look him in the eye or let him see what was in her eyes.

"Libby, I didn't tell you because I was afraid you wouldn't believe me."

Her head jerked up. "Of course I would have believed you!"

"Are you sure? You knew I was trying to win your hand, and you'd told me in no uncertain terms more than once that the only way you would marry me is if I shared your faith."

"That's why I don't understand why you didn't tell me. It was the only thing standing between us. Then when the barrier was gone, and you didn't tell me, I thought. . .I was afraid. . ."

"Afraid of what?" His voice held that gentle quality that had always unglued her.

She focused on his chest, the top button on his jacket, unable to look him in the face. "I'm afraid you've discovered you don't love me after all." The words were almost a whisper. Then, to her horror, she broke into quiet sobs.

"Ah, Libby, my dearest love." She allowed him to pull her gently against his chest. He wrapped his arms around her, and she buried her face in the wool of his jacket. "I thought I must live my faith for a while before you would believe in my change of heart. Then, too, after I faced the fact that I need God and spent more time reading the Bible, I began to see my past in a different light and saw how cruelly I'd treated you."

"You were never cruel!" *Sniff.*

"But I was. For years, I've felt sorry for myself. I thought you couldn't have loved me as much as I loved you, or you wouldn't have let anything stand in the way of our life together. I blamed God and your stubbornness and my drinking for the fact that we weren't together. It never occurred to me that I was the one who had abandoned you, abandoned us, abandoned the possibility of a life together. I was the one who was too stubborn to consider turning to God, even to the point of asking Him to show me whether or not He existed or loved me."

Libby wiped a tear from her cheek, hiccuping as her sobs dwindled. A gentle peace filled her breast. She had never thought he would talk like this with her about the struggles with his heart and his faith. His sharing made her feel closer to him than ever before.

"I never blamed you for not believing." She sought for the words to explain. "As much as I wanted you to know the joy of trusting Jesus, I always knew you couldn't do it just for me. Your heart wasn't ready to trust Him back then."

"I threw up so many roadblocks." His chest lifted in a deep sigh beneath her cheek. "Even if I wasn't ready to believe in Him, I could have ended our relationship in a kinder way. As you well know, the whole town soon knew the story of my elopement with Margaret. I was so concerned with my own anger and embarrassment that I never realized how abandoned and humiliated you must have felt in front of your family and the town."

Tears welled up again, but this time they were tears of release and gratitude. She hadn't allowed herself to realize how important it was to her that he understand how much he'd hurt her when he married Margaret all those years ago without even a good-bye to her.

"And I thought, I was afraid. . ." she could hear the amusement creeping into his voice as he repeated her earlier words, "that it wasn't fair to try to steal your heart from a man like Daniel, who would be so good to you and had, like you, loved the Lord most of his life."

"You can't steal my heart from a man who doesn't have it." Her sobs were subsiding, but her voice still shook from them.

"I guess I can't at that." He slipped a knuckle under her chin and lifted her face. He searched her eyes. "Do I need to steal your heart from anyone, or is it already mine?"

Joy-filled peace fell like a mantle on her heart. "It is yours, Spencer. It is yours."

He lowered his face toward hers. A heartbeat away from her lips he whispered, "I love you. I'll always love you."

His lips were tender, as if in awe of the gift life had finally brought him. She lost herself in his kiss, surrendering to the joy of love brought full circle from its youthful beginning.

"Harumph! Such behavior! On a public sidewalk."

Startled, Libby and Spencer jumped apart.

Judge Keyes and his wife were walking past. Mrs. Keyes's distinguished face was filled with indignation.

Libby caught back a giggle, remembering Mrs. Keyes's nosy questions in her millinery shop as she attempted to ferret out the direction of Libby's affections. She was sorely tempted to stop the woman and tell her, "I choose this one." *But Spencer hasn't actually asked me to marry him, not since he became a believer,* she reminded herself.

Spencer drew her arm through his once more. "Think that swing on your front porch is available? I plan to kiss you at least a few more times before we part tonight, and I'd hate to offend any more of the town's ladies when I do." His eyes twinkled in the glow from gas streetlights.

On the swing, hidden from curious eyes by the spirea bushes planted about the porch, Libby rested contentedly against his shoulder. Mellow light from the lamp in the parlor window allowed her to see the face that was so dear to her. Spencer had kept his word, and she'd been thoroughly kissed.

The dear little hat whose pin had saved the day rested alone at one end of the swing. Spencer's beard caught in Libby's curls as he moved his chin against her hair. She liked the feel of it.

"Ah, Libby, the wonder of being with you after all these years—it's like a miracle. I've imagined it many times, but it was never this sweet in my dreams." His lips touched her hair in a kiss, then the edge of her eyebrow, and the bridge of her nose. "Will you marry me, Libby?"

Libby closed her eyes and let the joy spill over her. "Yes! Oh, yes! In my heart, I'm already married to you."

His arms tightened, and she heard him sigh with love and contentment. "I feel the same way, but I want us to be married in the eyes of God and the world."

"I want that, too." She slid her fingertips over his cheek and looked into his radiant eyes. "I can't think of anything I want more than to spend the rest of our years together as man and wife."

They were silent for awhile, content to hold each other and revel in the wonder of their love. Spencer traced the line of her lips lightly with the tip of his index finger. "What are you thinking that brought that smile, my love?"

"I was remembering the Bible verse I hung onto while trying to learn to live without the hope we would one day be us. 'I waited patiently for the Lord; and he inclined unto me, and heard my cry.' I didn't wait so patiently, but He heard my heart's cry for you anyway."

Epilogue

Jennie Lee's dining and social hall shimmered with golden light. It shone from her crystal chandeliers, the brass-trimmed wall sconces, and candles within hurricane holders on the linen-covered tables. It sparkled off the crystal and silver at the place settings. Gold and ivory wallpaper and gold valances above lake-blue velvet draperies intensified the mellow light. Violin music added to the atmosphere the decorating created, and a background to the murmur of the wedding reception crowd milling about the room in the manner of the many crowds who had filled the salon during Jennie Lee's early days.

"You've done a beautiful job on this room, Libby." Constance's gaze wandered over the room.

"Didn't she?" Spencer slipped his arm around Libby's shoulders and gave her a squeeze. "It's elegant yet lighter than most I've seen, and I've seen a number."

Libby slipped a hand over Spencer's and smiled at him, then at Constance. Pleasure at the sincere admiration of two of her favorite people warmed her. As Constance was well aware, she'd used the colors of Constance's parlor as inspiration for the salon.

"When Spencer told me his intention to have the remodeling completed in three months, I didn't think it possible," Libby told Constance, "but with his business connections, he was able to arrange for all the help we needed."

"The room pales next to my bride, don't you think?" Spencer beamed.

"I do, indeed."

Libby ducked her head self-consciously, running the palm of her hand over the embossed satin of her wedding suit. It was quite simple, but elegant. She'd had Ida and Constance's assurance that it did not look too much like a wedding gown to be a proper outfit for a second wedding and a fifty-five-year-old bride. She loved the cream color, the leg-o'-mutton sleeves, the high collar, and dainty pearl trim on the jacket.

She still had no illusions about her beauty. She hadn't been born with a face that would launch a thousand ships and certainly hadn't grown into one through the years. Yet when she looked into Spencer's eyes and saw his love for her reflected there, she felt beautiful. She understood now that he didn't love her looks, he loved the essence of who she was, as she loved him.

"Captain and Mrs. Spencer Matthews." A smiling Pastor Green stopped before them, with Ida beside him. He and Spencer shook hands. "You've a fine wife there, Captain, and she has a fine husband."

"Thank you, Daniel. That means a lot, coming from you. Time was, I thought it would be you standing in this place today."

Libby's cheeks warmed. Her glance went to the toes of her satin shoes, which peeked out from beneath her skirt.

"You have my sincere wish for your happiness." Daniel turned to Ida and raised an eyebrow. "Do you want to tell them, or shall I?"

Ida's smile made little round balls of her cheeks. Her eyes sparkled. "We're getting married. He asked me last night, after your rehearsal."

Libby threw her arms around Ida's neck. "Oh, Ida, I'm so happy for you!" They drew apart, and she looked at Pastor Green with a laugh. "And for you, too, of course."

"I've you to thank for Ida, you know." Pastor Green's eyes twinkled.

"Me?" Libby laid a hand on her chest, surprised.

"Yes, you. If you hadn't stood me up so many times while seeing the captain, I might never have become so well acquainted with Ida."

The laugh the four of them shared was interrupted by Effie and Evan and Spencer's grandsons, two towheaded boys of five and six, as the children pushed in front of Libby and Spencer.

Effie threw herself against Spencer. "We told Lewis and Frank that we helped catch thieves who wanted the dead captain's gold, but they wouldn't believe us."

"Tell them it's true, Captain," Evan urged.

Spencer nodded at his grandsons. "It certainly is true."

The oldest of the boys crossed his arms over his chest. "I won't believe it until I see the treasure."

Effie rolled her eyes in exasperation. "They didn't find the treasure. But Evan and me are going to keep looking for it."

Evan nodded vigorously.

"Oh, dear." Constance's shoulders drooped. "Here we go again."

Spencer shook his head. "I'm afraid that treasure, if it ever existed, is gone for good. It's part of the legends of the Big Muddy, now."

"Maybe not." Effie didn't give up hope so easily.

The youngest boy turned large blue eyes to Spencer. "Did ghosts really try to find the treasure, Grandfather?"

"Of course not," Effie answered before Spencer could respond. "I told you, people only thought there were ghosts. There's no such thing as ghosts. You'll know that when you're older, like me and Evan. Real people tried to find the treasure."

The boy looked disappointed.

Evan turned to the boys. "Want to see the pilothouse? Come on!"

The four raced through the crowd.

Spencer's arm drew Libby close. His whisper in her ear sent delightful chills through her. "I thought my treasure had been lost for good, too. Now that I've found it, I'll never let it go."

"I didn't realize 'never' was such a wonderful word." She whispered, well aware of the crowd about them.

He chuckled.

"I'm glad your sons and their families came for the wedding, Spencer. I was so afraid they wouldn't want you to remarry."

"They only want me to be happy. They'll love you when they get to know you."

They'd have time to get to know each other. For a wedding trip, Spencer and Libby were taking the Jennie Lee to St. Louis. His sons' families and the Knights would be traveling with them.

He took her hand. "Let's go outside. There's something I want to show you."

It took them a long time to work their way through their friends and family to the deck. He led her up the stairs to the texas, then to the front of that level. His arms slid about her shoulders from behind, drawing her back against him. She rested there contentedly.

"I used to imagine how wonderful it would be," he murmured in her ear, "if you wore my name, and everyone would know by my name that you were my wife. But lately, I've been wishing tradition allowed a man to carry his wife's name, also, to show the world her heart belongs to him. I think I've found a way to tell the world you love me. What do you think?"

He pointed toward the pilothouse. Her gaze followed.

She gasped. Tears welled up in her eyes. Above the front windows, in large bold letters, a new name had been painted: THE LOVELY LIBBY. Her voice trembled as she read the words.

"I renamed the boat. Do you mind?"

"Mind? I think it's the nicest wedding gift any bride has ever received."

His lips touched her neck just below her ear. "Then perhaps you'd like to thank me properly."

"Why, Captain!" Her laugh trembled as she turned in his arms and raised her lips for his kiss. His mouth claimed hers with a passion that took her breath.

Giggles from above barely made their way through her consciousness.

"Libby and the captain, sitting in a tree, k–i–s–s–i–n–g!"

Libby jumped back as far as Spencer's arms allowed. "The children!" She whirled around, Spencer's chuckle sounding behind her.

Effie and Evan leaned out of the pilothouse window, with Spencer's grandchildren beside them. Effie waved. "We're teaching Lewis and Frank detectiving!"

"Oh, my!" Libby waved back weakly. "This is going to be quite a voyage, Spencer."

"Quite." Amusement filled the one word. His arms drew her back against him once more.

"No telling what Effie and Evan will lead your grandsons into."

Spencer stilled. He lifted his gaze to the pilothouse and groaned. "Oh, my!"

With a low laugh, Libby turned and slipped her arms around his neck. "Welcome to my world, Captain."

JOANN A. GROTE

JoAnn lives in Minnesota where she grew up. She uses the state for most of her story settings, and like her characters, JoAnn seeks to serve Christ in her work. She believes that readers of novels can receive a message of salvation and encouragement from well-crafted fiction. An award-winning author, she has had over thirty-five books published, including numerous novellas, several novels with Barbour Publishing in the **Heartsong Presents** line and novels in the **American Adventure and Sisters in Time** series for kids.

A Letter to Our Readers

Dear Readers:

In order that we might better contribute to your reading enjoyment, we would appreciate your taking a few minutes to respond to the following questions. When completed, please return to the following: Fiction Editor, Barbour Publishing, Inc., P.O. Box 719, Uhrichsville, OH 44683.

1. Did you enjoy reading *Minnesota Mysteries*?
   ❑ Very much—I would like to see more books like this.
   ❑ Moderately—I would have enjoyed it more if _____
   _____

   _____

2. What influenced your decision to purchase this book?
   (Check those that apply.)
   ❑ Cover   ❑ Back cover copy   ❑ Title   ❑ Price
   ❑ Friends   ❑ Publicity   ❑ Other

3. Which story was your favorite?
   ❑ *An Honest Love*   ❑ *Sweet Surrender*
   ❑ *A Man for Libby*

4. Please check your age range:
   ❑ Under 18   ❑ 18–24   ❑ 25–34
   ❑ 35–45   ❑ 46–55   ❑ Over 55

5. How many hours per week do you read? _____

Name _____

Occupation _____

Address _____

City_____ State_____ Zip_____

E-mail_____

HEARTSONG PRESENTS

If you love Christian romance...

$10.^{99}$

You'll love Heartsong Presents' inspiring and faith-filled romances by today's very best Christian authors...DiAnn Mills, Wanda E. Brunstetter, and Yvonne Lehman, to mention a few!

When you join Heartsong Presents, you'll enjoy 4 brand-new mass market, 176-page books—two contemporary and two historical—that will build you up in your faith when you discover God's role in every relationship you read about!

Imagine...four new romances every four weeks—with men and women like you who long to meet the one God has chosen as the love of their lives...all for the low price of $10.99 postpaid.

To join, simply visit www.heartsongpresents.com or complete the coupon below and mail it to the address provided.

- -

YES! Sign me up for Heartsong!

NEW MEMBERSHIPS WILL BE SHIPPED IMMEDIATELY!

Send no money now. We'll bill you only $10.99 postpaid with your first shipment of four books. Or for faster action, call 1-740-922-7280.

NAME _____

ADDRESS _____

CITY _____ STATE _____ ZIP _____

**MAIL TO: HEARTSONG PRESENTS, P.O. Box 721, Uhrichsville, Ohio 44683
or sign up at WWW.HEARTSONGPRESENTS.COM**

ADPG05